THE GAVEL:
From Verdict to Victory

A Novel

James C. Dodge

Webber Books

The Gavel: From Verdict to Victory

ISBN: Softcover 978-1-946478-06-1
Copyright © 2016 by James C. Dodge

This is a work of fiction. The characters, incidents, and dialogues are products of the author's imagination and are not to be construed as real. Any resemblance to actual events or persons, living or dead, are entirely coincidental.

To order additional copies of this book, contact:

Webber Books
1-423-475-7308

Webber Books is an imprint of Parson's Porch & Company (PP&C). Webber Books publishes books of noted authors, representing all genres, in support of The Robert E. Webber Institute for Worship Studies. For more information about IWS, go to www.iws.edu.

To Robert E. Webber in Memoriam

Acknowledgements

Every project bears the fingerprints of many contributors, as does this one. It began with a vision fired by Bob Webber over a couple dinner conversations more than a decade ago, while my wife and I were on an extended sailing holiday. He may have ruined my sailing life (broad smile), but he was the catalyst God used to set a course toward disciple-formation for which I am eternally grateful!

Many people have contributed to this story; I wish I could name them all. The few I've named here represent those who have had direct bearing on the outcome of the project. My great friend who is more like a brother to me, John Deller, carefully combed the draft manuscript offering both an editor's eye but also the heart of the Church. John helped soften the tone while preserving the message. I am grateful! Dr. Lester Ruth stoked the fires of the ancient Catechumenate – the pathway to disciple-formation – during his lectures and subsequent private conversations. Fr. Pius X Harding, spiritual director, Benedictine monk and dear friend opened my eyes to the broader church. Dr. Jeremy Wallace, dean at Canby Bible College, offered me an open environment to test my work. And my students at CBC provided an eager and honest sounding board. The RCIA (Right of Christian Initiation of Adults) catechists, sponsors and catechumen at St. Agatha Catholic Church in Portland, Oregon contributed significantly to my praxis based understanding of disciple-formation. Their contributions were indispensable. Since 2006 our Subway Kids, as we call them, have provided an endless stream of encouragement. Theirs is a story deserving a book of its own. To Robert E. Webber Institute of Worship Studies president, Dr. Jim Hart, and retired professor and thesis director, Dr. Gerald Borchert, I am forever grateful! Thank you, gentlemen, for the opportunity to offer this work under the Webber Institute Books imprint. Most of all thank you for your friendship in Christ. One of our Subway Kids, Jill Schulenberg, listened to more than her share of my ramblings during afternoon writing outings at local pubs where we pretended we were the "new" Inklings. Thank you! And to David Russell Tullock and the fine people at Parson's Porch & Book Publishing Company, I am grateful! Sadly, the risk exists that important contributors have been omitted – not by intention I assure you. You have both my apology and undying gratitude.

And to Judy, the lady of my dreams; who for forty-four years has been my wife, constant source of encouragement and best friend. I am most indebted to you with gratitude and deepest love. Thank you!

Foreword

The founder of the Institute for Worship Studies (IWS), Dr. Robert E. Webber, delivered a lecture in the early days of the school, advocating for "catechesis across the curriculum." What did he mean, and why is this a fundamental priority for an academic graduate institution that focuses on the biblical, theological, historical, cultural and missiological study of Christian worship? Why would IWS publish a novel about catechesis?

One key to reading the entire biblical narrative is this—God is calling his creation to right worship. The Bible is all about right worship. God ultimately wants his people to worship him aright. We need to worship because in that great act we become aligned and reconciled to God through Jesus Christ, the primary worshipper. Right worship leads to the rightly ordered or integrated life, the rightly ordered family, the rightly ordered church, city, culture, even cosmos. In worship we have the great privilege of telling the world its true story and bringing it to the right worship of the only God who is ultimately true, good and beautiful. This is why a focused study of right worship is at the very core of the Christian faith!

But how does this intersect with catechesis? "Catechesis is nothing other than the process of transmitting the Gospel, as the Christian community has received it, understands it, celebrates it, lives it and communicates it in many ways." (General Directory for Catechesis #105) The Gospel narrative is the content of Christian worship, and so is at the very center of Christian worship. Catechesis is an interactive process by which the participant or catechumen learns to live the Gospel. It is a lifelong practice of ongoing conversion and spiritual formation. Catechesis teaches Christians the way in which the Gospel is lived out in the world. It forms Christians into disciples of Jesus Christ with his compassionate heart for the world. Catechesis encourages the Christian to follow in his footsteps, being poured out for the life of the world. Catechesis starts and ends with worship, but embraces and implicates evangelism, discipleship, education, fellowship, apologetics, etc. The catechetical process develops hearts of service and lives of virtue, helping Christians to know God more fully, to love him more profoundly and to love the world with his love. In a word, when entered fully and wholeheartedly, catechesis leads believers into the fullness of the life of God and intimacy with Jesus Christ.

In *The Gavel*, Jim Dodge leads the reader through this well-told, realistic story to see the beauty, goodness and truth of the Gospel as it impacts just one life, a young man on the margins of society. As the story unfolds he is led by God working through a diverse "posse" of Christian leaders into participation, even immersion, in the life of God. The power of the Gospel, of community, of prayer, of apologetics, and of simple but deep love, all come to play in the conversion of our protagonist. And it is moving and inspirational.

Worship is famously referred to as the "source and summit of the Christian life." The catechesis of the Church fills in all the rest. Together worship and catechesis work hand-in-hand to lead all who find themselves on a search for meaning in life to the fullness of the true life of God. This book is rooted in that journey. Come along with us to learn, see and experience an example of Ireneaus' great dictum: "The glory of God is a human being fully alive."

Dr. James R. Hart, President
The Robert E. Webber Institute for Worship Studies

THE GAVEL

The gavel's fall echoed through the courtroom. "Guilty!" the jury foreman pronounced. Shackled at the wrists and ankles, the condemned, James Taylor Meyers, stood slump-shouldered in a faded orange jump suit stenciled "Stevens County Jail" across the back. His heart raced; his stomach wedged into his throat. James barely heard anything Judge Abrams said at the sentencing. When Abrams asked, "What happened, son? What went wrong," James stood motionless and stared blankly at the floor. His mother's muffled sobs could be heard behind him. He turned to face her – to face his entire family – but couldn't raise his eyes to meet theirs. Shame and humiliation prevented him.

The bailiff took him by the arm and led him silently out of the courtroom, down a dimly lit hallway and out the back door to a waiting van. "Felon; I'm a felon," he recited under his breath in utter disbelief. Suddenly his world went black. A thick lump raised in his throat, as he dropped onto the cold steel seat in the van's windowless prisoner box. Barely twenty years old, a felon heading to do hard time at the state's correctional institution – not the stuff of his boyhood dreams.

As the van bumped along, James' restless mind tormented him with scenes he wished he could forget. Judge Abrams' words burnt like hot irons, "James Meyers, you are hereby sentenced to six years confinement in the state's maximum security facility.... What happened, son?" If only he could go back in time, maybe he could answer Judge Abrams' question – maybe avoid it altogether. Images of his parents' faces, crushed in disbelief, haunted him whenever he closed his eyes.

"Six...years," he groaned between clenched teeth, and banged his head lightly against the metal wall. The guard riding with him shot a snide smirk in his direction. "Scared, kid? You should be." James ignored him and slouched into the corner, hiding tear-filled eyes.

A couple hours or so later – time seemed irrelevant – the van slowed and made a sharp right turn coming to a stop. What sounded like rusty iron gates opening rattled through the box. The van began moving again, slowly rumbling down a pocked roadway until it came to a final stop. "Get up kid," the guard ordered motioning toward the van's back doors. "Welcome to your new home."

Footsteps drew up behind the van; abruptly the doors swung open. "Alright, come on out," one of the prison bulls ordered. The shackles binding his ankles were too short for the long step and he stumbled, falling face down on the pavement. "On your feet," another guard growled. Two guards wrestled him from the ground; then flanked him as he waddled awkwardly toward an open door lighted by a single naked bulb. The gray pall of a rainy day darkened his already colorless mood. A light trickle of blood glided down the bridge of his nose, released from a small cut on his forehead caused by the fall. His head throbbed. Cold and frightened, his mind blurred and his mood sank ever lower.

Inside, the hellishness of prison struck him immediately. His eyes darted anxiously over the scene. Noise of slamming doors, guards barking at prisoners, and a putrid stench choked the atmosphere. Steel – everywhere – dominated the place, including the guards' steely expressionless faces. Clad in drab green uniforms and baseball caps, with piercing eyes and stone sober faces, the guards ruled. All day they bellowed orders at prisoners, shaking down those that appeared to be up to something. James shuddered, as the stark realization of life as an incarcerated felon crashed over him like an icy stream. Too frightened to cry, too numb to care, James felt his life end though his heart kept beating.

"Stand over there," a guard ordered pointing to a spot on the floor. James shuffled sideways until he stood in front of a barred door. A file labeled, James Taylor Meyers, was thrust into his hands. "Hold this, and follow me," the guard ordered. The echo of iron doors clanging shut further into the building sent a shock of terror down James' spine. He wanted to back away. He couldn't. There was no escape.

A buzzer went off, and the door in front of him creaked open. Two guards escorted him through it. Row upon row of narrow cells locked shut with solid steel doors stretched endlessly before him – two decks of them. Craning his neck he caught sight of a guard patrolling the upper deck above him. One by one he passed occupied cells, at times catching glimpses of expressionless eyes peering at him through the two by six inch slots in the doors. Sometimes his eyes met theirs. Then blankness, as the cell's denizens withdrew their glance and turned away. Florescent light cast surreal shadows that erased all features in the vapid cell block. Depersonalizing and hostile, the atmosphere grated on James. He could barely breathe and grew anxious. He worried that in time he'd become as anonymous – maybe as cynically callous – as the bodies behind the lifeless eyes. Judge Abrams was right; this entire tragedy could have been avoided. "If only…"

The interminable walk down Cell Block Alpha ended in front of a series of highly secured cages. Through them another barricade of solid steel-clad doors open to the prison yard on the far side of which resides the mossy gray stone administration office.

Suffocating from the imposing world inside, the blast of fresh – albeit damp, dank – air resuscitated him. "Maybe they'll let me do my time out here," James mused in nervous humor. "No chance," one of the guards smirked, killing the one thread of hope left in the boy.

The impregnably bleak atmosphere inside followed him into the yard. Rimmed by electrified chainmail fence fortified by coils of razor wire and over-lurked by heavily armed guards in towers, the yard was no Eden.

Shifts of thirty inmates could be found idling around the perimeter of the grounds during daylight hours. Today was an exception. It was playoff season, and the better-behaved inmates were huddled up in the rec hall watching Sunday's taped game between the Eagles and Giants. Pity the poor dude who spilled the score before the populace got to view the game on the small suspended TV. Violence was held to a minimum in the State House mostly because the guards had the authority to stifle it – harshly if necessary. But a few hot heads occasionally took matters into their own hands – then suffered for it. Cracking a few skulls was not out of the question for guards with edgy attitudes. More likely, however, was time banished to the stink-filled hole, an isolated cell in which hot-heads were dumped to cool off – typically for a couple of weeks.

James' eyes dropped once again to the scruffy turf; hopelessness squeezed him like the thick concrete walls inside. "What have I done?" slipped painfully from his lips. "Screwed up," one of his escorts snapped. For a solitary moment he managed an upward glance, only to find in the leaden sky another reminder of the numbing hollowness of his life. Like a wrecked car bound for the crusher, soon, he reasoned, he too, would be little more than a bale of scrapped humanity, crushed with no future. "At least cars get recycled," fell from his lips in painful resignation, an unintended but prophetic omen of things to come. The guards laughed.

Like every building in the compound, the administration building was entered through locked steel. Heavy footfalls from his guard escort echoed down the polished tile hallway. Weaving through the maze of corridors they finally arrived in front of the main office. The sign read, "Thomas W. Rowland, Warden." With no introduction, Rowland's matronly secretary ushered James and his escort into the ante room just outside the inner office. A few moments later, she directed them to go in, "Warden Rowland is waiting." James hobbled into the carpeted office, coming to a halt in front of the large cherry-wood desk behind which sat the lean, square-jawed warden who presided over the prison.

"James…Taylor…Meyers," Warden Rowland read in measured tones from a printed form. "That you?" he inquired, training his eyes on James.

"Yes sir: I am James Taylor Meyers."

Warden Rowland studied his new charge over reading glasses perched neatly on his nose. The fifty-five year old prison official appeared quite fit, a handsome man with a distinguished tint of gray about the temples. Educated in the east, Rowland held a law degree from Yale and a Master of Science degree in criminology from Princeton, the diplomas for which hung proudly over the fireplace mantle on the far wall.

Married with one grown child, a daughter, Rowland was a man of stalwart character with little or no toleration for shoddiness. A trial lawyer turn prison official, Rowland assumed his position nine years ago at the behest of the governor, a fellow Yale alum and good friend. Despite a respected practice as a distinguished trial attorney, Rowland set it aside believing firmly in his new calling. His office reflected his well-bred upbringing, as it also belied the ugly façade of the prison compound. Decked out in warm woods, densely stocked library, thick carpet and stately furniture, with family photos prominently poised on shelves and his desk, it would pass for a tenured Ivy League professor's office or that of a corporate executive – hardly what one expected to find inside prison walls.

"Sit down, Meyers," the warden ordered. James clumsily dropped into a leather padded wood chair beside the warden's desk. Gesturing at the file James held on his lap, Warden Rowland said, "Hand it to me." James stretched as far as his shackles allowed but came well short of the warden's grasp. Rowland snatched the file from him and studied the contents for several minutes, pausing over certain passages, which, by the deep furrows of his brow apparently disturbed him. Finally Rowland closed the file, straightened himself in his high-back leather chair and turned his attention to James. "You know why you're here young man?" he demanded in a tone that clearly commanded authority.

"Yes sir…I do," James said sheepishly.

"I find your circumstances especially desolating, James," Rowland offered, sounding more like a disappointed father than prison warden.

"From all indications you come from a healthy family, have a good education and spent some years of your life attending church." Rowland broke the words off in rapid staccato that made them sound more like an indictment than summary of James' life.

Rowland rocked back a bit and spun his chair so that he could peer out the window behind him. "James, I don't get it. Can you enlighten me?"

Warden Rowland had accurately summarized James' environment, but not all of it. James thought to himself, "how can I possibly make Rowland understand? How can I make myself understand?"

As his mind tore through the fated twists and turns that deposited him in prison, nothing made sense anymore – nothing. Caught abetting a notorious drug dealer in a buy that went south, James copped a plea with the DA that reduced his own sentence in exchange for turning State's evidence against the dealer. Despite the plea bargain and his "minor" role – setting up the buy – Abrams threw the book at him – six years hard time. Now age twenty and two months, he wouldn't smell freedom again until he was twenty-six. Good conduct might buy him a job of some kind within the prison, but nothing more. At least a job, any job, he reasoned, would get him out of the cell a few hours each day. Otherwise, within minutes of his meeting with Rowland, he would be processed into the system and locked up alone in a four by eight foot cell. Only ten minutes three times daily for meals, ten minutes for a shower every other day in the community shower room, and fifteen minutes a day in the yard was all he would taste of supervised "freedom."

James sat pensively, his eyes boring a hole in the carpet, as he contemplated Rowland's question.

"Well, son," Rowland insisted. "How did you get here?"

"Sir, I don't know," James said blankly. "I..."

Rowland cut him off. "James Meyers, you got here because you committed a crime. The court declared you guilty. You got here because somewhere along the line neither your parents, nor your teachers, nor the church meant anything to you."

"No sir," James protested. "They do mean something to me."

Rowland wasn't convinced and James seemed to know better than press the point.

"Something you'd better understand young man," Rowland said, his back still to James. "For the next six years prison will be your home, your church and your education system."

Spinning his chair back around, Rowland leaned across his desk toward James. "I wish it were not so for you or for any of the men locked in here." He paused. His lips tightened. Pointing an intrusive finger at James, he turned warden again: "But mark my words, James Taylor Meyers, you will be expected to toe the line. If you fall out of line you *will* be punished – severely if necessary. Do I make myself clear?"

James didn't need the message repeated. Rowland had made himself quite clear.

"Yes sir," James timidly responded his eyes firmly trained on the same spot of carpet he'd stared into since sitting down.

"Look at me!" Rowland demanded.

James raised his eyes, not wanting Rowland to notice the moisture that clouded them. A few tears betrayed him as they fled down his cheeks.

Rowland leaned closer and repeated his question for good measure: "James, I'm going to ask you again. Do you understand the consequences of failure?"

James nodded, dropped his head, and managed to choke out another, "Yes sir, I do."

"We'll talk again at another time," Rowland said rising from his chair. Then in an unexpected gesture, Rowland placed a fatherly hand on James' shoulder. "Son, I want you to make it. You've got youth on your side. You don't impress me as a bad kid. If you don't make twenty-year old mistakes here, you can make something of yourself after you leave." Then he added, "James, I'll be praying for you."

Rowland's parting words and warmth stunned and confused James. Rowland's reputation was that of a hard-bitten prison official nobody dared cross. James would later learn that the warden had two sides – one as a tough but fair prison official, and the other a father figure. Sometimes they seemed to merge as James had just experienced.

Rowland motioned to the guard who immediately stepped forward, lifting James from his seat. James had quite forgotten the guard's presence, lost as he was in Rowland's portentous words; so was a bit put off by the abrupt intrusion.

As the warden's office door closed behind them, iron-gates clanked open in front of them. Back out into the hallway, James was seized by a roiling contradiction of thoughts and emotions. "What was that about?" he mused silently to himself. His image of prison life prohibited any notion of nurture, only cold, even brutish punishment deserved or not. He was prepared to fear, maybe even hate Rowland whom the prison populace dubbed "The Iron Czar." But in the course of only a few minutes he'd witnessed more about the man than the indignant if maybe undeserved contempt fellow inmates held for him. James quietly wondered if every incoming prisoner got the same speech. He wanted to quiz the guard, but thought better of it. The answer would come on its own.

A cold mist draped the yard, chilling James through his dampened county jail jump suit. Water matted his medium length brown hair and streamed down his face. A slight quiver chased through his body. He wondered if it was from the cold rain or fear.

TWO

Rowland leaned against his desk as James followed the guard through the door. "Sad," he mumbled to himself, his face grimaced. In the privacy of his office, with no one to interrupt him, Rowland bowed his head in a long prayerful pause. Only he and God knew what stirred in his thoughts, but certainly young Meyers must have occupied a large part of them.

In meetings, Rowland frequently reminded his staff that the work of the prison exceeded meting out court-decreed justice. It included finding pathways to the souls of the men. He'd admonish them, "Never forget these prisoners are men – men with families who love them. They've failed not only themselves but their families – and society. Our job is not only to keep them in line; it's also to give them direction. We can't just turn them back out into society. We have to help them meet the obligations of living within it."

Rowland had long been a student of humane justice, and longer still of Christian ethics. To him, the two coalesced naturally. Public safety demanded justice for the offended and punishment for the offender. Yet, he reasoned, punishment must fit the crime with an effort to rehabilitating the criminal. Medieval cruelty toward prisoners has no place in humane justice, he argued. But neither, he believed, did modern indulgence. Both must be banished. Even so, Rowland was not naïve to the realities and set backs of the many failed rehabilitation efforts. His Christian faith taught him that transformation came slowly, and was cultivated through mentored, accountable relationships, not the dictates of the state penal system or some prescriptive formula.

Though not all of his staff fell in line with his ideals, none dared defy him. Rowland was as strict with his staff, guards included, as he was with the prisoners. He stubbornly refused favoritism, and accepted none for himself. Fair to a fault, some of his colleagues charged. Yet no one disrespected Rowland, not even those who opposed his philosophy.

The phone ringing – the white one – broke his concentration. A red phone sat beside it with a direct connection to the governor's office. Rowland picked up on the second ring. "Warden Rowland," he answered tersely.

"Good day, Tom, this is Father Ted," came a warm reply. The eternally affable Father Ted was a welcome intrusion into Tom Rowland's day.

"Ah, Father Ted, what can I do for you?"

"I just heard that the Meyers kid was moved into your hotel today."

"That so? Who gave you that tidbit?" Rowland probed.

"The kid's attorney," Father Ted replied. "He seems quite worried about him. How'd he seem to you?"

Rowland paused for a moment to gather his thoughts. "I think he's scared, Ted. James isn't a bad kid. I think, though, he's a very confused and messed up kid."

"Yeah, that seems to be the consensus, Tom."

"What can you tell me about James?" Rowland asked.

"Well, Tom, it's a hazy story," Father Ted said through a sigh.

"It usually is. But give me more background," Rowland insisted.

"From what I gather, the kid comes from a fine home. His dad's an executive with a major banking company and travels a great deal. His mom volunteers regularly at the hospital – reading stories to kids on the cancer ward, and generally keeping them company. I think the family attends a church not too far from our parish."

Rowland cut in: "I know the church. Mary and I used to attend there. Good church."

"I've heard the same," Father Ted offered. "Just the same, the family doesn't seem too connected. Word has it they're out shopping for a new one."

"An unfortunate habit of our times," Rowland acknowledged.

"Sadly true, Tom. But here's the rub: James never connected with the church – ever. In fact, he doesn't seem to have connected with his family either."

"I hear that a lot too. Got any siblings?"

"Yes he does – older sibs: much older. He's got a sister six years his senior and a brother two years older than her. They've got careers and families of their own now. I really don't think James knew them well."

"Sounds like an only child in a full house," Rowland groaned.

"More or less, I think. Friends say that by the time his sibs graduated and moved off to college, James was pretty much abandoned. Oh, don't get me wrong, his folks cared about him, I'm told. But they just didn't interact with him…kind of a superficial…on-off thing…. I really don't know what I'd call it, Tom. But James didn't seem to cause any problems, so I guess the folks just kind of left him alone."

"I get the picture. I see the syndrome every day." Rowland winced and pursed his lips. Too many such stories file into the state house all too regularly.

"I'll bet you do, Tom. It must be tough watching it repeat itself," Father Ted consoled.

"Yeah, it is. Give me more info," Rowland coaxed.

"Honestly, Tom, I don't have much more to tell."

"How'd he drop into the criminal world? That seems quite fuzzy to me."

"Me too: I'm not sure what happened. James wasn't a stand out student – did enough to get by. I spoke with one of his teachers the other day who said he had a lot more in the attic, but just didn't care to apply himself. He'd kind of closed himself off – isolated himself. He hung out more with his computer and books than he did with friends. His basketball coach was floored when he didn't show up for the team his senior year."

"So he was an athlete?" Rowland probed.

"Yeah, a good one, his coach said. He'd made varsity his junior year and got a fair bit of playing time – a sure starter his senior year."

"So what happened? Why didn't he show?" Rowland's juices were flowing.

"No one knows, Tom," Father Ted replied.

"Wait a minute, Ted. Why not? Who dropped the ball?" Rowland could feel his face flush.

"Good question. His coach didn't have an answer when I spoke with him. The teacher I called had no answers either."

"What about the school counseling office, or the administration?"

"No one seems to know."

"You mean no one seems to care!" Rowland barked.

"Calm down, Tom. This is where you and I come in. Granted the 'system' let the kid fall through the cracks – sadly the church did too. Prison is not the best of environments. But we're no strangers to this stuff. We can help this kid. You know that."

Rowland cocked his head and wiped a hand across his brow. "You're right, Ted. I needed to hear that." The strain he felt seemed to seep through the phone to Father Ted.

"Sure, Tom: I understand how you feel," Father Ted said in a soothing voice. "The kid's broken, but you know as well as I do, he doesn't need to stay broken. Are you ready for another long-term reclamation project?"

Rowland smirked out a short chuckle. "Yes, I guess I am, Father, as long as you work with me on this one."

"You know I will, Tom. How about getting together with the posse after work tonight?"

"Sounds good. How about seven o'clock at your office?"

"Sure. I'll call the others," Fr. Ted offered. "See you then."

"Good," Rowland responded and hung up the phone. Once more he dropped his head, arms folded. "Oh Lord, here we go again. Help us."

THREE

Bang! The steel door slammed shut and bolted. Suddenly alone, imprisoned, numb; James tumbled onto his bed and slung an arm over his face.

"Hard," he thought to himself; "Everything's hard. What have I done?" he begged again. From his steel bed to the steel cell, nothing warm just raw…cold…hard. "What a screw up," he blurted pounding his fist against the cement wall.

Every cell in his body ached from exhaustion. As he closed his eyes with his arm still resting across his forehead alternating pangs of resentment, disbelief and panic prowled his consciousness. Scenes so vivid he could neither deny nor escape them played endlessly in his mind: "How'd I get myself into this mess?" he groaned.

"Sh**!"

He flopped onto his side, drawing his legs up, his arms tightly to his chest. A small wooden table with no drawer sat between him and a stainless steel sink. The commode was bolted to the concrete floor next to it. James' eyes roamed the tiny space. At a slender five feet ten inches, he could lie in his bunk and easily rest his feet on the wall barely four feet across from him. A fluorescent fixture fastened to the ceiling poured white light into the room, sterilizing it of color and texture. The walls, a dull greenish gray, only added to the depressive atmosphere.

Again he closed his eyes, hoping everything would just go away. It didn't.

His bunk hung suspended by chains connected to ring-bolts screwed into the walls. It, too, was steel – a single sheet of steel with a thin foam mattress dropped on it. Plain white sheets, a pillow and pillow case with a beige blanket lay folded at the foot of the bed.

His eyes spied a pale blue book atop the table. Instinctively he reached for it, turning it so the title faced him. "Holy Bible," it read. "Gideons," he muttered, and shoved it back on the table. Footsteps outside his cell caught his attention.

He rolled off his bunk and peered through the slit in his door.

"Ray, the doc'll see you now. Get up," a gruff voice ordered.

"Must be a guard," James muttered to himself. He could hear shuffling and then the door slammed closed. Again footsteps went past his cell, and he faintly made out the face of a prisoner. Young, stocky built with cropped brown hair, the dude wasn't much older than himself. As he passed James couldn't help noticing the grim, hardened set of the kid's face. It was stone cold expressionless, like someone who'd had life sucked out of him. Would this be his fate, too? Blood rushed out of his face, his skin went clammy, and he felt he might vomit.

Falling onto the edge of his bunk, he cradled his head in his hands: deep groans his only words. Whether he liked it or not, he would be forced to confront the ugly failure of his life. He couldn't rewind the clock. Nobody was going to issue him a free pass or a do-over. His memories were his only companions in cell C201. Suddenly, if not mercifully, the light went out and darkness cloaked the room. He reached for the blanket, laid back and drifted off.

*****

"No, no, no! What the.... Leave me alone!" James shouted into the emptiness. His eyes flew open searching the darkness. Swathed in sweat and panting, he lay motionless, chest heaving. For a long moment he dwelt in the warped zone of dream and reality, uncertain of his bearings.

"Oh God, I can't take this," he whispered. He took in a couple of deep breaths and began to feel his body relax: his fists opened, the seizing tension from the hellish nightmare slowly released its grip. Ironically, the cold blackness of his cell felt eerily safe. To hear his heartbeat thump in his ears and the rush of air rush through his nose felt reassuring. But closing his eyes again was unthinkable. Sleep was dangerous. Real or fiction, the threatening force of his dreams seemed fatal.

Tonight was not the beginning of nightmares for James. They began the night he was caught. Like tonight he was alone in a cell. Unlike tonight, his fate was not clear. At some point everyone must face his demons. James had delayed his date with judgment as long as possible. But confronted with six years confinement, most of it in isolation, with only his thoughts for company, the season of judgment had arrived. However threatening was the experience of arrest, trial, conviction and sentencing, nothing compared to having to face the deep dark truth of his inner thoughts. The nightmares condemned him. Intense and vivid, whatever pain lay in standing up to the reality of his failures, the nightmares were worse.

Exhaustion finally overcame him forcing his eyes shut. Back in that ethereal zone between sleep and awake, his mind wandered to boyhood, age twelve to be exact. It was a bright and balmy late spring day just before summer break. He had jumped on his bike and raced for Sorrell Field, the lush baseball park named for its generous patron. His dad promised to meet him there after he caught up some things at the office. James remembered skidding his bike to a stop, grabbing his glove from the handlebars as the bike dropped to the ground and racing toward the field. His eyes searched the mostly empty grandstands that day as they had many game days – no dad. "It's early," he thought. "He'll be here. He promised."

A tear escaped out the corner of James' eye and dropped onto the pillow. "He didn't come," he mumbled to himself. "He never came – ever." James cut off his memory and drifted into an exhausted sleep.

FOUR

The "posse" gathered at Father Ted's rectory office as scheduled – four men all told. Tom Rowland arrived in jeans and sweater, his out-of-office attire. Terrance Hall and Mike Scanlon joined them a few moments later.

"How's Anne?"

"Who's asking?" Terrance replied as he walked through the door.

"Me," Fr. Ted said entering the room with a mug of coffee in one hand and muffin in the other.

"Oh, hi Father. Anne's good. Thanks for asking."

"Sure. And how's that strange church you lead?"

"It's good too. Just for the record, I pastor and God leads. But I wouldn't expect a priest to understand the distinction." The men laughed.

Terrance, with Anne's vigilant support, pastors a somewhat edgy new church that caters to at-risk youth. Their clever slogan seems to have caught on with a mostly lost tribe of kids, kids that just don't quite blend with the herd. "If you've been sat and spat on, so was He" hangs on a banner over the coffee-house-turn-worship café situated in a rough part of downtown.

"I never would have guessed you to become clergy, Terrance." Fr. Ted was known for good natured sarcasm that nobody took seriously. Terrance knew to take his comment as a sort of backhanded compliment.

"Oh, really?"

"It just proves God does work in mysterious ways. Just like you and Anne. Who would have guessed?"

Terrance dropped into his chair. "No kidding. That one had to be God."

Terrance and Anne didn't meet on the best of terms. Terrance was a gang leader, the alpha male in the Lobos Unit – tough, defiant... and violent. Arrested during a drug raid, he was pacing the floor in an agitated snit at the county lock up when Anne walked into the interview room. She was assigned to represent him. He made quite the first impression. Heavily tattooed down his arms, with slicked back brown hair, wearing a tight tank top and baggy jeans, Terrance looked every part of a gangland thug. How they got together can only be explained as serendipitous.

"Hello Mr. Hall, I'm Anne," the vivacious young attorney announced sticking out her hand, clutching a brief case with the other.

"What the! Don't tell me you're my lawyer!" he growled, turning his back on her.

"That's right, I am. Have a seat please. We've got a lot to cover."

"You're serious?" Terrance said. "The DA sent *you* to represent *me*?"

"That's right. Is that a problem?" Anne narrowed her eyes, her jaw set square.

"Do you have any idea who I am?"

"Yes I do. But I don't think that's the right question, Mr. Hall."

"Oh," Terrance sneered. "Then what is the right question madam lawyer?"

"Did you do it? Are you guilty?"

Terrance studied his adversary before answering. "What do you think?" he sneered.

Anne acted like she didn't hear him. "I'm going to ask you once more. Are you guilty?"

Terrance recoiled. "Hell no!" he raged in a loud defiant voice, slamming his palms down on the metal table not a foot from her face.

"Funny," Anne said with unruffled composure, fixing an icy stare on her belligerent client. "All this pile of evidence says otherwise." Without blinking, eyes clapped on Hall, she reached into the open brief case beside her and dumped out a thick envelope of photos, lab reports and other damning evidence onto the table in front of him. "Care to revise your statement?" She sat back and folded her arms as if having trumped his ace.

"That's bunk! Where did you get that stuff? It's bunk!" he bellowed almost spitting at her.

"Are you guilty? I'm not going to ask you again."

Hall glowered at Anne, his nostrils flaring with anger. Anne never blinked and waited for his next outburst. It didn't come. She took charge.

"Sit down and answer my question, or I'm going to get up and you are going to jail."

Out gunned, Hall had met his match. Not even the gang molls came off as tough as this pint-sized pest in a dress. He knew he'd been had.

"Okay, you won this one. But I don't like…"

"Don't like what, Mr. Hall? Don't like that I'm a woman?" Anne sat comfortably in her chair: legs and arms crossed, her eyes still focused on his. "How about we get down to business, Mr. Hall? You've been accused of crimes that will put you away for a very long time. So, do you still want to be cute, or do you want to be represented? Just in case you're a bit confused, as your counsel let me advise you, there's a right and wrong answer to the question. Choose wisely." Terrance Hall chose wisely.

Anne got her legal degree magna cum laude from Yale. She was also Tom Rowland's daughter, warden of the prison where Terrance would serve his sentence. Like her dad, she shared a firm and passionate Christian faith. Terrance would run head long into that reality not long after sentencing, though he caught glimpses of it beforehand.

During his trial and for years afterward the two of them – Anne and Terrance – butted heads often and hard. It came to a head one evening at her parent's house. Anne approached her father.

"Daddy," she confided. "I really don't think I'm cut out to represent Hall's case. I hate the jerk!"

Tom Rowland slipped an arm around his daughter's waist, "I know sweetheart. But it seems God thinks otherwise."

"Oh don't say that! I hate God too!" she whined sticking out her lower lip like a pouty school girl.

"Come on, now. Be a big girl," Rowland playfully scolded. "Pray for him, Anne. Pray for him like I'm praying for you." Oh she hated it when daddy played the "pray for so and so" card. It really ruined her mad.

"Alright but I'm not going to like it," she sassed, stomping off to help her mother with dinner.

After Terrance's sentencing Anne stopped by the prison to check on him. There was not one flicker of romantic interest in their meetings: strictly business. In process, God convicted Anne. She was his legal representative – purely attorney client. Nothing else. God, it seemed, wanted more. "Be my witness…" she read in her morning devotional. The words burnt into her heart. "To Terrance Hall?" she fairly begged. "God, aren't there men for that job?" She shoved the devotional book back on the desk. "Me?" Finally she relented, but only after a tussle with her soul lasting a few days. "Okay, Lord. I get the message. Use me." And he did.

Hall didn't take well to her "conversion tactics" at first, any more than he warmed to her legal counsel, pretty much telling her where she could "stick it." She persisted. In time, Anne, as well as her father, helped Terrance face himself. It was, though, God he couldn't face. Terrance hated God – the manically cruel villain he blamed for stealing his mother when he was six, killing his brother when he was ten, and abandoning him to the streets when he was fourteen. Reconciling a loving God with so many undeserved tragedies didn't square. But neither did the nurturing and fatherly concern Rowland extended him square with his impressions of prison life, or Anne's interest in his soul. It took most of the six years he was imprisoned before Terrance finally began to trust what they were telling him – and showing him. Then one morning Rowland said something that stuck.

"Terrance, my job here is to keep men confined. God's work in Jesus is to set men free. I want you to be free, son. I want you to *be* free." Terrance saw tears form in Rowland's eyes. In all the years of meeting together, he'd never seen tears; never felt them in his own eyes. Only alone, in the dark of night would he let moisture cloud his eyes. More than the words, the tears registered. In them, Terrance witnessed authentic vulnerability in a man he at first hated but had more recently come to respect – even revere.

"Freedom" he repeated softly to himself. The word startled him. He'd never known it; never trusted it; never felt he could have it. But suddenly it was in front of him. Rowland had just handed him the "get out of jail free" card he desperately craved. In that moment Terrance's world flipped – forever.

Staring intently into Rowland's clouded eyes Terrance's shoulders began to heave. Sobbing inconsolably, he bent over in the chair burying his head in his hands. Rowland rested a hand on Terrance's back. "Terrance, may I pray for you?" Too broken to speak, he merely nodded his consent. Rowland prayed, "Save my boy, dear Lord. Help him to let you save him."

"Terrance, are you ready to let God in?"

Terrance swayed up and down, "Yes! Please help me!" he shouted into his hands.

"Just let it go, son. Tell God everything. Ask him to forgive you."

Suddenly, Terrance found himself disgorging decades of hatred and contempt between convulsive sobs; begging God's forgiveness; crying out in anguish for salvation; praying to the God he formerly cursed, the one who had just set him free.

Moments later a broken but new man stood and met Rowland's open embrace. From that day forward their meetings took on a different tone. Before the week ended, Terrance joined an inmates' Bible study led by Fr. Ted, where he met other reclaimed prisoners – men reclaimed from a hell worse than jail.

*****

"Hi daddy," Anne chirped into her phone. "What's up?"

"Hi honey, I think you might want to check in with Terrance later this afternoon," Rowland said with a touch of vagueness in his voice.

"Why? You're being awfully mysterious," Anne replied, taking another sip of tea.

Rowland laughed, "Well, let's just say you'll be talking with a different man."

"Tell me daddy! You tell me now!" Anne could hardly contain her anticipation.

"Terrance became a new man," she heard her dad say. "Anne, Terrance broke and gave his life to Christ just a few moments ago."

Anne sat her cup aside, lifted her head toward the heavens and let out a loud, "Thank you Lord!" She began to weep.

"Oh, Daddy, that is the best news I've heard! Thank you! Thank you! Thank you!"

"No sweetheart; Thank God!" Rowland said leaning into his chair. "Now, Anne, the real work begins."

"I know," Anne said. "I'm ready. I'm truly, honestly ready!"

That was two years ago. Shortly after Terrance's release, Tom Rowland walked down a long aisle, Anne on his arm, and presented his daughter to this one time gangster now a reclaimed child of God – and preacher.

Terrance leaned into his chair. "You're right, Fr.," he smiled. "That was God!"

*****

Terrance stood when Tom re-entered the room. Tom greeted his son-in-law like he always did, with a warm hug and firm handshake.

"Ok, knock off the sap," Fr. Ted said rolling his eyes. "Where's Scanlon?"

Mike Scanlon entered on cue stirring cream into a cup of coffee from the rectory pot.

"This the same ink we drank last week?" he chided.

Mike Scanlon – Scanlon or Scans to the posse and his friends – owns an excavation company just outside of town, a second-generation operation begun by his father in the early 1950s. A medium height husky fellow with burly arms, Scanlon played linebacker in high school "a billion years ago," he'd say. He met Terrance through a prison ministry in his church, and has known Tom and Fr. Ted for several years.

Unrefined bordering on crude, Scanlon had overcome his own demons – alcoholism in particular. Of course he had help – his lovely, patient wife of twenty years most especially.

Sally loved her hulk of a man dearly. But after a decade of watching him waste himself in booze, the time came when she handed Mike an ultimatum: either he cleaned up or she'd move out. No one thought she would say it, certainly not do it. Despite being far from a timid sort, Sally still hated confrontation. Worse, she couldn't reconcile Christian faith with threatening to leave. It took her months to work up the courage and suffer through feelings of guilt before she put Mike on the line. Finally the night came when the inevitable could no longer be avoided.

Mike stumbled through the locked door drunk and tumbled onto the living room sofa. Sally strode into the room, arms folded, glaring angrily at the pathetic figure of her husband.

"Get up, Mike!" she demanded.

Mike squinted through bleary eyes, waving one of his thick hands at her, "Not now Sally. I'm not up to hearing about it now." He threw his head back on a sofa pillow and moaned.

"Get up," she insisted. "Get up or I'm leaving!"

"Wha...?" Sally had never threatened to leave.

"I mean it, Mike! I've had it! Look at yourself! Look at me! I'm telling you, it's either the bottle, Mike, or it's me...and the kids." Sally could hardly believe the words that fell out of her mouth, but she wasn't about to take them back. For Mike's sake as well as her own, and the sake of their family, she couldn't take them back.

27

Mike tumbled onto the floor trying to get to his feet. From his knees he studied Sally's stern and tear-swollen face. Surely she didn't mean what she said. "Look, Sally, I'm a mess. Let me clean up and we'll talk," he slurred while clumsily rising to his feet.

"No, Mike, we've done all the talking we're going to do. Time you make up your mind about what's most important to you. You've got one day to decide." With that Sally marched down the hall, slammed the bedroom door shut and locked it.

Sally's love never flagged. Her heart belonged to Mike, and it always would. But he had to do his part. He had to get and stay sober.

Sally threw herself on the bed, desolated by what transpired in the living room – angry at Mike, angry at herself. "Oh, God," she cried. "What have I done?" In desperation she phoned her best friend and confidant, Mary Rowland, Tom Rowland's wife. Mary had stood with her, offering a listening ear and voice of reason, not to mention hours of prayer. They had a *posse* of their own, other women who met regularly to pray and support one another.

Scanlon finally came to his senses. Of all the things he felt he could lose, losing Sally was not an option. The next morning, he phoned the local AA director and that night entered the door to recovery. That road also led him to faith in God.

Fr. Ted broke in again, "So gentlemen: Let's talk about young Mr. Meyers."

Fr. Ted could be counted on to get things rolling. The lone Catholic in a room of Protestants, he relished the mix. No one thought about it really – the Catholic and Protestant thing. Their purpose was clear – guide their charges to faith and freedom.

Listening to him, no one would think Fr. Ted a scholarly type. But like Tom Rowland, Fr. Theodore Charles Harding, held a doctorate of philosophy, his from Notre Dame in liturgical theology preceded by a Masters of Arts in moral theology from Loyola University. For a decade Fr. Ted served as assistant then associate professor of theology at Loyola. An ache for parish ministry, though, led him into the priesthood and to the congregation he has served for the past seven years.

This whole posse thing began with three of the men – Fr. Ted, Tom Rowland and Mike Scanlon. Shaken by a shared tragedy, they galvanized in a resolve to never let it happen again. A young inmate had taken his life, a young man each man knew well. How the kid slipped through the cracks remains a mystery. Tom Rowland took it especially hard. The incident occurred in his prison, under his watch. For the longest time, he blamed himself for missing the signs. "I'm too much an administrator and too little a mentor," he accused. Regardless, the incident shook each man; it shook them to their very core. The evening following the young man's funeral, Fr. Ted invited the men to his study, the very place they gathered tonight.

"I don't know what happened that brought Mark to kill himself," Fr. Ted began. "But I can't help thinking each of us should have seen it coming. Gentlemen, this can't happen again. Somehow we need to reach out to the Mark's of the world and guide them to hope – to Christ."

Somber heads nodded in agreement. Rowland shut his eyes and grimaced. Scanlon looked away in tears. Thus began a process of intervention, intercession and inter-relational mentorship – the posse. No young man need suffer the fate that tragically ended young Mark Dempsey's life.

"So, guys, about Mr. Meyers," Fr. Ted repeated. "What do we know and what steps do we take?"

"Ted, this Meyers kid reminds me a lot of Mark," Tom Rowland said, inflecting a grave tone in his voice. "He's a scared and confused young man, sickened by the circumstances that threw him in prison."

"I agree," Scanlon added. "You guys might remember that Mark stopped by my house the night he got busted. We spoke, not for long. But I'll never forget something he said to me. 'Mike,' he said, 'I don't have any hope, none.' At the time I just thought he was feeling sorry for himself." Scanlon paused. "Guys, I don't want to make that same mistake with the Meyers kid." The gut-deep conviction in Scanlon's voice drew a pained reaction from each man and a long pause before Tom intervened.

"Terrance, what do you know about James?" he asked, preparing to take notes on the legal pad that sat atop his crossed legs.

"Not a lot, I'm afraid. He came by the café on occasion, usually by himself. He never stayed long or hung out with anyone in particular. I tried to speak to him but he never really gave me much…barely the time of day."

"Dang it, that's just what Mark did," Scanlon blurted. "He never let anybody in." Scanlon shook his head and threw himself back in his seat.

"You're right, Mike," Terrance consoled. "That's what bugs me about Meyers."

"Did he ever talk about friends or his family?" Fr. Ted questioned, while shuffling through his own notes.

"No, not really," Terrance responded, raising his eyes as if searching his mind for more information. "He did mention that his dad was real busy and out of town a lot. I got the impression they didn't spend much time together."

"That's my impression," Tom interjected. "James blanched when I brought up his folks. He defended them, but I could tell there wasn't much real connection. The same for the church; he just blew it off."

Each of the guys paused to think. Tom Rowland scribbled notes on his pad. Scanlon stirred his coffee. "So," Fr. Ted re-opened the conversation, combing his beard with his fingers. "It appears we have a disillusioned kid, a frightened kid, with no one in his corner. Does that about cover it?" He searched the room for a response.

"Yeah, I think so, Ted," Tom nodded. Tom was the only one who got away with dropping the father from Ted's name, and Fr. Ted never corrected him. They'd been through enough of these ugly affairs together, respect was not in doubt, neither was their long and trusted friendship.

"Suicide watch, Tom?" Fr. Ted asked with a serious expression creasing his face.

"Definitely, Ted. He's being watched," Tom assured.

"Good! Now, where do we go from here?"

Terrance returned from the kitchen crunching on an apple, "Tom, how about I drop in on James early next week? Can I get cell time with him?"

"I can arrange it, Terrance," Tom replied, pulling his glasses down on his nose while looking up at his son-in-law. "I like the idea. We'll have to make other arrangements going forward, though. Protocol." Terrance rolled his eyes. Protocol wasn't his long suit – too much life spent bucking it.

"Protocol or not, I like the idea too," added Fr. Ted. "Ok men, looks like we have our assignment. Let's pray for our new charge. He and we will need it. Let's meet here same time next week."

The men of the posse bowed in their seats while Fr. Ted led them in prayer.

FIVE

"Go, go, go!" Loud shouting echoed down the long cell block. Lunging for the window slit, James spied a faint blur of uniformed guards racing by. He strained his vision as far as he could twist his eyes toward the ruckus. Other guards ran past, their hands stuffed in blue nitril gloves and carrying zip ties used to restrain out of control prisoners. "Oh no," James muttered. "Somebody got nailed."

"Back up to the door kid and drop your hands behind you!" a guard demanded in a gruff voice. It didn't register with James that the guard meant him. Suddenly the guard's eyes filled the narrow window. "Did you hear me? I said…"

"Me? What have I done?" James' first thoughts were that somehow he'd been falsely implicated in the mess down the hall. "Sir, honestly I've done nothing."

"Stop worrying, kid. You've got a visitor. Now give me your wrists." The rasp of a key twisted in a lock and a small plate-like gate somewhat larger than the window slit dropped open about waist high. James put his hands together behind him and backed up to the slot. The guard pulled his arms through the narrow slot as far as he could and clasped cuffs around each wrist. James grimaced against the pressure of the cuffs, feeling his hands begin to numb as the cuffs bit into his wrists.

"A visitor? Who?"

"You'll find out." A buzzer went off and the bolt securing the lock slid out with a loud scrape. "Step out and face forward," the guard ordered, as the door creaked open.

James complied, but his mind remained foggy. "A visitor: Who? Today?" Visitors come on Sunday not Monday.

His parents saw him yesterday, a rather tense, uneasy meeting. His mother's eyes never cleared of tears, and his dad's eyes never met his. Few words were spoken, and those that were remained surface level, a clearly intentional dancing around the proverbial elephant in the room. James hadn't really looked forward to greeting his folks, not here, not under these circumstances. He was still dealing with denial – so were they. Not once were the painful questions asked, "What happened, son? Where'd we go wrong?" After awhile they sounded more like rhetorical pleadings with an edge of indictment to them. They indicted him for ruining his – and their – life. They indicted his parents for their apparent failure.

Mercifully, visits had time limits – ten minutes. But those ten minutes took hours to psych up for and hours to unwind from. To James Sunday visits were sheer agony, one day each week he wished to avoid. Every one of them was like another day before the judge. That trend didn't resolve soon, and time was not the healer.

Standing outside his cell produced a welcome distraction from his thoughts. Thinking, endless hours of thinking drove many a man to the brink of insanity. Alone with only one's thoughts: could there be a more dangerous imprisonment? For James it meant long hours of profound sadness. Images of his life played in an endless loop, always coming to the same dead end – prison. And always he'd curl into a ball on his bed and beg for it to end.

In the week since incarceration at the State House, James had already formed indelible impressions of prison culture. The defiance registered by fellow inmates confused him. It seemed they made a lifestyle of it, justifying their behaviors by a cynical street code that for all the look of it was merely a means of surviving. It seemed more like a code between wolves than between men. He understood no such code. Despite his predicament he could not deny the many options he had available to him – options that did not lead to prison. Still, he could not reconcile the route he took or the reasons he took it. Loneliness? Bitterness: but at what?

"Ok, kid, let's move." The guard took James by his left arm and directed him down the block to the far door that leads into a wide, square-shaped prisoner's plaza with round red steel tables and mushroom shaped stools fastened to the concrete floor: the one colorful place in prison. Here better behaved inmates could sit and shoot the bull for a few minutes a day in a semi-relaxed atmosphere. Semi-relaxed! A prisoner never truly relaxes; he never turns his back or drops his guard, even in the plaza. Sudden fights, often for reasons of retaliation could erupt like the one that broke out moments earlier at the other end of the block.

Another buzzer sounded and a door swung open. Through it the guard led James to the same room where he met his parents yesterday. At first he was repulsed by the thought they might have returned. Instead, he found a medium height, slender built dude in jeans and denim jacket standing beside the dark wood table flanked by wooden chairs.

"You must be James," his visitor offered, extending his hand as the guard re-cuffed James' wrists in front of him.

"Yes sir, I am. But who are you?" James asked, coolie eyeing his visitor. He was momentarily distracted by a tattoo poking above the dude's collar.

"I'm Terrance, James. I used to hang out here."

"Oh yeah, what for?"

"We'll get to that later," Terrance answered, motioning for James to take a seat.

"You guys have ten minutes," the guard interjected abruptly. Both Terrance and James looked up at him. Terrance nodded and the guard stepped out. They seemed to know one another.

James was too puzzled to simply let slide Terrance's deferral. This guy whom he'd never met before made him uneasy. For all James knew, he might be a vengeful buyer who got stiffed the night the deal went bust. He clearly looked the part. But more likely, he was a NARC, a drug cop or a stooge hired by them.

"Ok, but why are you here and how do you know me?" James sat rigidly in his seat, his cuffed hands lying in his lap, his eyes riveted on the visitor.

"We have a mutual friend, James, a guy who watched out for me while I resided here. He asked I stop by. Besides, you might not remember but we met at the café." Terrance leaned on his elbows across from James.

"Café?"

"Yeah, the Cafe. It's a kind of gathering place for kids where we worship God and share life together. Sometimes we even call it a church," Terrance said with wry grin.

"Oh, yeah, you're the preacher there," James said smugly.

Laughing, Terrance said, "Well not too many call me a preacher. I'm just the dude who runs the place."

"You mentioned a mutual friend? Here? Who?" James shot in rapid fire. "I don't know anyone here unless you mean Warden Rowland. He's the only... Wait a minute!"

"You'd be right, James," Terrance filled in the blank. "Actually it's worse than that," he continued. "The Warden is my father-in-law too," he said through another wry grin.

"You've got to be kidding me," James fired back. "Ok, I'll bite. So Warden Rowland sent you in here to keep an eye on me?"

"Not quite. I offered and the warden thought it was a good idea."

"Why? Man, I'm lost," James shook his head and twisted in his chair. Terrance understood what James meant by lost but spun it another direction.

"Good response. You don't get in here because you've got stuff figured out. Believe me, I understand the word lost. Hell, man, I practically invented the word." Terrance shrugged his denim jacket off and swung it around the back of his chair. James immediately caught sight of a familiar gang tag, the snarling wolf tattooed on the inside of Terrance's right arm, with the word Lobos in thick gothic letters beneath it.

"Lobos," James said without thinking. "You a Lobo?"

"Was, James. Not anymore."

"You dudes are a bad bunch," James chided.

"Like I said, James...was but not anymore. I'm way done with that group and that lifestyle." Terrance shoved his thick dark hair back with his fingers, and shifted in his chair, crossing his arms on the table. "Look, kid, I'll be straight with you. I was the alpha Lobo? You know what that means?" Suddenly Terrance's face went taut and his eyes turned steely gray.

James felt his stomach tighten. He knew he'd been put in his place. "Yeah, I know what it means. You're the dude, the boss. You're a legend!"

"Was, James. Don't make me remind you. I no longer belong to that bunch."

"Yes sir," James acknowledged and sat a little straighter.

Terrance relaxed the tension and softened his voice. "Besides, I'm married to the man's daughter. She's the boss now, if you know what I mean."

James's jaw dropped. "You married the Warden's daughter? What were you thinking, dude?"

"Hey, stuff happens!"

Was this the fearsome gang leader he'd heard about on the streets – a gangland legend he'd never met?

"So, what does the boss do? She seems to have tamed you?"

Terrance threw himself back with a laugh, "Man, that's a great question. Well, if you've got to know, she's a lawyer."

"You serious? That's crazy, man. You married a lawyer! She's the warden's daughter and a lawyer?" James was incredulous.

"Oh it's worse than that. She was my lawyer before she was my wife. And believe me, James, I'm the winner." Terrance needn't wait long for a reaction.

"You're weird, man! She spring you from this place?"

"No, she didn't! I did my time."

James stared stunned at Terrance. He'd never met a man like him. Who'd go to prison as a felon gangster, hookup with the warden, then his daughter and come back to this stink-hole to see him?

Terrance pulled his wallet from his back pocket and showed James a picture of the two of them. "She saved my life, James. She gave me hope but she never made it easy. I was guilty, plain and simple. I deserved prison – maybe worse. I was definitely on the wrong path. Anne and Warden Rowland, well, let's just say I owe them."

"She's beautiful," James offered.

"I think so," Terrance confirmed, stuffing the wallet back into his pocket.

James sat motionless. He wanted to probe but got the impression there'd be a better time.

"They treating you okay here?" Terrance asked.

"It's prison. So far nobody's done anything if that's what you mean."

"Good. We'll hope it stays that way."

"You have any trouble here?" James asked hoping for a good report.

"Yeah, I did. But it was my fault. I was pretty hostile at first."

"What do ya mean?"

"Lobo wolves in the wild are a lot like our gang. They don't like borders unless they make them. I was penned up and fought it. In fact, I never really got over it."

"Like I said before, you seem tame now. How'd that happen?"

Terrance prepared to leap on the question. It was the opening he wanted.

About then the door opened and the guard stepped in. "Wrap it up guys. Time's up."

"Looks like we'll have to get into that later. Mind if I stop by again?"

"Sure. That'd be fine. Thanks." James stood as Terrance rose and the men shook hands best they could with cuffs clapped onto James' wrists.

"Look," Terrance offered. "For what it's worth I'm praying for you kid. A few of us, including Tom, I mean Warden Rowland, are. I'll tell you more next time." With that, Terrance slapped James on the shoulder and exited the room. The guard stepped over, took James by the arm and escorted back to his cell.

How utterly weird, James thought. He didn't know what to make of Terrance's visit or what would become of their acquaintance, but he looked forward to seeing him again. He definitely wanted an answer to his last question. Despite the uneasiness of having someone seem almost too familiar with his circumstances, James wasn't repulsed by it either. Something about Terrance said he could be trusted. For a rebellious sort, he certainly seemed at peace with himself now. But how?

SIX

No one would have called James a bookish kid. He was a loner, though – few friends, none close. And yet patrolling his room at home, it would become apparent the kid did indeed have a fertile mind, as one of his teachers inferred to Fr. Ted. An odd assortment of books lied in untidy stacks on the floor and strung across shelves laid over latticed pumice blocks – superhero sagas, text books from his three semesters of community college, and a biography of Magic Johnson. Interspersed among lesser known authors were titles by Dostoevsky, Camus, Sartre, and Foucault – deep reads. From appearances, he spent time with them. Dog-eared with Sticky Notes flagging particular pages, he also made copious margin notes, often with question marks behind one or two words, as if begging the author for clarity. On the bottom shelf rested a small stack of thin, narrow soft-padded books bound in dark red faux leather – his journals. They were tucked away as if given special residence on the shelves, the private musings of their author. Doubtful anyone knew about them or their contents. Doubtful anyone knew he thought on a level worthy of a journal, or held questions that plagued his conscience and made him wonder why he existed. Beneath his journals rested a Bible, a birthday gift from his folks, which from appearances didn't get much attention. On a small wood desk beside his bed sat a computer monitor and his lap-top plugged into a docking station. The remote keyboard showed wear, the slick oily prints of James' palms where he'd likely spent countless hours gaming, programming, web-browsing, interacting in a flat-screen environment. The computer was shut down, more or less like his life.

In his cell, James began scribbling notes onto sheets of ruled paper. In a week, he'd amassed several pages of scribbling, early ruminations about prison life, but mostly about ironies. "I met Terrance this morning. Curious dude," he began. From there he jotted quick impressions as if adding sums, taking a stab at what "all this stuff means." By all this stuff, he seemed to imply anomalies, out of the place intrusions like Terrance's parting words, "I'll be praying for you, James."

Rowland said those very words a week earlier. There was gentleness to them that felt like a reassuring arm around his shoulder. They also had an edge to them, the jabbing certitude that not all was right with his world, his life. The words seemed to come from somewhere deep within each man who spoke them, words they meant to say, conveying a message they intended James to hear. The words bothered James, though he wasn't sure why. He needed an arm around him but resisted it. Where was that fatherly, reassuring arm before he messed up? Only after all hell broke loose did he ever hear his dad say "I'm praying for you, son." Given the timing, the words sounded more like an excuse for failure, his and his dad's – like an added indictment. From Rowland and Terrance, they were different. He felt the intentionality of them in Rowland's squeeze of his shoulder, and in the seriousness of Terrance's eyes. "But what the heck do these guys mean? Do they think God, if there really is a God, actually cares about me?"

James continued to jot. "Prison, the death of my soul," fell onto the page. He dwelt on the words. "What soul," he sneered? Picking up the pen again he wrote, "My soul died before prison. I have no soul. I have no future. I have no life." What else he wrote remains with him. He took those sheets and tore them to shreds before chucking them onto the floor and curling up onto his bed dejected and alone.

He awoke in darkness. Just a faint glow from the hall light outside framed the steel door. With no light to read by he couldn't tell what time it was. The alarm clock his folks left with him wasn't plugged in. Time didn't matter. Calendars insulted whatever quiver of hope he mustered, reminding him that freedom lied a far distance into a nebulous future. To a twenty-year old six years was an eternity, nearly a third of the life he'd already lived. Too awake to sleep, too drowsy to concentrate, he lay motionless on his bed and let his mind drift.

A line from Foucault played in his thoughts. "People know what they do; frequently they know why they do what they do; but what they don't know is what what they do does."[1] James couldn't avoid the realization that his actions rippled wide, affecting a broadening stream of people. He cringed at the pitiful images of his parents' faces – pleading, inconsolable expressions staring at him in the darkness of his imagination. His brother hasn't spoken to him since his arrest. His sister attended the sentencing mostly to support the folks. She turned her head away from him when he was escorted from the courtroom, apparently too overcome with shame or anger – perhaps both – to look at him. No word from her since he arrived in prison. Estrangement, the most guilelessly painful reality of incarceration, abandonment by family and friends and ultimately of self, this would be his most plaguing nemesis. It would be the echo in his mind of how far and how penetrating his actions ranged. Then, too, James didn't have a good grasp on the why. All was doubt. Eventually, however, answers would come – ironies of another sort.

---

[1] Michel Foucault, *Madness and Civilization: A History of Insanity in the Age of Reason*.

SEVEN

"Scanlon! Answer the phone," Sally shouted from the bedroom. Mumbling under his breath and rubbing his head, Mike Scanlon reached for the receiver.

"Yeah," he said while hooking a chair with his foot from the dinette and scooting it over toward himself. "This is Mike."

"Hey, Mike, it's me, Terrance, got a minute?"

"Yeah, T, sure what's up?"

"I just met with the kid."

"Oh yeah, wha's he like?" Scanlon said while plopping down onto the chair.

"Cautious but not jaded, I'd say," Terrance replied adding, "I don't think the whole thing's sunk in yet. I think he's still in a daze. The uniform doesn't fit so to speak."

"Well, let's hope it never fits, if you get my drift."

"Sure do," Terrance replied. "Hey, look, you up for joining me say next Monday?"

"Hah, man, you sure he's ready for me? You weren't at first," Scanlon shot back.

Laughing, Terrance answered, "Well, everybody needs a loveable menace just to keep things on edge. Besides, I honestly think he'll listen to you."

"Fine, let's plan on next Monday. You meeting with the posse this week?"

"Yep. See you then. By the way, Mike, you don't sound so good. You okay?" Terrance could hear more than normal fuzziness coming out of Scanlon.

"Oh, I whacked my head getting out from under the kitchen sink," Scanlon groaned.

"Ha ha, you're a case dude! What the heck were you hanging out under the sink for? Sally banish you there?"

"Don't get cute, T. I can still handle you," Scanlon said mustering his best machismo. "I was fixing a clogged pipe. Now buzz off!"

"Okay, man. Have a nice day," Terrance chuckled in mock sincerity.

"Scanlon: Who was that?" Sally caught a bit of the conversation.

"Terrance, honey. He was filling me in about the new kid at Tom's joint."

"What's the story?" she insisted.

"T wants me go with him next week to visit the kid. That's all."

"Well, Mike," Sally entered the room and spied Mike straddling the dinette chair. "Good Lord, Scanlon, what have you done? You've got blood running down the side of your face!" Sally dashed for the kitchen sink, soaked a dish towel and thrust it at Mike.

"Nothin'," Scanlon muttered fumbling to place the towel on his wound. "I was just following orders." He lifted an eyebrow to see if Sally heard him.

"Orders! Scanlon, I never told you to clobber yourself, just fix the darn leak!" They both broke out laughing.

"Honey," she began with her arms folded around Mike's thick neck, "I believe in you. So does T and the rest of the posse. Just love young James as if he were your son. Show him what becoming a man means. You did it and I love you for the man you've become, Mike Scanlon. Lead James home. Lead him to Jesus." Sally then planted a kiss on Mike's cheek and dashed off to run errands.

For all his clumsiness in manners as well as plumbing, Mike Scanlon could be counted on. His word was a surety to anyone who knew him. Even during tough times, when work for excavators was sparse, Mike took care of his people and honored his commitments, a characteristic he got from his father. Instead of drowning his anxieties in booze as he did for more than a decade, Mike now appealed to God.

Though he had a bunch of trusted friends, Scanlon confided in just one person, Sally. Sally had a ruggedness about her, just sheer determination that never flagged regardless of circumstance. He'd occasionally quip, "Babe, I think you're a better man than I'll ever be." She'd jerk her head around and flip her ponytail at him, "Yep, Scans, you're right," wink and run down the hall giggling.

What Sally gave Mike Scanlon was stability, something he never had. Mike's dad lived to work. More of a boss than a dad, Mike never really got to know his father. Moral to the core but as distant as fire from ice, Mike's dad was unapproachable and demanding. He'd say, "If you've got energy to play ball, then you're shirking on me." Mike lived under a load of guilt and frustration throughout his teenage, never able to please his old man, never able to let his guard down. Home was a cold place. Sally spun that mold around. She came from exactly the opposite background. An electrician's daughter, she never had a lot but she had all she needed and much of what she wanted. Mostly, though, Sally had a daddy, a man who'd invite her to crawl up into his lap and watch Saturday cartoons together. He was there for her and her siblings even after long hours on the job.

Mike and Sally fell in love as high school seniors. She was the perky cheerleader and he the behemoth offensive tackle. She got great grades – salutatorian. Mike passed. Soon after graduation with plans for college, Mike's dad suffered a damaging heart attack that derailed Mike's football scholarship to Colorado. The eldest of four kids, he went to work for the company, and helped his mom who kept the company books and managed the office.

Unlike his old man, Mike's mom was kind of like Sally without the perkiness. Levelheaded, honest, no nonsense but welcoming – the guys that worked for Scanlon Excavation, Inc. stayed because Maggie kept them there. When the "old man" got surly, she somehow knew how to smooth the waters and keep an even keel. "Ah, heck, Chuck, just let it go in one ear and out the other," she'd say to a disgruntled but valued employee. "He's just being a crank. You're a great guy and we love having you around here." That usually stifled dissension. Maggie built and re-built the morale her husband, Mike Sr., destroyed. Make no mistake, though, Scanlon's employees worked hard for the old man, out of loyalty built up over decades of fighting through tough times together. For all his warts, Mike Sr. took care of his crew. Bruce Benning, Mike Sr.'s long-term foreman would say, "Senior'd take food off his own table before he'd let any of us go hungry." Senior died a year later from a third and fatal heart attack.

Ready or not and scared witless, Mike Jr. was thrust into running the company. His mom stood beside him, encouraging as well as teaching him the intricacies of the business part of excavation. In time, however, the pressure of living up to his dad's expectations drove Mike to booze. He'd never imbibed. As an athlete he'd climb all over his teammates for "poisoning themselves" with the stuff. Within a year of his first beer one Friday night with the boys, Mike had tumbled hard into alcoholism. It was Sally who rescued him. It was Fr. Ted who led him through AA and to faith in God. It took half a decade and the threat of losing all he cared about before Mike Scanlon beat the bottle and found his way to new life. Now, he was the rescuer – a job that unnerved him more than running the family firm. But it was a job he took seriously even if crudely.

EIGHT

Rowland walked the perimeter of the yard from the second story deck. Dressed in a neatly pressed business suit and wool top coat, he looked more the part of a banker than lawyer turn prison official. Two kinds of wardens ran modern prisons – those who mingled among the men and spoke their jive; and those like Tom Rowland, more authoritarian and removed. With him walked the chief guard, Harold Raynor, a man who'd worked in prison systems for more than two decades. Raynor held tenure over Rowland at the State House, and understood the climate. He'd watched three wardens come and go ahead of Rowland, none of them surviving more than a few years, each succumbing to trenchant realities that never conform to idealism. Almost comically the caprice of criminal minds outwitted the ideologues, regardless of their cultured and well educated theories. Rowland, though similarly educated, had witnessed these disillusionments from his work in trial law. Though not naïve to the realities, he, nevertheless, needed the benefit of a hands-on, well experienced – and well worn – tutor. In Raynor, he had that person.

"What do you make of the Meyers boy, Harold?"

"Well, for one he doesn't fit the mold."

"What do you mean," Rowland asked, facing Raynor.

"Most guys come in here with a chip on their shoulders. They want to blame society, their parents or somebody for their 'raw deal.'" Pointing with his head toward James, he said, "Meyers doesn't fit that description. The kid seems clear about what he did, maybe not why he did it."

"That's what Terrance seems to think also," Rowland replied. "Any worries?"

"No, none yet, Tom." Raynor paused then remarked, "Well, maybe one."

"What's that?" Raynor had Rowland's attention. He usually did, because he was usually right.

"I think, Tom, the kid's trapped in an isolated world. No one's paid much attention to him, so perhaps he created a reason to. Maybe he so to speak pulled the alarm and waited to see who'd show up."

"You think he deliberately got himself into trouble just to stir up attention for himself?" Rowland's voice rose as if questioning Raynor's opinion.

"No, not quite, Tom. I don't think he went out looking for trouble. I think trouble found him. I think he wanted someone to take him seriously and unfortunately the wrong guys did. They used him and he fell for it – most likely out of desperation."

"I can buy that." Rowland pushed his collar over his ears and shoved his hands into his pockets before continuing his walk. "You might be right on point," he added. Raynor, quietly walked beside him, each man with his eyes on the kid seated alone on a bench pushed up against the wall nearest the doors.

"What are you thinking, Tom?" Raynor broke in after they stepped back inside the warm building.

"I don't know, Harold. We tested him a couple days after he arrived. Do you have any idea what he scored?" Tom pulled open a door and waited for Harold to walk by him.

"No, I haven't seen the scores yet."

"They came late yesterday. Betty put them on my desk thinking I ought to see them before calling it a day."

"So, what'd they reveal?" Raynor stopped walking and looked at Rowland for an answer.

"Let's just say, Harold, the kid could do anything he puts his mind to. He's got an excellent intellect. He just hasn't used it intelligently."

"Maybe no one's given him the owner's manual. Has anyone ever shown an interest in his development?"

"Of course not!" Rowland growled. "The whole wretched world let this youngster slide unnoticed, untaught and unwanted."

Raynor shook his head then squared his jaw. "Well, maybe we ought to show him how to put that quality mind to good use."

Rowland smiled and took his friend by the arm. "You're right, Harold. That's exactly what we're going to do."

NINE

Living among felons was dangerous. It didn't take James long to find out how dangerous. Sitting idly in the yard, he attempted to go unseen, just fade into the wall. Men shuffled past, most of them seeming to ignore him. No one made an attempt to sit beside him. Still, he couldn't avoid feeling mildly anxious. Stuff happens in prison, often without warning.

The buzzer's blare announced the end of yard time. As he stood up to slip through the door, James heard the guy beside him gasp. Suddenly the guy fell to the ground grabbing his stomach. Blood oozed through his clothes, soaking his hands. No one stopped. One by one other inmates stepped over the fallen prisoner and shuffled idly down the hall as if nothing had happened. James crouched down to help the stricken prisoner. "Hey man, what's wrong?" Then he saw the blood. "Why are you bleeding, man?" James begged in stunned disbelief.

"I'm stabbed. Help me bro!" the guy pleaded writhing in pain.

"Hey, dude, get out of the way. It's cold out here," one of the inmates bellowed from just outside the door. Unthinking, out of sheer instinct James grabbed the victim's coat collar and drug him inside and out of the way. Frantic to get help, James grabbed the first guy he saw. "Forget it, man. Let'em bleed," the guy said jerking his arm free of James' grasp. James tried another man, then another, getting nowhere. Now in a panic, he began hollering for help! Two guards heard him and ran down the hall, one of them calling for backup on his radio. In moments a squad of guards had cordoned off the area, and locked down the block.

As the guards raced toward them, James tried to attend to the fallen inmate. Barely conscious, ashen and clammy, the victim appeared closer to death than life. "Hang on, man." James pleaded. "Just hang on. Help is coming." A guard grabbed James and shoved him to the other side of the hall, while two more guards tended the victim. "What happened here?" James' guard demanded.

"I don't know," James exclaimed with his eyes still fixed on the wounded inmate. "He just keeled over. I never saw what happened." By now James was feeling clammy and bit nauseous himself.

"Hey, you okay?" The guard insisted, taking James by the arms to steady him. James began to slump toward the floor. "Guys!" the guard barked. "I need some help here."

Disoriented and a bit rummy, James sat up on the bed but immediately fell back onto the pillow. "Oh," he moaned. "What's going on? Where am I?" A kindly nurse stepped over and placed a hand on his arm.

"You're in the infirmary, son. You passed out," she said.

James focused his eyes on her face – a middle aged lady dressed in pale blue scrubs with a pleasant smile. For a moment he thought he might be in a regular hospital. "Where am I lady? Infirmary? Where...?" He wiped his hand over his brow. "I don't feel so good."

The nurse laughed softly, "You're in the infirmary, son," she repeated. "You fainted, likely from shock. I'm sorry you had to witness that. But you'd better brace yourself. There'll be questions," she warned while winding a cuff around James' arm and putting her stethoscope under it. "I'm going to take your blood pressure now. By the way, my name is Barbara."

Nurse Barbara began squeezing the bulb and the cuff tightened around James' arm. He watched quietly as the gauge rose then ticked down as Barbara released the pressure. "Good, she said. One twenty over sixty-five: You're back up to normal. Just lie here and rest. I'll be back in to check on you in a little while."

"Just a minute," James interrupted. "What do you mean by questions?"

Barbara folded her arms and looked James squarely in the eyes. "You are new here aren't you?"

"Yeah, but what's that got to do with this?"

"When somebody gets stabbed or some other assault that injures another prisoner, there's always an inquiry. Standard policy. Did you have anything to do with it?" Barbara asked with a stern look.

"No I didn't. I just heard the guy groan and then saw him fall. I never saw what happened or who did it – honest."

Barbara studied James' with a wary suspicion. She'd heard more alibis and denials than she cared to remember. But James seemed legit. Frankly, he seemed too naïve and too new to the populace to have formed any enemies.

"Alright. You'll get an opportunity to tell them what you saw and heard. Just be straight. Got it?" Barbara held her stern look until she was convinced she'd made her point.

"Yes, I understand," James replied with a slight quiver to his voice.

"Good! Now get some rest. You'll need it. I'll be back in to check on you in awhile. Okay?" Barbara then placed one of her hands on James' arm and winked.

"Sure," James said in a whisper. "Thanks."

"No problem, son. Get some rest."

James' first real encounter with prison violence sickened him. It had become all too personal, literally a shoulder away. He had no stomach for it. Up till now he'd avoided it. It was always something that happened somewhere else but never touched him. As he lay in the hospital bed staring at the ceiling all he could see were vivid scenes of the dude lying on the floor, blood pooling around him. James' own hands were stained in it. He drew them to his face. Someone had cleaned them, thankfully. Suddenly tears began streaming from his eyes, down his face and onto the pillow, his shoulders began to shake. Try as he might he couldn't stifle the waves of emotion that poured over him. Yanking the pillow from under his head he buried his face in it, attempting to muffle the uncontrollable, convulsive sobs. They wracked him: condemning emotions, the emotions of a frightened child. He'd never come unhinged like this. Wave upon wave of irrepressible grief rolled over him like an ocean tide. Finally he regained his composure enough to wipe his face and sit up. His mind calmed and he could think again. Once more he was struck by an unexpected irony. Violence and kindness – He ached for the one and resented the other.

The infirmary bed felt like a sanctuary, an asylum from the callousness of prison, Barbara like a caring maternal figure quite apart from the severity of the guards. James took a deep breath and tried to relax. The dam had broken – it wouldn't be the last time – and he fell into a deep sleep.

Barbara returned and saw James had drifted off. "Good," she whispered, and dimmed the light. "Be with our boy, Jesus," she whispered again, and quietly left the room.

Fr. Ted walked in an hour or so later. James was still gone to the world so to speak. Not wanting to rouse him, Fr. Ted kept his distance and merely traced the sign of the cross over the sleeping young man, whispering a prayer for safety and mercy. As he turned to leave James awoke.

"Who's there?" James murmured in a groggy voice, peering through the dim light. "Do you need something?" With Fr. Ted's back to him, James mistook the kindly priest for a medical staffer. Fr. Ted turned his head toward James.

"Hi James," he said. "I'm Father Ted. Sorry for waking you, son. Just wanted to check on you."

"That's okay, Father. I'm awake now." James rolled onto his back and rubbed his eyes. "You're welcome to stay." James wanted company and who better than a salty-bearded priest? After what he experienced a couple hours or so ago, he needed a priest, a confessor, an ally, somebody who at least could reassure him that everything would be okay, even if it wasn't.

"How you feeling, James? I heard you got caught in a nasty situation awhile ago." Fr. Ted studied the young man, struck by his obvious vulnerability. He didn't belong in prison. He belonged at home. Fr. Ted waited for James to gather himself.

"I don't know." James raised his eyes and saw the bespectacled priest peering down at him. Of course James hadn't heard Barbara's parting prayer, but to awaken with a priest in the room seemed odd in itself. "I'm kind of numb. How's the other guy, the guy who got stabbed?"

Fr. Ted drew a breath and adjusted his glasses, "He didn't make it, James. He died about an hour ago."

James stared blankly at the priest. "He...died?"

"I'm afraid so, son. He wasn't much older than you either."

"Why? Who did this thing? What…" James' voice trailed off in disbelief. He hung his head and pulled his knees up under his chin. "I'm scared, Father," he said and he began to sob again.

Fr. Ted stepped across the room and rested a hand on James' arm.

"I don't want to be here. I don't want to be here," James said pleadingly, as if begging his circumstances to go away, just vanish.

"I know, James. But listen to me, will you?"

James looked up at the gentle priest through swollen eyes.

"The decisions and actions we make matter. They come with consequences. I know you don't want to be here. Son, I don't want you to be here either. But understand me. You will not be left alone. There's a group of people who know your name, your circumstances and care about you. In time you'll get to know them."

"Who? Is Terrance one of them?" James asked inquisitively.

"Yes, Terrance is one. So is Warden Rowland. And, so am I?" Fr. Ted smiled. "Look, James, I can't stay. I've got another stop before I leave." Reaching into his coat pocket, Fr. Ted pulled out a card. "On the front is my contact information. Just show it to one of the guards and I'll arrange to get in touch with you. On the back is a verse of scripture I take pretty seriously. Read it – daily. Okay?"

James took the card from Fr. Ted, studying the verse. It came from the eighty-fourth Psalm: "For the Lord God is a sun and shield. The Lord gives grace and glory. No good thing will he withhold from those who walk uprightly." James shrugged his shoulders to signal his understanding. "Yeah," he said. "Thanks, Father."

"Sure. Can I pray for you before I leave?"

"I suppose if you want to," James replied with another shrug.

Fr. Ted prayed a simple, short prayer asking God's mercy and protection for James and once more traced the sign of the cross over him. The men shook hands and Fr. Ted disappeared down the hall.

While James watched Fr. Ted stride away, Barbara swept through the door. "Isn't Fr. Ted great?"

"Yeah, I think I like that guy," James quipped.

Barbara chuckled. "We all do. He's helped a lot of guys around here. You'd do well to get to know him."

"I don't think I have much choice," James said with a twisted grin.

"Well, mind his words, James. He's full of good ones. Now let me take your blood pressure again."

As Barbara pumped up the cuff once more, James re-read the card.

TEN

Father Ted stopped by the morgue to perform last rights for the young stabbing victim. "Oh, Lord," he whispered softly, "how tragic, how utterly wasteful." His face grimaced, anguished for the lifeless body lying before him. "In the name of the Father, the Son and the Holy Spirit," he intoned, passing his right hand in the sign of the cross over the outstretched corpse and began the rites.

The slain prisoner wasn't new to the State House but he was young, barely two years older than James – just a kid like James. Apparently abandoned by his dad – his mother died shortly after he was born – he fell in with a gang at a very young age. They raised him more or less like a wild dog. Maybe that's why the tattoo looked so familiar to Fr. Ted. Lobos!

"Who would do such a senseless thing?" Father Ted whispered into the dimly lit room. Rival gang conflict wasn't out of the question, but neither was conflict among fellow gang members either. Still, how does one reconcile a stolen life? The boy was dead.

In his more or less "official" capacity as prison chaplain, Fr. Ted took responsibility for contacting the family when men died in prison. His cell phone buzzed. It was Rowland.

"Ted, can you stop by my office. I need to go over a few things before you call Nate's family."

"I'll be right there," Fr. Ted answered.

*****

Betty's voice outside his door advised Rowland that Fr. Ted had arrived.

"Go on in, Father, Mr. Rowland is expecting you," she said with a welcoming smile.

"Thank you, Betty. By the way, how's your mom doing?" Fr. Ted asked out of concern.

"Oh, she's doing much better, thank you," Betty answered.

"Very good to hear," Fr. Ted said twisting the knob to Tom Rowland's office. "Let her know she's in my prayers," he said warmly.

"I will do that, and thank you again," Betty replied in sincere gratitude.

"Ted, have a seat," Rowland said gesturing toward the same side chair in which James sat the day he arrived in prison, when he first met Rowland. "I've been digging through Chalmers' file. Not much to follow on, Ted, not in terms of family anyway. I'm afraid this one might be another 'John Doe' dead end."

"Ah, I see," Fr. Ted replied, swinging one leg over the other. "What can you show me?" he asked leaning over Rowland's desk.

"Well, his dad hasn't been heard from in years. We're not even sure he's alive. Whatever siblings Nate has seems spread out across the Midwest and East Coast, but no correspondence, not even any recent contact information. Betty's been cross referencing addresses and phone numbers, but so far we've only turned up a younger sister who seems to have problems of her own."

"Like what?" Fr. Ted inquired.

"Drugs: She's in rehab for what looks like the third or fourth time," Rowland replied leaning back in his chair, hands gripping the arm rests. "Ted, this is when I hate this miserable job," he said with a slight shake of his head. "I truly hate this part of my work."

"For what it's worth, friend, I don't much like it myself." The two men looked into the other's face and finally chuckled in feigned acceptance of the facts as they were. "So what do you want me to do?" Fr. Ted asked crossing his hands on top of the desk with his eyes locked on Rowland awaiting his response.

"I guess, Ted, we bury this young man." Rowland closed his eyes, exhaled loudly and swung his legs on top his desk. "Dear Lord," he sighed. "What do you want of us?"

Fr. Ted waited a moment until his friend finished rubbing his eyes, "Tom, I've got to ask you this. Did Terrance know the boy?" Fr. Ted worried that Terrance might take Nate's death quite hard.

Tom nodded his head, "Yes he did. This one will be terribly hard on him. Terrance had just begun working with Nate. They'd only met a couple of times, but Terrance knew the boy. I think he was involved in Nate's initiation."

"Oh, I see. You want me to call Terrance?"

"No. I'll talk to him tonight. He and Anne are stopping over for dessert. I'll tell him then."

"Okay, but let me know if you change your mind."

Rowland put a hand on Fr. Ted's wrist, "I will. Thanks, friend."

Fr. Ted nodded through a strained smile.

"One more question, Ted," Rowland said turning his head toward the priest. "How's Meyers? I heard this whole thing really shook him."

"It did, Tom. It shook him to his shoes. How will it go for him in the inquiry?"

"Good question," Rowland responded pulling his legs off the desk and sitting erect in his chair, hands folded in his lap, shoulders sagging. "It won't be easy. You know how it works. At first he'll be the one the panel will likely suspect. He was found standing astraddle of the body, the victim's blood on his hands." Rowland took a thoughtful pause. "I don't think, though, he ever touched the weapon. Forensics will sort that out. Just the same, James has an ordeal in front of him, another one."

"But Tom," Fr. Ted protested. "The kid couldn't have made any enemies in this short of time. He's not a killer."

"No, but that won't stop the panel from digging. A prisoner died at the hands of another prisoner and they've got to name a killer. James will be either at the top of the list or right up there with a handful of probables."

"You sure it was a prisoner who did it?" Fr. Ted knew the prison ethos rather well. Though his friend, Tom Rowland, had cleaned up a good bit of the mess left by his predecessors, some of the guards deserved a close watch.

"Without doubt Ted! This *boy* as we call him had a lot of potential assassins after him. He was a Lobo for heaven's sake. Every one of them is marked. I'm confident it was gang related, and likely set up."

Fr. Ted thought for a moment. Worry began to spread across his face. "Does that fact put Meyers in any danger?"

Rowland exhaled another heavy sigh and pinched the bridge of his nose. "It could." He stared into space a moment then said, "Raynor – I'll have him keep a careful eye out for the kid."

"Good," Fr. Ted responded feeling mildly relieved. "James doesn't need another complication. I fear he's on the edge as it is."

"Me, too, Ted. Well, posse tomorrow night?" Rowland asked as he escorted Fr. Ted to the anteroom of his office suite.

"I'll have the coffee ready," Fr. Ted replied as the two shook hands.

ELEVEN

"Oh no!" Terrance exclaimed in shocked disbelief. "Nate Chalmers is dead?" He could hardly believe his ears. "Tom, I just saw him the other day, right after I left James. He said the move to Cell Block C might have saved his life."

Tom rocked forward in his seat at the head of the dinner table. Anne rubbed her husband's back as he sat hunched over his crossed arms.

"Terrance, prison's a volatile place, you know that," Tom Rowland counseled, sounding every bit like a father. He bent lower to look more closely into his son-in-law's downcast eyes. "Violence," he began again, "especially gang related violence, goes on nearly every day. Fights break out and men get hurt. I'm very sorry about Nate, Terrance. Do you hear me?" Tom's words went unheard. Terrance didn't need to be convinced about the obvious. He lived in that environment for too many years. He wanted Nate back. But Nate was dead, a chilling fact of gang violence. Worse was the thought that he, Terrance Hall, had a hand in Nate's becoming a Lobo.

"Terrance, honey, did you know Nate well?" Anne asked.

Terrance raised an eyebrow and shrugged, "No, I didn't. He was initiated a few days before I was arrested. I'd just begun to crack him open a little on my visits. He'd spoken of wanting to stay clean once he was released." Terrance spent time with Nate and a couple other inmates. But winning their trust was a long ordeal requiring persevering patience.

"When did he expect to be released?" Anne asked looking toward her dad.

"I don't know, Anne," Rowland replied.

"One year," Terrance broke in. "He expected to get out in one year. He planned to move out of the area, to the West Coast."

Curious, Rowland asked, "Did he have family out there?"

"No, not family. He didn't have family to speak of. He knew of a guy, though, a mentor type, who wanted him to stay with him and his family. Get a new start. He owned a business and wanted to employ Nate. It sounded perfect."

Terrance turned toward Rowland, "Tom, I'm worried about James. Is there any chance I can get more time with him?"

Rowland thought for a moment, "Not without breaking a few rules. What I can do, though, is arrange it for you to be there when Fr. Ted makes his rounds. Then, of course, you can meet with him on Mondays. I can make that happen."

"Sounds good." Terrance reached over and put a hand on Anne's arm. "Sweetheart, would you look into James' legal file?"

"Sure," Anne replied. "But what do you think I should find?"

"I don't know. I just wonder if there's anything that can be done to shorten his stay. Isn't he a first timer? He has no priors does he?"

"I don't know, honey. But, sure, I'll look into it," Anne said smiling.

"He has no priors," Tom confirmed. "Other than the one conviction, his file is clean."

"Good. That's good."

Tom Rowland respected Terrance's advocacy and Anne's willingness to support him. Still he felt it necessary to add a test of reasonableness to the process. Leaning more heavily on his elbows he said, "But you two, I think we need to keep a couple of things quite clear. First, James broke the law and that has consequences." Terrance and Anne nodded. "Second, I don't want James knowing anything about this. You know how I feel about favoritism or any pretense of it. His actions deserve the punishment he's receiving. I will support early release only on the condition that his behavior in prison merits it, same as any other inmate. Are we clear on those terms?"

"Quite clear, Tom," Terrance said.

"Yes, daddy," Anne followed.

"Anne, do you know if your firm will even accept the case? You know it'll likely have to be pro bono," Rowland asked.

"I plan to check on it first thing tomorrow. If nothing else, perhaps they'll permit me to handle it on my own, off the clock so to speak."

Terrance pressed Anne's hand. "You're quite something, Mrs. Hall."

Anne smiled at him and said, "God rescued someone I love. I think he'll do it again."

She didn't quite catch the snafu she made and the men started laughing heartily.

"What's so funny?" she asked glaring at them.

"Look babe, he's way too young for you and in case you need reminding," Terrance tapped on her ring finger, "You're taken."

"Oh my goodness you two: You know what I mean," she said scolding them like misbehaving boys. She punctuated her ire with a solid elbow to Terrance's ribs.

"Ouch! Okay, okay! We're with you babe," Terrance cringed grabbing his side.

"By the way, Tom, Scanlon's joining me next Monday. I thought it'd be good for him to meet James," Terrance offered still rubbing his bruised ribs.

"Great!" Tom responded. "Scanlon will be a trip for the kid." They all laughed and moved out to join Mary in the kitchen.

*****

51

"Guess what, honey?" Anne teased.

"What?" Terrance could tell she was up to something.

"I pleaded my case with the partners this morning," she said coyly.

"And…?"

"They agreed to let me research James' case." She hesitated a moment and added, "Pro bono! Isn't that great news?"

"You're kidding! That's fabulous! What's the catch?" Terrance never took anything at face value. Nothing's that easy.

"You are so suspicious," Anne chided. "Well, in all honesty there is one little trifle."

"What would that be, dear?" Terrance said prying Anne for an answer.

"I have to do it on my own time. They won't give me company time until I produce reasonable cause for either a reversal of judgment or reduced sentence."

"That's not all bad is it?"

"No, it isn't. But I won't be available to you and the café while I'm doing the research. Will that be alright?"

"Of course, Anne. This case is worth the extra effort for all of us. I'm toying with the idea of pulling a prayer group together just for James. I was thinking Dirk and Tag along with me," Terrance tossed those names at Anne and waited for a response.

"Terrance, that's perfect! Dirk and Tag – former Lobos? That's great thinking, T!" Anne was ecstatic.

"Reclaimed Lobos, honey. Reclaimed!" Terrance knew that no gang member, Lobos especially, just walked away. They can't – far too perilous a journey. Brotherhood was the Lobos' mantra, a blood oath for life. Terrance suffered death threats from fellow Lobos when he left. One threat nearly made it to reality – a car bomb that fizzled. By God's grace no one got hurt.

It hadn't been any easier for Dirk and Tag. Like Terrance, they were deep into the gang. Dirk served as Terrance's lieutenant, a big brute of a guy built like a Scandinavian mountain who had Terrance's back and enforced the code: a toughened, streetwise kid from Chicago. Tag was younger, of slighter build with slicked back black hair he pulled tight into a ponytail. Both guys did time at the State House. In the joint they had each other's backs – "big brother and little brother," Tag quipped. "Yeah, but then *the posse* caught us," Dirk snarled through clenched teeth. "They brought us down so that Jesus could bring us up." Dirk's words expressed quite well Terrance's insistence on the word *reclaimed*. Before their faith in God they had no-one or anywhere to trust or to go. They had no home, no real place of belonging – just gang life. Reclaimed in Christ, they had an advocate as well as citizenship. They were reclaimed.

TWELVE

"Good Lord, who's breaking down the door?" Fr. Ted hollered from the other room.

"Scanlon, who else?" Terrance replied laughing.

"Sorry I'm late guys – traffic," Scanlon said panting.

"Traffic my…"

"Don't say it Terrance. We know Scanlon's excuses," Tom Rowland scolded in rare humor.

Fr. Ted returned from the other side of the rectory with a pair of file folders in his hands. "Well, guys," he remarked. "Looks like we have a couple of issues to deal with tonight."

"Other than Meyers, who else?" Scanlon asked as he poured a cup of coffee.

"Not so much who else, Mike, but what else," Fr. Ted replied. "Tom, why don't you fill us in."

Tom Rowland looked toward Terrance, "Actually, I think Terrance has a better bead on it than me."

"Okay, Terrance: You fill us in," Fr. Ted said taking his usual seat in the well worn thickly padded armchair, and placing a cup of tea on the small round table beside him.

"Scans, I don't know if you heard about the stabbing incident at the prison this week."

"Stabbing incident? No, that's news to me. What happened?"

"Yeah, well a kid I know from the gang, Nate Chalmers was his name…"

"Was?" Scanlon broke in.

"Was, Mike. Let me finish." Mike waved his hand to gesture compliance with Terrance's request.

"Nate was stabbed. Who did it we don't know, likely a gang member, a Lobo. He died from the wound. What complicates the matter for us is that Meyers was first on the scene. He witnessed it."

"Oh man," Scanlon said with a sagging jaw.

"Yeah, it really shook James," Terrance continued. "We don't know what the full scope of stuff he'll face amounts to yet, but there will be an inquiry."

"He didn't have anything to do with it, did he?" Scanlon was fidgeting with his cup.

"No, he didn't," Rowland broke in. "Still, regulations require an inquiry and anyone even remotely in the vicinity or connected with the incident will be questioned."

Terrance glanced over at his father-in-law, "The larger picture, guys, deals with James' safety. By helping Nate he'll be branded a traitor. That

53

won't sit well with the Lobos or rival gang members. Granted he reacted out of concern for Nate. But they'll see it differently."

"Oh man," Scanlon squirmed in his chair. "So what's next?"

"Well, Mike, that's what we're here to discuss," Fr. Ted replied. "Terrance, give us an update on what you and Anne have hatched."

Tom Rowland peered over his glasses at Terrance, while Scanlon leaned forward in his chair. "Anne went to her partners the other day who agreed to let her review Meyer's file pro bono on her own time. If she turns up reasonable cause for either a reversal of judgment or reduction of sentence, they further agreed to let her represent James formally, again pro bono. Mean time, we've got to keep an eye out for the kid. Tom's got his head guard, Harold Raynor, watching him, but still. Who knows? It's a crap shoot. The kid's in a bad way."

"Hell, guys, when will this kid get a break?" Scanlon moaned.

"Hold on big guy," Terrance implored. "I've begun a prayer group at the café, two of my reclaimed Lobo boys who did time at Tom's place. I think God is James' only hope just like for me...and for all of us."

Fr. Ted slowly nodded his head and fingered his beard. "If not for the Holy Child of God, none of us would have hope," he said.

"Amen," the three other men replied in unison.

Tom Rowland reached for the top file lying on the table between him and Fr. Ted. It read "Next Steps."

"What about moving him to a new block? Tom," Fr. Ted asked.

"Just as risky. The State House pipeline travels at the speed of the Internet. How, we don't know. But it does. Any of the other blocks will be just as dangerous for James."

"Oh Lord," Scanlon said scratching his head. "What about another prison?"

"I don't think so, Mike," Fr. Ted said. "I think we want him where we can reach him. I'm persuaded that God will watch out for young James. I'm also persuaded gentlemen the big job lies not with keeping the wolves at bay, and I mean the prison predators, but the predators of this kid's soul. He messed up but God saw it coming. That's why we're here. We're this kid's advocacy before God." Fr. Ted paused a moment before adding, "Gentlemen we are his protection. Our prayers, our counsel, our willingness to go the distance with him – we're it. Let's strap in. The Holy Spirit will give us all we need for the job."

"Great message, Ted," Tom asserted.

"Well, I didn't mean to preach. And Mike I didn't mean to step on your question."

"No apology necessary, Father. You're right. Time to raise the bar isn't it?"

Terrance reached over and laid a hand Mike's broad shoulder, "Well said, big guy. And well preached Fr. Ted. Not bad for a Catholic priest," he teased with a wry grin.

"So, how do we help the boy?" Tom asked. "Where do we go from here?"

"I think, Tom, we resolve together to do what we did for Terrance. We meet, we pray, we fast, we intervene and we don't stop until our boy is safely home first with God, then with us." Fr. Ted could be counted on to deliver the tough messages, because he could be counted on to walk them out.

"What are you thinking, Tom?" Fr. Ted asked. "You seem to have something on your mind." Fr. Ted noticed Tom staring off in the distance as if mulling something over.

"I do, Ted. James has been in prison for almost a month and I've met with him once, the day he arrived. Time has come for me to call him again. What do you think, Terrance? As I remember you weren't too fond of my office for awhile."

"It's the right thing to do," Terrance said looking intently at his father-in-law. "It doesn't matter what James thinks right now. He needs your iron-willed determination and the heart of a father. No one speaks more clearly or with greater authority than you do. I should know. You're right: I hated being called into your office. But do you know why? Have I ever told you?"

"No," Tom said quietly. "I don't recall talking about it. But I'd certainly like to know now."

"Because," Terrance paused to gather himself. "Because, I was so full of hatred all I wanted was revenge. You never let me get that revenge."

"What do you mean, Terrance? I don't quite follow you." By now Tom's face was stern, his attention rapt, and he was quite uncomfortable with Terrance's words.

"I hated everything and everyone," Terrance began, his lips taut and the set of his eyes hard as if reliving the moment. "The world sucked and all I wanted was to get even with it for all it took from me. So walking into your plush office and seeing that thick Bible lying on your desk drove me nuts. You stood for God, and to me he was the enemy. If he loved me as much as he loved you then why was I in jail instead of free? Tom, I hated coming to your office. It reminded me of every contemptuous thing in my life."

Tom's mouth dropped open, though he said not a word. Instead he composed himself and sat forward in his chair. "I knew you were angry, son. I knew you hated God. So what…what finally turned you around? When did you stop hating me…and hating God?"

Terrance's expression softened, his voice calmed. "It took a lot of time, Tom. Every time I walked out of your office, I found it harder and harder to resent you. You were the first man to ever treat me with dignity, as if I was a man too and not some castoff. I'm not sure exactly when – but you began to grow on me. I wanted what I saw in you – class, integrity, peace, and honesty. I saw the same stuff in Anne. I think that after a few years, maybe even a little sooner, I felt that I could trust you. Not once did you betray me. Not once did you let me off the hook either," Terrance said with a touch of humor.

A soft chuckle went around the room.

Terrance continued, "After that happened, trusting you I mean, I began to study you and to listen more closely to what you said. I wanted to know what made you tick. If you'd have started banging on me about God, you would have lost me. Like I said, God was the dude who hated me. To me, he was the judge who set me up, then sent me up. But how you dealt with me changed how I saw God. You obviously knew a different God than I knew." Terrance paused. "Do you really want to know what broke me, Tom?"

"Yes, of course."

"Remember the day I fell apart in your office and accepted Jesus into my life?"

Tom beamed, "I'll never forget that day, Terrance: One of the best days of my life."

"Do you remember what you said, but more importantly what you did just before I came unglued?"

"I remember telling you that my job was to keep men confined, but that Jesus' job was to set men free."

"That's right! That's exactly what you said. But, Tom, it wasn't just your words that worked on me. It was the tears…your tears…that sliced right through me," Terrance said pressing his index finger to his chest. "My gosh, Tom, here was a man I hated and now respected more than any man I've ever known standing over me, looking at me not as a righteous prig but with the look of a father. In that instant I knew…I knew you truly loved me. And that love crushed my hatred. You showed me the Father and led me to Jesus his son because, Tom Rowland, you were a man…the man!"

Terrance broke down and wept and Tom Rowland wept with him. Scanlon was an utter mess and even Fr. Ted could not resist tears.

"Friends," Fr. Ted said. "Terrance's story is precisely what I mean. If my Catholicism has anything to offer you Protestants," he said with a wink, "it teaches us that accountable relationships guided by God are what Jesus meant when he commanded us 'to make disciples.' Like Terrance was, James is presently a disciple of hatred and contempt. We need to saturate him with the same love Tom risked on Terrance and surround him with the community of the church. And gentlemen, to James we are the church. That is his only safe place. Jesus is his only hope."

Turning his attention to Terrance, "Your prayer group, the guys you've tapped at the café, keep them praying. Help them know how vital their prayers are."

"Don't worry, Father. They haven't forgotten the love dumped on them. They'll get after it."

"Excellent Terrance! I think we're on the right road. Mike," Fr. Ted said looking at Scanlon. "This kid can use a dose of your realism. But this time, cut him a little slack. Unlike T, here, James' shell is pretty soft."

"You calling me hard?" Terrance sputtered.

"Just your head, T," Scanlon mocked laughing at his friend, sloshing coffee out of his cup into the saucer.

The posse spent the next few moments reviewing the "next steps." Scanlon would join Terrance on Monday. Fr. Ted would look in on James during his rounds later in the week, probably Thursday. Meanwhile, Tom planned to arrange a meeting with James in his office before the inquiry. The kid was now surrounded by men intent on his rescue.

THIRTEEN

Wind blowing over the yard wall felt refreshing, making James yawn as he stretched his back and arms while facing into it. "You like that breeze, eh?" Harold Raynor caught sight of James and wandered over beside him.

"Yes sir, I do."

"Me too, James. I love these warmer breezes, kind of invigorates my old bones."

James felt at ease for the first time around one of the guards. Raynor seemed to know how to enforce discipline while being a real guy too.

"Before I forget," Raynor said. "Warden Rowland wants to see you next Tuesday in his office. He'll send for you. Okay?"

"Sure, but why? What's he want with me?" James' suspicions were aroused.

"He'll tell you. Don't worry, it's not because you've done anything wrong."

Not entirely convinced, James asked, "Is it about what happened to Chalmers?"

"That might come up. But I think he has other things to discuss with you. Stop worrying, Meyers. The warden just wants to talk with you."

James didn't like mysteries, no prison inmate does. There's always something hidden in the agenda, and James was feeling his guard rise.

"Enjoy your yard time, James," Raynor offered. "I'll see you around."

"Sure. Thanks." James shoved his hands into his pockets and walked toward the bench where he usually sat until the buzzer went off. "Hey," one of the inmates called abruptly from behind him. James spun around toward the voice.

"You talking to me?" James asked.

"Yeah, I am," said the tall, stocky inmate with a knit cap pulled down over his ears. "Piece of advice…Watch your back, kid."

"Huh?"

"You heard me. Watch your back," snorted the inmate as he brushed by James.

James wanted to pursue the dude but thought better of it. The veiled threat unnerved him and he began nervously peeking behind him and to the sides. Was someone sneaking up or was there something else he needed to mind? He made for the bench and sat down as if trying to make himself invisible. Immediately the buzzer sounded. This time instead of darting through the door ahead of the pack he waited, watching, studying the cold faces of the men. No one looked at him but they seemed to know he was there. James' heart raced and anxiety gripped him. Finally he edged off the bench and started for the door. Suddenly he felt a solid bump that sent him into the wall just inside the building. He turned to face his assailant. "Sorry, Meyers," a deep brusque voice said. "Didn't see you get up." It was one of the yard guards. James gasped and momentarily closed his eyes. "No problem," he sighed and started down the hall toward the stairway quickening his pace with every stride.

For the first time since arriving in prison, James couldn't wait to be locked in his cell, safely gated from anyone out to harm him. He tumbled onto his bed, his chest heaving. Terrified and bewildered he lie motionless, his mind churning. If ever he needed a voice of reason it was now.

"Hi James," at first he thought he was just hearing voices. "It's me, Fr. Ted." James craned his neck toward to the door. Peering through the slot was the bespectacled priest. "I was just walking down the corridor and thought I'd pop by. How you doing?" he asked.

"Not so good, Father," James replied.

"Oh, what's wrong?"

"A big dude just threatened me out in the yard. Told me to watch my back."

"I see," Father Ted replied pensively. "Have you told anyone about it?"

"No, not yet. I really don't know who to talk to. You, I guess. It really scared the crap out of me."

"I'm sure it did, James. Look, I'm heading over to Warden Rowland's office and will let him know."

"I'm not sure I want anybody to know. What if it gets back to the guy who threatened me?" James said nervously.

"James, the warden needs to know. He can have someone keep a closer watch. He has to know," Fr. Ted insisted.

"Okay, but Father I don't mind telling you I'm scared. I don't know how much more I can take."

Father Ted surveyed James' expression. The kid looked scared, even panicky. Once more he thought this boy doesn't belong in prison. For a flickering second he doubted his conviction that James should stay at the State House. Maybe, he thought, Scanlon was right, the kid should be moved. "No!" his mind argued. "God will protect him." "Look," he thought again to himself. "God had me stop by at just the right time. He's got it worked out."

"James, you keep your head on, okay? Just don't call attention to yourself and keep your head on. Don't show the guys you're afraid but don't do anything either. Do you understand me?" Fr. Ted asked looking quite intently at the pathetic figure of James stretched out on his bed.

"Yeah, sure, I understand. But…"

"Just do what I told you, James," Fr. Ted pressed. "Just stay cool." Fr. Ted spied the blue Bible lying on the table. "By the way, son, have you read that verse on the back of the card I gave you?"

James reached over and pulled the Bible off the desk. Stuck in the pages was Fr. Ted's card. James opened it, "Yes, sir, it's right here." He then got off the bed and walked to the door, holding the open text so that Fr. Ted could see. It was opened to the passage on the card, Psalm 84:11.

A large smile broke across the priest's face and a sudden race of assurance chased through his soul. "Good, James. Thank you. Just keep reading that passage."

"I will, Father," he replied. "I have it memorized."

Pointing through the window slot, Fr. Ted stated, "James, that book holds the key to your life. If you're up to another assignment, read the book of John in the New Testament. Do you know how to find it?"

"Yeah, I can find it. I guess it wouldn't hurt me to look it over. I guess I don't have anything to lose if I do," James said snidely.

"No kid, you don't have anything to lose reading that book. It's full of stuff every one of us needs."

"Suppose so, Father. Just the same, I'm not too sure about the God thing. If there is one, a God I mean, he hasn't convinced me I can trust him. But I'll read the book just the same. Mind if I ask you questions about what I read?"

"Not at all, James: I'd love the opportunity to discuss them with you." Father Ted was deeply heartened by young James' response. "See you later, James. Take it easy. And, oh, it wouldn't hurt to test your theory."

"What theory? What do you mean by test my theory?" Fr. Ted aroused James' curiosity.

"Oh, I was just thinking it might be worth testing your theory about God and his attitude toward you. That's all." Fr. Ted waited for a reply.

"How do you mean? How would I test something I can't see and don't even think really exists?" James was now more than a little curious. Actually he began to feel his blood boil a bit. Was the priest toying with him or was he serious? The thought of God repulsed James like few things could.

"When you pick up that book you're holding, and before you crack it open to read, just ask God to help you see what he wants to say to you. That's all," Fr. Ted said with a shrug. "That can't be so tough can it?"

"I'll see." That was all James would say.

"Okay," Fr. Ted said. "See you later. Oh, and before I forget, remember if you need anything, just show the guard my card and I'll get in touch with you."

"Yeah, I will. Thanks, Father. Thanks for stopping by."

"You bet, kid. Take care." With that Father Ted walked away down the corridor, through the door leading out of Cell Block C toward the administration office.

James slid the Bible back onto the desk, leaving it open to the Psalm passage. He picked up the card Father Ted left with him in the dispensary and read it again. A small dove symbol kind of like a flame poked out of a sunburst on the upper left corner in pale blue ink. It appeared aimed at a cross with the body of Christ on it – a crucifix – placed in the center of the card, also in pale blue ink. Father Ted's contact info traced through the crucifix in black block letters. In smaller letters along the bottom were the words, "May we never forget the cost." James either hadn't seen the words before or just noticed them differently. Regardless, they grabbed him. Biting his lower lip he pondered their meaning. "What cost?" he wondered. For whom or what were they said? He placed the card in the Bible, closed it and sat back on his bed. His mind raced.

FOURTEEN

"Not surprising, Ted. Troubling for certain, but not surprising," Rowland confessed after hearing Father Ted's comments. "Harold put two guys on close watch this morning but even then, they're not going to catch everything that happens in the yard." Rowland rocked back in his chair. "You still think this is the place James belongs?"

"I had a momentary doubt, Tom. But, yes, I still believe James will be best served here under our watch and mostly under our prayers."

"You know he's as good as dead here, Ted? The gang populace will be after him until they get him?"

Father Ted pulled off his glasses and rubbed his brow, "I'm aware, Tom, that keeping James here puts him at risk. And yet I cannot help but believe God will protect the boy." He looked directly at Rowland, "You know as well as I do God put this kid into our lives and made us responsible for him." Fr. Ted continued, punctuating his words by poking his index finger into Rowland's desk. "Sending him off does not protect him. Even if he makes it out of prison alive, what becomes of him then? No sir, I am convinced James is our responsibility until God proves otherwise."

Rowland carefully weighed Ted's response, swayed by his conviction. "Okay, I'll go along with you," Rowland said measuring his words. "But hear me: I'm feeling the pressure of protecting this kid. Ted, *the boy* as you call him has no reserve, nothing to fight back with and the vultures are circling."

"Tom, no one would criticize you, including me, if you decided to move James. I truly understand the gravity of the situation. But I can't deny the obvious – God put him here, not the courts. I believe that with all I am. It's not the first time we've faced this sort of thing, Tom. In fact we've both witnessed God's intervention time and again. I'm sure you need no reminder about the car bomb that nearly took Terrance," Ted said, his voice rising.

"You know I'll never forget it, Ted. It was one of the worst days in Anne's life, and not very pleasant for Mary or I either," he remarked with a trace of tension in his voice.

"What happened, though? Terrance walked away without a scratch. God won! Evil lost! I'm certain you haven't forgotten about that either! Have you?"

"No, I haven't," Rowland said slowly, biting his lower lip.

When convinced of a matter, Fr. Ted held his ground. Tom Rowland had learned through many an ordeal with this graying priest that he could not be easily dissuaded, especially when he got the bit in his teeth – a cleric with a pit-bull's fierce tenacity.

"You make your point well, my friend." Tom conceded. "For now James stays here. I trust Harold to keep his eyes open."

"Good." Fr. Ted stood to leave. "By the way, I challenged James this afternoon."

"Oh, how so?" Rowland asked.

"I suggested he'd benefit from reading the Book of John. I pretty much dared him to read it."

"Good assignment. Do you think he'll follow through?"

"Maybe. He's got a strong aversion to God, though." Fr. Ted began to chuckle, "It's almost like he's allergic to him."

"Well, perhaps we'll have to get him an antihistamine so he can breathe the Spirit better?" Rowland quipped.

"You're funny! Meanwhile, pray. I know you will, but pray even more."

"For certain, Ted. Why don't we offer a prayer for our boy now before you leave?"

"Great idea!"

The men bowed in Warden Rowland's office where they'd prayed many times for many men. This one young man, though, held a peculiar attraction for the posse. Likely it stemmed from both James' age and his obvious vulnerability. More likely, however, it resulted from their earlier blindness to the circumstances that led Mark Dempsey to take his own life. Certainly, the Nate Chalmers incident contributed. Prison held many young men, imprisoned in spirit as well as body.

*****

After Fr. Ted left, Tom Rowland asked Betty to call Harold Raynor to his office. He then opened a file on his desk. It chronicled recent gang related violence in not just the State House but other facilities as well.

"Warden Rowland, Mr. Raynor is here to see you."

"Thank you, Betty. Send him in."

"Harold thanks for getting here so quickly," Rowland said pointing to the chair beside his desk.

"Certainly, Warden. What's on your mind?" Raynor said while taking a seat. "I see you're reading up on the latest gang violence."

"I am, Harold. Quite disturbing information; I won't mince words, it unsettles me."

"Me too, and my staff. What do you make of your findings?" Raynor asked scanning the report in Rowland's hand.

"I was going to ask you the same thing," Rowland responded. "Since we implemented the gang watch protocol, we seem to have averted most of what might have gone down. It's this Chalmers incident that troubles me. Any intel on what happened?"

"Yes, I think we may have a lead. Like Meyers, Chalmers copped a plea for a lesser sentence. Unlike Meyers he snitched on one of his Lobo brothers. Word got into the State House about it and another of the Lobos got to him. We have a suspect in isolation. The cops and a court appointed attorney are interrogating him as we speak."

"I see," said Rowland, flipping a few pages in the file. "Any scuttlebutt on Meyers, retaliation or…?"

"No, Tom, the blocks are unusually quiet – eerie, too quiet. My staff worries that something's on the brew, maybe intra-gang retaliation for Chalmer's murder. It seems he had allies as well as enemies within the Lobos. Meyers doesn't seem to be on their hit list, at least we've not picked up on anything yet. We've got our eyes and ears open."

Rowland adjusted his glasses so he could look over them at Raynor. "What's your plan?"

"We've beefed up the C Block security team. County Gang Investigation has stepped in to help us here. They're shaking down anyone they suspicion and we're isolating known agitators."

"Alert status?" Rowland queried.

"Orange, Tom. We think some kind of action is imminent, but we're unsure of when or by whom."

"Orange?" Rowland repeated. Red was the highest alert and orange was just behind it. At orange the guards walked on tenterhooks. It signaled imminent danger.

"Yes, orange. I'll let you know the instant we sense a change."

"Good. About Meyers; is he safe?"

"He's as safe as we can make him right now. Until things settle down I suggest he take his meals in his cell and limit his yard time to once or twice a week when we can increase security. It'll be tough for the kid, but it's for his protection." Raynor handed a form to Rowland for his signature. It was a temporary change of orders for James Meyers.

"I'll agree to the change, Harold. Nice work," Rowland said. "There's always something isn't there?" He added through an anxious grin.

"That's why it's called prison, Tom, and not recess," Raynor replied.

Rowland smirked and signed the document. "Have your guard go easy on the kid when he presents this to him. I think he's on the edge."

"Actually, Tom, I plan to review it with him myself," Raynor said as he took the paper from Rowland's hand.

"Thank you. I appreciate that."

*****

Raynor left Rowland's office and returned directly to Cell Block C. He found James seated on his bed with the small wooden table pulled up in front of him, scratching notes on a growing pile of paper – his prison diary. The door opening gave James a start, but he relaxed a bit when Raynor stepped in.

"Mr. Raynor," James said cautiously.

"Relax, I have something for you."

James sat his pen down and reached for the paper Raynor handed him.

"James," Raynor began, "Warden Rowland and I think it best if you spend more time in your cell, at least anyway until the inquiry is over and things have stabilized."

James heard Raynor but was more troubled by the wording in the document.

"This says it's for my protection. Am I in some kind of danger?"

Raynor furrowed his brow, "I won't lie to you son. Yes, we believe you are in a potentially threatening situation by being exposed to the prison populace at this time."

"Just because I helped a guy?" James asked, perturbed by the action.

"In a word, yes. Prison life makes little sense. And violence… shoot, kid… it never makes sense. Inside these walls a senseless culture of violence is what my staff and I spend most of our time stifling." Pointing at the paper, Raynor continued, "Taking this action is truly for your protection. We don't need any more casualties and honestly, James, you're not prepared for the rough stuff inside here."

James stared back at Raynor, clutching the paper like it was a death warrant. "All I tried to do, Mr. Raynor, was help the guy. How can that put me in danger?"

"It's absurd, James. As I said, a culture of violence is a senseless thing. But it is a fact of prison life. You helped a guy. The gang thugs in here think you interfered. You know why none of the other inmates responded to Nate?" Raynor asked.

"Because they were afraid…afraid of the gang?" James replied haltingly.

"That's exactly right." Raynor sat down on the bed beside James. "Look young man, whatever you do, don't let prison harden you to the place you won't help another man. What you did you did naively, but you did it out of your instinct to help someone who needed help. Hold onto that, James. The time will come again when you'll have to choose against your own safety to do what's right. That, James Meyers, is the measure of a man. It's dangerous no doubt, but it's right." Raynor took a moment to give James time to think. He continued, "Let me tell you this. If you want to walk out of here a man, I'll help you. While I can't promise with certainty that you'll survive this place, I can promise that I'll do everything within my authority to keep you safe. It's what we try to do here – keep the men safe."

James looked into Raynor's stern face. He could tell the guard meant his words. Raynor stood up to leave.

"Mr. Raynor, thank you. I haven't met many men who ever kept their word. Mostly they've lied to me – said they'd be there for me but weren't. Somehow I get the feeling I can trust you, sir."

"I'm glad. Now mark my words. Do the right thing regardless of the cost." Raynor gave James a reassuring pat on the head before leaving the cell. As the door slammed shut it left a different impression. James didn't feel locked in as much as he felt harm had been locked out.

FIFTEEN

"Terrance, where are you?" Anne asked loudly as she roamed the café looking for her husband.

"Oh, hi Mrs. H – Terrance is in the Bear's Lair," came a voice from behind the espresso bar, situated to the right of the entrance door.

"Thanks," Anne responded and strode back to the closet-sized room that served as Terrance's makeshift office – the Bear's Lair. His desk was a two-by-twelve plank over stacked pumice blocks. Pictures, mostly of him and Anne, as well as the kids that hung out at the café adorned the walls. A few books sat on a short flimsy bookcase that tilted awkwardly to one side. Terrance's study Bible was flopped open on top of the desk.

The door was closed but Anne could hear the drone of voices behind it. She listened. Finally a loud "Amen" was said and the door opened. Out came Dirk, Tag and her man. They'd been praying – standing because the office had room for just one chair, Terrance's folding chair that he propped up against his desk when others entered.

"Hey babe," Terrance said smiling admiringly at his lovely bride. "You been out her long?"

"No," Anne answered. "I just got here. You guys wouldn't have been praying for James would you?" She asked.

"Sure was Mrs. H," Tag replied. "Been praying for him pretty much every day at this time."

"That's cool, Tag. That's way cool," Anne said with a broad smile.

"So honey, what brings you here at this time of day?" Terrance asked glancing at his watch.

"I've got some news. Can we talk, privately?" Anne's expression changed.

"Sure, how about you drive me home? We'll be less distracted there."

"Sounds good." Terrance jumped into Anne's car and they drove away from the café.

"Good news or bad?" Terrance inquired looking at Anne who seemed lost in her thoughts.

"I'm not sure, honey. I'll explain more when we get home."

Terrance didn't pry. He waited sensing Anne's apprehension. Terrance might not have had the benefit of formal education, but he was a keen observer of people's behavior. Anne trusted her husband's intuition as he trusted her intellect.

Inside their cozy little house, Terrance and Anne plopped down beside one another on the living room sofa. Terrance draped an arm around Anne, who snuggled up to her husband.

"From the expression on your face, I'd guess it's mostly bad news," Terrance began.

"Honestly, I really don't know what to make of it. From what I can tell the courts treated James fairly. It even seems to me the presiding judge, Judge Abrams, made an effort toward leniency. But there's something that troubles me."

"What's that," Terrance said angling his head to see if he could read Anne's face.

"James got six years for essentially abetting a known dealer. Do you know what the dealer got?" Anne sat up facing Terrance.

"Three years and two years of probation," she said through pursed lips.

"What! You've got to be kidding. The court gave James six years! How could that be? Was Abrams trying to make an example of the kid?" Terrance stood up and began pacing the room.

"I don't think so. From what I can tell, the DA's office has the dealer in its pocket. They use him as a snitch. He tells them what he knows and they go easy on him."

"That stinks!" Terrance recoiled. "They throw a kid into prison and let an asshole drug head loose on the street."

"Hey, knock off the language! I don't like it."

"Sorry for offending your delicate ears, babe. But I kind of think what happened to James trumps my bad mouth." Terrance was quite worked up.

"Okay, so what happens next?" Terrance asked with his hands on his hips.

Anne slouched back in the sofa, "Good question! The courts really can't help James. What they've given him is well within their authority. In fact, they could have stuck him with up to twelve years. Abrams backed it down." Anne reached for Terrance's hand. He settled down, took her hand and sat on the coffee table facing her. "There is one possibility we can explore. If James behaves himself he could get parole in four years. That would mean he'd finish his sentence on probation for two years."

"That's something, Anne."

"Yes it is, but like daddy said: James can't know about it yet. I...I mean we've got a lot of work ahead before we let him in on any of this stuff," Anne said staring sternly at Terrance.

"I got you babe. I'll keep my mouth shut," Terrance promised.

"Not even the posse can know yet."

"I'll be mum."

"Good."

"You mentioned a lot of work. What kind of work?"

Anne reached for her briefcase and pulled out a pad of notes. "First, James has to satisfy the panel during the inquiry that he had nothing to do with Nate Chalmers' death. That's numero uno. Not a steep climb per se, but he must acquit himself of this crime. Though most of the prison officials suspect gang retribution, no one saw what happened. They only saw James."

"Okay, then what?" Terrance probed.

"Well, then he has to behave himself at the State House. Keeping a low profile would be a good start. Getting a job when one comes available and performing well would help. Until he's deemed safe by daddy, Raynor and others, that'll have to wait. Then there's another item."

"What other item?" Terrance was obviously bothered. More complications it seemed.

"He needs a new lawyer."

"That doesn't seem so tough does it?" Terrance quipped somewhat relieved it wasn't a bigger deal.

"No, not really. But before you ask, I can't do it."

"Why not?"

"My office thinks it would be looked upon as conflict of interest. If James was anywhere but the State House, I could represent him." Anne shoved the file back into her briefcase and reached for her husband. Terrance rejoined her on the sofa.

"Well, is there anybody in your firm who could take his case?" Terrance inquired lacing his fingers around Anne's shoulders.

"Maybe, but we still have to await the panel's inquiry. Then we'll see."

"Oh Lord, help our boy," Terrance groaned.

SIXTEEN

James sat fumbling nervously with the Blue Book, the term he used to describe the Gideon Bible on his desk. He hadn't taken Fr. Ted's dare yet, reticent for some inexplicable reason. He pushed it aside and reached for the small stack of paper in front of him. Resting on his bed with his back against the wall, he reviewed the contents again.

To the best of his recollection he recounted the events of Nate Chalmers' stabbing. Of course there was one huge black hole he couldn't account for – when he fell unconscious at the scene. Still he captured a fair amount of detail, items that came to mind at odd moments, colors, smells, sounds, even words. But what he could never pull out was the incident itself. If asked about it, he had nothing to offer. The guy – Nate – just keeled over. That was it! The only thing he heard was Nate moaning. No flash of a hand, no blade or anything, just a huddle of men trying to cram through the same doorway – that was all he witnessed. The harder he tried to reconstruct the scene the murkier the details became. He poured over his notes again, straining to close the gaps in his story.

"They'll never believe me," he whispered aloud. "With this stuff, they'll think I did it and lied about it." He threw the papers onto the bed. Some of them scattered across the floor.

James couldn't wish away the fact he was found straddling the victim, with the victim's blood all over his hands. Sure he yelled for help, but by then it was too late: Nate's fate was sealed and he was the only one who stopped to lend aid. But will the panel think he meant his actions for good or ill? In the end his – James' – fate lay with seven anonymous inquisitors whose judgment would make that determination.

Suddenly it dawned on him! He never saw the weapon. Consequently, he never touched the weapon. That was his out and he began to regain composure. He stared into the wall across from him as if staring into a gray mist, "I never saw it. Nate had his hands on it," James blurted into the emptiness of his cell. He gathered up his notes again, and searched them for anything about the weapon. Nothing! He saw nothing. He touched nothing. Furiously he scribbled brief jots that he felt would exonerate him for sure.

Next, James remembered waking in the infirmary and wondering what the black ink was smudged on his right thumb and fingers. "They must have fingerprinted me while I was out," he conjectured. "That'll tell them I never touched the weapon." Suddenly his confidence buoyed and the strain he felt eased. He jotted the ink stains in his notes. Faint traces of ink could still be detected in the creases of his thumb and fingers.

Over and over again he replayed the events, jotting more things as he remembered them. Finally he could think of nothing else and dropped the stack of paper back on the desk and reached again for the Blue Book. He flipped it open to the Psalm passage and pulled out Fr. Ted's card once more. "For the Lord God is a sun and shield...nothing will he withhold from those who walk uprightly." Spontaneously he muttered under his breath, "If this is true, I need it to be true now." A prayer! The words caught James by surprise. He'd never prayed, never intentionally prayed. His own words drew to mind the cautious guidance he'd received from Rowland as he set foot in prison, Nurse Barbara and Fr. Ted in the dispensary, and just hours earlier from Mr. Raynor. So God dealt in quid-pro-quo James mused. I behave and he takes care of the details. It wouldn't be long before he'd discover the Psalmist had much more in mind.

Footsteps stopped in front of his cell. "James, your folks are waiting for you. Let's go."

"My folks? What day is this?"

"Sunday. Now get up and let's go," the guard ordered in a brusque voice.

James pushed the table back to its place against the wall and rose from his perch on the bed. The cluster of notes he tucked under his pillow away from eyeshot.

"What's that you just shoved under your pillow, kid?" The guard stepped over and pulled the pillow off the bed. Seeing the sheets of paper made him suspicious. "Stand against the wall," he demanded pointing across the bed from him. There was barely room for one person, so standing against the wall was about the only thing James could manage. The guard began examining the sheets of paper. Unsure of their meaning he asked James to explain them.

"They're my notes...for the inquiry, sir. I've been trying to piece the details back together and these are my notes. That's all." The guard studied them a little longer, occasionally asking for explanation. James stood sweating, worried they'd be confiscated. Finally the guard put them back down on the bed.

"Ok," he ordered. "Turn around and give me your wrists." James complied. With the cuffs secured the guard led him into the corridor while the door was shut. James took a quick look over his shoulder to see if the guard had grabbed the paper. No, his hands were empty. James exhaled and blinked his eyes with relief. As they strode down the long corridor the guard offered him some advice.

"For the future, Meyers, don't try to hide stuff in your cell. Keep things like those sheets of paper in plain sight. Turn them over, but leave them where we can see them. Otherwise we'll think you're up to something. Got it?"

James nodded his understanding but saw the guard was looking directly at him. "Yes sir, I do."

71

"Good. Just do as you're told!"

"Yes sir, I will."

*****

The guard escorted James past the row of visiting rooms where he met his parents and Terrance the week before to a secure area partitioned with thick glass panes. The cramped cubicle was barely large enough for one person. Just as he dropped into the wood chair he spied his dad enter a similar space on the other side of the glass partition, apparently unaware that James had just sat down. About then a voice came through an overhead speaker, "You have ten minutes gentlemen and your conversation will be recorded."

James' dad looked up, startled to see his boy sitting across the pane of glass from him.

"Good morning, son, how you doing?" Don said awkwardly like he wasn't quite prepared to start a conversation.

"I'm fine, dad, and how are you and mom?"

"We're okay. Mom's out in the waiting area. They would only let one of us in to see you this time — something to do with increased security." James' dad furrowed his brow and asked again, "Are you sure you're okay? Do you need anything?"

"Like I said, dad, I'm fine." James spoke tersely, more or less hoping to end the conversation before it began.

"Well, we wanted to stop by and check in on you: Let you know we're praying for you."

"Good. Thanks," James returned.

"Uh, son, we're not sure where to go from here?" His dad said nervously.

"What do you mean?"

"It seems that the prison has you under tighter control until the inquiry is over."

James wasn't even sure his folks knew about the inquiry. His dad continued, "Evidently, until you're through this thing the investigators want to keep everyone at bay. I guess that means we won't see you for a little while."

His dad might have meant his words as an apology but James wasn't the least bit disappointed.

"I suppose so, dad. But don't worry. I'm sure things will work out fine and we'll see each other again real soon." James managed a warm, albeit forced, smile that seemed to comfort his dad. Prison he thought, while watching his dad gather himself, wasn't the best place to start the first real conversation you've ever had with your dad. From indications, Don felt the same way.

"Honestly, James, I really don't have much to report," Don said with a slight shrug. For a cool, buttoned down corporate executive, the man was anything but comfortably composed. It was clear that neither the surroundings nor his son in cuffs and prison garb appealed to James Donald Meyers, Sr.

"I understand, James said," letting his dad off the hook. "Tell mom I said hi."

"Sure will, son. Anything else?"

James paused. "Yeah, tell her I love her too."

Meyers Sr.'s mouth dropped open. He clearly hadn't expected to hear those words from his son. "I will, James. I will definitely tell her you love her. She'll be pleased."

"Thanks. Take care of yourself." With that James stood up to leave. Before he got out of the cubicle, though, tears began to well in his eyes, tears he did not want his dad to see. Too bad really: Because had he turned to face his dad one more time he would have noticed moisture clouding his eyes too.

SEVENTEEN

Scanlon swung his crew-cab diesel pickup alongside Terrance's very used Corolla in the State House parking lot. Terrance was leaning against the fender of his car waiting for his tardy friend.

"You're late Scans!" Terrance barked all in good humor.

"Give it rest or I'll find a reason to have you readmitted," Scanlon snapped pointing toward the prisoner admittance door.

"C'mon you jerk," Terrance said, "Let's go visit the kid. You ready for this?"

"Man, what do you mean, am I ready? Buddy, don't forget who came to visit you when this place was your address. Got it?" Scanlon was in rare form, amped up like he was playing in the Super Bowl or something.

"You kill me, Scans. You really do. By the way, do you think you ought to leave that lump of keys in your truck?" Scanlon looked at the huge ring of keys to sundry truck, tractor and building locks hanging from a clip on his thick cowhide belt.

"Oh, these," he said snapping them off and tossing them onto the floorboard of his truck before slamming the door shut and arming the lock that made an annoying "whirp, whirp" sound as they walked away.

"What's our agenda here today, T?"

"Just spend ten minutes with the kid, see what he needs and maybe learn something," Terrance said as they approached the front door to the admin building.

"Sounds about right," Scanlon agreed. "We plan to stop by Tom's office?" he asked.

"Not sure, Mike. Maybe on the way out. I don't like to just drop in on him unannounced. Right now, he's got a lot on his plate if you get my meaning."

"I'm not sure I do," Scanlon replied.

"Well, things are a little edgy with some of the gang types in here. In fact, I don't think we'll get to see James in one of the casual rooms. They'll probably stuff us into one of the secure spaces instead."

"Great! Like you and I can fit in one of those," Scanlon gruffed.

"We'll take turns, Scans. I'd like him to meet you so let me set it up, okay?

"Sounds like a winner," Scanlon replied, holding the door open for Terrance.

Though Mike Scanlon was familiar with the visitation protocol, Terrance was an insider. He knew many of the guards and most of the admin staff.

"Hey Terrance, good to see you again," a familiar voice announced.

"Good to see you too, Rick. By the way have you met my friend Mike Scanlon?"

"No, I don't think I've had the pleasure," Rick Baker said sticking out his hand toward Scanlon.

"Nice to meet you, Rick," Scanlon said shaking hands with the entrance guard.

"So, who you here to see, Terrance?" Rick inquired.

"James Meyers. Any chance we can visit with him in one of the casual rooms?" By casual rooms, Terrance referred to the small four-walls and a table arrangement in which he first met James.

"Let me see," Rick studied the manifest. "Nope, doesn't look like it, Terrance. Looks like I'll have to squeeze you guys into a secure slot."

"My friend was afraid you'd say that," Terrance said with a laugh.

"No problem boys. We can work you both in during the ten minutes you've got."

"Great. Let's do it," Terrance said clapping his hands together.

"Well then, empty your pockets on the table and step over to the 'bone glow,'" Rick instructed. The "bone glow" was prison speak for metal detector.

Both guys pulled out their wallets, keys and coins, removed their wrist watches and coats then stepped in front of the detector and waited for Rick to signal each man through.

"Go ahead, Terrance, step through then raise your arms so I can wand you," Rick said with a wave of his hand. Once through the x-ray scanner, Terrance lifted his arms while Rick passed a long wand over his profile, just one more precaution before admitting him to the visitation area. Mike Scanlon waited his turn then stepped through on Rick's cue. As the men gathered their personal items, Rick keyed the radio microphone clipped onto his shirt collar and asked for clearance, as well as let whoever he called know that James Meyers had visitors.

"Feels like you've increased security some, Rick. Any worries?" Terrance inquired.

Rick really couldn't answer directly so he gave Terrance the usual prison side-step. "Nah, making sure not just anyone gets by us," he snorted.

"Yeah, yeah, yeah," Terrance sputtered. "The usual non-answer to an obvious question."

Rick just kept walking, leading the men down the hall to the steel cages that open into the prison proper. "You know the drill, Hall. Has it been that long since you resided in our house?" he said while punching in the security code.

"I see. Security *is* tighter," Terrance replied with emphasis, taking stock of the additional protocol that was absent last week. Rick smirked but said nothing.

"Okay guys, wait here. I'll be back," Rick said then exited out a side door and down the next corridor.

"What do you make of this security thing, T?" Scanlon asked with an edge to his voice.

"Not much. I've been through it before. If the house was on red alert we wouldn't have gotten this far. But it does mean they've got their eyes on something."

"Like what?" Scanlon wasn't satisfied with Terrance's answer.

"If I was to guess – gang activity."

"Are you talking riot, like a full-scale in prison gang war?" Now Scanlon was in full army readiness of his own.

"Not quite, Scans. Usually a small group of toughs think they have a score to settle and start a fight. It could escalate into more, but the staff around here knows how to handle that stuff. Don't be such a worry wart!"

"Okay, you're the guy around here as far as I'm concerned."

"Just do as you're told and it'll all go fine. If something comes up, they'll hustle us out of here," Terrance said, looking at his nervous friend. "Besides, Scans, you're bigger than most of these dudes. They'll be more worried about you than anything," he said sarcastically.

"Oh that's reassuring, T. Like I'm probably the biggest pussycat you know."

Terrance was still laughing when Rick reentered the room. "Alright guys, follow me," he said ushering them down the corridor to a small anteroom outside the secure visitation cubicles. "Another guard'll come out and take you in one at a time. You'll have ten minutes altogether."

"Thanks, Rick," Terrance replied. Then looking at Scanlon he said, "Man, Scans, you look like a wreck! You've been through this! So what's the problem?"

"Look T, I've gotta be honest with you. I'm not comfortable meeting Meyers. I'm not sure how to approach him."

"Mike, look; There's a reason I wanted you with me today. You and James share a few things in common beginning with dads who didn't give you the time of day. I think that might be a starting place – common ground."

Scanlon tugged on his ball cap as he seriously considered Terrance's observation. "Alright, I'll go with that."

"Besides, bro, God knows – He just knows. Let's take a second and pray now."

"Good! I'd like that," Mike said reverently dropping his head.

Terrance prayed and they both took a seat and waited for James to arrive.

*****

76

"So Terrance came back to see me?" James asked the guard as they walked toward the secure visitation area.

"Think so. I doubt Warden Rowland would let anyone else in on a Monday."

"Probably not," James reasoned, stuffing his left foot back into the unlaced sneaker. "Well, unless it was Fr. Ted, I suppose."

"Fr. Ted?" the guard laughed. "Yeah, that guy's pretty much got a free pass."

A buzzer sounded and the last door opened in front of them. James stepped ahead of the guard who then reached for the cubicle door. "Go ahead, Meyers. I'll let the security officer know you're ready."

James scrunched himself into the tight space and looked through the thick pane of glass into the space across from him. A moment later Terrance appeared, smiling and taking a seat.

"Good morning, James. Great to see you again! How things?" The flimsy microphone made Terrance's voice sound scratchy.

"I'm fine, thanks. Good to see you too." James said his cuffed wrists resting on the ledge in front of him.

"I brought a friend I'd like you to meet. He was a great help to me when I lived here a few years ago. Would that be alright with you?"

James thought for a moment then said, "Yeah, that'd be fine. But can I ask you a question?"

"Sure. Shoot!"

"I don't mean any disrespect but why are you coming all the way out here to see me? I mean we really don't know one another."

"Well that's a good question. Last week I came at Warden Rowland's request. Today, I'm here on my own. I know what it's like to be confined in prison. And I know what it was like to have someone take an interest in me and help me get a fresh start. James, I'd like to apply for that job with you. I'd like to offer you what a few other people offered me. You game?" Terrance leaned closer to the window and waited James' response.

"Yeah, I'd like that," James said, still unsure of what to make of Terrance's offer, but what'd he have to lose?

"Like I said last time, James, there's a few guys I'm close to who have you on their mind." He hesitated then added, "Not to make you freak, but in their prayers too."

"Okay, thanks," James replied. "Is the guy you brought one of those guys?"

"Yeah. I'll send him in. His name is Mike Scanlon, but we just call him Scanlon. Like you and me, he's had his things to deal with but managed to get past them."

"Like what?" James broke in.

"He'll tell you. But so you know, he's had his problems with booze. Mike's a recovering alcoholic: A great guy who's been knocked down but got back up."

"Okay, I'll meet him," James' interest began to grow.

"Hang on, then. I'll go get him." As Terrance rose to leave he looked back and leaned into the microphone one more time. "Ah hey, we know you're in a rough spot with this inquiry and tighter security. Like I said, don't freak, but just so you know we've amped up our prayers for you. God'll get ya through this stuff." Terrance gave James a warm smile then left to get Scanlon.

"Alright Mike, you're up," Terrance said as Mike stood waiting his turn.

"How's the kid seem?" Scanlon asked rocking on his feet.

"He's fine, Mike. He doesn't seem as suspicious as last time." Scanlon poked out his lower lip and headed through the door. The space was almost too tight for him to swing a leg over the chair and sit down. James was momentarily amused by the clumsy effort of this oversized man.

James spoke first, "You must be Scanlon," he said still amused by Mike's entrance.

"How could you tell? Terrance tell you how gracious I am?" Scanlon said playfully.

"Something like that. Tells me you've had stuff to deal with same as him and me."

"You don't waste any time cutting to the chase, do you?" Mike said while still wrestling with the chair.

"Don't have time to waste when I get visitors," James smarted back. "So, are you going to answer my question? Sounds like you've had some junk to get over too."

"Kinda, but different. My prison was booze and it nearly cost me everything – my business and mostly my family." Scanlon didn't hold back. He laid it right out there in front of the kid.

"How long if you don't mind me asking?"

"Too long, James – ten years. Toward the end I was literally a fall-down drunk." Mike finally got comfortable and began to relax. Terrance was right, there was a connection and the two seemed to meld quickly.

"That's a long time."

"You're not kidding, kid. It's a hell-of-a long time – the worst prison I've ever been through." Scanlon doffed his ball cap and scratched his head. "Don't make that mistake," he said with seriousness in his eyes.

"I won't." Curious, James delved deeper, "How'd you get out of the ditch?" Just as Scanlon was opening his mouth to answer the security administrator broke in, "Time's up gentlemen." The door behind James opened and a guard stepped in to take him back to his cell. Before leaving, though, James said, "Huh, looks like we got cut off. I'd like to get an answer to my question. Can you come back?"

Scanlon wasted no time in saying, "You bet, kid. I'd love to continue our chat." Then the guard took James by the arm and out the door. Mike returned to the ante room where Terrance had been sitting, quietly praying for the two men.

"That was brief! So how was it?" Terrance asked with raised eyebrows.

"Fabulous!" Scanlon enthusiastically responded. "The kid and I clicked from the start."

"Praise the Lord," Terrance said softly. "I kind of thought you would."

"Yeah, he wants to continue our conversation." Mike put his cap back on then looked at Terrance. "Know what he asked me?" he said with a wry grin.

"No! What?"

"He asked me how I managed to get clean. T, he wants my story."

"Now then, Mr. Scanlon, that's a start. I'd call it progress, just exactly what we'd hoped for." Terrance popped his friend on the shoulder and strode behind the guard through the security exit and into the parking lot. The men could hardly wait to share their info with the posse.

EIGHTEEN

Just as Terrance and Mike were approaching their vehicles for the drive back to town, Rowland came bolting through the door after them.

"Hey guys, hold on a minute." He said motioning for them to wait. "If you're not in a hurry I've got Fr. Ted in my office. How about giving us a report?"

Terrance looked at Mike who shrugged and said, "Sure. I can manage the time."

"Me too," Terrance added and the three walked back into the building and entered Rowland's office where Fr. Ted sat waiting for them.

"Take a seat, gentlemen," Rowland said gesturing toward the couch across from his desk. "Want any coffee or tea?" Rowland never kept soft drinks, but Betty kept the coffee pot and hot water on tap.

"I'm fine," Terrance replied.

"Yep," Scanlon chirped agreeing with Terrance.

"So, how'd it go with young Mr. Meyers?" Fr. Ted inquired, taking a sip from his coffee cup.

"Well, he survived Scanlon," Terrance smarted off, which drew a chuckle from everyone but Scanlon. "Honestly, Mike spent more time with him than I did. So what do you think? How'd it go," he asked facing his snarling friend.

"Better than Terrance's nasty's comment." Scanlon waited for the laughter and trailing banter to ease up then continued, "T must have tipped him, because he jumped me about my drunken past before I got the chair under my butt." Again the group roared with laughter.

"Just a minute, Mr. Scanlon," Terrance interrupted. "Not once did…" He caught himself midsentence. "Well, maybe I did clue him in, but only because he asked."

"T, you're going straight to H…," Fr. Ted stopped the finger waging before Scanlon could finish his epithet.

"Should we believe you guys really got nowhere with James?" the jovial priest jested. "How about we get to the point?"

Rowland nodded his head in agreement.

"I'd say we connected," Scanlon replied. "We didn't get to talk that much – took too long tryin' to wedge myself into that stupid cube – before the guard called time on us. But he asked me how I managed to get out of the ditch. That's where we left it."

"I'd definitely say that's a good start, Mike," Rowland offered.

"Tom, any chance I can bring Mike back and we can get more than ten minutes?" Terrance asked.

"I'd have to break the rules, Terrance. As much as it pains me to say it, I won't do that," Rowland answered.

"I understand. Sorry for putting you in an awkward spot," Terrance apologized.

"No apology necessary. As for Mike, I can make that work. We'll put you guys on a special visitation schedule together with you, Terrance, as an auxiliary chaplain under Ted. That okay with you?" Rowland asked turning to Fr. Ted who'd put his coffee cup down and sat with his feet crossed and hands folded taking in the conversation.

"Fine idea – I'd go along with that for sure," Fr. Ted replied through an assenting smile.

"Work for you?" Rowland asked next, this time facing his son-in-law.

"Yeah, absolutely! How'd you manage that, Tom?" Terrance asked pleasantly stunned with the idea.

"I'm the warden," Rowland smirked leaning smugly into his thick leather chair with an air of elitism in his voice. The men got a jolt of pleasure out of Rowland's out-of-character humor. The buttoned-down Ivy Leaguer could let down his well groomed hair once in awhile and this was one of those rare moments.

"Seriously, Tom," Terrance coaxed. "What rule did you break, as though you would?"

"I didn't. Terrance you're a minister aren't you?"

"Yes, but I'm not ordained or anything."

"How far are you in your seminary training?" Rowland asked.

"Two years…a little more than two years," Terrance answered with a quizzical edge to his voice.

"So, how much do you have left?" Fr. Ted asked.

"A year," Terrance responded. This time curiosity overcame him. "Okay, what's going on here with you two?" Terrance stood up and leaned against the office door like he wasn't sure if he wanted to stay.

"Come on now, Terrance, we're not ganging up on you. Sit down and relax," Fr. Ted chided.

Terrance returned to his seat but kept his eyes clapped onto the two older men as if measuring their motives. His old gang-life preservation instincts kicked in, which made the room somewhat uncomfortable.

"Your dad-in-law and I've been talking. You have an internship to complete your final year, don't you?" Fr. Ted asked.

"I do," Terrance said letting his guard down a bit.

"Well, why don't you do it here under me?"

"That's it? That's all you guys were hatching…an internship?" Terrance moved from defensive to tacitly compliant with the idea.

"Knucklehead," Scanlon sniped. "Gang banger knucklehead," and waged his head derisively.

Terrance scoffed, "Well maybe I am. Sorry guys, I just hate surprises, even good ones."

"We'll work on that too," Fr. Ted said.

"Terrance, what we're thinking is that you'd be named auxiliary chaplain like I said. Here's the rest of it. In your new role, you'd be assigned to a very limited number of inmates, James Meyers being your primary focus. Does that agree with you, or should we offer it to Scanlon," Rowland asked with an icy stare like he'd give an inmate he suspected of mischief.

"Uh no…I'm, yeah…that would be great!" Terrance sputtered, obviously caught off guard by Rowland's piercing persuasion.

"Oh, so you want Tom to offer the job to Mike? Fine with me," Fr. Ted teased.

"No, I want it!" Terrance blurted. The room erupted in another fit of laughter at Terrance's expense. Regaining his composure, Terrance said, "I'm stunned. I'd love to work inside, Tom. I'd love the assignment. What a gift!"

"We thought you would, son," Tom said warmly.

"When do I start?"

"Right away," Fr. Ted said for Rowland. "We'll work out a syllabus that complies with the seminary's requirements. I have a few we can work from. You'd not be the first student to complete an internship at a prison. But I want to see you in my office tomorrow morning if that works for you."

"I can make it work," Terrance replied reaching for his cell phone. "What time?"

"Make it 10 o'clock," Fr. Ted said looking at his pocket planner.

"Ten it is!"

"Hey, what about me?" Scanlon grumped. "Where do I fit into this little scheme?"

"Actually, Mike, that's a good question for a change," Rowland inserted. "With Terrance working on the inside so to speak, that opens the visitor privilege to you as long…" Rowland hesitated.

"As long as what," Scanlon moved to the edge of his chair.

"As long as you're willing to become an associate pastor under Terrance at the café," Rowland finished.

"What!" Both Terrance and Scanlon barked in unison.

"No offense, Tom, but I have a day job already," Scanlon said tapping on his chest. "Sally likes the income I bring home. I doubt T pays as well."

"Mike, no one expects you to quit your day job. What we're proposing to both of you guys amounts to an accommodation that allows you both on site to visit Meyers. The associate pastor title would be in name only. Unless, of course, Terrance can talk you into volunteer work," Rowland explained.

"I get it," Scanlon said calmly. "If T buys it, I do."

"Yeah, sounds great. So if I understand the arrangement, I become an auxiliary chaplain while completing an internship that still has to be approved by the academic dean, and Mike becomes my associate at the Café. Effectively, then, he takes my visitation privilege while I have pretty much fulltime access to the kid. Right?"

"That's pretty much the idea guys," Rowland confirmed. "Are you on board?" He asked sweeping his eyes from Mike to Terrance as if reading their expressions.

"I'm in," Scanlon said not waiting for Terrance.

"Count me in, too. I think it's inspired," Terrance said.

"Well, that makes four of us," Fr. Ted chimed in. "If we do our jobs right, more than James Meyers stands to win. This, gentlemen, is the picture of disciple formation. It makes each of us accountable for the kid." Turning to Rowland he added, "I applaud Tom's resourceful thinking and courage to put such an unorthodox idea in motion here. Tom, that took ingenuity and guts. Well done, friend."

Tom Rowland acknowledged appreciation for Fr. Ted's words. "Gentlemen, our roles are defined. I suggest we consecrate ourselves and this plan to God. Truly, men, it didn't come from me. It came in the middle of the night two nights ago from God. I awoke with it on my mind and immediately knew its source. Ted and I met yesterday and laid out the details. I'll announce it to my staff later today. Okay, let's pray."

The men leaned forward in their chairs and Tom led them in prayer. Fr. Ted concluded the prayer with a blessing over the men, including James Meyers, and then sat back into his chair with a satisfied smile creasing his face.

"What are you thinking, Ted?" Rowland asked.

"Do you guys know what my favorite part of mass is?"

"Not a clue," Terrance said.

Tracing the sign of the cross in front of the men Fr. Ted said, "Mass is ended. Go to love and serve the Lord."

"Really!" Terrance replied. "Why those words?"

"Because he's done and can get some lunch," Scanlon piped. Terrance punched him and Rowland rolled his eyes.

"No gentlemen," Fr. Ted said patiently. "It's the point of mass, the underlying meaning of the word itself. This short dismissal sends us. It tells us that since we have heard from God and feasted on His Word, we are sent to be his hands and feet and heart to the world…to fulfill His commission."

"I love that," Terrance said quietly under his breath.

"That's a really good message my friend," Rowland said. .

"So then, friends, 'Mass has ended. Let us go to love and serve the Lord…and young Mr. James Meyers."

"Amen," the men said as they rose to leave.

NINETEEN

Back in his cell James began fidgeting with the stack of yellow paper on his small wooden table. Unlike other parts of the legal process which can take an interminably long time to develop, when prison violence breaks out, inquiries convene rapidly. Already a panel had been formed, its judge appointed and announced to Warden Rowland. A date had been set, too, but not announced to James. "Any day now," was all he got when he quizzed the guards. Any day until what, an announcement, the real deal or his execution – he was left to stew on his own. And he did, pacing the short crawl between the commode and bolted door, thinking, tapping on the wall then scribbling hastily onto a yellow pad.

Still no news about the forensic report: Had they discovered his fingers never touched the weapon? And what was the weapon – a filed fork, melted coffee cup lids molded into a long stiffened shiv, bed spring mounted to tightly wound newspapers? James worked his checklist. The weapon issue headed it. Immediately behind it was the blood on his hands and shoes. How would he explain that if asked? And without doubt he would be asked. He ticked down the items, most them inconsequential but worrisome just the same. Obviously the stabbing was the work of another inmate. The only other item apart from the weapon James felt might help his defense was his newness to the populace and his lack of gang ties. He had no known enemies, no axes to grind, no grudges to settle. He paced some more, picked up the pile of pages and rehearsed them in his mind, searching for any omissions – forgotten details.

*****

In the administration office the story was different.

"Judge Parker, glad to see you again good friend," Warden Rowland said welcoming the esteemed jurist into his office. "Please have a seat."

"Good to see you again, Tom. Wish the circumstances were different however." Judge William Parker took a seat, dressed nattily in a navy suit and red tie, with a halo of gray hair wrapping his mostly bald head.

"I see you have your panel and inquiry date, Judge," Rowland noted while perusing the memo Betty handed him before announcing the judge's presence.

"Yes, we do, Tom. The inquiry panel convenes day after tomorrow. We'll want to interview James Meyers on day one and go from there."

Not wanting to reveal his bias for Meyers, Rowland tossed an obvious and hopefully innocuous question at the judge, "Any likely suspects yet?"

"Actually just one," Parker said without offering a name.

"Just one?" Rowland quizzed still studying the summary documents in front of him mostly to disguise his rising anxiety about Parker's likely response.

"So far the evidence points to Meyers, Tom."

Holding onto his best poker face, Rowland quizzed, "Oh, what makes Meyers your mark?"

"Honestly, it's fairly circumstantial," Judge Parker replied, dropping a file onto the floor beside him and bringing his hands together with his elbows resting on the armrests of his chair. "Meyers was the only one seen by other prisoners. His shoes and hands were stained with the victim's blood. No one else had blood on their hands or clothes. Plus two witnesses stepped forward with corroborating stories that point to James Meyers."

Rowland looked up from his desk on that last piece of information, resting a finger on his temple. "Reliable witnesses, Bill?"

"It's a prison, Tom: As reliable as prisoners can be. Of course we're not through with the investigation and might not be before we complete the inquiries."

"Not exactly overwhelming or damning evidence, then?" Rowland said.

"No, not really, but it's what we have."

"I see," Rowland said offering nothing more.

"What do you know about the situation, Tom? In particular, what can you tell me about Meyers and these other two prisoners, the witnesses?" Parker asked, retrieving the folder from the floor and handing it to Rowland.

Rowland took a few moments to peruse the file content. "I can tell you immediately that the two witnesses have ties to the Lobo gang, same as the victim, Nate Chalmers. You'll see in their resident files they've each received disciplinary actions for a variety of incidents, fighting mostly." He paused a moment. "Ah, I see you have that information right here," pulling a page from the file and sliding it over to Parker who pressed his glasses higher on his nose.

"And Meyers?" Parker asked lifting his eyes from the sheet of paper.

"James – to be honest, Bill, I'm surprised he's your top priority. In fact, apart from the circumstantial material, I'm surprised he'd be considered at all," Rowland said, closing the files and returning his attention to the judge.

"Really, why?"

"James has no gang ties," Rowland said with a flick of his hand as if waving the matter off as if irrelevant. "Besides, he's been here just a short while, not long enough to create any enemies. He's been kept in Cell Block C as much for his safety as for punishment. And he's an awfully naïve kid – intelligent but naïve."

"I see," Judge Parker said, stuffing his glasses into the vest pocket of his suit. "What about his conviction? According to the court transcripts, he doesn't appear so naïve to be inculpable of complex drug negotiations. They paint a pretty damaging story if you ask me. It seems he was mired up to his neck in that botched deal."

"I said he was intelligent. That doesn't mean, Bill, he really comprehended his actions. The kid was looking for attention." Rowland could tell his arguments didn't hold a lot of water with the judge. Frankly, they didn't sound all that credible in his own ears.

"Come on now, Tom. I understand your position but let's be honest with one another. Meyers was the only one seen, the only one tainted with evidence and the only one fingered by the populace."

"Granted, but no one has said anything about how it went down have they? I just reviewed the charges and filings again today. All they say is that Meyers 'did the deed,' I believe is how your witnesses put it. What they don't say is how he did it or with what." Rowland was now pleading James' case reminiscent of his days as a defense lawyer.

"It was with a filed spoon, Tom. You'll see that in the depositions. I'll concede the means are murky. The witnesses insist it went down pretty quickly," Parker offered not needing to and perhaps ill advisedly. The inquiry hadn't formally begun, but that wasn't noticed in Rowland's office.

"A filed spoon?" Rowland smirked. "Bill, James Meyers has not been anywhere in this prison that would give him access to tools. How could he have filed a spoon?"

"You know prisoners, Tom! Was his cell inspected?"

"You know it was! Immediately after he was taken to the infirmary guards practically ransacked the place. Isn't that in your files? They found nothing! Nothing, Bill! Nothing more than a few scraps of paper and a ballpoint pen." Rowland's face flushed. Parker said nothing. Rowland broke the pause. "What did the lab report say, Bill?" Rowland alertly knew the smoking gun in this case would be evidence contained on that report.

"I can't divulge that, Tom. You know I can't."

"But you can accuse a frightened kid. Bill, I'm shocked to think this is as deep as the investigation has gone. So far I've read nothing or heard nothing about motives. You're going to have to go deeper. Or..." Rowland stopped his own words.

"Or what, Tom?" Parker asked wary of Rowland's threatening snarl.

"Or I might represent the kid myself."

"Huh, well that would be a first. You really believe James Meyers to be innocent don't you?"

Rowland softened his tone, "I do, Bill. I think this kid has made terrible mistakes in his life. But he's not a murderer. Besides, what do you have for a motive?"

"Honestly, motive is murkier than method. We don't have one yet."

"Hmmm," Rowland muttered. He drew in a long breath and let it out as he contemplated the situation more thoroughly. "In light of that admission, old friend, I stand on James Meyers' innocence."

Judge Parker knew Tom Rowland well, well enough to recognize that his long-time friend would not put himself on the line if he didn't have a case. "I'll take your words under consideration."

"Thank you."

Parker paused then said, "Off the record, Tom, I admire your advocacy. You and I go way back, back to our first jobs out of law school. As I recall you've always had a penchant for kids like Meyers."

"Have I been wrong?"

"No, no you haven't" Parker said through a knowing smile. He sighed deeply himself before concluding, "You have my word; we'll keep our options open – and go deeper."

"I appreciate that, Bill. That's all I can ask."

What bothered Rowland most was the absence of any discussion about the suspect taken into custody and held for questioning soon after the incident. Parker's only conversation had been about Meyers. Why not this other guy?

"Bill, I am troubled about something else, something we've omitted in our discussion."

"What's that?" Parker asked with deeply furrowed brow.

"What about the prisoner taken into custody by my staff? They were all but certain he committed the crime."

"Tom, that one bothers me, too. But here's the problem, nobody places him at the scene. In fact, corroborating evidence has him in the laundry at the time of the stabbing. We looked into it, but it appears that guy was framed by other Lobos. We're not sure why, but it's clear this guy had no direct responsibility for Chalmers' death – no DNA on his clothes or body, no blood, no motive, no opportunity, nothing."

Rowland tapped his desk and stared blankly at Parker. "So that makes Meyers not just your primary but your only suspect?"

"Yes, yes it does. Does that news alter your opinion of Meyers' innocence?"

"No, it doesn't. I'll agree that as it stands it doesn't look good for him. But, Bill, I'm still persuaded of his innocence."

Rowland rose to shake Judge Parker's hand and see him out the door. "Bill, I don't often take a personal interest in my prisoners, certainly not to this degree. But this one is different. I want to see the young man get turned around. He doesn't need another mountain to climb, especially where I am confident beyond doubt he's innocent."

Judge Parker pursed his lips and studied his colleague's face. Rowland's granite stare evinced a determination he'd seen before, years ago when both men were young, zealous trial lawyers. His friend was esteemed for many things, his intelligence and perhaps more for his bulldog tenacity, but not careless tenacity. Tom Rowland held the reputation of a rock solid trial lawyer, skilled and meticulously prepared. Still, for whatever reason, Parker felt the need to press the matter one more time for good measure. "Can you be that sure? Can you be that sure James Meyers did not commit the crime?"

"I'd stake my career on it, Bill."

"That's some trust. I hope you're right. If the tables were turned, I'd want someone like you in my corner. Actually, I'd want you." Judge Parker gave Tom Rowland's arm a firm squeeze, nodded toward Betty and exited out the door.

Rowland closed the door behind the judge and could sense Betty looking at him. "I hope I'm right, Mrs. Morrison."

*****

Of course James had no idea what just went down in the warden's office. It was another stomach-acid-for-lunch day as he fretted away time alone in his cell. Impressions, recollections had ground to a halt. He was drained. All that remained was waiting, interminable, anxious waiting. He'd given his deposition. He'd probed the guards for information. Waiting to know, to simply know the judgment of his fate however unfair it might be was all he could do, and pace.

TWENTY

"Meyers! The Warden wants to see you."

James' eyes darted to the window slit. "The Warden?" Then he remembered. Tuesday!

"Yeah, Warden Rowland," the guard snapped. "Let's go!"

James pushed himself off his bed and backed up to the slot as the guard unlocked it. The cuffs seemed to bite sharper than usual. James clenched his teeth.

En route James paid little attention to the other inmates, though it felt like they had their eyes on him. The plaza was empty, a good sign. All the visitor rooms were empty, too. It was Tuesday, no visitors should be here. Neither the guard nor James said anything. They just walked briskly toward the administration office, connected by a short breezeway that offered James the only jolt of fresh air he'd had in days. He gulped in a deep swig of the reviving air just before the guard swung open the door leading to the Warden's office.

As James stepped into the ante room an unfamiliar but cheerful voice welcomed him. "You must be James."

"Yes ma'am I am."

"I'm Betty, Warden Rowland's assistant."

"Nice to meet you," James said, feeling strangely comfortable in Betty's company, a matronly lady professionally comported in her mid-fifties. Her pleasant demeanor tended to relax him, as if he'd been invited into her living room not the warden's office.

"Can I offer you some tea, James?" Betty asked smiling at him from her desk.

"Oh, no thanks ma'am, I'm just here to meet with Warden Rowland. But thank you."

"You're quite welcome, James. The Warden will be with you in just a few moments."

James stood facing out the window to a world beyond the razor wire, a world that had suddenly become alien to him. It seemed so surreal. Between him and that world was six years of time, a barrier more impenetrable than the walls and fences surrounding the prison. A sickening anxiety swathed him like the cold gray mist that greeted him on his arrival a few weeks ago.

The cadence of Betty typing returned him to the moment. He surveyed the room. His guard escort stood a half step behind and to the left of him. The coffee pot made unnatural gurgling sounds. He noticed carpet under his feet, the first cushioning feel of carpet he'd felt since…well…the first day he arrived.

Betty's phone buzzed. "Go on in gentlemen," she announced. "Warden Rowland is ready to see you." Betty's smile seemed reassuring but didn't begin to melt the weight of dread James carried into the Warden's office.

"Good morning, James," Warden Rowland said coming from behind his desk to welcome him. "Have a seat."

Rowland sat down on the sofa across the dark cherry wood coffee table from James, a distinctively casual approach in contrast to their first meeting. James awkwardly twisted his chair around to better face the Warden. For a moment the men merely sat studying one another. The hard drawn expressions that etched Rowland's face during their first meeting were clearly absent. Instead, he appeared relaxed, his composure inviting.

James, though, was the picture of edginess, tense and uncomfortable. He'd entered the populace a frightened and disillusioned boy. In just a very few weeks he'd assumed the demeanor of wary prey, fearful, distrusting and still very frightened.

"James, I wanted to visit with you again in light of recent events but mostly to see how you're holding up." With these words Rowland set the agenda.

James said nothing in response, but simply shrugged his shoulders in tacit acknowledgment and waited for Rowland to continue.

"I can only imagine what you've gone through since arriving here, particularly in light of the Nate Chalmers incident." Rowland swung his arm up on the back of the sofa and crossed his legs.

James listened but made no reply. He wondered where Rowland was going. Rowland was right, James reasoned to himself. He had no idea at all what plagued his mind, what dreams tormented him in the dark of night and awoke him in a cold sweat. Rowland's next words caught him entirely off guard.

"I want you to know, James, I've read the depositions, including yours, spoke with the judge who'll preside over the inquiry and come to the conviction you are innocent. I told the judge precisely that earlier today. While I have no authority over the proceedings, this is my conviction. Now I'm going to ask you, am I right? Are you innocent of the murder of Nate Chalmers?" Rowland bit off those last words like he was snapping a tree limb.

"You believe I'm innocent?" James asked furrowing his brow, shocked by Rowland's admission.

"I do." Rowland paused. "But I need you to tell me in your own words that I'm right, that you are as I said, innocent of Nate Chalmers' murder."

James parted his lips but the words formed slowly. "Yes sir, I am innocent of Nate Chalmers' murder. I truly am, sir." James instinctively knew that Rowland had put himself on the line for him. But why; why would he stick his neck out like that?

"May I ask you a question, sir?" James said.

"Yes, of course."

"What makes you sure I didn't do it?"

"I think I told you when we first met that you didn't impress me as a bad kid. I do think you've done some stupid things, committed serious errors in judgment. But it's my guess that you did them for reasons other than criminal intent." Rowland took a breath and rested a hand against the side of his face. "James I read your test scores and frankly they didn't surprise me. When I put it all together, it confirms my suspicion."

"What do you mean...suspicion?"

"You're a bright, capable young man with a lot of promise, who with solid direction and the appropriate attention could make something significant of his life. That's my suspicion. Your test scores tell me you are capable of whatever you put your mind to."

James was stunned. He swallowed hard before responding. "Nobody has ever said anything like that to me." He felt warm moisture flood into his eyes.

"Never? Not even your parents? A school teacher? A coach?"

"No. I've never heard those words before...from anybody." James wiped a sleeve across his eyes.

"I'm surprised but not surprised," Rowland said gently shaking his head. "Why do you think no one has recognized your gifts before now?"

"You mean before prison? Good question."

"Seriously, what's your take on the matter?" Rowland wanted to hear it from James own mouth.

"Honestly, I just don't think anyone ever noticed me. My folks were always busy. My brother and sister have lives of their own. I just kind of became invisible."

"Yeah," Rowland said. "The kid left out, left behind, left alone, and left to figure out life on his own. Does that about sum it up?"

"Yes, sir, I think it does. No one abused me or took advantage of me. They just never seemed to notice I existed."

Rowland wanted to dig a little deeper – see how far James might let him probe.

"How'd you spend your time at home?"

"Mostly hanging out in my room," James replied.

"Doing what?"

"Surfing the Internet."

Rowland swiftly broke in, "Porn?"

James recoiled, "No offense, sir, but that's kind of personal."

"So?"

"I'll leave that for you to figure out." James could feel his blood begin to boil.

Rowland didn't press him. In effect he got his answer.

"What else? Watch sports, read?"

James' cooled his rising ire. "Not so much of a sports nut. Mostly I read quite a bit."

"Like what? What are some of your favorite authors?"

James wasn't certain he wanted to answer another nosy question. Just the same he recited names of authors that caught Rowland's attention.

"Those are fabulous writers, James. They're some of my favorites, too. I'm especially fond of Dostoevsky. What drew you to those authors? They're not exactly easy reads."

"No, they're not easy reads but the authors seem to understand me." James repositioned himself in his chair, trying to get comfortable with Rowland's insistent prying.

Rowland glanced over his shoulder to the bookshelves behind him. "If you like those guys, I think I have a read you might really get into." He stood up and walked over to one of the upper shelves and pulled down a book.

"Here, take this with you. Of course I'll want it back, but I think you'll like spending some time with this guy." Rowland held the book out to James then sat down on the arm of the sofa.

"Orthodoxy: the Romance of Faith," James read slowly taking it from Rowland. "Who's G.K. Chesterton?"

"Given your selection of titles and authors I'm a little surprised you haven't heard of Chesterton. He was considered, and really still is considered, one of Great Britain's finest journalists. His writing bridges the nineteenth and twentieth century. I suppose you'd say he was kind of an odd fellow really, a nerd – brilliant mind, massive obese body and searing wit." Rowland broke into a smile on that last bit.

James hadn't noticed how relaxed he felt. Suddenly he was enthralled with this unexpected common interest between him and Rowland.

"Thank you, I'll definitely read it."

"And report on it," Rowland said sternly. "Seriously, James, I want you to dig in with that fine mind of yours and let's plan to discuss this book."

"Alright, that sounds great," James said patting the text on his leg. "Thank you again!" Holding the book up he said, "This was not expected, Mr. Rowland."

"You're quite welcome." Rowland sat quietly for a moment and watched James flip through the pages of the book like it was the most important thing he'd ever received.

"James, do you remember what I said to you during our first meeting?"

"You said several things, sir. I'm not sure which one you mean."

"I told you that I want you make it, son. I want to see you leave here a different man than when you came, a good man."

"Yes, sir, I remember you saying something like that to me."

Rowland leaned forward with his hands on his knees. "Do you know that I meant that? I truly want to see you succeed."

"I'm beginning to, sir. I just don't know what to make of your interest in me, though. There are so many men here, why me?"

"There are many men in this prison and I care about them all. James, I pray for them. I pray for you. It is my strongest conviction, son, that God has placed you here for more than correction. I am persuaded he wants to go way past penal correction all the way to transformation. In a word, James, God wants to give you a new life."

James stared intently at Rowland. Never in his life had any man shot that straight with him or showed that level of concern about him.

"I don't know what to say, sir. Why would God care that much about me? I'm nobody. Besides, I'm not sure about God, I mean if there is a God or what kind of God he is."

"First of all, Mr. Meyers, you are somebody. To God you matter. To those of us who love God you matter. As for whether or not God exists or if he's a worthy deity, well, I think our book reviews will get us down that road."

"I see. Will this guy Chesterton talk about that stuff?" James asked holding up the book again.

"Pay close attention, James. You'll see another perspective than the one you have now. Chesterton will cause you to rethink your assumptions and readdress your opinions not just about God but a number of things."

"Like what?"

"Read the book. We'll talk about them."

James held the book in both hands, "Okay. I'm down."

"By the way," Rowland added. "I understand Fr. Ted practically dared you into something."

James furrowed his brow wondering what Rowland hinted at. Then it dawned on him.

"You mean the Bible reading thing?"

Rowland nodded, "Yes, the Bible reading thing. Fr. Ted said he dared you to read the book of John."

"Yeah, he did."

"So?"

"I'm sorry, sir?"

"So are you going to take him up on his challenge?"

"Ah, I've got to tell you, I'm not so sure about that. Let me get into this book awhile and I'll see."

"Fair enough. But for what it's worth, you could do a lot worse with your time. The Book of John is remarkable. The first few verses will keep your mind busy for a good long time."

Rowland's comment struck a chord. "Oh yeah, how?" James asked.

"Just read the first dozen or so verses in the first chapter. I think you'll get my point."

"Okay, I might just take you up on that."

"Good!"

Rowland stood up and went behind his desk, picked up a folder and returned to the sofa.

"Before you leave we need to talk about the inquiry, James."

"I was afraid that might come up."

"Why? Nervous?"

"Scared to death is more like it."

"I'm sure you are. Let me give you a little heads up." Rowland pulled a document from the folder and perched his glasses on his nose.

"The inquiry, James, will convene at 10 o'clock Thursday morning. A law school colleague of mine, a good and fair man, Judge William Parker, will be presiding. You will be his first witness."

James sat raptly intent, absorbing everything Warden Rowland said. Being the first out of the chute bothered him.

"Why am I the first one?" James asked.

Rowland gave it to him straight. "Frankly, because Judge Parker thinks you committed the crime."

"But you don't?"

"That's right. I don't think you did it. Now bear in mind, he must produce sufficient evidence to indict. Right now that evidence seems sketchy. Still, it won't be easy, James. Regardless of what I think, due process must be served and that will entail an exhaustive inquiry. You might be called on to give testimony more than once." Rowland put the paper down and pulled off his glasses. "There is one thing you must bear in mind at all times. Be truthful! Don't hedge the truth. Be forthright in all of your answers. You will not be able to hide anything. Sooner or later all of the details of what happened that day will get pieced together." Rowland's eyes narrowed and he pointed that intrusive finger at James, "James if the verdict goes against you and you told the truth you have the recourse of appeals. If you lie, all of that goes away. Do you understand me?"

"Yes sir. I appreciate you being straight with me. It actually helps."

"Good."

Rowland retrieved another item from his desk, a file.

"I hear from the guards that you've been keeping copious notes. Is that right?"

"Yes, sir, I have."

"You will not be able to have them with you during the inquiry but keep them just in case you need them later."

"Will they be safe in my cell?"

"For now they will be." Rowland continued, "James in addition to being entirely truthful, the most important thing you can do for yourself is to relax. You have friends, some of whom you've already met, who are praying for you. They believe in the God you doubt, and believe him to be a loving and merciful God. That might not mean anything now, but it will."

"I don't know what to say, Mr. Rowland. To be perfectly honest, I was scared out of my mind coming here to see you today. I still don't get why you're helping me, but I want you to know it means a lot."

Rowland smiled.

"Oh, sir, how long do you think this inquiry will take?"

"I really don't know, James. I've seen them last as little as a day and as much as several weeks. The good news, if that's what we can call it, is that you are only one part of the inquiry. It is possible they will come to a determination about your guilt or innocence early even before the inquiry itself has concluded."

"Will they tell me?"

"Oh yes. They'll tell you. Hopefully, they'll let me tell you."

"I'd like that, sir."

"We'll see what we can do. Right now, it's time I get back to work. James, I'm going to ask you to recall one more thing I said to you during our first meeting." Again that finger pointed at James' nose. "I still expect you to toe the line. Is that clear?"

"Yes, sir, it is quite clear," James replied catching the full weight of Rowland's authority.

"Well, goodbye, James. I'll send for you again in a week or so. Let's see how much of that book you get read by then," Rowland said gesturing toward the book James held in his two hands. "I'll expect a report."

James rose and shook Rowland's outstretched hand, turned and left the room. It hadn't occurred to him that his guard escort wasn't present in the meeting. Instead, he waited in the anteroom. Apparently Rowland didn't feel he needed the security. James later discovered Rowland broke the rules. For reasons of security, regulations require a guard always present in meetings with the warden whether of an official or personal nature.

"Good to meet you, James," Betty said. "Take care of yourself."

"Good to meet you, too, ma'am. Thank you."

*****

More ironies, James thought to himself. He expected his visit to the Warden's office to yield anything but a book club invitation. He entered the meeting thinking he was going to have his head handed to him. Instead he left with fresh content for his head. But it was more than all that. Rowland did what no man had ever done for him — stuck his neck out, took a risk, believed in him.

"C'mon kid, we've got to move," the guard ordered, pushing James along. Put off by the guard's abruptness, James balked. But the guard pushed harder. Then James saw why. The big, heavyset dude who threatened him in the yard came walking toward them, his right hand shoved in his pants pocket, his eyes steely cold and directed right at James' eyes.

"Bates, what are you doing out here? Get back to your cell," the guard demanded.

Just then the burly inmate swung his arm out of his pocket in a slashing motion toward James's mid-section. Instinctively James jumped back. The shiv ripped through his shirt then dropped to the floor. James stumbled and fell a short ways from it. Another guard saw the commotion and came charging, while James' guard wrestled with the assailant. More guards came, one of them leaping onto the downed inmate's back, while another wrapped zip-ties around his ankles and arms. They hauled the cursing man to his feet, blood streaming from his nose. A mouse was already forming under his right eye, evidently caused during the fracas.

"Bates, you're heading for the hole," one of the guards bellowed. "Move it!" he ordered, shoving the assailant past James. James squirmed to avoid the man's foot, which swept by, missing his head by inches. For a split second their eyes met. Stone cold malice etched the inmate's face, anger unlike anything James had ever experienced. He lay frozen in fear on the floor gasping from shock.

TWENTY-ONE

Quickly James' guard dropped on his knees beside him, looking for signs of injury. A blood soaked jagged tear in the side of James' uniform revealed a nasty gash in his side.

"Let me help you up, kid. We're going to the infirmary."

"Oh god, not again!" James groaned. "What next?" The guard threw James' arm over his shoulder and fairly hauled him down the hall.

"Hold on Meyers, we're close," the guard urged. Each step weakened James, until finally he collapsed two steps from the door leading into the brightly lit whitewashed treatment room. "Don't quit now, kid. We're almost there. Hang with me." The guard laced his fingers around James' mid-section and bear-hugged him the remaining steps.

Barbara was there to greet the men as they crashed through the door, James bleeding quite heavily by now.

"Oh my goodness," she said. "Put him up here on the table."

Barbara rammed her hands into a pair of surgical gloves and grabbed a pair of scissors. Quickly she cut away the bloody side of James shirt and opened it wide.

"This doesn't look good," she said. "Let me get Dr. Kearns in here right away."

James lay on the table still breathing heavily, and still unsure of what went down.

Dr. Kearns strode through the door, shoving his scrubbed hands into a pair of gloves as he stared at James' wound. "Did anybody get the weapon?" he asked.

"Yeah, I did," the guard said, placing the hand-made shiv on the metal tray beside the treatment table.

"Serrated," Dr. Kearns exclaimed. "That accounts for the messiness."

"Is it bad, doctor?" James asked nervously.

"You'll make it kid. Just relax. We're going to have to transport you to a local hospital for surgery."

"Surgery!?" James groaned. "That bad?"

"Like I said, kid, you'll be fine." Dr. Kearns said, patting James' knee. As he stripped off the gloves, Dr. Kearns instructed Barbara to alert County Hospital and call for an ambulance.

By now James was feeling searing pain in his side, and like he was about to empty his lunch.

On the ride in the ambulance his mind kicked into high gear. Would there be more retributive strikes between now and the inquiry?

*****

Meanwhile word got to Rowland about the slashing. Immediately he called Fr. Ted.

"Ted, we've got a situation," Rowland said tersely.

"What do you mean?" Fr. Ted replied.

"James was accosted on the way back to his cell after leaving my office. He's being transported to County Medical's penal ward right now. Can you get there?

"Absolutely! Mind if I call Terrance? I think he should be there with me."

"No. Do it. I think it'll help if James sees both of you." Rowland hung up the phone and immediately called Anne.

"Hi sweetheart," Rowland said.

"Hi daddy! What's up?"

"I need you to pray for James right now," Rowland said calmly but in a grave tone that Anne knew meant something serious was up.

"You know I will. What's happened?"

"He was assaulted this afternoon. Honey, it happened after he left my office."

"You mean James?"

"Yes, James."

"Oh no! When will the insanity stop for this kid?" Anne said rubbing her forehead. "How much does God think he can take?"

"I know, sweetheart. I ask myself the same question. Look, I need you to amp up James' appeal process if you can. I don't think he's likely to survive here."

"Okay, I'll get on it," Anne said. She knew it would be a steep climb, but circumstances demanded action. And she knew her dad's tone. It meant failure was not an option.

*****

"Hello!"

"Terrance, this is Fr. Ted. Do you have plans that can't be broken?"

"Just the Café tonight. Why?"

"Can someone else take your place? I need you right now!"

"Sounds serious, Father. James?"

"Yes, the boy's being transported by ambulance to County Medical as we speak. Tom called me just a moment ago and asked if I'd get over there. I asked him if I could take you with me. I think James would benefit from both of us there. Besides, I could use the backup."

"Oh Lord, what next? Yes, of course. Let me make a phone call and I'll get right back to you. Better yet, can you pick me up on your way to County?"

"I'm on my way!" Fr. Ted said and hung up the phone.

Terrance immediately contacted Dirk. "Dirk, I need you to stand in for me. James has been hurt and Fr. Ted's asked me to go with him to the hospital."

"Yeah, you bet, T. I can do that."

"Great, man. I owe you."

"No worries. Hey look, mind if I just ask the group to go to prayer for James tonight. Like, I think that would be the best thing we could do."

"You're right on the money, pal. That would be fabulous. I'll keep you posted."

"You've got it T!" Dirk said.

Fr. Ted pulled up a few moments later. Terrance had been praying and pacing the yard in front of his and Anne's small house. He and Anne had spoken a minute earlier.

"I'm free. Dirk will fill in for me," Terrance said sliding into passenger seat.

"Nice work!"

"Yeah, he's going to have the kids who show up pray for James. That's all they'll do – just pray for him."

"Well done! That's what we need to do right now. 'Dear Lord, be with our boy, your child, James. Be with him right now. Amen.'"

"Amen!"

"Look, Terrance. I don't know what we're about to find. Let's just hope we can do some good here. You know what I mean."

"With you, Father. God knows what's up. He'll have everything under control."

"Indeed! Indeed he will!" Fr. Ted said, striking the steering wheel with his fist.

*****

The ambulance came to a lurching stop and the rear doors flew open. Quickly hands grabbed for the stretcher, as orders came flying from someone outside the vehicle.

"Looks like a nasty wound," a female voice said.

"Yeah, it is," one of the EMT's confirmed. "He was stabbed."

Lifting James' blood soaked shirt the female voice blurted, "Stabbed? This looks more like a hack job. The dude must have used a chainsaw! Get me a sponge and open ER2 STAT!"

Wide glass doors swung open and curtain swept aside.

"What's his name?" The female voice insisted jogging alongside the stretcher.

"Meyers! James Meyers."

"He's diaphoretic, Doctor."

"Yes, I know. He's in shock!"

"James, listen to me. We're going to prep you for surgery and get you fixed up. Okay? Try to relax. You're going to be alright," the female voice said.

James' eyes blurred, his breathing grew increasingly shallow and rapid. He only made out faint images that seemed to swarm around him. A searing pain burnt through his right side. His lips tingled, and hands began to go numb. "What's…your…name?" he asked with a breathy slur.

"Linda!" the voice returned.

"You…my…doctor?" James' tongue seemed to thicken.

"I am, James. My name is Dr. Linda White. Just call me Linda."

"Okay…thanks. What's…happening…to…me?" Images grew even fainter and sound more muted.

"Look, James, you're going to get some drugs to help with the pain and stabilize your blood pressure."

"Fine. Thanks….My b**k" and he drifted off.

"What was that last part?" Linda asked. "What'd he mean?"

"I think he was referring to this," an EMT said handing her the book James was clutching when he fell on the hallway floor. It was bloodied.

"Oh, okay." Linda replied. "Good! James, we'll get you ready to read that book." She said to her unconscious patient. "Let's get him to surgery STAT!"

*****

"May I help you, Father?" A polite voice said from behind the reception desk.

"Yes. I'm looking for James Meyers. I think he was just brought in by ambulance."

"Meyers? Oh yes, he's being wheeled into surgery as we speak."

"Where will he be taken after that?"

"Recovery to begin with. Just a moment, here comes the ER doctor. Maybe she can help you."

"Doctor," Fr. Ted called.

"Yes, may I help you?"

"Dr. White, these men are looking for James Meyers," the receptionist interrupted.

"I see. He's heading into surgery right now."

"We know. What can you tell us and where will he be taken?"

"Are you family members?" Dr. White asked in a clinical tone.

"No, I'm the prison chaplain, Fr. Ted Harding, and this is my assistant Terrance Hall."

"Well okay. James is in pretty bad shape, gentlemen. He's lost a lot of blood. We're not sure about internal injuries yet. The cut's a deep one; a very ragged laceration that we hope didn't catch any internal organs. As for where he'll go after surgery: If he survives the operation he'll be sent to recovery then the OR ward on the penal floor, floor nine."

"If he survives surgery?" Terrance asked, obvious worry in his voice.

"Like I said, he's lost a lot of blood," Dr. White repeated. "Look guys, we're on his side with you. We'll do all we can."

"Thank you," Fr. Ted replied. "We're confident you've got our boy's best interests at heart." With that Fr. Ted and Terrance turned to leave.

"Just a moment, guys," Dr. White said. "Can you tell me the circumstances of James' stabbing?"

"We're really not at liberty to discuss those details, doctor. I can tell you, however, he's had a rough time of it."

"Prison you mean?"

"Life," Terrance stated abruptly.

Dr. White closed her eyes and sighed, "I'm so sorry to hear that."

"We're sorry, too," Fr. Ted said, giving Dr. White's arm a gentle squeeze. "Thank you for taking care of our boy," he added with a warm smile.

"Sure. I'm glad I could be here for him."

The men strode off to the elevator and OR Recovery to wait in vigil for James.

TWENTY-TWO

"Dirk! What are you doing here?" Terrance asked in astonishment. "We're all here, T." Dirk stepped aside to let the men onto the elevator with him.

"Who's here?"

"Actually the entire café came to the hospital. We're hanging in the chapel praying."

Fr. Ted's mouth dropped open and a broad smile began to stretch across his face.

"Well done, young man!" he said. "Well done!"

"Dirk, I can't tell you what this means to me. Thank you my man!" Terrance beamed.

"The guys would like it if you two would come up and fill us in – maybe stay and pray with us awhile."

"You've got it, Dirk. We'll follow you," Terrance said.

The men arrived at the cozy chapel, finding it crammed with kids from the café, some crowded into three small pews and others sitting wherever they could find floor space, even spilling into the hallway. A narrow pulpit stood centered in front of a wood carved crucifix. Terrance stepped over kids and took a place beside the pulpit, pausing momentarily in front of the crucifix. The eyes of Jesus starring compassionately from the cross moved him. His eyes flooded and a he felt his chin quiver.

"I don't know what to say," he began looking out across the tumble of teenagers and twenty-somethings. "Thank you! Thank you for coming here on behalf of a friend, a friend who needs you right now." Pointing behind him to the crucifix, "James needs Jesus. We need to pray he will find him…soon." A collective affirming "amen" came from the group. Terrance turned to Fr. Ted, "Will you fill the kids in on James's condition and lead us in prayer?"

Fr. Ted nodded assuredly. Placing a hand on the shoulders of kids as he maneuvered through them he made his way beside Terrance. "You guys are too much," he began. The kids chuckled politely. "James is in serious condition – not critical, but serious. As you've perhaps heard, he was stabbed while being returned to his cell at the State House earlier this afternoon. I would only be speculating, but it might have been an effort to silence him. He's due to testify Thursday about the stabbing death of a fellow inmate. Stabbings happen all too often in prison." He paused. "Guys, the wound on Jesus' side right here," he pointed to the crucifix. "This was the stabbing he took for us. His death brought life, because he defeated death, sin, hell and evil. James needs this life. He needs Jesus. Will you help him find the way?"

A collective "Yes" rose from the group.

"Wonderful. Thank you." Fr. Ted said. "Now please pray with me."

Tracing the sign of the cross over the group, Fr. Ted prayed, "In the name of the Father, the Son and the Holy Spirit, our blessed Lord we commend to your care the life of James Meyers. We trust you will guide the surgeons and restore James to health. More importantly, Lord, we beg you for James' soul. We pray he will find his way to you, to perfect freedom and safety in you. We know you love him as you love each of us. Please hear the prayers of these young people who've come in your name on behalf of James. Thank you for your salvation in Jesus. Save James! In the name of the Father, the Son and the Holy Spirit, amen."

"Amen" rose from the kids, each one wiping tears from his or her eyes.

Terrance stepped in, "It's going to be a long night guys. Whether you stay or leave, please keep praying. Fr. Ted and I will send word to you of James' condition through Dirk. Watch the café web site for info. You're welcome to stay as long as you want. Thank you again. You're the best."

Dirk stepped out with Fr. Ted and Terrance, where they put together their communications strategy. It was simple. Terrance would call or text on his cell phone, and Dirk would post the updates on the café site from his phone. Dirk then returned to the group – Fr. Ted and Terrance to the surgical recovery area.

"That's quite a group you have, Terrance," Fr. Ted said as he stepped onto the elevator.

"They are – thanks. Most of those kids have been in trouble themselves – drugs, gangs, and stupid mischief. It wouldn't surprise me if they stayed all night."

"It will be an all night vigil, my friend," Fr. Ted sighed. "You up for it?"

"It's what I signed up for, Father. I signed up to wait for kids to find their way home."

Fr. Ted broke into another broad grin. "Home indeed!"

*****

"Please have a seat Mr. and Mrs. Meyers. I'll call you as soon as I have any report."

Fr. Ted overheard these words as he and Terrance stepped off the elevator. He nudged Terrance. "I think that's the kid's folks."

"How do you know?"

"I just heard the attendant tell them to sit down. She called them Mr. and Mrs. Meyers."

"You think we ought to check it out – see if she's right?"

"I do. C'mon."

"You wouldn't be James Meyers' parents would you?" Fr. Ted asked as he approached an obviously worried couple seated against the wall.

"Yes we are," Mr. Meyers said, standing to greet the men. "And who are you if I may ask?"

"I'm Fr. Ted Harding and this is Terrance Hall. I'm the chaplain at the State House and Terrance is my associate."

"So you've met our son?"

"We have. In fact, we've spent some time getting to know him." Fr. Ted placed a hand on Mr. Meyer's arm, "Mr. and Mrs. Meyers, we are so very sorry about today's circumstances. Has anyone shared details with you?"

Mr. Meyers shook his head. "No. We were just told that James had been injured and was transported here. What can you tell us?"

"Please sit down." Fr. Ted pulled a chair around in front of the couple and Terrance parked himself on the end table beside him.

"We're not sure exactly what happened ourselves. Like you we received a call and were told to get over to the hospital. What we know is that James has been knifed...by another inmate. The attending physician in ER told us the wound is serious, requiring surgery to repair. There is some risk but how much she did not say."

"Risk?" Mrs. Meyers broke in.

"That's all she told us ma'am."

"Please, call us Don and Kathleen," Don interjected. "Does anyone know why? It seems so random...senseless."

"It is random...and senseless," Fr. Ted replied. "Every act of prison violence is nothing but senseless and, as you said, random."

"Don and Kathleen, if I may," Terrance said. "I was a prisoner at the State House myself, up until a couple of years ago. I've witnessed prison violence...actually been a part of it. Prison culture plays by its own rules set by the inmates, usually gang rules. To law abiding people it makes no sense, none at all. To a gang member it's all about survival; it's the code. You live by it or you suffer. I'm quite certain James unintentionally got trapped by that code and never saw it coming."

Don was struck incredulous. "You were a prisoner?" he asked, his voice rising.

"I was, sir."

"What were you in for? What did you do?"

"I was a gang leader."

"Oh my," Kathleen said. "But you seem too nice to have been a gang leader."

"Thank you, but it's true. I was."

"If you don't mind me asking, how'd you get straightened out? I believe Fr. Ted said you're his assistant?" Don asked.

"It's a long story and, yes, I have recently been appointed Fr. Ted's associate. I am completing graduate studies at Grace Seminary and operate what my wife and I call a worship café for at-risk kids, teens mostly."

"But your story – you were a prisoner and now you're a chaplain?" Both Don and Kathleen's expressions were inquisitively incredulous. It was like they were staring at a freak of nature and had no idea how to react.

"That's right. It took nearly all of the six years I was in prison before I was ready to trust and then accept the kindness and message of hope Warden Rowland, Fr. Ted and a few other people offered me. The good news is I did. I gave my life over to God, submitted to the mentoring of these people and quite literally became a new man."

"Amazing!" Don said.

"We so hope James will turn around, too. I don't know where we went wrong…" Kathleen's words drifted into a muted sob she stifled with a tissue. Don held her in his arms.

"This whole thing with James going to prison has been almost unbearable. It's crushed our family quite hard." Don offered in somber tones.

"We can only imagine your grief, Don and Kathleen," Fr. Ted consoled. "I want you to know that the two of us, as well as Warden Rowland and another friend have committed ourselves to helping James get on track. Even now as we talk, members of Terrance's worship café are in the chapel up stairs praying for your son."

"Oh my! How wonderful!" Kathleen beamed through her tears. "Please thank them for us. I can't begin to tell you how much that means."

"Would you like to thank them yourself?" Fr. Ted asked in a sweet priestly coaxing tone.

"Oh, I don't know that I could," Kathleen said looking at Don hoping he wouldn't push her. "I'm not sure I could face them."

"Kathleen, please believe me," Terrance began. "These kids know what you're facing. Each one of them has been in trouble and put their parents in tough places. Some of them were members of the same gang I led. They would be the last people to point the finger at you. If anything, they'll jump at the chance to help, even offer a warm hug. I really think it would help if you took Fr. Ted up on his offer."

"What do you think, Don?" Kathleen said through bloodshot eyes and quaking voice.

"I think we should, sweetheart. I don't know what to expect, but it can't be any worse than what we've endured so far."

Don turned to Terrance, "You mentioned a code, a gang code, and said James might have inadvertently gotten trapped by it. Can you explain how?"

"Don, the code is known only by the members. Each gang has one. It's like a way of living that stakes out turf, protects it and the members within it. If someone interferes, well, they're dealt with…usually violently."

"I still don't understand how James fell into it. Wasn't he just trying to help a guy?"

"True, Don, but the gang sees it differently. They were out to get the guy James helped. James interfered and they went after him. Whether he intended to or not he became the enemy; he violated the code."

"My God! How utterly primitive!" Don's faced flushed red. He calmed himself and asked, "So, how can James avoid such a thing in the future? Isn't he kind of a marked man now?"

"He is, Don. Honestly, only God can save James. And we believe God put us in James' life to help him best we can."

"What about another prison? Wouldn't he be safer out of state, at another facility?"

Fr. Ted broke in, "Not necessarily. The prison system is populated by gangs, including rival gangs. Even if James was moved, he'd likely encounter other members of the Lobos who would have received word about him."

"Oh, this is so unsettling," Kathleen sobbed.

"Don and Kathleen, Terrance is absolutely right. God is James' salvation. If anyone should know, it would this young man," he said gesturing toward Terrance, who was now on his feet ready to escort the couple to the chapel. "We can't guarantee James' safety. We can help him start down the right path. We're willing to go the distance with your son. But we'll need your help too."

"Yes, of course," Don said. "We know we're in part to blame, maybe mostly to blame for our son's condition."

"It won't help to blame yourselves. Like your son, we want you to turn down a new pathway, allowing God to lead you. Are you willing?" Fr. Ted was most insistent.

Don and Kathleen looked at one another. Then turning his attention to Fr. Ted, Don answered, "We are."

"Well then, let's go meet the kids. Please, follow us," Fr. Ted said as he stood up and motioned for the Meyer's to do the same.

TWENTY-THREE

"Bill, we've had a situation here at the prison that will likely affect the inquiry."

"What do you mean, Tom?" Judge Parker laid down his pen and sat back in his chair. "Something wrong?"

"I'm afraid so. James Meyers was stabbed on his way back to the cell after leaving my office this afternoon. He's in surgery at County Medical right now."

"No! What happened?" Parker asked rubbing a hand across his head.

"One of the inmates, a member of the Lobos, went after him. From what I've learned about the wound, the knifing nearly claimed James. As of ten minutes ago, he's still not out of the woods."

"Tom, I'm very sorry to learn this news. You're right; we'll likely want to push back the inquiry." Parker paused then asked, "How you holding up, Tom? I know that this young man means a lot to you."

"He does, Bill. I'm doing well, thank you."

"Well, keep me posted."

"You know I will, Bill. Talk to you as soon as I get more information."

Rowland hung up then called Terrance.

"Any updates?"

"Not yet. James is still in surgery. We met his folks, though. Fr. Ted's with them now. We're about to introduce them to the kids."

"Kids? What kids?"

"The kids from the café. Dirk brought the whole bunch to the hospital. They're piled up in the chapel praying for James."

"Oh, that's great news, Terrance! How are the folks?"

"Pretty shaken. They're nice people, Tom. Not the kind of people who would intentionally neglect their kid."

"Well, they've got a rough road ahead. Glad they're with you guys."

"Hey, dad, you don't sound so good yourself."
"Oh, don't worry about me. My thoughts are on the young man…and his family."

"I understand. Look, get some rest. We're going to be here for the long haul. The kids plan to stay all night."

"Terrance, I don't think I've told you recently how very proud I am of you. But I am."

"Thanks! Now don't go getting sappy with me. You know I can't do sappy," Terrance was laughing.

"I might just stop by in awhile and check on things," Tom replied.

"Do that! I think you'll like what you see."

Rowland snapped off the light and shut the door to his office. Betty had left a few hours earlier. Just as he was leaving his cell phone buzzed – it was Mary.

"Hi honey!"

"Hi to you! When are you coming home?"

"On my way."

"Anne called me, Tom. Are you okay?"

"I am, sweetheart. It's just been a rugged day. I'll tell you more when I get home."

"Look, why don't we go out for dinner and then drive over to the hospital together," Mary offered.

"You're quite something, Mrs. Rowland. I'll be there shortly."

Mary knew her husband well. His penchant for taking some of his prisoners very personally was a source of both admiration and concern. Tom didn't always protect himself, allowing the ills of these men to grind on him. She'd waken in the middle of the night to find his side of the bed empty. Predictably, she'd find her husband sitting alone in his den, the lights off just thinking or praying. Occasionally he'd be out in the living room, staring through the window into the black of night. Her gesture tonight was for his sake. He wouldn't be able to rest until he knew James Meyers would be okay.

TWENTY-FOUR

"Bates, I want a straight answer," Raynor demanded. "Who put you up to this?"

Bates sat stoically, flint faced as if he never heard the question. About then officials from the County Gang Investigative Force (CGIF) walked in.

"Can we see you outside Mr. Raynor?"

Raynor took his eyes off Bates long enough to acknowledge the CGIF detective then stared once again into the chiseled, defiant face of the perp. "Don't think we're done Bates. We'll get to the bottom of this and when we do you'll have a lot to explain."

"Yeah, Tony, glad you came," Harold Raynor said running a hand through his thick salty hair. Tony Harrison had served in numerous gang related law enforcement agencies for nearly twenty-five years. He was hired by County two years ago to get a handle on the upsurge in local gang activity.

"No problem, Harold. What's the story?"

Raynor walked Tony through the details and had him sit with the two guards who witnessed the stabbing, as well as took Bates into custody.

"Lobos," Tony sneered. "Man, they're thick as thieves and deadly as snakes." He got up and walked over to the one-way glass on the other side of which sat Bates, his hands folded on the worn wooden table and his shaved head rigidly erect. "You won't break him," he said. "Not this guy."

"What've you got on him?" Raynor inquired.

"More than he thinks we have. Racketeering through the prison system, attempted murder, drug smuggling and myriad gang related assaults, all masterminded from right here."

"Accomplices?"

"Oh yeah; he has plenty of those, most of them coerced."

"I take it they're in the State House," Raynor pried.

"Most of them, but not all, Harold. The dangerous ones are outside, even spread among other prison populaces. We haven't cracked their communications network, but we have a bead on some of it."

Tony paused, ramming his hands into his jacket pockets. "These dudes are real dangerous, far worse than when Hall was in here," he said referring to Terrance. "They're tied to organized crime in a big way and recruit through violence. Rats don't live long."

"We've seen it, Tony. But how do we deal with it?"

"You're going to want to get Bates out of here. He's the de facto head of the State House Lobos. They're not calling him the Alpha yet, but it's only a matter of time. Once he throws his weight around a little more, hurts a few more vics, he'll have all the allies he needs to take charge."

"Okay, so we move him. Then what? "

"Tell me about this kid, James Meyers. How's he messed up with these guys?"

Raynor leaned up against the wall, his arms crossed. "He's not other than by being in the wrong place at the wrong time." Tony shrugged his shoulders like he'd heard that one before. Raynor continued, "He helped a guy who was stabbed and that seemed to throw him in harm's way too."

"Yep, that'll do it. Any report on his condition?"

"Not yet. He's in surgery now. All we know is that he's lost a lot of blood…in pretty bad shape."

Tony shook his head. "Look, Harold, this guy here, Bates, won't budge. If he does, he's a dead man too. Like I said, the Lobos are the most dangerous mob in the region. Bates is their heavy, the dude who kills in cold blood. Extradite him as soon as possible. Isolate other known Lobo bangers and keep the Meyers kid in C Block under close surveillance. Even with Bates out of here, the kid's still at extreme risk."

"What about moving Meyers out?" Raynor asked, hoping Tony might agree with him.

"No, that won't help. We can put a couple undercover guys in here for awhile, a few weeks, and keep an eye on Meyers that way, along with what you guys are doing."

"Alright, I'll inform Warden Rowland of your advice. What else?"

"Tell Meyers to keep a low profile…say nothing, do nothing, just stay to himself. If you transport him to places take different routes. Don't let the populace think he's snitching. Tell that to Rowland also."

"Got it," Raynor said. "I've got a guy on each shift who's specially assigned to Meyers."

"Don't do that, Harold. Rotate the duty otherwise these thugs will catch on. Keep a tight eye on the kid, especially until the inquiry goes down, but broaden the base of protection. Can you do that? Do you have the manpower…I mean the manpower you can trust?"

"Yeah, we can manage it," Raynor replied. "I'll create a roster only I'll know about, and appoint a new guard every day."

"Good. One more thing; how many more Meyers types do you have in here? I mean how many guys are at risk? Any idea?"

"Right now just James," Raynor said. "He's the mark as near as we can tell."

"Good. We'll keep our eyes and ears open, Harold, and let you know what we catch."

"Thanks, Tony."

"No problem. Say Hi to Tom for me. We'll be in touch."

*****

110

"Harold, what's up?" Tom Rowland said tersely into his cell phone, as a hot plate was placed on the table in front of him.

"Tony Harrison just left, Tom. He recommends we get Bates out of the populace."

"Move him?"

"Yes, move him. Seems he's behind a lot of bad stuff here, Tom."

"Okay, meet me in the morning and we'll discuss it."

"Sounds good."

"Anything else?"

"Yes, how's our kid?"

Rowland softened his tone. "I don't know, Harold. We haven't gotten any recent reports. Mary and I are heading over to the hospital after we finish dinner."

"For what it's worth, Tom, Steph and I will bring it up in our small group tonight."

Rowland sat his fork down. "I didn't realize you guys attended a small group of any kind."

"Yes we do. We're part of Fr. Ted's parish and have a group that meets for Bible study and prayer each week. We'll definitely pray for James...and for you."

"Harold, I had no idea. Thank you!"

"Glad to extend the grace, Tom. See you in the morning."

Rowland sat his phone beside his fork and looked across the table at Mary.

"That's an odd expression," she said peering at her husband.

"Harold just told me that he and Steph will ask their small group to pray for James tonight. And us."

"So?"

"Mary, I didn't know he was a Christian."

"Here's a flash for you, Thomas. Steph and I have been attending the same Bible study for nearly a year now."

"And why was I kept in the dark?"

"You never asked," Mary said with an impish grin.

"Remarkable!" Rowland grumped. "My head guard's a Christian and I'm the last to find out."

"Well, Warden Rowland, open your eyes," Mary said, flicking water in his face from her glass.

The two laughed out loud before bowing to say grace and diving into their meal.

TWENTY-FIVE

The droning of soft voices filtered into the hall as Fr. Ted, Terrance and the Meyers approached the chapel. A few kids sat in a huddle outside in the hall, bent over their knees, deep in prayer. The kids massed inside barely noticed the intrusion.

"Honey, this is amazing," Kathleen whispered to her husband. "Look at all these young people."

Terrance pressed into the chapel and edged his way to the pulpit.

"Hey guys, pardon the interruption, but I've got some people you'll want to meet."

Immediately all eyes moved toward the entrance where two rather timid adults stood smiling awkwardly barely inside the doorway in front of Fr. Ted.

"Guys, say hello to Mr. and Mrs. Meyers, James' parents," Terrance said.

"Oh, you're James' folks!" one of the kids, a teenage girl seated on the floor chimed. "Please join us."

The others chimed in also, "Yes, come on in. We'd love to pray with you."

Terrance motioned for Don to join him at the pulpit. At first he resisted but the kids persuaded him. One by one kids began standing to clear a path for him to make his way to Terrance. As he crept along toward the front of the chapel, Don felt hands gently touch his shoulders. He turned and looked into bleary, tear-filled eyes, welcoming smiles and warmth. "Troubled kids?" he thought privately to himself. Tattooed, pierced, wild hair and shabbily clad, they were that. But their faces revealed a different reality: Angelic came to mind. From ruin to righteousness, these kids were nothing if not the incarnation of hope Don and Kathleen needed.

"I hardly know what to say," Don began. "I'm told that each of you were like our son is now – troubled. But look at you? I see the miracle of new life in you." He paused. "I want to see it in my son. Please pray that he survives tonight so he can find his way to God." Don's head dropped and his eyes squinted shut. Biting his lower lip he forced back deep emotion and concluded. "Pray for Kathleen and me too. Pray that God will forgive us and show us how to love our son to Him."

Two young men standing to his left stepped over and draped their arms around Don. Kathleen put her hands over her face as a few young women gathered her in their embrace. Terrance began to pray, "Jesus, please hear Don's words as his heart poured out to you. May healing happen tonight in this place for now and forever. Amen"

Kids seated in the front pew moved out and ushered Don and Kathleen into their place. "Oh, thank you," Kathleen said. "But I think we want to go back downstairs and wait for word from the surgeon."

"Yeah, guys. The Meyers need to be close to James right now, as close as the nurses will allow them. We'll keep you posted."

As the Meyers made their way through the jumble of youth, hugs abounded and words of encouragement followed them into the hall. Nothing more was spoken as they followed Fr. Ted and Terrance into the elevator and back to the waiting area outside the operating room to await the outcome of their son's surgery.

TWENTY-SIX

"More suction!" the lead surgeon demanded. "Damn, what a mess!" Dr. Phelps sponged away blood searching for the laceration hidden in gurgling red pools. "Hang on kid! Don't run out on us!"

A nurse daubed perspiration from Phelps' brow as his fingers probed inside James' abdomen.

"Another liter of blood, doctor?" One of the attendants asked.

Dr. Phelps gazed over the loupes attached to his glasses to see the empty bag of whole blood dangle from its hook.

"Yes! Do it!" he snapped.

Quickly another bag was hung – the fifth.

"Where the hell is this leaker?" He kept probing.

Suddenly he straightened. His eyebrows raised in thick hairy arcs.

"Got it! By damn I've got it!" he exclaimed. "Clamp!"

The pooling abated. "Sponge!" One after another he and the assisting surgeon sopped the blood away, flinging drenched fabric squares onto the floor.

Outside the OR Don paced. Kathleen sat quietly with her arms crossed. Terrance and Fr. Ted said nothing, glancing occasionally at the worried couple. Time barely moved. It had been two hours since James was wheeled into surgery and no word. Don approached the nurse's station. "When do you think we might hear how our son is doing?" he asked.

"I don't know, Mr. Meyers. It could be awhile. I'm sorry," the nurse said with a note of sadness.

Don nodded and slowly walked over to Kathleen. She reached for his hand. "No news yet, honey: We'll have to wait." Kathleen tightened her lips and let out an anguished sigh.

About then the elevator doors opened and out stepped Tom and Mary Rowland. Terrance went over to greet them.

"Any word?" Tom asked; obvious concern in his voice.

"No, not yet."

Mary noticed the couple over by Fr. Ted. "Is that James' parents?"

"Yeah, it is," Terrance replied. "You want to meet them?"

"Please," Tom said and began to move their direction.

Terrance motioned toward the Meyers, "Don and Kathleen, I would like you to meet Tom and Mary Rowland."

Don shook Tom's outstretched hand. "Our pleasure. But please forgive our ignorance. I'm not certain who you are."

"Of course," Terrance said rather embarrassed. "Don, Tom is the warden at the State House."

"Oh, Warden Rowland," Don replied with sudden recognition. "Yes, James has spoken well of you." Don alertly recalled James' brief description of his first encounter with Warden Rowland, but said no more. He was quite taken, however, with Rowland's demeanor – polished yet engaging.

"We are so very sorry about what has happened to James. Please know that we are praying for him and for you," Tom said reassuringly.

"Yes," Mary interjected. "We are both concerned and praying, as well as members of our church community."

Kathleen looked into Mary's eyes. "Who would think that the warden and his wife would show up at a time like this? And here you are. I hardly know what to say."

"No words are necessary. We've known similar heartbreak...And we've known the healing that follows," Mary assured. Mary's mind swept back through the long conversations around the small table in the kitchen where Anne would pour out her frustrations with this most irritating client – Terrance of course – over a cup of tea.

"Oh, I wish we could be sure of the healing part. I'm so very frightened," Kathleen choked out the words between sobs.

Mary sat down beside Kathleen, placing a consoling arm around her shoulders. "I know. I truly know."

"How do you know?" Kathleen protested. "How can you possibly understand what we're feeling right now?" Anguish knows only its own pain and Kathleen had lived in a long drought of arid anguish.

Mary smiled while looking directly at Terrance. "Our son-in-law put us through quite an ordeal for awhile."

Terrance shifted awkwardly acting as if he hadn't heard Mary.

"Your son-in-law was in prison?" Kathleen then caught sight of Mary staring at Terrance, and Terrance squirming uncomfortably on the end table where he sat. "Terrance?" Kathleen looked back at Mary who was now grinning. "He's your son-in-law?"

"Afraid so," Mary replied in mock resignation.

Kathleen's jaw dropped open as she looked intently back at Terrance.

Caught without escape, Terrance sheepishly confessed, "Guilty."

Suddenly the atmosphere erupted into loud laughter. Kathleen had the look of astonishment on her face.

"Oh what that boy put us through," Mary moaned derisively. "But now look at him: the picture of innocence."

"I don't know about the picture of innocence. That might be stretching it a bit, Mary," Fr. Ted joked.

"I'm shocked!" Kathleen exclaimed.

"It's a long story," Mary remarked. "The short version is that our daughter, Anne, was Terrance's attorney. As you can see, she got more than she bargained for."

Again peals of laughter echoed in the waiting area. Humor broke the tension.

"So you do understand," Kathleen replied.

"Sadly yes, Kathleen," Terrance once again confessed. "And so does Tom. I owe them and their daughter – my wife – big time; more than I can repay them."

Fr. Ted chimed in again, "You see, Kathleen, you and Don know the pain, suffering, and yes perhaps embarrassment as well as sense of betrayal of James' imprisonment. But these people," he motioned toward the Rowlands and Terrance, "they know the other side of picture too. They know what healing, and dare say forgiveness, looks like."

Tom stood close to Don, "We're here to help as we can. For what it's worth, Don and Kathleen don't try to shoulder the load alone." Tom added. "And what's more, self-condemnation doesn't help either."

"We've been down that road already," Don confided. "You're right, though. It hasn't helped." Many nights Don held vigil alone, unpacking the years wondering where he'd failed as a father.

"We feel a huge sense of responsibility for our children and their lives. It comes with being parents," Mary offered giving Kathleen's shoulders a tight squeeze.

"Occupational hazard," Fr. Ted said with a chuckle.

"Amazing," Don said shaking his head as if bewildered by what just transpired.

"What's amazing?" Fr. Ted asked.

"It has been so long, so incredibly long since our world fell apart. I think we'd all but given up any hope that it would…or could actually be any different. But you all seem to be living proof it's possible."

"Oh it's quite possible, Don," Tom said. "But it takes a lot of patience, prayer and perseverance."

Don turned to Terrance, "So, how long was it before you came around?"

Terrance chuckled and reflected a moment before answering. Images of angry outbursts and smoldering resentment returned to his memory like another life, another person ago. He was a changed man. "A long time, Don; a long time. In all about six years."

"That is a long time," Don sighed. "What was it like for all of you?" He anticipated it might have been a strain, but he needed to hear it from Tom and Mary.

Looking into Mary's face Tom replied, "It was rough. It takes a great deal of time, and personal vulnerability to inspire trust within someone who has never been shown trust. Who's spent his entire life just surviving."

"Yah," Terrance groaned. "I put these folks through quite a lot until it finally dawned on me that they were the real deal."

"But you made it," Don exclaimed.

"Honestly Don, I'm still working it out. What I have are people who have given me every reason to believe in myself, as well as in them and definitely in God. And they've given me space to work it out. It was all so foreign to me. Sometimes it's still hard to just trust."

"I see," Don replied. "And it will probably be a long road for James, too."

"Yeah, it will, Don, "Terrance affirmed. "Just don't give up hope…Whatever you do, keep hoping and keep praying. I am living proof that hope pays off."

Fr. Ted, always intuitive…and nosy…couldn't resist asking a delicate question. "How has your church supported you?"

Don and Kathleen looked at each other – sad expressions fell across their faces. "I wish I could give you a good report," Don answered tactfully. "But in honesty, Father, the church has been absent."

"Oh, I'm sorry." Father Ted replied apologetically.

Kathleen spoke up, "It's a large church with a lot of programs and good teaching. We attend on Sundays but really don't know very many people. We don't even know the pastor responsible for people living in our part of town."

"It's pretty impersonal, Father," Don added. "They have a support group for parents of troubled youth, but…"

"But you're not comfortable exposing your problems to strangers," Fr. Ted finished Don's thought.

"Yes, exactly," Don answered.

"For what it's worth, Don, programs seldom succeed outside of committed and trusted relationships. That's in part why the Church is a community that shares in the life of its members."

"Yeah, well, that part has been missing, Father." Don didn't mask his irritation and disappointment. At the nadir of his own anguish he reached out to the church. When asked the nature of his concern by the receptionist, he reluctantly revealed that it dealt with his son's imprisonment, and was immediately transferred to Congregational Care, a soft sounding euphemism for family counseling. It was during that session with a person he'd never met before the suggestion was made that perhaps a support group would be his best answer. "A support group?" he mused. "I thought this was a church not a clinic." Where, he wondered, was this family of God that showed up on all the advertising?

He shook himself from the fog of a bad memory and began pacing, obviously pained by the circumstances surrounding his son and family. Turning on his heel he stopped in front of Fr. Ted like a light had just come on, "You're Catholic!" he said as if the cleric's collar hadn't already given him away.

"Yes I am." Straightening his glasses Fr. Ted teased with a wry grin, "That's kinda why they call my Father Ted."

Don directed his attention to the Rowlands and Terrance, "You Catholic too?"

"No, we're not, Don, not anyway in the Roman Catholic sense," Tom qualified for the rest.

"Does that surprise you?" Fr. Ted asked enjoying Don's confusion.

"Well, I'm not sure," Don hesitated. "You all seem so comfortable with one another."

"We are," Terrance confidently confirmed.

"And what exactly do you do, Terrance?" Don was now in full puzzlement.

"Actually, I'm a pastor...of sorts."

"Of sorts..." Fr. Ted barbed.

"Oh knock it off," Terrance scolded giving Fr. Ted's arm a swift brush of the back of his hand. "Those kids you met upstairs. They're my flock so to speak."

"Really!" Don said with astonishment.

"Yep, I pastor a kind of lost tribe of young people who're seeking for something to believe in. We meet at what we call a worship café downtown. The kids show up with their questions and attitudes, and we show them God." Terrance snapped his fingers like something flashed to mind. "By the way Don, James has come by a few times...not many but a few. He never really hung out with anyone in particular or stayed long."

"I didn't know that," Don replied. "Surprising," he said in a thoughtful whisper.

"Why? What's so surprising about that?"

Kathleen entered the conversation, "We really never knew where James spent his time...or who he spent it with." Facing Mary she confessed, "I guess that means we weren't that tuned into our son."

"Kathleen, it's not too late," Fr. Ted reminded them. "We would appreciate the opportunity to travel that road with you."

"We?" she asked. "You mean all of you...here...now...with us?"

"Yes and one other," Fr. Ted answered. "The 'we' I mentioned is what we call the posse. Another man, Mike Scanlon..."

"Scans!" Terrance blurted. "Sorry to interrupt Father, but has anyone told Scanlon what happened? He'll be torqued if we don't!"

"I doubt anyone has," Tom responded. "Why don't you give him a call now, Terrance?" Terrance immediately headed for a quiet corner to make the call.

"Well, before I was so hastily interrupted," Fr. Ted remarked, "The four of us, Tom, Terrance, Mike Scanlon and myself formed this small group a few years ago to help young men like James."

Don crossed his arms, "You've got my attention. What kind of help?"

"We take a very active role in praying for them and doing everything within our God-enabled ability to proclaim the Gospel and help these young men find their way home."

"Remarkable!" Kathleen fairly wept with excitement.

"I'll say," Don added. "And James is one of these young men you've…ah…decided to help?"

"Well really, Don, it's more like God brought James to us," Tom said. "We feel a strong conviction that God saw what was coming and placed James under our care. We knew when he arrived that God had redemptive ambitions for your son."

Kathleen broke into joyous tears. "I don't know what to say. Don, this is more than we hoped for! We've prayed so hard and so long." She took a moment to wipe her eyes. "Honestly, it has felt like praying into thin air with no one listening. To meet you here tonight: I just don't believe it! Apparently God has been listening," she said, astonishment rising in her voice.

"Oh, he was listening alright, Kathleen. And do believe it!" Mary admonished. "We struggled just like you have, and suddenly seemingly out of nowhere light broke through the darkness. Oh yes, indeed, he was listening!"

Don knelt down in front of his wife. Looking deeply into her face he smiled and said, "Sweetheart, I just get this feeling that it's all going to work out somehow. This whole hideous mess – God has shown us that he truly has heard our prayers. He knows, and now I truly believe I know that He knows…and that He cares."

Kathleen broke into intense sobs, "I pray you're right! I so want our son back."

"Don and Kathleen, just like Mary said, God does know, and He is your answer as He is James' answer," Fr. Ted affirmed as he sat on the edge of a chair leaning toward the couple. "Those kids upstairs, they know too. Each one of them is a miracle."

Terrance returned. "Scans'll be here in bit."

"He didn't need to stop by tonight," Tom said.

"Yeah, I told him that, but you know Scans."

"So who is this Scans," Don asked.

"Comic relief," Fr. Ted shot back before anyone else could offer a polite answer.

Laughter lightened the atmosphere.

About then the doors to the surgical area swung open and an obviously exhausted doctor pushed through them, still clad in blood splattered scrubs. The grave look etched into his creased face was not reassuring. Don and Kathleen clasped their hands together in anticipation of the news. Tom sidled up to Mary. Terrance stood close to Tom, while Fr. Ted remained seated. Dr. Phelps swept the hat from his head and brushed a hand over his short-cropped graying hair, craned his head toward the group and announced, "He'll make it."

"Ahhhh," Kathleen sighed and began to weep again.

"Thank God!" Don and the others exclaimed in unison.

"I'll be straight with you," Dr. Phelps said in a grave tone. "He's still not completely out of the woods, but I'm confident he'll pull through. He lost a hell of a lot of blood. But the knife didn't hit anything vital. We'll keep him here at least a couple of days to monitor his condition as well as watch for any infections."

"Infections?" Kathleen asked with a hint of worry.

"Infection is always a risk," Dr. Phelps answered. "But we have him on some pretty strong antibiotics and will keep a close eye on him. You need to know, too, that he's awfully weak. I would recommend just a short visit tonight – parents only. Okay?"

"Thank you so much, doctor," Don said, his voice quaking with deep emotion.

"Don't mention it. Glad we could save your son." Dr. Phelps acknowledged the group with a nod then strode back through the doors into the hospital's inner sanctum.

"Excuse us," Don said taking Kathleen by the hand. "We need to see our son."

"We'll be here praying for you," Tom said.

"Thank you!" Kathleen stood and gave Mary a tight hug. Together the couple approached the nurses' station for directions to James' room.

TWENTY-SEVEN

Tom, Mary and Terrance were so emotionally spent they fairly fell into the chairs behind them. Just then the elevator door opened and a mass of human confusion stumbled out of it.

"What'd I miss? Where's James' folks?"

"Obviously Scans has arrived," Terrance joked with mock sarcasm in his voice.

"I'd have been here sooner but got lost in that maze downstairs. Man, I needed a GPS to find my way up here."

Scanlon hadn't noticed everyone looking at him like his fly was down.

"Whatcha you guys staring at?"

"Just you," Terrance barbed again.

Fr. Ted wasn't listening to the banter. His eyes searched the obscure crucifix tacked to the wall behind the sofa, a gaunt, pathetic figure of Jesus hanging from a bent metal cross: "Christ of God or cosmic therapist?" he mused under his breath.

"What's that Father?" Terrance asked, hearing what for the sound of it was mere mumbling.

"Oh, I was just pondering, Terrance."

"Pondering what?"

"I was wondering, what do Protestants really think about Jesus' passion?"

Terrance followed Fr. Ted's eyes to the crucifix, a symbol of revulsion to a great many people. Terrance himself wondered why Catholics insisted upon leaving Jesus hanging dead on the hard beams of a cruel, unmerited death. Did they not celebrate His triumphal victory? Was their focus so attuned to his ransom for our sorry sinfulness they had displaced his resurrection and ascension? "I guess," he began, "they think it was the price Jesus paid to save us."

"Hmmm...," Fr. Ted inflected while shaking his head.

"Do you think otherwise, Father?"

"No Terrance, no I don't and neither does the Church. But let me ask you this, why do you think we Catholics leave Jesus hanging on the cross. Why do you think our cross is never barren?"

"I'm not sure Father. Why...why do Catholics leave Jesus hanging so to speak?"

Fr. Ted's chin began to quiver as he pointed toward the crucifix and said softly, "So we will never forget the cost."

Terrance looked at his mentor-friend, and saw tears welled in his eyes. By now the others became conscious of Fr. Ted's contemplative mood, training their concentration upon the crucifix as well.

A long pause ensued, a silence no one, not even the irreverent Scanlon, betrayed.

"You see," Fr. Ted began, "the Cross in early antiquity long before hierarchies and sacramental rites, was seen as the altar of the New Covenant. It represented the final sacrifice to end all such sacrifices. It never lets us forget the God who sacrificed heaven for the life of the world." Pausing again to reflect, Fr. Ted brought his hand to his chin and a finger across his lips. His eyebrows knit in a thick blanket imaging him as the picture of erudition. Continuing, he said, "The early centuries of the church were stained in blood, so much blood, Tertullian, the venerable third century historian remarked, 'The streets of the cities ran with the blood of the martyrs.' The cross, dear friend, is never naked. It wears the flesh, the sweat and the blood of the Christ of God. It of all images reflects his glory. From it the Church took courage and shouldered its cross in the face of persecution and death. We must never forget that. The price came before the victory, and certainly the victory must be celebrated. It, too, must never be forgotten."

"I see," Terrance said in hushed voice. "I…"

"Permit me to finish," Fr. Ted said raising his hand.

Terrance waited.

"Perhaps you noticed I went silent when Don commented about the disappointing meeting at his church. I was disappointed too. Not because of differences between Catholics and Protestants or anything of the kind. Lord knows, a good many Catholics fail in a similar way. No, I was disappointed, brokenhearted actually, by the failure of that particular community to gather Don and Kathleen in their arms and place them before the Cross…and the empty tomb." His teeth clenched, "They simply didn't get it. In that moment they demoted Jesus to cosmic therapist, not the victorious Christ of God."

"Oh my," Mary recoiled. "I would have never caught that. Have we become so insensitive that…"

"Not insensitive, Mary – narcissistic. In the end, Mary, two kinds of people face God, those who have said 'Thy will be done,' and those to whom God has said, '*thy* will be done.'" He paused to let these words search deeply into his own soul. "Do you know who I took that last part from?"

"No, I don't," Mary answered.

"C.S. Lewis. I took it from his wonderful little book *The Great Divorce*. Have you read it?"

"No, but perhaps I should."

"We all should. We all need to look into the face of Jesus and answer the only question that mattered to him. And Lewis understood that question."

"What is that, Father?" Mary waited for the answer.

"Who do you say that I am?"

TWENTY-EIGHT

Blurry holographic images swept across his vision while indecipherable voices spoke above him. "Who's there?" James asked in a tone so weak only a faint moan was heard by the people hovering around him. A hand clasped gently around his arm. A voice spoke into his ear, "James can you hear me?" He managed only a muted "yes" before fading into a deep slumber.

"He's still heavily sedated, Mrs. Meyers," a kindly sounding voice said.

"How long do you think he'll be out?" Kathleen asked.

"Oh, it's really hard to tell. He's been through quite an ordeal. I wouldn't expect him to rally much before morning." With that the nurse reached for the IV bag suspended from a t-shaped bar above the bed, checking the drip, and then turned her attention to the beeping monitor that registered James' vital signs.

"Good," she said. "His condition seems to have stabilized. I'll inform the doctor."

"I take it that's a good thing," Don remarked to the nurse.

"Yes, very good, Mr. Meyers. The doctor might be able to upgrade your son's condition."

"What is it now?" Neither Don nor Kathleen inquired about James' condition when they arrived at the hospital; neither had anyone volunteered his status.

"I thought you knew," the nurse replied.

"No, we weren't told," Don said with a bit of edge to his voice.

"He's listed in critical condition presently, Mr. Meyers." "Perhaps the doctor will revise that, though it his judgment to do so, not mine."

"I see," Don said stepping over to the head of the bead. "When will we know?"

"Later tonight after the doctor makes his final rounds. He should be by here within the hour."

Don acknowledged the nurse who offered a reassuring smile before placing material back into a cart and pushing it out the door and down the hall.

Kathleen stood beside her obviously worried husband. Don, in turn, slipped an arm around Kathleen's waist as they both gazed helplessly at their son.

"Maybe," Don said with his eyes closed and deep heaviness in his voice, "…just maybe tonight's the bottom." He paused. "Maybe tomorrow we'll start to climb out of this mess."

"Lord may it be so," Kathleen whispered.

TWENTY-NINE

"Ted, I don't think I've ever observed that kind of tension from you," Tom commented to his emotionally distant friend.

Exhausted, Fr. Ted wiped his hands across his eyes and repositioned his glasses. "Yeah, I'm not entirely sure where that came from, Tom." He cocked his head, "Well that's not entirely true. To be honest I was reacting to something very important that used to be and no longer is."

"Oh?"

"Somewhere along the way the Church seems to have forgotten its mission…forming disciples of Jesus Christ."

"How so?" Tom pressed.

"Doesn't it seem apparent that if Jesus' last word to his disciples was to make disciples that he meant it to be the work of the Church? Think of his concluding words and the events of Pentecost, Tom. Those words, 'lo, I will be with you always to the end of the age' were not an aside, something he tossed off the cuff." Leaning forward in his chair and gesturing like a professor, he continued. "Those words are spoken with the authority he claims earlier, just before the commissioning statement. They tell us 'this is how I will relate to the Church. When you are forming disciples in my Name, I am with you.'"

"Okay," Tom replied, his mind engaged. "But you also tied these words to the events of Pentecost, Ted. How does that work?"

"Oh, don't you see!? To be with us He poured His Spirit out onto or, better, into us and the very first action of this new mob called the Church was to proclaim the good news in one voice as he did, Tom! Think of it this way. When we proclaim the cross and salvation, it's not our story but his, and it's never absent his Spirit. Thus, 'lo, I am with you!'"

Rowland's eyes narrowed. "I'd never thought of it in those terms. Never put those verses together like that."

"You're not alone," Fr. Ted dismissed with a wave of his hand. "There's more to it, though." By now Fr. Ted was at full throttle.

"Like what?"

"This startling event, this manifestation of God was unusual for another reason. Remember God appeared only briefly to Moses. He called Samuel's name. He broke in upon Elijah and Isaiah. And dare say through an angel he startled a young virgin, Mary. All individuals, Tom! All individuals! But never had he swept into a community of people – certainly not like he did on that fateful day of Pentecost. This event is radically unusual, though Jesus hints at it in his prayer to the Father before he and his disciples enter the garden where he is betrayed." Fr. Ted halted his impromptu lecture, reached for the Bible sitting on the end table beside him. Opening it to the Book of John, he read the following from chapter seventeen. "'I do not pray for these only, but also for those who believe in me through their word, that they may all be one; even as thou, Father, art in me, and I in thee, that they also may be in us, *so that the world may believe that thou has sent me.*' That's the big story within the story, Tom! But get this!" Fr. Ted continued reading, "The glory which thou has given me I have given to them, that they may be one even as we are one, I in them and thou in me, *that they may become perfectly one,* so that the world may know that thou has sent me and hast loved them even as thou hast loved me." Laying the Bible back on the table, Fr. Ted took up his lecture, "Then too, don't forget that these people, this first community gathered after Christ's passion, resurrection and ascension were waiting, Tom. They were waiting for the Father's answer to Jesus' prayer without a farthing's clue as to how it would be manifested. Little did they expect that it would be manifested through them – One body in Christ! Proclaiming him not as a therapist, but as Savior!"

"So, what's the point?"

"The point good friend is that the Church was formed as a community for the purpose of proclaiming Christ and walking the journey of faith together...*as one.* There was no such thing as anonymous conversions. There was no such thing as unaccountable, private faith. Never was conversion neat and tidy. Often it was dangerous and messy. On their way to their baptism, I believe it was St. Cyril who said something like, 'Don't worry if you die for your faith before your arrive at your baptism. You will have been baptized in your own blood.'"

"Honestly, Ted, I'd never put those pieces together like that. I've got to ask, are you suggesting the lack of this sort of thing in the church today?" Tom quizzed rhetorically, knowing his friend would blanch at this impertinence but risked it anyway.

"Oh, Tom, it has been lacking for all too long! It got lost in the detritus of philosophies that removed God from the equation, began doubting Christ's divinity and elevated man to the place of sovereignty. You know, Thomas More's 'Man for All Seasons,' man as the measure of all things. And it seeped into the church with hardly any notice."

"That's a serious indictment, Ted, but I cannot disagree with you. The State House is populated by these 'men for all seasons,' guys made in their own image."

"Exactly!"

"But, Ted, where do you see this sort of...what do I call it...devaluing of redemption... showing up in the church today?"

"Let me ask you, how do people come to faith in your church?'

"That's a great question, Ted." Tom took a moment to think about it and form his thoughts. "I would say..."

"Let me stop you right there, Tom. That you had to think about it and don't seem entirely certain of the answer suggests that disciple formation may not be top of mind in your church."

"Well, sadly, you may be right. Evangelization, so to speak, seems to be the focus, such as it is."

"What do you mean, 'such as it is'. Finish your explanation."

"Usually at the end of Sunday morning worship, whoever is preaching extends an invitation to the congregation for anyone who hasn't responded before to 'receive Christ.'"

"How does the preacher go about this invitation?" Fr. Ted was toying a bit with Tom. He'd attended a few such services, but that's another story.

"The preacher asks the congregation to bow their heads and close their eyes while those who wish to accept Christ raise their hands."

"In other words the church hides while the – hopefully – penitent person signals their intent to accept Christ?" Fr. Ted said incredulously.

"That's one way of putting it, I suppose."

"Well how else would you put it?" Fr. Ted pressed.

"I guess you could say at least the penitent, as you put it, got to make a great decision without undue scrutiny."

"My friend, decisions don't make disciples, and more, scrutiny is essential to the process." Fr. Ted shifted in his chair, "Take James for instance. How far would he get in your church if at the moment of his 'decision' no one was looking, no one knew about this climactic moment in his life and let him leave as anonymously as he came?"

Tom winced with disgust at the thought. "Not far I'm afraid."

"Not far indeed! Tom, he'd become one of the horde of stillborns who heard the story, agreed with it, and then starved for lack of nurturing."

Right then the Meyers emerged through the doorway that leads to the Intensive Care Unit.

"How's James doing?" Tom inquired, while Mary and the guys stood to greet them.

"Oh my," Kathleen responded with a gasp. "He's so pale, as white as the bed sheets."

"He looks like death warmed over, Tom. But thankfully the weapon missed anything vital." Don added.

"Oh, that is good news! But will he be alright?" Mary asked with urgency in her voice.

"He's still listed in critical condition, but his vital signs have stabilized. We're hoping the doctor will reevaluate him tonight and upgrade his condition," Don reported.

Terrance walked toward the elevators.

"Where you going?" Fr. Ted inquired.

"Gonna fill the kids in."

"Good! Mind if I join you?"

"Not at all, Father; I'd like the company." Terrance also wanted to probe Fr. Ted a bit more about his comments.

"Hey, what about me?" Scanlon blurted like a forgotten child.

"Hop on big man," Terrance said holding the elevator door open for his friend.

THIRTY

"You look tired, Father," Terrance observed as his mentor-friend stepped onto the elevator and leaned heavily against the back wall.

"I suppose I am, Terrance. Sorry if I got carried away…too preachy."

"Not at all," Terrance assured. "In fact you raised some curious questions."

"Yeah, it really messed with my head, Father," Scanlon said.

"What doesn't mess with your head?" Terrance joked, swiping Scanlon's ball hat off his head.

Father Ted ignored their antics. Returning to Terrance's comment, "Good!" he said. "That sort of discussion should raise questions. It should honestly raise more than questions. It should cause a deep introspective stir into the soul of the Church."

"It definitely stirred me." Terrance recomposed himself, lost in thought as he was. In truth, Father Ted's *lecture* cut quite deeply. His own personal experience was proof enough that Fr. Ted was dead on point. There were times he and Anne were tempted to peek during the invitation while attending Tom and Mary's church just to see if any of their café kids raised their hands. "I just get the impression that you have more insight into Tom's church than meets the eye."

"You've got a keen sense of observation there my good protégé," Father Ted replied with a wink.

Terrance chuckled. "Are you going to leave me hanging?"

"Let's just conclude for now that I haven't always been a Roman Catholic, Mr. Hall."

"That's it! You *are* going to leave me hanging!"

"For now. We've got bigger fish to fry tonight. Let's check on the kids."

"Okay, I'll let you off the hook for now. But…"

"Not to worry, my friend. I'll fill you in."

"When?"

"Not tonight."

Scanlon just stood wordless in his two feet of space, wondering what the big deal was anyhow.

*****

The soft drone of hushed voices met them off the elevator a short ways from chapel. Terrance peeked into the tightly packed cloister of kids huddled in prayer and motioned for Dirk to join him in the hallway.

"Hey Terrance, we've been wondering what's up. How's James?"

"Resting but still in pretty tough shape," Terrance answered.

"C'mon in man, and give us the low down," Dirk said leading Terrance and Fr. Ted into the chapel.

"Hey guys," Terrance began. "Tough night, eh?"

A collective moan rose from the group.

"Here's what we know so far. James made it through surgery and is in ICU. As of a few minutes ago he's still listed in critical condition. That's the bad news. But his vital signs have stabilized. That's the good news."

"Ok, but will he make it?" one of the kids demanded.

"We don't know…not yet. He lost an awful lot of blood. Fortunately, no vital organs were injured."

"His parents expect to hear from the doctor later tonight. If all goes well and he remains stable, his condition might get upgraded," Fr. Ted said to fill in the blanks a bit more.

"So how are the folks?" Tag asked.

"Tag, it's been rough on them," Terrance responded. "In all honesty, they're somewhat in shock. Nothing much has gone right for their son – this incident didn't help."

"Man dude," Dirk said. "We've been praying that this might be where stuff starts to go in the dude's favor. Like, man, he's been through the grinder. He needs a break."

"What he really needs, Dirk, is an advocate," Fr. Ted said emphatically. "He needs people in his corner just like you guys have been doing tonight."

"We're here for him, Father," came a reply from inside the room. A collective "yeah" arose from the group like a hearty "amen" from a Sunday morning congregation.

"I can see that," Fr. Ted said through a broad smile. "Because of you, James has never been in a better place. With God's mercy, he will survive. Then we can all help him recover…all the way."

"That's awesome man!" Blurted a shaved-head kid with a thick mangy beard; dressed like his clothes just kind of fell on him, colors and patterns purely optional. "We're God's army for this dude, man! We'll keep the devil off his back! God'll save him!"

"That's the spirit!" Fr. Ted enthused pumping his fist into the air. Immediately the entire mass of kids jabbed their fists into the air with a volley of "right on!"

"Right on!?" Fr. Ted exclaimed. "I haven't heard that expression since I was your age."

Loud laughter spilled down the hallway drawing the attention of a nurse who stuck her head into the room, "Shhhhh," She said sternly with a finger to her lips. "Keep it down! Patients are sleeping."

Dirk raised both hands over his head gesturing for the kids to pipe down. "We'll cool it," he said to the nurse, who left with a scowl. "Might want to keep Nurse Cratchet in our prayers, too," he mocked. The kids snickered quietly. Even Fr. Ted couldn't resist a muted chuckle.

"No worries, guys," Terrance said. "Let's keep our voices down but our prayers heading up. Okay?"

Heads nodded agreement across the room, which for all the cramped humanity stuffed inside its walls was taking on the ambiance of a locker room. But nobody cared. James' existence in all dimensions of the word was at stake, and these were his advocates. God would accept their sweaty odor as the welcome aroma of prayers rising like incense.

THIRTY-ONE

"Good morning, Harold." Rowland said through his grogginess. "Sounds like you didn't get much sleep."

"No I didn't. Neither did Mary or anyone else."

"You must have gone to the hospital," Harold said inquisitively.

"We did. We spent most of the night there with the folks."

"We? Sounds like you weren't alone."

"I'll say! Fr. Ted, Mary, Terrance, Mike and I were with the folks. But the chapel was full of Terrance's downtown café kids."

"You're kidding!"

"No, I'm not." Tom rocked back in his chair. "Harold, I think our kid has people on his side for the first time in his life."

"Incredible! So how is he?"

"Stable...serious but stable."

"I'd gotten word that he was listed in critical condition. So I assume he's improved some since."

"He has. The attending physician advised the family just before we left that James's condition had improved. He wouldn't go so far, though, to say he's out of danger."

"Well, that's at least a starting point, Tom. If you don't mind me saying you sound like critical condition yourself."

Rowland chuckled. "I think you're right! But I've got a plate full of stuff more critical than my condition to deal with. Can you stop by at nine? We need to talk about Bates and the overall complexion of things around here."

"I'll be there. As for the prison atmosphere – so far so good. We've got its pulse...quiet, almost too quiet."

"Okay. Well, see you at nine."

Betty entered Rowland's office with a glass of water and a couple of aspirin for him.

"Here, this should help."

"Thank you," Rowland said taking both the water and pills from the tray Betty held out to him.

"How you holding up?" she asked.

"Oh fine, thanks. Just a little tired."

"I'm worried about you, Mr. Rowland. It's not my place to ask, but are you maybe taking James a little too personally? I mean..."

Rowland held up his hand to stop her. "I understand your concern. I honestly do, Betty. But no, I am not taking him too seriously." Looking up into her eyes he said, "For the first time in his life people are taking him personally, including his folks."

"Aw, that's wonderful" she said, smiled politely and quietly left the office.

*****

Harold Raynor showed up for the meeting promptly at nine.

"What's the atmosphere at this hour, Harold?"

"Tense but restrained."

"No evidence of potential disruption?"

"Or eruption either, Tom. Like I mentioned before, it's almost too quiet."

"What's the status on Bates?"

"I brought his file and some papers for you to look over."

"Transfer?"

"Yes. To answer your first question, he's being held in solitary until we sort out the next steps."

"Good." Rowland took the file from Raynor, scanning the documents. "It all looks in order. I'll sign it." Rowland reached for a pen and signed the transfer orders. "That should take care of Mr. Bates."

"Bates isn't my only concern, Tom. He had accomplices."

"How do you know that?"

"Let's take a walk."

Rowland looked warily at his trusted guard but grabbed his suit coat and followed Raynor out of the office.

As the men walked down the hall, Raynor began to fill Rowland in on what he knew. "Look, Tom, I just spoke with Tony from County Gang before leaving for our meeting. He has evidence to suggest that an infiltrator got to Bates, pretty much made him an offer he couldn't refuse."

"Like what?"

"James or his own life."

"What?" Rowland had seen and heard a lot since becoming warden. But this one had a sinister knell to it that put his teeth on edge. "Are you telling me the hit on James was a conspiracy from outside the prison?"

"Afraid so, Tom. Listen, Tony's going to meet us at the walk-around," referring to the secured walkway that overlooks the prison yard. "He's got the details."

"Fine, but why outside and not my office?"

"I think he's got something to show us."

Tony was already out on the deck, studying the prisoners massing at the far end of the yard away from the doors. About then a guard bellowed from the tower above, "Hey, break it up down there." Nobody moved. The guard bellowed into the bullhorn, "I said break it up." More guards came onto the deck, weapons drawn. Finally a few of the less belligerent prisoners walked away, back to the opposite side of the compound. Slowly the others followed. A few stayed put and loitered around the wall.

"What's happening, Tony?" Raynor asked as he and Rowland approached.

"Not sure, Harold. That whole bunch of guys you see down there had their heads together at the far end. The tower guard barked at them a couple of times before they broke it up."

"No altercations?" Raynor probed.

"None that I saw." Tony noticed Rowland beside Raynor. "Oh, hi Tom. Very sorry to hear about the kid."

"Thanks, Tony. Pretty difficult night," Rowland replied.

"Any updates."

"Not really. Nothing new: We're all just hoping and praying."

"Gotcha."

"Harold tells me you have some information for us," Rowland said while scanning the prisoners now roaming aimlessly around the yard.

"I do, Tom. It's not the stuff we want, but it's stuff we'd better pay heed to."

"Like what?" Raynor asked. Raynor and Rowland both felt an uneasiness lurking around them.

"We got word yesterday that confirmed earlier suspicions. Meyers definitely got in the way of a major hit." Tony shoved his hands deep into his waist-length leather biker coat pockets and turned to face Raynor and Rowland. "I'll give it to you straight. Nate Chalmers ratted out a Lobo, and the Lobo he ratted out was Bates."

"Oh my gosh," Raynor braced. "So Bates went after Meyers thinking he was in on the snitch?"

"Pretty much, Harold. The Lobos had Meyers listed long before he got here."

"Listed?" Rowland asked thinking there was much more behind the word than just the fact James' name found its way onto a piece of paper.

"Yeah Tom, listed. Bangers 'list' guys they plan to liquidate, you know, kill. Top on their list are rats. James was right under Chalmers on 'the list.'"

"How did you come by your information?" Rowland asked.

"One of our street stooges, a guy who works both sides for a buck or a break," Tony answered.

"Reliable?" Raynor asked.

"As reliable as a frightened felon can be. He's produced for us before."

"What's in it for him?" Raynor wasn't convinced yet.

"Protection. He supplies information and we keep him safe."

"I see," Rowland said. "So what do we do with this information?"

"Getting Bates out of here will help, but it won't get Meyers off the list."

"Move him?" Rowland asked pensively.

"No, as I've said to you guys before, that won't make him safe. Keep him in his cell. Move him only short distances and with tight supervision…never during general population movements."

"Do you fear more attempts on the kid?" Raynor asked.

"Yes, I do. Just who I'm not sure, but that's why I wanted to meet you guys out here." Gesturing with his head, Tony pointed toward a short, stocky guy in a denim jacket, shaved head and ruddy face standing off to himself against the far wall away from them. "See that guy there? He's the one we've got our radar out for."

"Chavez?" Raynor inquired.

"Yeah, him…Chavez."

"What do you have on him?" A couple of Raynor's guards had suspected him of trafficking contraband into the prison. No hard evidence, just suspicion.

"We intercepted a communication between him and one of his guys on the outside."

"Rival gang?" Raynor pressed.

"A Latino version of the Lobos. They call themselves Nuevo Lobos." Tony let out a snide humph, "What's worse, they're far more violent than the Lobos Hall led. They kill for sheer sport; prove their allegiance and crazy, angry crap like that. They showed up in the states about a year ago."

"What's their deal? Why here and why now?" Raynor continued to ask questions while Rowland kept his focus on Chavez.

"Turf! They want to put the old Lobos out of business. They want their drug trade."

"So our Lobos aren't necessarily the ones with their sights on James?" Rowland broke in. "In other words, we've got the makings of a serious war on our hands."

"That's right, Tom," Tony affirmed. "But here's the deal. These new thugs recruit by coercion. They started by consolidating smaller rival gangs, gangs too small to stand up to the Lobos. Pretty soon they were big enough to enforce consolidation."

"Join or else, eh?" Raynor quipped, feeling his adrenaline rise.

"Exactly! They're big business now and Chavez is the alpha."

"Wait a minute, Tony. How can Chavez be the alpha if he's locked up in here?" Rowland snapped.

"You want it straight?"

"Yes I do!"

"Well here it is guys: Your joint's got leaks like a rotting boat headed for the bottom of the ocean."

Tony's descriptive evaluation of security at Tom's "joint" had a visible affect on him. Tom practically went ashen: His face sagged, as did his shoulders and entire frame. Beneath the heavy woolen topcoat he wore, a man shaken by too many tragedies stood square jawed but with quivering knees. Even Raynor's two decades patrolling maximum security prisons hadn't thickened his skin enough to take this news without wincing.

"Don't look so glum, guys!" Tony scolded. "Yeah, you've got a leaky boat, but compared to the others around the region, yours aint so bad."

"Encouraging," Raynor snarled. Several obvious questions raced through both his and Rowland's minds: Source or sources and means topped the list. Where were the leaks and how were they getting into the prison?

"Look, men," Tony could see his words struck like a punch to the gut. "Chill! We don't think like those creeps," he bit his words off like spitting out bad food. "You guys don't sit around all day trying to think like criminals. Those guys do. You're playing chess with creeps who change the rules all the time. They're ahead of you. Hell, they're ahead of all of us."

Raynor grabbed his ball cap and twisted it tighter onto his head. "Like I said, encouraging."

"What's our options?" Rowland was businesslike; ready to solve this mess and restore order. His contempt for slovenliness and clutter included how the prison ran. Leaks sounded all too much like poor leadership more than invasive ingenuity.

"I think it's time to infiltrate the scum."

"Okay, what does that mean?" Raynor asked.

"I spread a few of my guys undercover here, among the populace."

"Won't that be a bit obvious?" Rowland wasn't quite buying the idea.

"If we do it right, no it won't be. My guys are trained for this sort of thing. The ones I have in mind have been on the inside a few times."

"As cops or inmates?"

"Both."

"So they're accustomed to the risks and culture, eh?" Rowland was beginning to warm to the idea a little.

"They've got the drill down pretty well."

"Who do you have in mind?" Raynor inquired.

"Only I'll know their names. You'll have to trust me on this one. You'll know them by codes names. Their safety and the success of the operation demand it this way."

"What do you think, Harold?" Rowland deferred to his more experienced colleague.

"Makes sense to me. I think it's worth a shot."

"When do we start?" Rowland asked.

"I'll set things in motion later today. The guys'll be in here by delivery time tomorrow." By delivery time, Tony meant the normal new prisoner arrival time.

Rowland needed more assurance. "How will we be informed of any activity or information?"

Tony looked at Raynor. "I'll be in touch with you at least twice daily. Anything that comes to me you will hear about. You'll have to keep Tom informed. Okay?"

"Works for me," Raynor acknowledged. Looking at Rowland he asked, "How about you, Tom?"

Rowland nodded cautiously, "I'm on board."

"You guys go ahead if you don't mind. I want to watch the dude for awhile." Tony was referring to Chavez who was now standing alone with his back to the wall and a navy blue knit cap pulled down over his ears.

As the men stepped away to leave Tony on recon so to speak, Rowland was struck with another concern. "Tony, I want immediately any information that potentially affects Meyers."

"Will do, Tom. I'll get any developments to Harold ASAP!"

"Good! Thanks for the help."

"Don't mention it."

Rowland and Raynor headed back to Rowland's office, leaving Tony on his own.

"Security level?" Raynor asked.

"Orange or were you thinking higher?"

Raynor's hesitance wasn't encouraging but he agreed, "Orange...for now."

THIRTY-TWO

"You're looking perkier than last night." Fr. Ted said poking his head into James' room. "How you feeling?"

"Oh hi, Father," James replied sluggishly. He was sitting up in bed dozing in and out, still under the effects of anesthesia. "I think I'm better. Anyway the nurse tells me I am."

"Well you gave us quite a scare young man." Father Ted approached the side of James' bed, gripping the raised side rail with both of his hands. It pleased him to see some color in the young man's face, although energy was observably flagging. The pale blue smock hanging like a bag from James' shoulders wasn't much improvement over the dingy white prison jumpsuit, making him seem even more pathetic looking to the concerned priest.

"Scared me too, Father," James said again with feeble voice, straining to straighten himself in bed. "Guess the dude got me pretty good."

"That he did, James. Thank the Lord, though, he didn't penetrate anything important."

"No joke!"

Father Ted spied the book open on James' lap. "So what are you reading?"

"The book Warden Rowland gave me." James handed it to Fr. Ted. "I just opened it. Not really feeling like reading just yet."

"Great book," Fr. Ted offered. "One of my favorites."

"Yeah, that's what Warden Rowland said, too. Said it would challenge my assumptions."

"Oh, it will do that," Fr. Ted said with a hearty laugh. "It'll definitely do that and then some. It'll challenge pretty much everything you ever believed."

"Maybe that's a good thing," James conceded with a glint of hope in his voice.

"I think so, James. You're due for some good news." Fr. Ted said obliquely referring to the Gospel.

James nodded his agreement. "Look Father, I don't mean to be rude…"

Fr. Ted interrupted, "I understand, James. Let me say a brief prayer and I'll let you get some rest."

As before Fr. Ted concluded his prayer with the sign of the cross over James, a gesture James had come to not just expect but welcome. It had the feel of a comfortable wrap, something secure though unseen.

James drifted off to sleep while Fr. Ted stood over the bed looking down on the young man. "Dear Heavenly Father, can this be the time when James' life changes direction?" With his words evaporating into the air, Fr. Ted left the room clutching to this prayer. Somehow he felt that despite unseen perils, James had reached bottom; that his trajectory might be about to change.

*****

Mike Scanlon spied Fr. Ted leaving the hospital as he crawled out of his pickup. "Fr. Ted," he called to the priest who seemed lost in thought. "Fr. Ted," he called again, this time getting his attention. "You coming from James's room?"

"Hi Mike. Yes I am. He's pretty wrung out right now. Fell asleep while I was with him."

"Not a good time for a visit then?"

"Probably later. I'm sure, though, he'd like to see you." Fr. Ted bit his lip as if pondering an idea.

Sensing Fr. Ted's mood change, Scanlon remarked, "Looks like you've got something on your mind."

"I do. Mike do you mind if I ask; when did things finally begin to turn around for you? I mean, when did you get serious about getting clean and accepting God into your life?"

"That's easy. Right after I hit bottom…hard bottom."

"When was that?"

"The night Sally threw me out." Mike Scanlon might not have been the sharpest pencil in this box of characters, but bitter experience made him one of the more keenly observant. "Where you going with this?" he asked Fr. Ted.

"Would you say that maybe James has hit bottom, or do you think he's got further to fall?"

"Depends," Mike shot in reply.

"Depends on what?"

"Father, I will never forget that night," referring to the night Sally confronted him. "I've never had my chain jerked that hard; scared the crap out of me. Then and there I knew I stood to lose everything I ever cared about. Maybe getting knifed will do that for the kid."

"Maybe so, Mike. Maybe so."

"Look Father, this kid has been bottom dwelling for a long time. He doesn't like it anymore than I liked being a drunk. But no one's ever shown him the light. Yeah, I think he's gotta be close to the bottom if he's not there already. Now he needs the light, the way out. You know, the Gospel."

"Mike you're a better theologian than I am," Fr. Ted said, giving his burly friend's arm a manly squeeze. "I'm down with that."

"Now you're starting to sound like one of T's hoodlums," Scanlon chortled. Then they both laughed.

"Hey, would you mind giving the guys a call? Let's get the posse together at my place tonight. And ask Terrance to invite Anne."

"Sure! No offense to T, but why Anne?"

"She might hold an important piece to Mr. Meyers' future. Just go with me on this one, okay?"

"I'm good. I'll call the guys."

"Great! Let's make it seven."

The men shook hands and went off to their respective tasks, Scanlon to make a couple of calls and Fr. Ted to whatever was on his agenda.

THIRTY-THREE

There was a buzz to the gathering at the rectory, energy quite unlike the gloom of the last few days. Tom brought word from the hospital that James' condition had been further upgraded to fair and stable. That news bolstered already rising spirits. No one seemed quite certain why this new thread of optimism apart from general agreement that perhaps despite the circumstances the kid was in a good place. Good if because the only recourse remaining for him was up. The nadir had been reached. What an irony, one more that wouldn't even escape James' keen notice, that lying flat on his back up was the only available option. But how?

"Okay, Ted, you called this gathering. What's on your mind?" Tom asked ever businesslike.

"You're right I did, and thank you Michael for making the calls."

"Michael? Who's Michael?" Terrance fairly wailed with laughter. "You can't mean Scanlon?"

"Well, actually I do mean Michael Richard Scanlon, Mr. Hall," Fr. Ted responded in professorial brogue.

"Why thank you, Father, for recognizing me with such courtesy," Scanlon replied with his nose to the air and pinky held out from his coffee cup, a cartoonish image of bulk and civility. "Now can we can the crap?" he blurted, obviously done with being the butt of the joke and ready to get down business.

"You put it so delicately, Michael. But, yes, let's do turn our attention to Meyers," Fr. Ted quipped. Tom rolled his eyes and gestured for Fr. Ted to get on with it.

"Gentlemen, I asked Mike this morning," Fr. Ted began. "Do you think James has reached bottom yet?" Looking at Mike, "Tell the guys what you told me."

"Yeah, I think so. I think that getting knifed might have scared him enough to finally open him up."

Tom's face assumed a serious cast, lost as he seemed in Mike's comment. "What are you thinking, Tom? You seem preoccupied," Fr. Ted asked, feeling his friend's apparent apprehension.

"Don't you think getting hauled off to prison hadn't already accomplished that?" Tom asked.

"I think it made him mad, Tom," Mike replied. "I think it made him madder than hell that nobody cared enough to prevent him from self-destructing."

"Huh, mad but not scared?" Tom reflected as he settled deeper into the thick easy chair. "What's your take, Terrance?" Tom inquired turning toward his son-in-law.

"Oh I think Scans nailed it!"

Tom Rowland wasn't buying the idea yet. "What *more* than getting locked up would he need to jolt him to reality?" Tom snapped.

"Death!" Scanlon and Terrance shouted in unison. Scanlon continued, "Look Tom, like I told Fr. Ted this morning, I knew I was in prison as a drunk. I hated every minute of my life and circumstances, all of it. But when Sally threatened to leave me:" He tugged on his ball hat. "Oh man that woke me up! When she slammed the bedroom door shut, guys that was like…like I'd died. Nothing ever scared me like that. Nothing!"

"Okay, Mike, I'll concede your point." Tom took a moment to contemplate the matter a little further, adding, "Actually your point seems quite plausible. I'd not put it together quite like that until now. I understand the anger, the sense of betrayal and abandonment. New inmates import that stuff into the prison every day." Again he turned his attention to Terrance. "Is that how it went for you?"

"No, not quite. I stayed angry. In some ways anger gave me something to live for. It was when the lights went off at night and my mind went to work on me that I'd feel afraid."

"Of what?"

"I don't know if I can put it into words, Tom."

"I think I might be able to help you with that, T," Scanlon piped up. "Do you remember when you finally came around – took a hard look at who you'd become?"

"Well yeah. But what's your point?"

"You were afraid of what you saw – dead end. You saw no way out."

"You're right big guy; you're absolutely right."

Fr. Ted seized the opening, "So Mike, what was Terrance's answer?"

"The Gospel, of course!"

"And…," Fr. Ted persisted.

"Like T, James has looked in the mirror and what he sees staring back at him scares the crap out of him, just like Tom said. But getting knifed, well that just confirmed what the mirror tells him every night the lights go out. He's as dead as dead gets. Now he needs to see the light. Guys, we've got to show him Jesus!"

"Nothing has made more sense to me than what you just said," Tom remarked, now leaning forward in his chair. "I gave James a book out of my library."

Fr. Ted cut him off, "I saw the book today, Tom. Heavy read. Is he up to it?"

"Gentleman, that young man has a fabulous mind. He's a smart kid: Poorly programmed but more than capable of comprehending the book's point."

"How do you know this?" Fr. Ted wanted more confirmation.

141

"His test scores. They confirm he has ample intellectual acuity. And he's curious. He won't leave many rocks unturned in his search for truth, or answers to his life."

"Okay, I give. What book?" Scanlon asked."

Fr. Ted answered, "Tom gave him G.K. Chesterton's *Orthodoxy* to read."

"Not exactly a stick-figure Gospel tract, huh?" Scanlon snorted, scratching his head under his ball cap.

"Exactly," Fr. Ted replied. "But if the kid's as bright as Tom says, there's not probably a better book for him to digest than that one."

"That's what I felt, Ted. Chesterton will open his mind to a new world of thought that will lead him to the reality of God."

Now Terrance was scratching his head. "How do you plan to track his progress, Tom?"

"Weekly book review sessions. I plan to invite him to my office for an hour a week to talk about what he's read, answer his questions and ask a few of my own."

"Brilliant!" Terrance remarked. "I love it!"

"So do I," Fr. Ted said with thoughtful composure. "Truly inspired, Tom."

"But gentlemen," Tom's tone became grave. "James' perils are not over."

"Explain yourself," Fr. Ted urged.

"It's the opinion of the county gang squad that James' problems with the Lobos began before he got sent up. They began when he ratted out his assailant."

"What does that mean for James?" Fr. Ted probed more insistently.

"Tighter security for one – both for him and the prison. Tony said our facility leaks like…I believe he said a sinking ship."

"Listen, Tom," Terrance broke in. "It leaked like that before now and it's far from your fault." He stood and paced a moment. The guys followed Terrance with their eyes. He seemed lost in thought if not in memory. "Look, no prison is pristine or even close. You've heard the old song and dance before – the prisoners run the asylum. It's no different but I'll grant you, it's more dangerous." Turning toward his father-in-law he concluded, "Tom, there's little or nothing you can do that will stop it or even slow it down. I suppose you got your intel from Tony, right?"

"That's correct."

"Look, no one knows the system better than him. Does he have his operatives moving in?"

"He does."

"That's good. It will at least alert you…and us…to any possible actions. But you need to know one more thing."

"What's that?" Tom squared his eyes directly at Terrance.

"Tom, whether you knew it then or not I don't know, but I was in exactly the same spot James finds himself right now. And somehow, only God knows, I got through it. I am totally sold that God has James under watch even better than the guards at the State House."

Tom studied Terrance's face. It evinced unwavering conviction. Terrance had advised Tom on thorny issues in the prison before and been right on the money: None more important than this one. He bit his lip before responding.

"You're right, Terrance. And you reminded me of something I'd quite forgotten – your own ordeal with the populace. Okay, where do we go from here?"

"It's cosmic, Tom!" Terrance snapped. "It's always cosmic!"

Fr. Ted sat forward, "What do you mean – cosmic?"

Terrance grabbed up his nearly worn out Bible, assertively flipping through its pages. "It's right here guys! Right here in Paul's own words. Listen! 'For we are not contending against flesh and blood, but against the principalities, against the powers, against the world rulers of this present darkness, against the spiritual hosts of wickedness in the heavenly places.'" He sat the book back on the armrest of his chair, and sat himself down beside it. "I am convinced, guys, that we cannot lose sight of this battle. It's the one that matters most. It's the one that has taken down so many people, and has infected the populace" referring to the State House inmates.

"I feel your passion, T. I'm with you bro!" Scanlon offered.

"Well said, Terrance. I needed that assurance, and if you will that accountability. As the warden, it's easy to feel the burden is yours and yours alone. I think it's also easy to forget that the battle is, as you put it, cosmic."

Fr. Ted cut in, "That's why we're here tonight gentlemen. The cosmic importance of what lies ahead is what we must address. I have some thoughts on that." But before Fr. Ted could continue, the front door opened.

The guys stood as Anne entered the rectory. Immediately she noticed two empty chairs in the living room where the posse convened. "What's this chair for?" she asked, pointing to the other empty chair. "Expecting someone else?"

"Ah, yes, you noticed," Fr. Ted beamed. "None of these dolts caught the second empty chair," he barbed, poking his thumb toward the guys seated around him.

"So, who's it for?" Anne asked again.

"That chair, my dear, is reserved for an expected guest who can't be with us just yet," Fr. Ted said with certain piquancy.

Now the other guys were bemused by the airs and mysteriousness of the friendly priest.

"Oh, who?" Terrance asked wryly.

"Why James, of course. I've reserved this chair for him, for the day he steps out of prison and joins us as a member of the posse. Let me say it this way," he added, "When the cosmic battle goes in his favor."

"Fantastic!" Scanlon beamed. "What a great idea!"

"Nice touch, Ted," Tom added with a broad smile.

"I want us to think of James as always among us," Fr. Ted instructed. "I want to think of him as with us and never apart from us. When we meet, let's assume he meets with us. Let's begin now to think of him as part of us, not as a project, but as a man presently in search of himself. Our task is to help him find that answer – to find it in Christ. To beat those cosmic forces through the power of Jesus Christ!"

"Ted, I've been thinking along those same lines," Tom said. "That's in part why I've asked him to join me each week for the book review discussions. I want to get into that kids' head…and his heart."

"Wow, it's like we all have something to give the kid," Scanlon gleamed. "T's been right where the kid is and knows the way out." Waving his hand toward Tom and Fr. Ted he exclaimed, "With you guys it's like he has two granite rocks to lean against. You know; father figures." He caught himself. A quirky smile crossed his face. "No pun intended…Father." Fr. Ted rolled his eyes, "Only you, Scanlon. Only you."

"Yeah, and what about you Scans?" Terrance asked. "Where do you see yourself in this picture?"

"Man I don't know." Scanlon pushed his ball cap back and scratched his head. "Can't see it yet. Not sure."

"You're the enforcer, Mike. If you push him like you pushed me, accountability won't be a problem. But…"

"But what!?" Mike stiffened.

"I was gonna say, you don't always have to make him mad."

"Ah, you guys are such wimps," Scanlon moaned with a wave of his arm. Tom and Ted just shook their heads and chuckled.

"Hey, don't get me wrong, Mike. You are the enforcer. You come across tough, but you've got this… I don't know…ability to dig the dude out of a hole. No one wants to let you down."

"Thanks, T." To Mike no one validated him more than Terrance. Their friendship had galvanized through difficult circumstances that demanded trust where trust was the hardest thing to give.

"That's right, Mike," Tom affirmed. "You've got credibility at the core of the man. He'll trust you."

"Really?" Scans tugged his cap tightly into place. "Okay, I'll buy it. I'm the…whatever…enforcer dude."

"Well, we've practically forgotten Anne," Fr. Ted said, extending his hand in her direction. Anne sat quietly smiling at this display of manly approbation. "Don't mind me, Fr. Ted, I've been quite amused." Another round of laughter ensued.

"Well," Fr. Ted added, "You, too, play quite a role in young Meyers' life. Why don't you fill us in on the legal side of things?"

"Thank you Father, and thanks for inviting me to the posse," Anne acknowledged through a playful grin.

"Just honorary, love," Terrance winked.

Anne flicked her hand, "Whatever."

Reaching for her briefcase she extracted a legal pad on which she had written several notes. "As I've already told Terrance and Daddy…"

"Daddy?" Scanlon just couldn't let it go. "Who's Daddy?" The entire room except Anne snorted with loud laughter. Tom just shook his head and closed his eyes. "Not here, dear. I'm daddy at home, but not here."

Anne glared at Scanlon and then at her dad. "Sorry Warden, I forgot I was with your male wilderness bonding group. And you, Mr. Scanlon, can keep your trite comments to yourself." Scanlon came to attention without a whimper.

"As I was saying," she started again. "Both Terrance and *my father* know what I've already found, that James, despite what we think of him or hope for him, has been given a reasonable sentence. Judge Abrams could have gone further but seemed to apply some leniency in light of James' first offender status. Just the same, James was convicted of a serious felony which the law stipulates must include up to twelve years in prison."

"Twelve years! The judge did take it easy on him," Scanlon blurted.

"He did, Mike," Anne continued. "But, I have also discovered that because James is a first timer, he has some options."

"So more than the one you've already told me about?" Terrance inquired.

"Yes, honey. Let me proceed." Terrance nodded. "As Terrance inferred, I'd learned that James could have up to two years of his sentence commuted to parole, which includes pretty stiff compliance to court stipulations. But there is one more possibility." Anne flipped through her notes. "In light of his present circumstances brought about by apparent gang related activities within the State House that threaten to further imperil his life, the courts have been known to grant clemency to first time offenders who demonstrate exceptional behavior while in prison, and whose advocates can assure the court that the convict has…well…learned his lesson and presents no further threat to society."

"Clemency? Exactly what does that mean in terms of James' prison time?" Tom inquired suspiciously.

Anne sat a little straighter in her chair as though on trial herself. "It could mean anything from early release and parole with a very long tail on it, something in the neighborhood of six or more years, or house confinement again with a long parole, or worse case it could mean nothing more than tighter security right where he is."

Anne had the men's attention, each one now leaning her direction.

"That's quite a revelation, Anne," her dad observed, with both arms poised on the cushioned armrests of the overstuffed easy chair in which he sat. "What corroborates your finding?" he asked sounding like the trial lawyer he once was.

"There are actually three cases, two quite recent, where the courts acted favorably toward a prisoner who behaved himself, but whose life was threatened by the populace. The third case involves a young woman who was married to a made mobster, and who ultimately was murdered in prison before her case was heard. Hers became the *stare decisis* by which similar cases are tried; this despite her death."

"What motivated the court to continue the case after her death," Tom probed.

Anne studied her notes more closely. "Apparently the case had gone to court but action had been delayed by a variety of motions, including a motion to vacate the case. One day before her murder the judge had ordered the case be heard and decision rendered. Despite the prisoner's death, it was the court's opinion that a gesture of clemency deserved the force of law under the conditions suffered by the now deceased inmate, and was so ruled."

"But why was she murdered? Just her association with this made mobster?" Terrance asked.

"No, it goes deeper than that. Apparently she was in the wrong place at the wrong time and witnessed a mob execution."

"So the mob silenced her?" Terrance probed.

"That's where the record seems vague but the conjecture seems reasonable."

"What about other cases, those that didn't receive favorable ruling?" Rowland continued his interrogation, unconvinced that any of this discovery was relevant to Meyers.

"Well, that's interesting for this reason. Only four cases have been tried on this basis and only one petition was denied. According to the ruling, the prisoner was a repeat offender, evidently connected with the mob. I found his case so intriguing I read the newspaper stories surrounding it. The bottom line is that the guy was murdered in his cell two days after the judge ruled against him."

"Really?! Who did him in?" Terrance was totally drawn into the story.

"That's the interesting part, honey. Even though the case was tried over seven years ago, all I could find was that it's still under investigation."

"Another inside job, Tom?" Terrance asked.

"Sounds suspiciously like it might be. I'll ask Harold if he knows anything about it."

"Anne, how old is the girl's case?" Tom inquired.

"It's quite dusty actually. Let me see," she rifled through her notes again. "Oh my, twenty-five years ago."

"That's awhile. And you say the other three cases, including the denial, are more recent. How recent?" Tom wanted more details.

"They're all within the last six or seven years. The most recent appears to have been tried just two years ago. Actually more like a year and a half ago."

"Wonder why the lag between the first case and the more recent ones." Now Scanlon had his brows raised.

"Good question, Mike. It appears the original case went into the books with little notice. It wasn't until about seven years ago it was rediscovered."

"By whom, Anne?" Tom asked.

"Well, by a good friend of yours, Daddy...er' Mr. Warden." Anne shot her dad a wry smile and waited for him to ask.

"Okay, I'll bite. Who?"

"Judge William Parker."

"Bill? He never said anything to me about that in any of our conversations."

"Well, he's on the other side of the court now: Prosecutor not attorney for the defense."

"Still, I would have thought he'd say something." Tom Rowland was displeased with his former colleague's less than forthcoming omission...or silence...or convenient lapse of memory.

Something seemed to bother Terrance. "What's on your mind, Terrance," Anne asked.

"Isn't Parker pretty convinced that James is responsible for Nate's murder?"

"He was while in my office, but I may have planted ample doubt in his mind," Tom rejoined.

"My hunch, Tom, and it's only a hunch, is that Judge Parker likely wasn't aware of how dangerous James' situation is at the State House," the conciliatory Fr. Ted interjected. "You might want to cut him a little slack until you can talk further with him."

"Good thought, Ted," Tom conceded. "I'll give him a call in the morning. But I might just play along awhile before suggesting what we've learned from Anne."

"By the way, sweetheart, great job of lawyering," Tom said with fatherly and professional pride in his voice.

Terrance shot his bride a huge smile, "Thanks, babe. Maybe we caught a break thanks to you."

"My pleasure. Of course nothing is etched in stone here. We just have a thread of hope for James. But I must caution again, he can know absolutely nothing about what we've discussed this evening. I hope I am quite clear about that, guys," Anne emphasized.

"Yes, of course," Fr. Ted answered for the group. "You're sounding more like your *daddy* every day."

Tom and Anne both rolled their eyes.

Anne surveyed the room for general agreement. Confident she had it, she added, "I'm not entirely sure yet what our next steps are, especially in light of the pending inquiry. That's my next job, find a path."

"I can probably help you with that," Tom offered. "The inquiry takes precedent. What we need to pray toward, folks, is a good outcome there."

"Agreed," Anne affirmed.

"Well," Fr. Ted said, "I think Anne just joined the posse."

Once more the room filled with good natured laughter.

"Anyone disagree?" Fr. Ted asked almost daring dissention.

"Not from me," Terrance quickly answered.

"Me neither," Scanlon said. "She's definitely got my vote."

"Tom?" Fr. Ted asked. "How does *Daddy* vote?"

"Daddy votes aye," Tom returned with a wink and nod toward his daughter.

"What about me?" Anne replied in mock derision. "Don't I get a vote?"

"Sorry, dear, but no," Fr. Ted returned dropping his hand on Anne's arm. "You're in."

"Well," she said with a flick of her hand. "In that case, I accept."

"Good! Let's pray people." Fr. Ted then led the posse, including its newest member, in prayer concluding with, "And, blessed Lord, may James soon fill this chair beside me. May the cosmic forces be defeated!"

A rousing "Amen!" ensued, accented with a feminine voice.

THIRTY-FOUR

"How's the young man doing, Tom?" Judge Parker inquired while perusing documents on his desk. He seemed to know without asking why his friend and colleague had called.

"Improving, Bill, but still quite weak. Thank you for asking."

"Any new developments?"

"From what I was able to get from the staff, James will be kept in the hospital for a few more days."

"So you visited him?"

"Yes, I did. I stopped by on my way to work this morning."

"How'd he seem to you?"

"Well, he was asleep so I really didn't get to speak with him. But he still looks like death warmed over; terribly pale. They're keeping a close watch on him for possible infections."

"Good, glad to hear they're watching him. Tom, I'll take your lead in terms of when we can reschedule his part of the inquiry."

Tom hesitated before replying. "That sounds fine, Bill, but am I to conclude you're proceeding with the inquiry without James at this time?"

"I am, Tom. We have other people to question and additional research to investigate. I'm easing up on Meyers for now."

"Alright, I understand. By other research, do you mean you've come up with some new evidence?" Rowland kept mum, but in his mind he was hoping Parker would tip his hand, maybe let slip that no evidence was found that connected James to the murder weapon.

"You know, Tom, I'm not at liberty to discuss the case or any portion of it at this time. As a trusted friend...and off the record...I'll just say we have some doubt about Meyer's role."

Rowland withheld the onrush of elation that swept over him. In lawyerly decorum he simply replied, "I'll take that as good news, Bill. And thank you for it."

"Keep it to yourself."

"You know I will."

"Tom, I must add, you well know Meyers isn't exonerated of anything yet, and he is a suspect."

"Of course, Bill. I thoroughly understand that." Still, Rowland had no misgivings that Judge Parker's inference about doubting James' "role", as he put it, was a hopeful sign. He pulled back his own trump card – Anne's discovery. It might be needed later, he thought to himself.

Certainly, Rowland would comply with Parker's stern caution: But the posse needed to know.

*****

Fr. Ted pulled his buzzing cell phone from his shirt pocket, "Fr. Ted," he answered. No one responded. "Ah darn techno, cyber pest," he muttered, stabbing the green answer button with his index finger. "Fr. Ted," he answered again, this time a mite brusquely, at least that's how it came across to Rowland.

"Ted, you sound distracted. Is this a bad time?"

"No, not at all, Tom," he replied recognizing Rowland's voice. "I just suffered a techno lapse. Couldn't figure out how to answer this blasted new phone my parish insisted I just had to have. What kind of egoist names their product I-something anyway? Darn things! Not fit for humans. If you want to make something from Mars, then let Martians use it!"

Fr. Ted's cyber meltdown humored Rowland, who was already feeling his tension ease.

"Well, let me know when you're through swearing at your phone. I've got a bit of news about James I think you'll want to hear."

"I'm not sweating at my phone! What about James?"

"Well you old curmudgeon, the young man's no longer on the top of Judge Parker's suspect list."

"No kidding! How'd you find that out?"

"Thought that news might get your attention. He couldn't divulge anything and even this bit of information must stay between me, you and the posse."

"Yeah, sure. So what did he say?" Fr. Ted leaned forward, elbows resting on the desk with his phone pressed snugly to his ear.

"It's both what he said and what he didn't say, Ted. What he said was that he now harbors some doubt about James' role in Chalmers' murder. What he didn't say may mean even more."

"Great news, Tom! But what are you surmising about the unspoken message?"

"He swore me to secrecy as you might expect, but if he really thought James was culpable of the crime, he wouldn't have offered me anything, certainly not this kind of concession. Not now when the panel hasn't even convened."

"So you're assuming that his absence of further details or assumptions might mean the evidence points another direction?"

"Precisely! My dear Watson," Rowland affirmed in his best Sherlock Holmes imitation.

"Curious!" Father Ted responded. "Would that take James off the suspect list altogether and make him more of an eye witness?"

"Something like that but not yet. Parker's not going to tip his hand too soon. He'll keep James on the suspect list until he's absolutely certain of his innocence. Parker's as tenacious as…"

"As Tom Rowland, attorney for the defense?" Fr. Ted inserted with a wry chuckle.

"I was going to say bulldog, which I in no way resemble." Rowland continued on before Fr. Ted could distract him further. "If Bill thought James was culpable he simply would have remained silent about it. He was throwing me a collegial courtesy. But, Ted, it's just one more little piece in a very messy puzzle. Even so, it seems like maybe our boy's catching some positive momentum."

"By the grace of God it will continue!"

"Yes, let's hope so! Look Ted, could you help me out? I've not spoken with anyone else in the posse, just you. Would you call Mike? And please put the muzzle on him! I'll see Terrance and Anne tonight."

"Glad to," Fr. Ted said letting out another chuckle.

"What's so funny?"

"Muzzle Mike? Where did you come up with that?"

"I guess I've been hanging around him and Terrance too much lately," Tom replied, now laughing at himself.

"Well, muzzle Mike I will do. Talk to you later." Fr. Ted went to punch the "end" button just as a new thought struck his mind. "Wait a minute, Tom! You still there?"

"Yeah, I'm still here. What's on your mind?"

"Curious really. What was Parker's notion of Anne's findings?"

"Ah, well, I didn't tell him what Anne dug up. Saving it for later if necessary."

"Got it," Ted replied. "Just baiting the trap, eh?"

"Yes perhaps I suppose. I'm thinking it might become important when negotiating Meyer's next steps. We'll see."

"Oh very good!" Fr. Ted was quite impressed with his friend's legal savvy. Now that matter of muzzling the big guy. "I'll give Mike that call you asked me to make."

"Good! We'll chat a bit later."

THIRTY-FIVE

With this new wrinkle the posse met at the rectory to hash out a new game plan, Anne among them as the newest member.

"Anne, what do you make of Judge Parker's concession," Tom asked his daughter.

"Honestly, I really don't know what to make of it. On the surface it sounds like he was sending you a signal. On the other hand he hedged his position as I would expect him to do." Another possibility came to mind. "As I think about it, I'm not convinced it was a concession he made, Dad."

"Oh, what then?"

"I'm wondering if the evidence might be sending him somewhere else."

"That was my take, too," Tom registered. "I came away with the sense that he might have another suspect in mind."

"Possibly. That would make sense," Anne offered.

"So what do you two attorney-types think is the bottom line here?" Fr. Ted jumped in to ask.

"Again, I'm not really certain," Anne responded ahead of her father.

"I'll go out on a limb, Ted. I've known Bill for awhile. He wouldn't offer anything if he was at all concerned it could come back and bite him. If I was to hazard an opinion, I think James will become more of an eyewitness than suspect by the time the panel calls on him. My mind hasn't changed about that since we talked earlier today."

"Plausible," Anne said with a hint of reservation. "Still, Parker didn't quite let the kid off the hook. So I'm sure, Dad, you'd agree we need to stay alert."

"Absolutely," Tom agreed. "But I think that's where we really dig in and seek Higher wisdom. James' whole situation seems to me to be teetering on the sharp edge of the blade. I just pray it doesn't slice him."

"Wow, that's quite a metaphor, Tom, since it's a blade, so to speak, that put him in the hospital." Terrance said: his face stressed with obvious concern. "So despite your confidence in Parker's whatever we call it – admission or concession or something else – you both seem to be more than just a little cautious."

"Call it professional gamesmanship, Terrance," Anne said. "I think Dad and I are aware that despite all the investigative discoveries and legal maneuvering that go into this sort of inquiry, James' innocence or guilt is still up to a panel of people and a judge. That's where it all seems so subjective, and at times unfair."

"Quite true, Anne," her dad affirmed. "That's my point exactly, that this whole matter appeals to Higher Wisdom and Higher Judgment, otherwise it devolves to a court of human inquiry leaving the door open to prejudice, which does not always result in honest justice. It's that cosmic thing Terrance brought to our attention."

"So what do you suggest, Tom?" Fr. Ted asked.

"Prayer and fasting."

"Go on," Fr. Ted urged.

"I would like to propose that as a group we convene nightly for the next week to fast and pray for James. I know we're busy, you Ted and Terrance especially with your respective ministries. But the circumstances justify the urgency. The panel convenes tomorrow and will begin its investigation. James is still on the suspect list albeit no longer at the top of it."

"Appealing to the Judge of all justice makes great sense, Tom. I can clear my calendar," Fr. Ted confirmed.

"Yeah, I can too," Terrance agreed. "Dirk and Tag can take over for me. They'll probably have the kids in every night to pray and fast too."

"Mike, you've been unusually quiet. Where are you on Tom's idea?" Fr. Ted probed.

"I've been muzzled," Scanlon smirked. "But count me in."

"Muzzled! What's that about?" Terrance blurted with a snarky snort.

Fr. Ted and Tom dropped their heads and then stared across the room at one another.

"Why did you say that to him?" Tom asked Fr. Ted with pained resignation.

"Because you told me to say that to him," Fr. Ted answered with an impish grin.

Tom rubbed his forehead, "Mike, that 'muzzle' order is for all of us. Nothing we've discussed here tonight can leave this room."

"No harm, guys. I kinda thought it was funny. The Book says to muzzle the ox, and who's a bigger ox in this group than me?" Scanlon said, poking good natured fun at himself while easing the tension between the two senior members. Loud laughter pealed throughout the rectory. Terrance reached across and gave his big buddy a manly hug.

"We love you bro," Terrance said, squeezing Mike's thick shoulders.

"Hey okay can the sap, I'm good," Scanlon said shoving his friend back into his seat.

"Well, now that we solved that issue, are we on board with Tom?" Fr. Ted asked surveying the room for an answer. He needn't wait long. Everyone emphatically bonded in a commitment to pray and fast over the next week – or longer if deemed necessary, meeting nightly at the rectory.

"Oh," Scanlon broke in before the group bowed for Fr. Ted's benediction. "What about asking our wives to join us? T's already got his bride here."

"Love it!" Fr. Ted remarked. Around the room Scanlon's suggestion met strong approval.

"Great! I know Sally will definitely want to participate," Scanlon confirmed.

"Mary will too," Tom added.

"Well, then," Fr. Ted concluded, "Posse and spouses tomorrow evening at seven."

THIRTY-SIX

"Orthodoxy: The Romance of Faith," James whispered to himself after seeing the book Warden Rowland lent him resting on the cart-like table on which the nurses served his meals. Reaching for it he flipped aimlessly through the pages stopping at the Table of Contents. A few chapter titles caught his attention: "The Maniac," "The Suicide of Thought," and the "Ethics of Elfland." "You're kidding! What's this stuff about? Okay," he muttered aloud, "you've got my attention." Turning the page he stopped on the opening line, "The only possible excuse for this book is that it is an answer to a challenge." James stared at that line as if he were its target. A strange twist of the words entered his foggy mind. "The only possible excuse for *my reading* this book is a *possible* answer to *the mess of my life*." The book flopped onto his chest as he drifted off to sleep with these words wafting through the mists of grogginess.

The nurse crashing through the door pushing her weird beeping monitor in front of her woke James, a box poised on a pole with wheels that for the look of it made him think of a brainy little sci-fi geek. "Back with the droid, eh?" he mumbled in a sleepy voice.

"Yep," the nurse chirped. "Got a pulse for me?"

"Think so," James mumbled again.

"Well let's see," the nurse said winding the cuff around his arm. She punched a couple of buttons and the *droid* sprang to life. "Yep you do," she quipped. "Hey, that's the stuff!

"What stuff?" James asked turning to look the droid in the face.

"Best pulse I've seen from you – nice and strong."

"Improving, huh?" James asked wriggling to sit up a little straighter in bed.

"Sure are." The nurse looked up from the folder in which she entered some notes. "Hey you've got color in your face, too. You don't look like a bleached bed sheet anymore."

James chuckled at the comment.

"And that sounds like improvement, too. Don't think I've heard you laugh since you got here."

"Haven't felt much like laughing," James snorted.

"I suppose not." The nurse caught sight of the book. "Been doing a little reading it appears."

"Not really. I just opened it before I fell asleep again."

The nurse snapped it up and thumbed a few pages. "Ugh, this looks heavy. You must be smart or something."

"Hah, not hardly," James slurred. "I'm just a dumb kid stuck in prison."

"Hey, knock it off," the nurse snapped. "Nobody reads this kind of stuff if they don't have a brain. Besides, I didn't think you got to have books in prison."

"Oh, it's not mine. Warden Rowland loaned it to me."

"Oh yeah, so you're in tight with the Warden, huh?" The pesky young nurse was now toying with James. She could tell she was getting his goat a little.

"It's not like that at all," James said, annoyed by the inference.

"Oh, it's not huh?"

"No it's not. May I have my book back now?"

"No, I'm not done with it yet." The nurse turned a few more pages then began reading. "Whoa, this is really cool!" She blurted.

"What's cool?" James asked in a snotty tone.

"Something I'm sure wouldn't interest you," she shot back in an equally snotty tone.

"C'mon, read it!" He snarled.

The nurse cleared her voice, "You may alter the place to which you are going; but you cannot alter the place from which you have come." Stopping she glanced over the top of the book to catch James' reaction.

He flinched like he'd been punched. "That's a load," he said and let out a long sigh. "Yeah well, I've actually been thinking about that *a lot* lately."

"Thought you'd like it," the nurse said, flopping the book back down on the table. "Well, I'd better go check on some more patients."

"Just a minute," James stopped her. "What page was that?"

"Oops, dunno!" She said with a shrug. "I think it was like around page one hundred and something. It's at the top of a page though," she said flippantly.

"Great! Guess I'll go hunting for it later."

"Sorry!" the nurse said again with a shrug, stuffing the cuff into the basket behind the droid's face. "See you in awhile."

"Hold it!" James said just before the nurse got out the door. "What's your name?"

"Terri," she said with a smile, and then slipped through the doorway into the hall.

"Terri, eh? Terri the Terror!" James snarled under his breath. But it was apparent young nurse Terri had left an impression – maybe more favorable than James was willing to admit.

The door opened again and in stepped the doctor. Scanning the contents of an open folder he said without looking at James, "Looks like you're on the mend young man. For giving us one heck of a scare the other night, I think you'll be out of here in a day or two."

"Great, back to prison: some release," James remarked.

"Well young man, as close as you came to dying, prison isn't so bad." The doctor closed the file, shoved it under his arm and looked straight into James' face. "You *are* a young man, Mr. Meyers," he stressed. "You'll still be a young man when you get out. I'd encourage you to adjust your attitude to that reality. Your choice of reading material suggests you know how to think. Put that mind of yours to good use."

"How'd you know what I was reading?" James growled, bothered that his limited privacy had been invaded…again.

"I saw the book here on my earlier rounds. You were asleep. I didn't think you'd mind me thumbing a few pages." The doctor thumped the book resting on the cart-like table.

James relaxed. "No, it's okay. Sorry for sounding like a jerk."

"Not to worry, we all get upset, James. But look, you do have a future if you want it. That is," the doctor paused, "if you've got the guts to straighten up and fly right."

James wasn't ready for that kind of straight talk from a stranger, doctor or not. But he kept his mouth shut. It would have been futile to argue. The words, after all, struck the right nerve.

"By the way," the doctor said while checking his pager. "Looks like you put a smile on Terri's face."

James snuffed, "Yeah, right."

The doctor laughed as he exited the door. James stared at the ceiling, "Why is it everyone thinks I've got a future but me?"

THIRTY-SEVEN

James fell asleep again but awoke to find a visitor beside his bed.

"Hi! I was just leaving for the day. Um, I'm like off duty and just wanted to pop by to check on you before taking off."

"Terri?"

"Yep! How you doing?"

"Okay, I guess," James said sitting up and rubbing the fuzziness from his eyes.

"The buzz says you might get out of here pretty soon." Terri said projecting a little disappointment.

"Oh, what'd you hear?" James asked projecting a little disappointment of his own.

"Wow, you don't sound all that enthused about leaving. Like it here, huh?"

"You didn't answer my question."

"Uh, like maybe sometime tomorrow, probably afternoon," Terri said, her hands shoved into her coat pockets.

"I see," James sighed. "Don't get me wrong. It's not that I like hanging out in the hospital, but I feel safe in here."

"Yeah, I'll bet."

"Will you be on duty tomorrow?" James asked not trying to be too obvious.

"Yep, sure will. I'm on another twelve hours – seven to seven-thirty shift."

"Nice. Maybe we can talk more then." He pulled the covers up around his shoulders. "I don't mean to be rude, but I'm not feeling so good."

"Oh sure, you need your rest."

"I do, but thanks for stopping by. It means a lot."

"No problem." Terri hesitated a moment and bit her lower lip. James could tell she had more on her mind.

"Something bothering you?" he asked.

"No, I'm just not sure I should say what I want to say," Terri said rocking awkwardly on her feet.

"Go for it. I promise not to embarrass you."

"Well, it's just that I want you to know I care. I know you've been through a lot of really scary stuff. That's all; I just want you to know I'll be praying for you."

"Praying for me, huh?" James muttered. "Another prayer *warrior* sent from God?"

Terri scowled. "Hey, what's up with that? Did I say something that bugged you?"

"No, no, not at all," James rebuffed half apologetically. "It's just that everybody I meet seems to think I need their prayers."

"You want the 4-1-1? Trust me, you need those prayers."

"Yeah, well we'll see. I'm not so sure, but I'm grateful for your concern."

"Really? You still sound kinda pissed."

"Oh no, don't get me wrong. I really do appreciate your concern. It does mean a lot. I just feel surrounded by religious types – Fr. Ted, Warden Rowland, Terrance, this big guy named Mike, the nurse at the pen, and now you."

Terri shrugged, "Did it ever occur to you that maybe God's got something to tell you?"

"Sure, like I'm in deep…"

"Don't say it, James! Look, I should go and let you rest." Terri reached for the door then stopped and looked back at her ill-tempered patient, "For what it's worth, I used to not believe, mostly because I hated God." She hesitated and drew a breath. "I think that's your problem too."

James' mouth fell open but no words fell out. It was like this perfect stranger had unmasked his darkest secret. Who died and made her the oracle of his conscience, he thought? "So you think I hate God, a god I'm not sure even exists?" James glowered indignantly.

"Yeah, I do," Terri answered in a soft voice. "But, James, I get it."

"Get what!?" James bristled. "What do you really know about me that makes you think you get it? Where do you get off thinking you've got anything on me? I'm a con – and you're not!" He seethed. Jerking the covers tighter around him he fairly shouted, "Why the hell does everybody think they've got me figured out? If you think you've got the key that unlocks the screwed up mess I'm in I'd sure like to have it. Otherwise just leave me alone and shut up about this God crap! Okay? I'm sick of people dropping the God-bomb on my head."

Terri's eyes filled, her heart sagged. But she held her ground. "Look, I didn't mean to upset you. I just wanted you to know that you're not the only one in this room to have gone through a dark place and made mistakes."

"Oh really!"

"Yeah, really!" Terri shot back angrily.

Her reaction shocked James. Shocked her too. Looking into her eyes he could see there was a story held behind them, deep inside places that still evinced great pain when probed. James felt his own flood of anger dissolve. He relaxed his guard. Just perhaps he'd met someone who truly knew his story in her own way. "I'm sorry, Terri. I had no idea. I'm truly sorry. I'm just so…"

"Angry? Really pissed off? Abandoned? James, I get that, I truly do. But…" She bit her lip once more and carefully selected her words. "But I know the God you hate, and I know what it means to be set free."

James' eyes clouded. His head dropped. He swept the moisture from his face. A deafening silence filled the room. Finally the only words that came to him fell involuntarily out of his mouth, "Thank you."

Terri's face streamed tears too. "Like I said, James, I'm praying for you…And I care. Don't mock me…and…don't doubt me."

James said nothing. He laid in bed feeling helplessly absorbed in contradictory feelings none of which he could fully trust.

"See you tomorrow," Terri said softly, a gentle smile creasing her face, as she pulled open the door and left James to the frightening poverty of his own torments.

THIRTY-EIGHT

Rowland spied Raynor walking down the administration building hall, "Harold," he summoned.

Raynor spun around, "Yes, Warden, you want to see me?"

"Yes, I do. Can you meet with me for a moment right now?"

Rowland opened his office door and snapped on the light. Raynor stepped in ahead of him.

"What's on your mind?" Raynor asked.

"My daughter Anne came up with some interesting if not sobering information while researching Meyers' case."

"Like what?"

"What do you know about clemency for well behaved prisoners?"

"I've heard of it, Tom, but it's rarely considered. If I were to guess, I'd say there probably haven't been ten cases even tried on that basis."

"That's what Anne discovered."

"If I can ask, Tom, where are you going with this?"

"Nowhere for now, Harold. I'm especially concerned, however, about one case where the prisoner was murdered in his cell a day or so after the judge granted his petition. Do you have any insight on that one?"

"I heard about it. Must have been, oh, six or seven years ago. If I'm not mistaken the prisoner was connected with the mob and ratted out some guys pretty high up in the organization."

"Was it a plea bargain, his case I mean?"

"It seems it might have been. But I don't think it was a 'clemency' trial like Anne might have thought. The guy was offered a deal of some kind and it might have smacked of clemency."

"Where was the prisoner being held?" Rowland was somewhat worried that it might have been at the State House.

"Don't worry, Tom, it wasn't here," Raynor seemed to be reading Rowland's mind. "I don't exactly recall where. But it occurs to me it might have been one of the New York prisons, maybe Attica."

"I see."

"Back to Meyers, Tom. I don't mean to be prying into something that's not my business, but is Anne proposing that the kid might be eligible for clemency?"

"I really can't answer that, Harold. We're just quite concerned about the risks in front of James while he's incarcerated. Just exploring any recourse that might relieve him of being the target of more violence."

"That makes perfect sense."

Fearfully reluctant, Rowland asked, "What are his chances of survival in your opinion?"

Raynor shook his head, his face sagged, "Not good."

Rowland looked away, "I don't know, Harold. I just don't know if leaving him here is in his best interests."

"Tom, you know he can be moved but you heard Tony's opinion about that."

"I know."

"So what does Fr. Ted think?"

"You could probably guess."

"He likely thinks that God dropped him off here."

"That's exactly what he thinks, Harold."

"For what it's worth, Warden, so do I."

Rowland studied Raynor wondering if he and Ted were in collusion. "Don't worry, Tom. We're not taking sides against you."

"So you two have spoken."

"Yes, of course. We've gone beyond just talking, we've prayed together with both yours and James' interests in mind."

"Really? Harold I apologize for not paying attention. I had no idea you were, well, a believer."

"Oh, it's much worse than that, Tom. Stephanie and I attend Fr. Ted's parish."

"So it is a conspiracy?"Rowland good naturedly sniped.

"Well, it's a conspiracy only in the sense we all share the hope that young James Meyers will get straight with God, himself and the world."

Rowland chuckled in agreement. "Harold, has Ted mentioned anything about getting together in the evenings this next week to pray and fast for James?"

"No, actually he hasn't. Is this part of your posse thing?"

"Yes it is. So why don't you and Stephanie join us? Seven tonight at the parish."

"Tom, that's a great idea! Thank you. I'll call Steph and we'll probably be there."

Suddenly the posse was expanding – Anne, the wives, and now Raynor and his wife. James had no idea how many people stood with him. But it wouldn't take long before he found out.

THIRTY-NINE

"Father, you might want to see this," Terrance said poking his head into Fr. Ted's office.

"See what?" he answered rising from his chair.

"Just trust me. You'll want to see this."

"Okay, let's go look."

Terrance held the door open between the office and the narthex to the church's nave (sanctuary where the congregation meets for worship).

"Oh my goodness! Terrance, you brought your hoodlums!?"

"I brought who?" Terrance glowered.

"Your kids! What are they doing here?"

"They insisted on coming! They're down for this fast and prayer thing for James."

"Wonderful! Absolutely wonderful! Like I said before, you've got a great tribe of kids!"

"What do you think the rest of the posse will think?" Terrance asked.

"They'll love it!"

"Hey, what's this hoodlum stuff?" Terrance quizzed, ruffled by the priest's impertinence.

"Oh that's what Scanlon calls them."

"Scans huh? I'll fix that."

"Don't bother, Terrance. It's Scanlon. Need we say more?"

Terrance laughed as Fr. Ted took him by the arm and led them both through the door to join the kids.

*****

"Dude, this place creeps me out," one of the hoodlums said in a whisper.

"Hey, cool it, dude. This is the house, you know Church."

"Yeah, but look at all this stuff." The guys peered through the door into the nave to scope out the scene. Mary with the Christ child in her arms stood on a small pedestal to the left in the north transept. A figure of Jesus hung from a larger-than-life cross behind the massive altar in the apse. A square golden box rested serenely beneath an iconic image of Christ to the right in the south transept. "Man, I feel like I'm being watched."

"You are," Fr. Ted answered, approaching from behind them. "All of Heaven has its eyes on you."

"Hey guys, you probably remember Fr. Ted from the hospital. He's the pastor here," Terrance said.

Pretty soon a huddle of kids formed around the priest. "So this place creeps you out?" Fr. Ted remarked with a chuckle. "How many of you feel creeped out?" Several hands raised and a few kids shrugged their shoulders. "From your gestures I'll assume most of you feel like that." The clutch of hoodlums began laughing. "Well, how about a tour? Maybe you'll feel differently afterward?"

"Yeah, that sounds cool," a couple of the kids exclaimed.

"Follow me," Fr. Ted said as he led the group to the front entrance.

"Okay, here is where it all begins," Fr. Ted said, standing at the front doors. "The entire point of the architecture and symbols is to remind us that we've stepped out of our daily lives and entered into the presence of God. When we walk through those doors," he said pointing to the large double-paneled wooden swinging doors across the narthex," it's as though we've left earth and entered heaven. We call it the nave – or gathering place. You likely call it the sanctuary."

One of the kids piped up, "Actually we just call it the café." Everyone laughed.

Fr. Ted pushed open the doors to the nave, pausing to dip the fingers of his right hand into a small brass bowl of water fastened to the inner wall. With water dripping from his wetted fingers, he traced the sign of the cross over his chest.

"Wow!" one of the kids exclaimed. "That's freaky."

"What's that for?" one of the girls asked kind of sarcastically.

"It's a symbolic gesture to remind me that I have been buried together with Christ that I might rise with him to newness of life. It calls me to live in my baptismal covenant with him."

"Whoa, that's cool," said another kid. "Where does that come from?"

"The Bible," Fr. Ted answered.

"Really!?" A couple other kids replied in unison.

"Yes really. The Apostle Paul reminded the believers in Rome that their baptism into Christ was both participation in his death, as well as in his resurrection. Dipping my fingers into this small basin of water reminds me that when I walk through these doors I'm about to confront the crucified and risen Christ. It puts me on notice. It makes me stop and confirm the covenant in his blood that Christ made with me." Sweeping his hand as if gathering the group within its reach he concluded, "…and with us all."

"Oh wow!" one of the guys exclaimed in an audible whisper, followed by a reverent hush as the kids thought about what they'd just witnessed. A few even dipped their fingers in the bowl and clumsily signed themselves while bowing their heads. Just then the outside doors opened and in walked the Rowlands and Raynors. Immediately behind them came the Meyers. "Looks like a full house," Fr. Ted remarked as he made his way to see them in. "Welcome! I was just about to give the kids a tour of the church. Care to join us?"

"Certainly," Tom Rowland answered for the group.

"Very well," Fr. Ted replied as he made his way to the front of the group. "Fall in with the gang."

Fr. Ted swung open the large doors which groaned as he pressed his hands against them. Inside the vaulted nave, the faint smell of incense and an array of images situated around the room piqued everyone's senses. Eyes roamed the space as Fr. Ted led the group down the center aisle to the front row of pews. There he genuflected before the host and bowed before the altar, a large granite table spread with a green cloth. The kids stopped in their tracks. "Can you explain what you just did, Fr. Ted, and why?" a young lady with pierced nose and short jet black hair asked politely.

"Certainly! When people in the Bible – like Moses for instance – came into the presence of God how did they respond?"

"They fell on their faces!" The girl responded.

"Indeed they did. When I bowed just now, it was because, like them, I had come before his presence and reverent humility was the only proper response."

Without prompting, the kids each bowed or curtseyed before the altar. They seemed to grasp a sense of its sacredness, its place of importance. The images and gestures grabbed their attention, and suddenly they felt themselves swept up into the story as if characters in its plot.

"What's that box?" another girl asked pointing to the golden box situated on the table beneath the iconic image of Jesus.

"That my dear girl is the Host."

"Host?" she inquired again.

"Yes. It's where the pre-consecrated bread representing Jesus' body is kept for communion. It signifies that He is risen and with us, and that he has invited us into his presence."

"It's like everything in here tells his story!" Another of the kids, a boy, exclaimed.

"Exactly," Fr. Ted replied.

"Okay," another kid piped up. "But what's with this statue?" he inquired pointing toward the figure of Mary holding the Christ child. "It's like you guys worship her or something."

"Look real closely at the statue. What is she doing?"

"Holding Jesus out in her arms."

"You're absolutely right," Fr. Ted responded. "You see, whenever Mary shows up in the New Testament she has just one job to do – show us Jesus."

"But don't Catholics kind of like…well…worship her?"

"No, that would be idolatry. We esteem her, though. Do you know why?"

"Probably because she was willing to give up her body to have Jesus," one of the girls answered.

"Yes and even more than that," Fr. Ted offered. "When the angel appeared to her and told her this extraordinary prophecy that she would be the mother of the Messiah, do you recall her response?"

The kids thought for a moment but said nothing. "She said, 'be it unto me according to your word.' Think of it." Looking into the faces of the young women in the group, Fr. Ted asked, "Would you have been willing to risk what Mary risked to obey this radical proclamation?"

"Oh wow, that's really huge!" A girl dressed in a pink sweater with a short skirt covering black leggings responded. "I don't know if I could have done that."

"You see guys; Mary shows us how to obey God and how to trust in her son." Another long hush came over the entire group. The images began to speak to them like all of the stories of the Bible came to life and took shape. One of the kids remarked, "I feel like I'm in the story, like I'm walking with all of these dead people who aren't that dead."

"No kidding," said another.

Fr. Ted walked over to the kid, a young man maybe sixteen, put his arm around him and asked, "Where do you think they are right now?"

"Heaven, I suppose."

"Yes, Heaven. So if they are in Heaven, are they dead or alive?"

"Oh man, I'd not thought about that. T tells us that when we die we have eternal life because of what Jesus did. So, I guess they're alive."

"Quite correct young man. So these dead folks aren't quite that dead after all are they?"

One of the girls, the one with the jet black hair, then walked to the center of the nave, crossed her arms over her heart and said, "I feel His presence. I can worship here."

Others chimed in, "Yeah, me too," they said.

"So, do you still feel creeped out?" Fr. Ted playfully asked.

"No! It's kinda weird or different, but it makes sense."

"Good enough. Let's go pray for James."

*****

Fr. Ted's object lesson wasn't as much about Catholicism as it was about reverence before God, and the awareness that all of Heaven prays for the least and lost. He led the posse, all of its members – including this so to speak lost tribe of pierced and inked youth – to a wing off the left side of the church where they gathered in a warmly paneled, cozy chapel. The sound of creaking wood resonated throughout the room as each person either sat down in the wooden pews or knelt on the rails in front of them.

"Our posse seems to have grown," Fr. Ted said, taking his place behind the small pulpit called an ambo at the front. A soft titter of comfortable laughter swept the room. Adjusting his glasses he opened the thick Bible lying in front of him.

"I'm not going to preach. We are here to pray for James, a young man in deep need of God's mercies, His protection and above all His saving grace."

A quiet "amen" rose from those gathered with him.

"Let's permit Scripture to talk to us. Listen and meditate on these words from our Lord's brother, James. 'But the wisdom from above is first pure, then peaceable, gentle, open to reason, full of mercy and good fruits, without uncertainty or insincerity. And the harvest of righteousness is sown in peace by those who make peace.'" Fr. Ted closed the Bible and rested his crossed arms on it. "I have thought a lot about these words lately, especially in light of James. Where he has been is the very antithesis of the wisdom this James, our Lord's brother, speaks about. I pray these men will meet one day, and that our James will say to the other James, amen."

Once again Fr. Ted crossed himself as he bowed his head. "Father of mercy and peace, you gave us your Son Jesus for our salvation and the salvation of the world. We who have gathered here in this room cry out to you dear Abba, in the Name of your precious Son; save James. Save him now and for all eternity. Keep him safe and heal his wounds, most especially the wounds that have scarred his soul."

Muffled "amen" broke out around the room. Several of the hoodlums wrapped arms around one another, forming a knot of kids whose own scarred memories held images quite like the mess James was in. They were broken, empty and screwed up kids who for the look of it might be mistaken for the unwashed and unredeemed. But redeemed they were. They knew how lost they had been, and their prayers were, if nothing, hearts gushing anxiety over a friend lost as they had been lost, hoping against hope that he might find The Way and join them at the cross.

Don and Kathleen knelt and around them gathered the Rowlands, Raynors, and Terrance who had just been joined by Anne who arrived late. It wasn't long, however, before they were all surrounded by the kids just like at the hospital days earlier. From all appearances the scene had the look of extended family; the kids seeming to feel unison of heart and spirit deprived from their youth but present here, in this place at this moment. And now the entire room became a cacophony of prayer and prayerful sobs.

Fr. Ted remained alone at the pulpit, his arms crossed over the thick Bible. What was to be an hour of prayer turned into two hours, but no one noticed the clock. Heaven touched the room and hearts galvanized in solidarity for one broken human being – James Taylor Meyers. What a scene it was – a place where the Ivy League and the street mingled and embraced, young and not so young, the prim and the pierced, the Body of Christ.

"Tomorrow night?" Fr. Ted asked as the group rose to sing the doxology.

"Yes," the group intoned in unison. He then turned to his friend and asked, "Tom, would you pray a benediction over our time here tonight?"

Tom Rowland smiled, bowed his head and lead the group in prayer, ending with "Blessed Jesus, we pray that James has reached bottom, and that his journey upward to salvation and hope has begun." Hugs and handshakes followed as the group filed out of the church in silence.

FORTY

James awoke and found the book still in his hand. He'd begun reading it before drifting off for the umpteenth time. A yellow pad sat beside him, a few notes hastily scribbled on it. Wiping the bleariness from his eyes he glanced over his jottings. A few stuck out – one struck him forcibly. "The poet only asks to get his head into the heavens. It is the logician who seeks to get the heavens into his head." "Yeah, really," he mused. He thumbed ahead finding an underlined passage Rowland must have liked. This one stopped him short:

> As I read and re-read all the non-Christian or anti-Christian accounts of the faith, from Huxley to Bradlaugh, a slow and awful impression grew gradually but graphically upon my mind – the impression that Christianity must be a most extraordinary thing. (84)

"Huh?" he snorted. Flipping back to where he'd paused before falling asleep he read, "Every remedy is a desperate remedy. Every cure is a miraculous cure. Curing a madman is not arguing with a philosopher; it is casting out a devil." (22) "What devil?" James argued in his mind. The devil himself, or some fiction invented in his own mind that drove him to self-implosion? He shook his head in disgust and confusion.

Just then Terri walked in on him. Seeing his eyebrows knit into a knot she quipped, "What's that grumpy face about?"

"I don't get this guy?"

"What guy?"

James waved the book at her.

"Oh, that guy," Terri replied. "What don't you get?"

"I don't know. He's got an odd way of making his point, but he's hard to argue with."

"Well, maybe Warden Rowland can help you sort it out."

"Maybe," James snorted. "I think he's out to convert me or something."

"Just listen to him, James. Please!" Now Terri's eyebrows knit into a pleading face.

"Okay. I'll listen. Just don't push me."

"I won't. But I'll be…"

"And don't tell me you'll be praying for me."

"No problem, grumpy. I'll just do it and not tell you."

That bit of humor broke the tension. As he looked into Terri's face, James felt a strange, somewhat welcome yet uncomfortable sensation well up. "You know, Terri…I'm going to miss you when I leave here. You've been kinda…well… a friend. Thanks."

Terri almost blushed. "Wow! I didn't expect to hear that from you." She grinned, "I kind of figured you took me more for a pest or airhead or something."

"At first," James remarked.

"But not now, huh?"

"Nah. Not now. You've been…well…somebody I think I could trust."

Terri smiled at her new, unexpected patient-friend. "Well, for what it's worth, James, I'll miss you too."

"Oh?"

"Yeah…not sure why, though," she playfully chided with a coy wink.

"I'm sure," he mocked. "Maybe, somehow, we can stay in touch," James offered.

"Yeah, maybe. I'd like that," Terri smiled.

"Hey," she said glancing at her watch in part to break the awkwardness she felt. "I've got other patients to see. Catch ya in few!"

"Sure. See you later."

*****

Father Ted spied Terri leaving James' room.

"Just a moment, nurse."

Terri turned around to see the cardigan clad priest in his usual black shirt and stiff white collar striding toward her, "You talking to me, Father?"

"I am. How's our patient?" he inquired pointing at James' door.

"Pretty good, really. I think he's going home…er' back to…" Her voice trailed off.

"I gotcha. Back to the State House."

"Yeah."

"When?"

"Probably this afternoon. At least that's what I heard last night."

"Ah, I see," Fr. Ted said as he reached for the door handle.

"Just a minute, Father. Can I ask you something…privately?"

"Of course," Fr. Ted replied, stepping away from the door.

Terri took him by the arm and walked him over to a small lounge area.

"What's on your mind young lady?" Fr. Ted asked cocking his head in curiosity.

"Uh, I really don't know how to put it. Kind of awkward. I'm a nurse not a nun. So…"

Fr. Ted couldn't resist a chuckle.

Terri made another clumsy attempt to say what was on her mind. Fr. Ted broke in.

170

"I take it you've exceeded your duties as a nurse and snuck into mine as a chaplain. Would that be a fair guess?"

"Kinda, I suppose. Something like that," Terri replied rocking gracelessly on her feet. "It's just, Father, that I felt God nudge me and I said a few things to James that I hope were okay."

"Like what, my girl?" The concerned priest inquired.

"Like I was praying for him. You know, like, well, the only way James is really going to find help is if he finds God."

"Oh my dear young lady, you did jump into the deep end."

"Did I mess up?" Terri asked anxiously, fearing she had screwed up an important moment.

Fr. Ted broke into a broad embracing smile as he placed a hand on Terri's arm. "No, not at all! Not at all, indeed!" He paused, "You couldn't have said anything more appropriate! Proud of you! Well done!"

Terri let out a huge sigh of relief. "Oh, Father, you don't know how glad I am to hear that. Thank you. But, hey, how'd you know my name?"

"Your name tag. It says, Terri. That is your name I presume?"

"Ha…yeah…sorry," she said with a silly grin on her face. "So I didn't mess up?"

"No dear, Terri, far, far from messing up; you did a truly great thing. In fact, you've joined a special club."

"Really! What club?"

"A growing group of people praying for James."

"You're kidding. I'm part of a real God-thing?"

At that Fr. Ted roared with laughter. "Yes, my dear, you are part of a real, honest to goodness conspiracy of hope – a real God-thing!" he affirmed, rising on his toes and leaning toward her to emphasize the seriousness of the occasion. "I want you to keep praying for our friend. And," he emphasized, "I want you to keep talking to him. Will you?"

"Sure! I'll definitely keep praying," she hesitated. "And talking as long as he wants to talk."

"I know he can be a bit snarly. But it's not because he dislikes you or any of us. He's frightened, Terri. He needs true friends."

"Okay, I'll try to remember that – especially when he snarls at me."

Fr. Ted broke into laughter again. "You do that, my dear. Always remember it cost God a lot to give us Jesus. It costs us something to hand him to others."

"Oh, wow!" Terri exclaimed in a near whisper. "That is so cool! I needed to hear it that way."

"When James snarls, remember what I said."

"I will, Father! I definitely will!"

"We'll chat again," Fr. Ted said with his hand still on Terri's arm, that typical broad smile assuring her of his approval.

"I so hope so, Father. Thank you!" Terri started to dash off to her next patient but stopped in her tracks, spun around and gave Fr. Ted a warm hug. "I needed you today! Thanks for stopping me!"

Laughing, Fr. Ted concluded the conversation. "My dear, Terri, I needed you too. We make a fine team. Someday our boy will thank us."

With that Terri's face brightened as she headed off on her rounds.

*****

Fr. Ted was still laughing to himself as he entered the room. Finding James deep in thought, he let slip a quiet cough to get his attention.

"Yeah, hi Father. I didn't hear you come in."

"I see you've been doing your homework," Fr. Ted interjected pointing to the book and pad as he walked up beside James' bed.

"I suppose. At least when I can stay awake I am."

"Looks like you've been taking notes, too."

"Yeah, this dude is really deep," thumping the book with his left hand. "He's kinda got my head spinning. Not sure about some of this stuff."

"I totally understand. Chesterton's made a lot of people think, me included." Fr. Ted remarked. "Say, do you mind if I sit in on your book discussions with Warden Rowland?"

"No, not at all. That would be fine with me if it's fine with him."

"Good. I will."

"So you've read this before?" James followed inquisitively.

"I have – a few times. Every time I read it I find something new, something that causes me to go a little deeper in my own introspection."

"So, I'm not as lost as I feel then?"

Again the affable priest chortled. "Not hardly, James! You're in good company. A lot of folks squint hard at Chesterton. I'm sure you're bumping into some strange sounding stuff, but hang in there. It'll start making sense."

"No joking, it sounds strange!" With that James flipped his note pad to the quotes he'd written. "I have some questions about some of this stuff," he said running a hand through his unkempt hair. "But not now; I'm too wrung out."

"Not to worry, James. We'll get to your questions later. Tell me, though, how are you feeling about things?"

James dropped his head and heaved a long sigh. "I'm still really scared, Father." He drew another deep breath, "I really don't know what to expect...mostly scared." Looking into Father Ted's face he said mournfully, "Father, I really don't want to go back."

"You mean to prison?"

"Yah...prison."

"Alright, I get that." Father Ted said thoughtfully. "Hey, look, would you like me to meet you back at the State House when they transport you later today?"

Tilting his head to the side unsure of what he heard, "You would do that?"

"Sure."

"That would be great, Father. I would like that…I would like that a lot."

"Okay, I'll get the details and plan to be there when you arrive." He wheeled around to leave but stopped and looked back at James. That typical mischievous expression came across his face. "By the way, young man, I think that cute young nurse has taken a liking to you."

"Wha…Terri!? Oh Father, give it rest! You've got to be joking! Don't you think you're kind of poking your nose in the wrong place?"

"Oh, not at all. I specialize in meddling. It's a priest thing."

"Oh man! Even if I liked her, do you honestly think she'd fall for a con? Besides she's kind of a…well…air head?"

"Au contraire my son! She's cute and got more on the ball than you think. Besides, don't rule her out of your picture, not at least as a friend."

"No, I get that. She's already a friend. But not a…"

"Girl friend," Fr. Ted finished James' thought for him with a wink.

"Yah, girlfriend. Now will you leave it alone?"

"I'm just saying, James, I've seen stranger things in my lifetime. Furthermore, dear young man, she might be a piece to the puzzle of your life. Someday you'll be an *ex-con*, with a new start. Don't throw yourself under the bus kid and think your life's a washout. No! Don't do that! You have a future."

A long silence ensued. James surveyed the priest's face, realizing he wasn't joking any more. "A future?" he thought mockingly in his mind. "These guys think I have a future," referring to the posse though he knew them only as warden, priest, preacher and ex-alcoholic. But then the doctor and this perky little nurse; they all put the thought of a future in this troubled you man's head too.

Staring at Fr. Ted in puzzlement, James remarked, "Huh, what kind of future?"

"Well, son, as I've suggested before, that's a great question to ask Terrance someday. He made a bigger mess of himself than you have. And from where I stand, he's done quite well. For that matter Scanlon would be a good guy to consult, too. Look, James, I wouldn't blow smoke up your pant leg. You're an intelligent young man. Like I said before, if you've got the guts to face your failures and turn them around, you've got a future."

"That's quite a load, sir."

"Think about it."

"I will. I promise, I will."

Fr. Ted stuck out his hand. James took it. "See you in awhile, kid."

"Yes sir," James replied with a polite nod.

FORTY-ONE

Rowland slipped into the back row of the conference room, a sparsely furnished, fluorescent lit, windowless square. A few youngish legal aides occupied the seats in front of him, each one pouring over documents members of the panel would likely demand. So busily consumed with their work, none of them seemed the least distracted by the warden's presence. Neither had Judge Parker noticed Rowland's entrance; instead appeared to be sternly instructing one of his aides in some manner of protocol. Rowland couldn't make out what they were saying. No matter – it would come to light once proceedings began. It wasn't immediately clear if anyone seated in the gallery around him were potential witnesses Parker and the panel might call to give testimony. That intrigued Rowland. Who would be called? Meanwhile panel members began taking their place behind placards bearing their names and titles. Besides Parker it appeared two other jurists had been empanelled, a Mr. L. Hinson, esq., and a Ms. M. Kesten, appellate court judge, neither of whom Rowland recognized; possibly lawyers from out of state. The two other panel members included an official from the State Attorney General's office, and one State House administrator, Harold Raynor. Raynor's inclusion surprised Rowland. For obvious reasons, his head guard couldn't self-identify without breaching strict rules of conduct pertaining to panel confidentiality. Their eyes never met.

Suddenly the door swung shut and two armed policeman stood guard immediately outside them. Parker turned his attention to a docket passed to him by an aid sitting directly behind him. From where he sat, Rowland could plainly see over Parker's shoulder but couldn't make out what was written on any of the documents. Curiously, Parker seemed distracted by what he read. He paged through the items as if looking for something. He turned to an aide who flipped through a large file case before pulling a sheet of paper from it and handing it to Parker. Nodding his head, Parker laid the sheet atop the others, straightened himself and addressed his colleagues.

"The Inquiry pertaining to the death of Nathaniel Richard Chalmers is now in session." Avoiding pleasantries, Judge Parker cut to the chase. "We have the unenviable task of identifying Mr. Chalmers' assailant and remanding him for prosecution. While we have been presented with suspects who either had motive, opportunity and intent, evidence suggests we have no one person with all three. Those with opportunity apparently lacked either motive or intent. And those with motive and/or intent appear to have not had opportunity. That leaves us, it seems, with the task of identifying who might have been either bribed or coerced into this act and why. Our primary subject, an inmate, James Taylor Myers, while having opportunity seems to have had no plausible cause to stab Chalmers. Moreover, the murder weapon has revealed that Mr. Myers never had it in his possession. It bears neither his fingerprints nor DNA. The only evidence of DNA matching that of Mr. Myers was found on Chalmers clothing where, it appears, Mr. Myers had grabbed the victim in order to move him out of the way of prisoners entering from the yard." Parker paused, lifting the single sheet just handed him from the stack of papers in front of him. "This form just handed me clarifies that matter." Laying it aside, Parker continued, "Nonetheless, Myers was named by several alleged eyewitnesses as the person who inflicted the fatal wound. While the credibility of these witnesses presents challenges, our obligation as I see it is to verify either their veracity or its lack with respect to this matter. Given the evidence as we have it, it is my belief that while Mr. Myers is likely innocent of the stabbing death of Nate Chalmers, he represents a key if not vital witness."

Rowland could scarcely believe what he heard. Parker's opening statement all but exonerated James. Where to from here, he wondered? Right then his phone vibrated. A text message read, "James will be here in one hour." It was Fr. Ted announcing the kid's return to the State House. Rowland of course knew he could say nothing.

"Mr. Warden, I didn't realize you'd entered the room."

Rowland looked up to see Parker staring at him. "I did, Judge Parker, moments before you opened the inquiry."

"I see," Parker replied. "You know, however, that nothing you heard can be repeated outside this room." Parker seemed to know Rowland would avoid breaching confidentiality or tainting the inquiry, but was compelled just the same to advise him.

"Yes, of course," Rowland answered.

"Good. Will you be staying?"

Rowland took Parker's question as a hint to leave, which he did immediately and without further comment. His emotions raced but his mind raced faster. What recourse did he have but to divulge what he'd just heard to the posse or to Anne? None! He needn't bother with that for the moment, despite every urge to announce the good news. Instead he strode back to his office. Betty couldn't help noticing the broad smile on Rowland's face as he entered the office suite. "Good news or just a cheery mood, Mr. Rowland?"

"Both!" He announced as he dashed inside his own office. He didn't disguise his joy but withheld jubilation. Pacing in front of his desk, he prayed quietly and intensely, at times lifting his arms toward heaven. The staid scholar of jurisprudence, the tough prison warden was overcome by this almost too-good-to-be- true news. The kid caught the break the posse, the family and the entire range of James' supporters had hoped he'd catch. God was to be praised!

Betty buzzed the intercom. "Fr. Ted is here to see you."

"Send him in, Betty."

176

The door opened and in stepped the grinning priest-friend. "It's a good day," he announced knowing nothing of Rowland's discovery.

"It is indeed, my friend," Rowland replied taking a seat on the sofa. "Sit down, Ted. What's got you in such fine fiddle today?"

"That's a rather arcane greeting don't you think?" Fr. Ted chuckled as he took a seat.

"I suppose it is. It was the best I could come up with. So, again, what brings you by in such good spirits?"

"You know, Tom, I'm not sure. I just have the silly hunch that our kid is in a good place…a very good place, even with all the junk he's endured lately."

"Really!"

"Yes! I just have this curious sense that God has wrapped our boy in his arms. That's it! That's the best I can do!"

Though deeply conflicted, Rowland nonetheless withheld what he so badly ached to divulge. But how could he deny the obvious? Prayers had been heard. God was stirred to answer.

Gathering himself, Rowland asked, "I get the same feeling, Ted. Isn't it ironic?"

"What's that?"

"Prison – this place of all places."

"You mean, who finds salvation in a prison?"

"Yes, exactly."

"We've seen it happen before, Tom. We watched Terrance hit bottom in this place and dramatically change. Why shouldn't we believe it for James?"

"Wisdom, my friend. You are full of it."

"Better wisdom than some other stuff I can think of."

Rowland grumbled, "For a priest, you're utterly incorrigible!"

"I'll accept that as a compliment. What's really on my mind is James' return to the State House later this afternoon. I told him I'd meet him here."

"Good. Anything else?"

"Yes. I've asked Terrance to join me. As my associate, I didn't think this would be out of line."

"No, not at all; I like the idea." Rowland confidently affirmed.

"What's on your mind, Tom? You have the look of someone about to ask a favor."

"I am going to ask a favor." Rowland agreed. "I would like it if you joined me for the book sessions with James."

"Oddly, I asked James if he'd be open to that very idea."

"Oh?"

"Yeah! He agreed."

"Another God thing?"

"Maybe so. I'm beginning to think this whole ordeal has been…and is…a God thing."

Both men sat quietly for a few moments as if caught up in thought.

"Tom, I never felt so certain of anything in my priestly life."

"Certain of what, Ted?" Rowland inquired.

"It's been hell for the kid – literally hell. But for the life of me, I feel as if heaven is about to break through for him." Fr. Ted clenched his teeth and shook his head. "Tom, I just feel it!"

Rowland's heart raced. If only his friend knew. "I'm inclined to believe you're right, my friend. I'm inclined to believe you're right."

"Tom, let's pray."

FORTY-TWO

"Hi there!" a timid voice chimed from behind the door. About then a lovely face appeared.

"Oh hi Terri," James replied. "C'mon in."

Terri slipped in; hands stuffed in her pants pockets and smiling from ear to ear. "Guess what?" she asked.

James sat a little straighter, "I have no clue."

"I'm riding with you to the State House this afternoon."

"You are!?" James exclaimed in disbelief. "How'd that happen?"

"Well, your doctor agreed that it would be a good idea if a nurse went with you. And…well…I'm a nurse."

"The doctor agreed? Agreed with who?"

"You mean with whom."

"Okay, with whom?" James repeated mockingly.

"With me," Terri chirped.

"You're kidding!"

"Nope! I'm not kidding. That alright?"

"I guess so."

"You *guess* so? Would you prefer I didn't go?"

"Oh no, I didn't mean it that way. Yeah, sure, I'd like it if you went. I'm just kinda surprised."

"Why?"

"What do you mean why? Who wants to go to prison? I don't get it."

"Well, it doesn't really matter. I just thought you could use a friend. You know; someone who's in your corner."

"Oh! Wow! I don't know what to say. Thanks!" To say James felt somewhat awkward masks just how awkward he felt. But he couldn't deny it would be good to have a friendly face with him in the ambulance.

"You know Fr. Ted plans to meet me at the prison?" James announced.

"That's great! I really like that guy. He's the best."

"I'm beginning to think so too. Honestly, Terri…" James' voice trailed off. He looked away for an instant unsure if he wanted to say what was on his mind.

"Honestly what, James? Tell me! Please!"

"It's weird, man. It's really weird."

"What's weird?" Terri waited but James said nothing. She poked him on the shoulder, "Can I make a guess?"

"Sure. Okay. Go ahead."

"Maybe it feels weird because…well…you haven't had people care about you before now."

"Suppose. But it still feels weird."

"Why? Because you're afraid they might ditch you or something?"

"Yeah. Maybe. It's been the habit."

"Look, I know the feeling. I truly do. But I don't think Fr. Ted's faking it. I think the man feels your pain like it was his own." She paused, "And so do I."

Terri's aside jolted James. He looked up into her eyes. He could see she wasn't kidding. Even more, there was something about her words and how she said them, as well as the look etched on her face that made him realize she had a story too. "What do you mean? How would you possibly know about my pain?" he asked indignantly.

"Well, you're not the only one in this conversation to have gone through hell."

"Okay, I'm listening."

Terri sighed, "It's my story and kinda personal."

"Look, I won't put you down or treat you like a loser. I'd really like to know."

"Well, maybe another time. I'm just not sure..." Terri's voice dropped and she started to walk away.

"Hey, don't leave me hanging," James pried. He softened his tone, "Like I said; I'd like to know."

Terri turned and looked at James. It'd been awhile since she divulged her grimy past. Did she really want to tell him? Would he get it? Even though he said he wouldn't look down on her, she wondered how he could possibly respect her if she gave away her dirty little secret that wasn't so little.

"Look Terri, my life's a mess. I'm a prisoner but you don't seem to hold that over me." He squeezed his lips together unsure of what next to say. Finding his words he said, "For what it's worth, you've treated me like a real person and not like a scumbag. Trust me, I won't treat you that way either."

"Good; I'm glad you feel that way. And for what it's worth, I don't think of you as a scumbag. But what does that have to do with me...my mess?"

"Maybe nothing. But maybe your story will help me with mine."

"I don't know, James." Terri played it close to the vest. Could she disclose the ugliness of her past to a guy who only a couple days ago was a perfect stranger?

"Can it be that bad? You're a nurse." James pleaded. "You don't get to be one of those if your life's a screw up."

"I haven't always been a nurse," she replied.

"So?"

"I don't know." Terri folded her arms snugly around her, rocked awkwardly on her feet while staring up at the ceiling. James waited but Terri offered nothing. He could tell there was a dark hole inside her she didn't want to dig up.

"Look, if it's too painful, I won't pry. But just so you know, you've become…well, like a, you know." James felt his face flush. Suddenly he was embarrassed.

"Like what?" she asked curiously.

"Like a friend," he blurted. "I haven't had many of them."

"Honestly?" Terri sheepishly replied.

"Yes. Honestly."

"Wow! Thanks! That makes me feel good," she said, as a narrow smile spread across her face. "I want to be a friend. I didn't have many either." James' kind words disarmed her a little. She studied his face as if searching for a sign. "You really want to know about my stuff?"

"I do. It matters."

Terri closed her eyes, letting out a deep sigh, "Okay, I'll tell you." She ran a hand across her face, "I didn't have the best of childhoods," she began. "My dad beat my mom…and me. Then he left us." Her shoulders heaved, "When I got a little older I ran away. And then a boy in high school I thought loved me got me pregnant and then he split." She bit hard on her lip, "By then I felt so alone, so rejected." She hesitated unsure if she wanted to say more.

"Go on."

Terri drew a breath, "Scared, I did something…" She paused again. Covering her face with her hand she began sobbing. James looked intently into Terri's anguished face, and felt something he had not felt for a very long time, maybe ever. He felt compassion. He felt it for a person who in the moment was as needy, as broken and as despairing as him. Unthinkingly, almost involuntarily he reached from his bed and placed a hand on Terri's arm. "Go ahead, Terri."

Terri gathered herself, "I'm so ashamed, James. It feels like yesterday." Again she wiped a sleeve across her face; tears streaming like rivers fell onto her scrubs. "I aborted my baby." She broke down and sobbed inconsolably. James kept his hand gently resting reassuringly on her arm. Suddenly his world didn't seem so dark. In the shock of Terri's admission, he felt an odd if not profane solidarity with this nurse. In that instant, she stopped being one of them, the people on the outside sneering condescendingly on him for his failure. She was like him – broken, and in need of a friend. Terri laid her hand on James' hand. "I haven't told that to anyone outside of my church family. I'd like you to keep it between us for now. Please."

"You have my word."

"Thank you," Terri said in a whisper. "Thank you."

For a solitary moment neither of them spoke a word. Terri stood staring at the floor, her hand poised on James' hand. James kept his eyes on his friend, studying her expression, uncertain of what to say or do. It hadn't occurred to him that the roles had flipped; he assuming the role of consoler and confidant.

"Terri?"

She looked through tears into his face, "Yeah?"

"I'm sorry. I truly am."

Terri nodded and choked out, "Thanks. It means a lot." Dropping her head she asked, "Are you ashamed of me, James?"

James paused before answering, "No. No I'm not. How can I be? I'm in prison."

"Yeah, well, so was I."

"Prison?" James asked uncertain about what she meant.

"Oh not prison with bars and guards and that stuff, but prison just the same." She drew another breath, "I hated myself, James. I hated myself so badly I tried to kill myself. I felt so trapped in a…I don't know…a very dark place. I felt," she winced as if in pain, "I felt nothing…no hope, no love. I felt dead." She looked searchingly at James, "Does that make any sense?"

James nodded silently, "It does. It makes sense. I feel like that a lot." He pondered his thoughts a moment. "But you seem to have gotten turned around. You don't seem to be that person anymore."

"I'm not, James. I'm not that person anymore."

"What happened? Can you tell me?" In Terri's confession James witnessed a profound contradiction. He'd just witnessed a young woman relive the painful events of a desperate existence, but was this the perky, pesky nurse who seemed so vibrantly full of life when she burst into his universe? Which Terri was she? What changed? And how?

Terri shifted on her feet, "I guess you could say I hit bottom. After the abortion I just wanted to disappear. I felt so dirty, so…guilty."

"And then what?" James gently coaxed.

"That's the weird part. I'd just finished nursing school and started working here." Terri smirked, "On the neo-natal ward of all places." She continued, "I was assisting a couple who'd just had their first child, a baby boy. He'd had a tough go at first and spent quite awhile in NICU. I watched these young parents literally beg for that baby's life. I'd see the dad in the chapel bent over in his seat crying to God. At that time I was pretty jaded about the idea of God. But watching him…well, I'd never seen anybody call out to God like that. When she was up to it, his wife joined him. They'd sit for the longest time just holding hands and praying." Terri looked intently at James, "I'd never seen anything like it. I'd never seen love like that…ever! And I wanted it! I wanted it really bad!" She raised her eyebrows in wistful arc, "I'd have traded places with that baby to be loved like they loved him."

James remained silent, pondering Terri's words. But something stirred inside his soul unlike anything he'd ever felt before. What it was he could not describe. But in Terri's story as well as in the truth of her eyes he realized there was more.

Terri looked at James, "Do you want me to continue?"

"Yes. Please go on."

"Well, I don't know really what I was thinking, but I found myself inside the little chapel one afternoon on my break. I just sat in one of the seats staring at the cross hanging on the wall in front of me and thinking about this young couple and their baby. And oh, James, they were so young…my age." Terri took a tissue from her pocket and wiped her eyes. "Okay, well, I hadn't gone to church before. I didn't know what to think. That figure of Jesus hanging on the cross really got to me. Why was he there, I wondered?" She paused as if reliving the scene in her mind. "About then another nurse walked in, my charge nurse. She saw me sitting there, and saw tears in my eyes. 'Terri,' she asked. 'Is something wrong?' I couldn't speak and just nodded. She then asked me if she could help. I didn't know what to tell her, I was so confused. But I couldn't hold it in any longer. It was like the dam broke. Without thinking I began spilling the whole story to her…the whole thing."

"About your abortion, too?"

"Yes…that too."

"What did she do?"

"That's what's so amazing. She sat down beside me and listened. She never once condemned me. What she did next was the most compassionate thing anyone ever did. She put her arm around me like I was her daughter or something and just held me. I sobbed like a baby. I'd never felt so secure, so accepted…ever. She held me for the longest time and let me cry."

"Did she say anything else to you?"

"She did. After I stopped crying, she told me that God was my Heavenly Father who understood my needs even better than I did. She then pointed at the cross with Jesus hanging on it and said, 'That's why he sent him.' What's funny, she said it with such love it didn't sound at all like preaching. It sounded like hope. And I needed a bunch of that. Boy did I need it. Then she asked if she could pray for me. I didn't know what to say so I said alright. I can't ever remember praying, not ever. I don't think I ever heard anyone pray before then. But when she prayed it was like she really, truly knew God; like they were friends or something. I just felt warmth." Terri could see that her story had affected James. His eyes clouded and his chin quivered.

"Have you ever felt like that, you know, warmth?" she asked him.

James slowly shook his head, "No. No I haven't."

"I'm so sorry."

"Yeah, well, that's okay." James wanted to hear more. "Did she just leave you then? I mean after praying for you?"

"No, she asked if I'd like to know Jesus. I had no idea what she meant. So she explained what it meant to ask Jesus to forgive me of my sins and let him come into my life."

"Did you?" James inquired.

"Not then. I couldn't get this forgiveness thing. How could God forgive me for killing my baby? I couldn't forgive me. How could he?"

"Well, something happened. What was it?"

"She asked if I'd like to join a nurses Bible study so I could learn more. I had no idea that nurses got together to do such a thing. I had nothing to lose by going so I said sure. And I went."

"What was it like?"

"At first it felt strange. I felt really awkward, like I stuck out. But they…the other nurses…never treated me like that. They took me in like I was one of them. I think that's what began to make it easy for me. They didn't care about my past; at least they didn't act like it. They were just glad I was with them. It's kinda like how Fr. Ted treats you. You know?"

"Yeah, like a friend."

"Right! Like a friend. That's how these nurses treated me. Some were my age and others were like my mom's age. I didn't have a Bible so they gave me one. They all chipped in and gave me a Bible of my own on my second visit, and each one of them signed it. They showed me how to use it. No one made fun of my stupid clumsiness. They just helped me. After awhile I felt comfortable to ask questions. They let me doubt God. They let me get stuff off my chest." A warm smile spread across Terri's face, "And then one day it all came together. We were praying like we always did at the end of our study. It was always a special time. I could close my eyes when they closed theirs and very quietly mumble a few words toward God. I'd never done that before. But it seemed like the thing to do. And the funny thing is; I truly began to think he was listening. That must have been when it happened."

"When what happened?" James' curiosity was piqued.

"When it all spilled out. During our prayer time one day, I suddenly broke down. All of a sudden I felt this strange thing deep inside. The nurses told me it was the Holy Spirit speaking to me. They said he was convicting me of my sins. If he was convicting me it sure felt like love. It was powerful. I really can't describe it." Terri looked away as if lost in a dream, "I still can't explain it." She shook her head as if coming out of the dream and continued, "One of the nurses noticed me crying. She asked if she could help. Pretty soon other nurses came over. They all put their arms around me or their hands on me. I just began blurting out stuff to God like I was throwing up in his hands. I told him everything. And then I asked if he'd please forgive me." Terri's voice grew soft, "Oh James, I cannot even say what happened.

But I knew I was different and it felt good. The nurses said I was saved. Honestly, that's what it felt like. It felt like I had been rescued. I didn't feel dirty anymore. I didn't feel dead. I never felt so alive."

James listened intently but privately cynicism nagged him. Could it be that simple? But how could he deny Terri's story? The evidence of change was too obvious. If it was true, wasn't this the sort of thing he needed? But *God*? Did it all have to come down to God? He chafed at the idea. Couldn't there be another plausible way; one that didn't lead to the God topic? The thorny thing about Terri's story, though, was the undeniable change in her life; a change she credited to God, a personal God of love not vengeance or condemnation. It seemed so terribly real – so irrefutably, terribly real. And it was staring him in the face…literally.

James broke his train of thought to ask, "Do you still meet with the nurses?"

"Every week. They've helped me so much. They're like my sisters…and moms."

Sisters and moms – James could accept the family thing. After all, they birthed his new friend into a new life. But could he accept it for himself, especially if it led to God?

FORTY-THREE

James had been back at the State House less than a week when Rowland summoned him to his office. Still quite weak and colorless, he needed assistance to make the long trek from the infirmary where he was recuperating. A guard helped him into a wheelchair, but James insisted on pushing it himself, grasping the wheels, stroking them forward, while the guard followed a step behind. Despite his stubborn determination, each stroke sapped him of energy, and it wasn't long before was out of gas so to speak. The guard noticed James breaking into a sweat. "Here," he said, "let me do the driving." James couldn't avoid the assistance anymore than he could avoid feeling vulnerable. The guard noticed his anxiety. "Worried, kid?" he asked.

"Yeah, a little," James replied.

"I've got your back."

James looked up behind him. The guard's eyes were straight ahead as he relentlessly strode down the hall as if tasked with guarding James' life more than enforcing prison protocol.

Betty heard them pull up and went to open the door. "Welcome, James. I hope you're feeling better."

"Thank you, ma'am. I am."

Just then Rowland's door opened, the one into his private office, and out stepped Fr. Ted grinning like he'd eaten the canary. "Hey, where's your friend?"

"What do you mean?" James answered.

"You know what – and who – I mean," Fr. Ted retorted giving Betty a wink.

"You mean Terri?"

"Who else!"

"Oh man!" James groaned and buried his head in his hands.

Both Fr. Ted and Betty laughed. "So are you going to tell me who this person is, James? Or am I going to have to get it from Father Ted?" Betty playfully prodded.

"She's a nurse…a nurse from the hospital."

"That's all?" Betty pressed. Fr. Ted was enjoying the scene.

"That's all. Just a nurse who…"

"Who spent a lot of time with one patient," Fr. Ted humorously interjected, playfully poking James on the shoulder. By now even the guard was smiling.

"Can we get this over with?" James snarked.

Rowland appeared in the doorway. "What's this I hear about a nurse?"

"You too?" James recoiled. "Can I just go back to the infirmary?" The room erupted in laughter.

"For what it's worth young man," Betty began in a motherly tone. "A friend is not something to be ashamed of."

"Yes, ma'am," James consented.

"Especially one who'll hold your hand while riding with you in the ambulance," Fr. Ted chimed. Again laughter broke out at James' expense.

"I think I'd rather spend a week in the hole than put up with this." James snorted indignantly. But down deep, beneath the façade he was throwing up for the jokesters, the kid was enjoying the inferences. Terri had held his hand in the ambulance. She held his hand as the guards escorted him down the hall to the infirmary in a wheel chair. And she gave him a sweet hug before leaving to return to the hospital. All the while, the wily old priest was absorbing the details.

Before Terri jumped into the ambulance for the ride back to the hospital, Fr. Ted caught up to her. "Terri," he shouted. "Just a minute."

"Hi Fr. Ted!" she beamed. "Are you riding with us?"

"No, no, I'm not," he answered breathlessly after nearly sprinting to catch up before the ambulance pulled away from the prison. "But I did want to see you a moment before you left."

"Oh? What's up?" Terri asked with more than a hint of curiosity in her voice.

"You know young lady; you've made an impression on James. I just want you to know I'm grateful. We are all grateful!"

"I did?" Terri replied in surprise.

"You certainly did. You must have taken our little chat to heart."

"Wow! Thank you, Father. And yes I did! You really helped me sort it all out. It really, really helped!" Terri cocked her head, "But you said we. Who's we?"

"The posse...and others."

"I'm confused," Terri said with a shake of her head.

Fr. Ted chuckled, "It's quite a story my dear. But the long and the short of it is we're a group of four men out to help young men like James get a fresh start."

"That's so cool! So that's why you're hanging around James then?"

That description threw Fr. Ted into a fit of joyous laughter. "Yes it is! Well put! And you, dear nurse Terri, fit in so perfectly."

"I do?" Terri's eyebrows rose inquisitively.

"Indeed you do! James needs a friend and from my observations you've been that friend. He let me in on a little of your conversation. Not to worry though! He was very discrete. He protected your confidence. But let me say, you've made him think." Fr. Ted placed a fatherly hand on Terri's arm, "Young lady, I've never been prouder of someone than I am of you."

"Really?!" Terri shrieked, immediately clapping a hand over her mouth to stifle her outburst. Peeking around the ambulance to see if she disturbed anyone she whispered, "Sorry! Got excited!"

"Well," Fr. Ted replied in a whisper, "would you like to be a member of the group?"

Terri's eyes widened with excitement, "Are you kidding? I could be a member of the posse?"

"Well of course you could," Fr. Ted answered with gravitas in his voice. "You reached into the soul of a young man who truly believed he had no soul. You exposed his cynicism and confronted his anger. Mostly, you showed him Jesus. Bravo, young lady! Bravo!"

"I had no idea," Terri exclaimed. "All I did was tell him my story."

"Yes, but your story may very well have cracked open his soul to the possibility that he can have a new story."

"Oh, I hope so, Father Ted. I really, truly hope so."

"So do I, and the other people praying for James."

"Others? You mean there's more posse than the posse you mentioned?" Terri was all ears. She could feel anticipation that something wonderful might be brewing.

"It was intended for *the* posse, the four guys, but it has grown to include their wives, the head guard at the prison and his wife, and young people like you who attend the Worship Café downtown."

"You're kidding!" Terri shrieked again, and again clapped her hands over her mouth. "I used to attend that place."

"Well then my dear girl, how would you like to join us at my parish tonight to pray for your new friend?"

"Seriously! I'd love it!" Terri's enthusiasm spilled out like she'd been asked to the prom.

"Then I'll expect to see you at seven sharp," a very pleased Fr. Ted said with a gleam in his eyes.

"I'll be there! Your parish? I know where it is. Yes, I'll be there! Count on me!" Terri could barely contain herself. "This is so exciting!" With that she jumped into the back of the ambulance.

Fr. Ted was still relishing this conversation as he ribbed James in front of the others. Rowland's impertinence simply spiced the moment.

As Rowland stepped aside, the guard wheeled James into the carpeted office, and Fr. Ted followed close behind – still amused. Rowland politely dismissed the guard, sat down in his usual spot on the sofa with Fr. Ted plunked down beside him. James remained in the wheel chair across from them.

"I see you have the book with you," Rowland said pointing at the worn paperback resting on James' lap.

"Yes, sir, I do."

"With all you've been through, I don't imagine you've had much time to read it," Rowland offered though hoping to be proven wrong.

"Actually I have been reading, sir, at least when I could stay awake."

"So it bores you?" Fr. Ted quipped with a smirk.

"No, it doesn't bore me at all. Actually, I'm kind of intrigued by some parts. It's just I've not been very with it."

"Understood," Rowland remarked. "James," he continued, "I just received a phone call I'm certain you'll be interested in. That's part of the reason I summoned you."

James could tell by Rowland's tone that it was something quite important. He felt edgy, wondering what else could go wrong. "A phone call?"

"It was from Judge Parker who's presiding at the Inquiry."

The Inquiry! James' spirits sagged. He felt his stomach wedge in his throat. He'd hoped – falsely – this mess would go away. He gripped the arms of the wheel chair wondering, what next? "Another bomb?"

"Actually, James, to the contrary. This time I have good news...very good news."

James remained cool but anticipation was rising. He said nothing. Just sat waiting for the shoe to fall.

"You've been cleared of any and all responsibility for Nate Chalmers' death. You're free of all charges." Rowland waited for James to respond. But for one long moment, James only stared back at Rowland as if in shock, as if he hadn't heard a word Rowland said.

"Did you hear me James? You're free of all charges and suspicion. You're not guilty."

"Not guilty?" James echoed as if unsure of what he had heard. The words sounded so foreign he was certain they weren't meant for him.

"If the Warden says you're not guilty, young man, well, you're not guilty," Fr. Ted clarified with a broad smile widening his beard.

"I don't know what to say," James said with a look of stunned disbelief etched into his face.

"How about whew, glad it's over!" Fr. Ted joked.

James never broke a smile, never twitched a muscle, afraid that if he did he might wake from a dream only to find what he'd heard was only a dream. The longer he sat motionless, the more Rowland's words enlarged in his mind.

"If I can ask, sir, how'd the judge decide I was innocent?" James asked timidly.

"There simply was no hard evidence that corroborated the accusations brought against you," Rowland stated with a dismissive wave of his hand. "The weapon had no traces of your fingerprints on it. What DNA matches that were found came from blood splattered on your shoes and pants, but none from the weapon. And…" Rowland paused, "a couple inmates stepped forward in your defense."

"Someone stood up for me?" Again James was struck incredulous. "Who? Who were these guys?"

"Their identities are going to have to remain anonymous, at least for now," Rowland stated. "The Inquiry is still in session. No information will be available until it concludes."

"You still look stunned," Fr. Ted remarked.

"I am, sir. That's exactly what I am." James shook his head.

"Something wrong?" Rowland asked.

James hesitated, "No. No, nothing's wrong. I just can't believe I'm free." He shook his head again, "I can't believe anybody stood up for me. Can't remember when that ever happened?"

"You mean you can't ever remember anyone taking your side?" Rowland questioned.

"No, sir, I can't. I've mostly just been anonymous to use your word. Like I was invisible or…dead."

Rowland leaned forward, "James, it's time you wake up to the fact that there are some people on your side." Pointing his head toward Fr. Ted seated beside him, Rowland added, "Two of them are seated in front of you right now."

"That's right, James," Fr. Ted interjected. "Did you think I stopped by your room just because I was doing my chaplain routine?"

"Honestly, yes," James shrugged.

"Just so you know – I fulfilled my obligation well before popping in on you. And I was there a couple of times when you were zoned out asleep. So I just prayed for you quietly and left."

"James, I once told you that the book on your lap would challenge your thinking. Has it?" Rowland asked.

"I suppose, but what's that got to do with this stuff?"

"There's a phrase about mid-way or so through the book that always strikes me." Rowland looked into James' face as he recited, "It goes, 'There are an infinity of angles at which one falls, only one at which one stands.' Do you recall reading that?"

"Yeah, I've got it marked." James had several small tags of paper sticking out between the pages. "It's right here." He flopped the book open and scanned the words. "Okay, I see the words, but I'm not seeing your point."

"I'm not so much making a point as asking you to consider an alternative."

"Okay, what did you have in mind?"

"You haven't, to my knowledge anyway, fallen into any of those things Chesterton mentions, any esoteric philosophies or odd religions, but you have dropped into a myriad of other dangerous pitfalls. In other words you've tested the angles but haven't found the one that will hold you up – just those that have let you down. Perhaps, in light of today's news, and with the support of the people in this room and others, you might just consider the possibility of another angle – the one that will support you. Can you at least accept that possibility?" Rowland laced his fingers together across his chest, and looked directly into James' face.

Again James waited, measuring Rowland's words. He let his eyes sweep the page again. No denying the fact that all the angles against which he leaned had to this point been false fronts. None of them held up. All of them fell out from under him like a bad joke. But perhaps this warden and priest, and the other members of the posse had something to offer. What did he have to lose by giving them a shot?

"Maybe I can, sir." He very desperately wanted what he'd just experienced, the kindness – and wisdom – of these guys, and the things Chesterton wrote to be true. But could he trust it? Was it true? Did it lead to truth – the truth that stands up and holds up?

"James you're tired. I can see that. But you asked if I'd be the one to break any news to you. I said that if permitted, I would. Fr. Ted and I wanted to tell you ourselves, both of us." Looking at his be-speckled friend he continued, "Fr. Ted and I have been down this road before, James – different young man with different circumstances, but in similar deep water. We let him down, James. We failed him. Because of that, we made a pact between ourselves as well as two other men you've met – Terrance and Mike – to never let that happen again." Returning his eyes to James, "And James, we haven't let it happen again. Neither will we let it happen with you. Our jobs here are one thing, and we will enforce them. Our responsibility as men – Christian men – goes beyond our jobs. It cuts to the core of why young men like you end up here." Lifting a finger and pointing it gently toward James, "But that's the other part of the story, James, the part you have yet to discover, and we feel responsible to help you find. Your story doesn't have to end up here. It can start new. We want to help you find that angle against which you can lean but not fall."

James allowed Rowland's words to soak in. At this moment, he was vintage Rowland, the warden-father. James glanced toward Fr. Ted, who had a ponderous expression on his face and seemed to be muttering something under his breath. Curious, James remarked, "Looks like you've got something to say."

"No James, I am in firm agreement with Warden Rowland. I was just praying."

"Praying?"

"Yes, praying. I was just thanking God for this news. And I was asking him for wisdom."

"Wisdom?"

"Yes wisdom – wisdom to help you."

James pondered these words too, overcome by what seemed like undue attention. In reality, the attention – this kind of attention – was overdue. Having never experienced it, though, he had no capacity to trust or understand it. He felt awkward, but at the same time protected.

"I don't know how to take this. I've never heard this kind of stuff before. If there is some grand plan, maybe this is the start. I just don't know. I don't get you guys. No one's ever acted like I was worth the effort. I've never felt wanted. It's hard. It's just damn hard." James sighed and looked away as if lost in his thoughts.

"What's hard?" Fr. Ted pressed.

James opened his hands, "Who to trust? How to trust? What to believe?" Then he looked at the men seated on the sofa on the other side of the coffee table from him, "But if I can't trust you guys, who can I trust? You're the only men who've thought I was worth the effort. I don't know; maybe I can trust you. At least you haven't tried to screw me."

"Trust is a difficult thing, James," Rowland offered. "It takes time, and it takes evidence. Consistent evidence over time will furnish you with the confidence to come to your own decisions about what's real and what's fiction. Judge us on those terms, James."

James nodded but said nothing.

A soft knock on the door distracted the men's attention. "Yes," Rowland answered. Betty poked her head in, "There are a couple of men here to see you Mr. Rowland."

"Oh, who?" Rowland asked inquisitively.

"Terrance and Mike, sir."

Rowland waved to have them enter the office. Scanlon had his ubiquitous cup of coffee in hand and his sleeves rolled up, while Terrance was decked out in denim with his hair slicked back like the gangland thug he used to be.

"I don't remember calling for you guys," Rowland said half sarcastically.

"Actually you didn't," Terrance answered while pulling a chair beside James.

"Who did, if I may ask?" Rowland inquired, this time suspiciously.

"That guy," Scanlon blurted pointing his finger accusingly at Fr. Ted.

Fr. Ted tapped his fingers on his coffee cup and looked across the room as if not hearing any part of this conversation. Rowland glared at his friend as if put off by his apparent impertinence.

"And who authorized you to fill my office with these characters may I ask?" Rowland scolded.

"I was just thinking since you called a meeting with James and me, you might just want the rest of posse present," Fr. Ted said with shrug and smirk.

"I see," Rowland replied smugly. "It's my office but you've arrogated to yourself authority to hold court with anyone you choose?"

"Well, I wouldn't put it in those terms but okay, I'll buy it."

Rowland just shook his head. Looking at James, "Obviously I don't carry the weight of authority I think I do."

Suddenly the room relaxed, including the edginess inside James. He felt his guard drop a little, the tension ease. This was no tribunal. It was a gathering of friends, colleagues, and decent men. He was among them, not as a prisoner but as a peer.

As Terrance sat down in the chair he pulled over from Rowland's desk, he gently slapped James' knee, "How you holding up kid? You gave us quite a scare."

"I'm good. Sorta tired, but okay."

"I'll bet," Scanlon added. Looking at Rowland and Fr. Ted, he asked "So what's this news you wanted to tell T and me?"

"Not only do you invite these guys but you tell them I have news for *them*?" Rowland poked his priestly sidekick.

"It may not be public, but I didn't think you'd mind these guys knowing," Fr. Ted replied.

"Actually for once, you're right," Rowland quipped before dropping the news. "Well, gentlemen, James is off the hook insofar as the Inquiry goes," he stated matter-of-factly.

The latecomers' mouths fell open and in unison exclaimed, "Off the hook!"

"That's correct, men," Fr. Ted replied. "He's no longer under suspicion."

"What else does that mean?" Terrance asked, his prison experience reminding him that nothing's ever as it first seems.

"It means," Rowland cut in, "That though James is freed of all charges, he will likely have to furnish testimony. When that will happen, I'm not certain. Judge Parker offered me no timeline."

"That's all?" Scanlon asked as if surprised there wasn't more to the deal.

"Yes, that's it, Mike," Rowland said. "Parker's words to me included nothing more."

Terrance turned to James, "How's that make you feel, kid?"

"Shocked!" James replied.

"I'll bet," Terrance stated. "Doesn't seem real does it?

"Exactly!"

"Man, kid, I remember wondering if I'd ever see the light of day again. When things began to go in my favor, I felt just like you – shocked. You know, I think I had a harder time with trust then than ever. I wondered when the trapdoor was gonna fall out from under me…again. It always did."

"Yep, I felt the same just about the time it seemed like I'd finally kicked the bottle," Scanlon added. "I was scared spit-less I'd fall off the wagon."

In as many days James had heard three similar stories, each one different but the same. A gangbanger, an abused kid and a recovering alcoholic – each one somehow had managed to rebound from a dark place. If anything seemed common among them it was that each person had a bottom he or she hit, a nadir below which hell might have seemed merciful. It was at that point light appeared to crack through the darkness with hope riding on it. But James wondered; had he reached that point or was there more to come? And still, there was one more thing each person shared alike – faith in a merciful, forgiving and loving God. Once more he wondered; could it be that simple? He harbored doubt. If such a being existed, he questioned, why hadn't he shown up before prison? Why hadn't he shown up when he was a kid at home? Why did he seem so real to everybody else and so hidden to him?

"Hey, what's the book?" Terrance noticed. It seemed the book caught as much attention as the kid himself. Books weren't frequently found in a con's possession. "Contraband you got caught smuggling into your cell?" He smugly snorted.

"Not hardly," James shot back with a snide edge to his voice.

"Not contraband, no not at all," The petulant sounding priest joked. "The warden thought prison wasn't harsh enough, he made the kid go back to school."

"Oh yeah! Let me see it!" Terrance snorted again snapping the book off James' lap. "Huh! Not a bad read," he smirked. "Yeah, well, this warden has that reputation. If it's hard, make it harder. If you can't do hard labor, he'll send your head to the salt mines."

"Alright you loosely considered gentlemen. I'll take it from here," Rowland interrupted seizing back the meeting he called.

"About that book, James" Rowland asserted gesturing for Terrance to hand it back to James. "You said it intrigued you? Anything in particular?"

James flipped the pages while gathering his thoughts. "His backward logic," I think.

"Backward logic?" Rowland asked in a quizzical tone.

James continued to fumble through the pages as if searching for something. "There's this one thing that stuck out." James had marked the page. He began to read, "The poet only asks to get his head into the heavens. It is the logician who seeks to get the heavens into his head." Looking at

Rowland, "It's stuff like that I'm not sure about. It's like this guy's got it backwards. Isn't enlightenment a good thing? So what if we find out that matter and science is a better philosophy than philosophy itself? Don't we all just die and become dust? He hasn't convinced me that life has a point. It all seems so pointless to me. Guess I'm not much of a poet."

"I see," Rowland thoughtfully mused. "But I wonder, James, if pointlessness as you put is a result of reason or circumstance. How much of your own philosophy is governed by what hasn't gone right in your life rather than that science is a better arbiter of reality?"

Scanlon sat scratching his head but said nothing. Terrance was squinting as he thought about Rowland's questions. Fr. Ted, on the other hand, seemed to enjoy the repartee.

"What do you mean?" James had a hunch but wasn't going to divulge it without forcing Rowland to tip his own hand.

"It's been my experience here and other places that when confronted with tough experiences the tendency is to find an out, a safe escape. I'm just wondering James, if science or reason isn't the out you've chosen because nothing else makes better sense to explain your circumstances."

"I don't know that I'm so sold on science or even reason as you say, Mr. Rowland. I just haven't found better explanations."

"For your circumstances?" Rowland probed.

"For my life, sir." James raised his eyes and looked directly into Rowland's eyes.

"Perhaps we can help you with that, James," Rowland offered pointing to each of the other men in the room.

"The posse?" James asked deadpan.

"That would be correct," Rowland confirmed. "To a man, James, we've sworn to support you and help you get on a better road than the one you've been on to this point. But…" Rowland paused. "It also depends on you."

"How, sir?" James asked.

"Most posses go out looking for the bad guy to bring him to justice. We see ourselves as men committed to helping someone who wants to get on a better road to find it. That implies two things, James. That you want a better road, and that you're willing to explore new alternatives to find it."

"Okay, I see your point. But what if I don't buy everything you guys think I should buy? What then?"

"You mean will we give up on you?" Rowland asked in reply.

"Yeah. Exactly." James confirmed.

"James, the only person in this room who will quit on you is you. We've been down this road a few times. Yes there has been a guy here and there who said he wasn't ready to take important next steps. We didn't quit on him. He quit on himself. We still stand with him. It's just he's decided to stand alone. That, James, is your prerogative too. But we hope you'll see things a little differently. Maybe for the first time in your life you'll see people standing with you, for you and with your best interests at heart and in mind." Rowland paused. Looking James squarely in the eyes he asked, "Are you game?"

James thought a moment, his mouth open and his eyes riveted. He could feel the gravity in Rowland's words and sense it in the guys seated around him. Rowland had just asked him if he could trust these men. Trust – that fated word that never quite held up. Could he risk it on these guys? Still somewhat unsure he nonetheless answered, "I'm game."

Immediately Scanlon and Terrance reached over and gave James a stiff pat on the shoulder. "With you kid," Terrance said with obvious conviction in his voice. "I've been right where you are and I know these men will not let you down." Strong emotion welled inside James and flashed into his eyes as pools of salty water blurred his vision. "We get it, James. We get what you're going through. Hang with us man. Just hang onto us." James could only nod his head and choke out, "I'll try."

"That's good enough for now James." Rowland said. "We wanted to be here with you when this news about the Inquiry was announced. But more, we want you to know you're far from alone young man. Prison as odd as it might seem could be your turning point." For good measure Rowland repeated, "You're not alone, James."

"Far from it," Fr. Ted chimed in. "For the last few nights while you've been in the hospital quite a number of people have gathered at my parish just to pray for you."

James' mouth fell open again and he furrowed his brow. "What do you mean? Who?"

"The wives of these guys. Mr. Raynor and his wife."

"The kids from the café," Terrance added.

"You mean your hoodlums," Fr. Ted joked.

Terrance just shook his head. "Pretty redeemed hoodlums, Father."

"Indeed they are, my friend. Indeed they are," Fr. Ted said while laughing.

"You look surprised, James," Rowland observed.

"I am, sir."

"Got you surrounded, kid," Scanlon stated like a big brother. "Like Tom, er' Warden Rowland said, we're with you. But like he asked, are you with us?"

"How can I not be?" James shrugged. "Like you said, you've got me surrounded."

Laughter filled the room. James wiped his eyes and broke into a smile of his own.

But as soon as it appeared his smile faded and he became sullen.

"What's on your mind, James," Rowland asked.

"There's something I still don't get. There are a lot of men in here. How come I'm the lucky guy?"

Rowland leaned forward in his seat, "James we want to reach out to all the men here. I've said that to you before. But there's too many for us to treat everyone the same. We can only hope they have a posse somewhere in their journeys. Fr. Ted is working on that through both his parish ministry and outside interests. But if you'll let me say it this way, we don't choose who we will stand beside, God does that for us. He chooses. And we believe he has chosen you as our guy. And like I said, we hope God is raising posses for the other guys."

"Alright, I'll buy it. But if you call yourselves the posse, what's your game? What do you call this thing you're doing for me? Have you got a name for it?"

"Yeah," Scanlon broke in. "It's called harassment! We harass the hell out of you until you wake up."

"Knock it off you big ape!" Terrance growled. "Give the kid some room." Looking at James, "Now you know why we call him the enforcer," he said with a wink.

"Actually, James, there is a name for it." Fr. Ted conceded.

"Like what?" James asked inquisitively.

"In Catholic speak, it's called inquiry. It's a time when someone who's thinking about faith and the church gets a free opportunity to ask questions without worrying about what everyone around them thinks. It's the same process for anyone who's puzzled about life, truth and the things like Warden Rowland asked you. All questions are fair game as long as they're asked with respect and out of honest personal concern."

"That's cool," James said smiling. "Inquiry – In other words I get to put faith and the church on trial instead of it putting me on trial."

"Well, I hadn't quite thought of it in those terms. But I get your point. Yes, you get free reign to interrogate the faith." Fr. Ted affirmed. "But let me ask you something. How will you handle it if in putting faith on trial you end up accepting it as plausible – as true? Are you up for that possibility…of crossing that bridge?"

"In all honestly, sir, I need a bridge. I can't stay where I am. It's killing me – literally. But what if I find that it isn't true, at least true for me? Are you up for that?"

Rowland broke in, "James you made a strong case for reason. But something in your background provoked me to pull this particular book from my shelf. Why do you think I chose it?"

James took a moment to consider the question. "Because it's about reason."

"That's right. Because it's about reason. It's about reason seen from a perspective your background suggests you do think about – philosophical reason."

Rowland obviously had James' attention. The kid bristled but said nothing.

"That's right, son. I know what you've read. It's right there in a file," Rowland pointed toward the large locked file cabinet in the corner behind his desk. "I'm firmly persuaded Chesterton sees more clearly than most philosophers into the big questions that plague us all. That's why I handed you that book. You're not the only person to harbor such questions. And you're entirely right to say you need a bridge. I think you'll find that what seems backward in Chesterton's logic may well be straighter and truer than the logic you've presumed correct so far. It might even lead to that bridge. Even some of those post-modern authors you've read might agree, wouldn't they?" Rowland sat back and let James tumble that question through his mind.

"They would. But, sir, I've got to know."

"No, James. What you've got to do is trust, at least take one step toward it – toward trust." Terrance admonished. "Let me put it this way. A drug dealer screwed you, your parents ignored you, the church let you down, but four guys are sitting here who have no axe to grind with you. We have no reason to be here other than for you. We're not selling dope. We're not setting you up to screw you. But the only way you'll know that is if you have the guts to test us. Put us on trial! See if we let you down!" Terrance was at full throttle. "Look, James, no one in this room has a better idea of what you're facing than me. So do you know why I'm here – with you and with these guys?"

"I'd like to know."

"Because of these guys! They saved my life! And because of what they gave me I've joined them to give it to someone else – to you! But do you have the guts?"

James surveyed the room – eight eyes riveted on him. Eight eyes fairly dared him to accept Terrance's wager. But did he have the guts?

"So I'm gonna ask you one more time, are you in or out, kid?"

"I'm in."

"Right answer!" Terrance snapped.

It might have been heavy, but to James, Terrance's dare felt right. It felt worth the risk. Something inside him said, "Take it!"

FORTY-FOUR

Terri pushed the creaking old wooden door open. Faint traces of incense lingering from morning mass invited her into the foyer. A female voice greeted her, "Terri!" She turned in the direction of the voice. Her mouth dropped open, "Robin!" The girls met in the center of the open space with the embrace of long lost friends.

"It's been forever! Where have you been?" Robin excitedly asked.

"Working mostly. You know I went to nursing school?" Terri replied.

"That's right! And now? What's up?"

"I'm a nurse! I work at County Medical," Terri replied enthusiastically, but withholding the specific floor – too many questions about "why the prison floor?"

"That's so cool!" Robin exclaimed.

"And you?" Terri asked deflecting the conversation from herself.

"I finished my degree in social work last spring. I'm going back for my masters this fall."

"Fantastic!"

"Hey," Robin blurted, "What brings you here, to this place?"

"I was going to ask you the same thing," Terri shot back in reply.

"Fr. Ted and Pastor T of course!"

"Okay, but why?"

"For a kid in prison." Robin grabbed her friend's arms, "Oh, Terri, he's in such a bad place. We come here every night just to pray for him."

"His name wouldn't be James would it?" Terri shyly asked.

"Yes! How'd you know?" Robin asked in stunned excitement.

"Um, well, I was his nurse at County Medical. I work on the prison floor."

"Oh, wow, Terri! I had no idea! So you met him there?"

"Yep! We sorta became friends too."

"That's so cool! It's got to be a God-thing!" Robin exclaimed with a massive smile spread across her cute face. "So you must have bumped into Fr. Ted there too?"

"Sure did. Actually, I think he bumped into me. Anyway, he asked me to join the group here, tonight."

"Oh wow! Terri, this is just the coolest ever! Hey, let me introduce you to the rest of the Café!"

Robin grabbed Terri by the hand and led her briskly over to where the huddle of kids had gathered in the center of the foyer. "Hey guys got somebody for you to meet?" Robin announced.

"Terri!" shrieked a pair of girls decked out in raggedy garb with rings looped in their noses.

"You know these girls?" Robin asked with a look of shock.

"I do! Hi Tina! Hi Markey!"

"Holy heck, how do you guys know each other?" Robin queried again.

"It's a long story," Tina offered while looking at Terri. "We'll save it for another time."

"Thanks, Tina," Terri whispered back to her.

By now the rest of the gang had gathered around. "So who's your friend?" one of the guys in the group asked Robin.

"Hey guys, this is Terri. She used to hang at the Café a billion years ago. Fr. Ted invited her to hang with us tonight – you know, pray for James."

Fr. Ted entered the foyer through the side door from his office, "Well, well, well. It looks like you found Terrance's hoodlums," He said with a wink to Terri.

"Yep, I sure did! Robin introduced me," Terri said excitedly.

"Wonderful! How about joining the others in the chapel?" With that Fr. Ted led the procession of kids into the small chapel where the adults were already gathered.

"Welcome everyone!" Fr. Ted began. "I have someone to introduce, someone who has become important to James' journey quite recently." Stretching his arm toward Terri, he said, "Please greet Terri. This young lady has been James' nurse during his hospital stay."

Polite applause ensued, with several respectable hoots from the hoodlums. Terri bobbed her head in response. Terrance stepped up beside her and slipped an arm around her, "Good to see you again. It's been way too long."

Terri beamed, "It has Pastor T. But it's all good."

"That's great, Terri. Glad you're here."

"Me too," Terri replied.

Fr. Ted motioned for everyone to take a seat while he took his place behind the ambo. "Tom and I met with James just a few hours ago. Mike and Terrance joined us a few moments later. In that meeting, Tom let James know that the Panel of Inquiry has dropped all charges against him. Don and Kathleen found out this afternoon, shortly after our meeting." Huge sighs of relief could be heard across the room, embellished with "Amen!" and "Thank you Jesus!"

"I think it's safe to say, God has heard and answered our prayers people. We still have a ways to go. Our boy harbors deep doubt about God – and about himself. But I can't help being impressed by what has transpired in the last few days." Smiling at Terri, he continued, "God has faithfully brought people into James' life at important moments that have left him with a great deal to think about." Positioning his glasses tighter to his face, Fr. Ted opened the large Bible resting on the ambo and read, "I will never leave you or forsake you. Hence you can confidently say the Lord is my helper, I will not be afraid; what can man do to me?" He closed the Bible and rested his arms on top of it. "This passage from Hebrews neatly sums up what has just happened in this young man's life. Though he doesn't recognize God in the picture, it is God who has stood with James as he has stood with each of us. Indeed, what can man do to me – to us?"

Silence filtered through the chapel filled with hopeful family and friends – a thought-filled pause ahead of another evening of intense prayer.

FORTY-FIVE

James sat with his back against the wall contemplating his first session with the entire posse. As he browsed his space it struck him that his cell no longer felt like punishment but more like a sanctuary, a safe environment in which to contemplate new thoughts, to send his mind into a more habitable place of clear and honest hope.

But what kind of hope? To this point, the notion of a loving God vexed him with insoluble complexities that left him a rigidly confirmed agnostic. Evidence that to some proved not merely the existence but gracious character of God – or a god – sent him the other direction toward the nonexistence of such a being. Yet in the presence of the men with whom he'd just met, within Terri's story and within the odd circuitous meanderings of Chesterton's *Orthodoxy*, his long-held contempt toward this non-being seemed almost irrational. He began to ask himself different questions, and found it odd that he would consider them reasonable. For instance, if this being – God or a god – didn't exist, why would he spend so much mental and emotional energy denying it? Why contempt toward such a being if no such being existed? What responsible explanation permitted anger and doubt toward God or a god if there were no such being? Dismissing such questions now, despite his contempt toward the very notion of God, seemed – if not irrational – certainly irresponsible, if the objective was to arrive at truth, especially truth that made life more than a cruel slog through banality until death finally and mercifully ended the mess. Maybe it was time to accept Terrance's dare and test new assumptions. That thought, however rational it seemed, set his teeth on edge.

He flopped Chesterton right side up to the page that sent him into this quandary, and began scratching questions onto the yellow pad that already held several pages of notes and queries. Formerly his questions dealt with his own guilt or innocence with regard to the Inquiry and the reason he was sent to prison in the first place. Now they changed course as he put God on trial – a different kind of inquiry. There was even a quixotic wisp of hope that perhaps God did exist, that he was the merciful being Terri portrayed him to be. That door, though not locked any longer, still sat closed. He couldn't quite risk opening it. Was it proof he needed or something else, like faith perhaps?

These words struck him, "Every act of will is an act of self-limitation." He paused. Grabbing his pad he jotted a quick note, "Self-limitation! Does that mean that because of my stupid decisions I've trapped myself in a life that leads to dead ends?" The next few statements fortified his concern, "When you choose anything, you reject everything else." And, "Every act is an irrecoverable selection and exclusion." He found himself staring at an intellectual fence that held real life implications. "Choices lead to behaviors that lead to consequences," prowled his thoughts. He scribbled something like that on his pad. He also jotted, "I'm where my decisions – and actions – led me for sure. I deserve prison. But forever? Is there a way out?" The God-thought struck him again. Was God the way out of his miserable circumstances or the cause of them? If these words he read held any answer, it appeared the responsibility rested on him. So where was God?

"Meyers, on your feet!"

James' head snapped around toward the cell door. Peering in at him were the stern searching eyes of a guard.

"I said on your feet, Meyers. You have a visitor – two visitors."

James pushed the small table back to its spot, cleared his bed of the scribbles of paper and stood facing the guard. "This isn't a visiting day is it?"

"No matter," the guard grumped. "There's people here to see you. You know the drill, back up and let me cuff you."

James put his hands behind his back and stood in place as the guard snapped the tight biting cuffs onto his wrists. Once more he was on a long, mysterious walk to meet with people he had not invited, but somehow chose to see him.

The route passed the secured cages reserved for more dangerous types or for times of tight security, back toward the more relaxed meeting rooms. As they approached he could hear voices at near whisper – one a female voice. "Terri?" he mused quietly. Sure enough, there she sat beside whom else but Fr. Ted wide beaming smile spread across his bewhiskered face.

"Bet you didn't expect to see me so soon did you?" Fr. Ted asked with a hearty laugh.

"That's for sure," James said as he rubbed his raw wrists after the guard removed the cuffs.

"Bet you didn't expect to see me either, huh?" Terri beamed.

"No, I didn't. So what's up?" James queried while plopping down in the lone wooden chair across the table from his visitors.

"Wanted to say hi," Terri replied with a sparkle dancing in her eyes.

"Missed me eh?" James smirked.

"Honestly, yeah, I did," she said feeling her face flush.

Fr. Ted was enjoying this awkward moment between these two youngsters. It rather amused and delighted him. He rocked back in his chair; arms crossed over his prominent belly, that silly grin still spread across his salty bearded face.

"You having a good time?" James sniped as he looked over at the priest.

"Oh yes, quite a good time," Fr. Ted chuckled.

"At my expense," James fired back.

"Somewhat, I suppose," the priest replied with a wink.

"So, aren't you glad to see me?" Terri interrupted.

"I'm sorry," James sputtered. "Yes, yes I am. How are you?"

"I'm good. Was wondering how you're doing?"

James shrugged, "Okay, I guess. Been doing a lot of thinking."

"About what?"

Fr. Ted's smile faded into a curious thoughtfulness as he awaited James' reply.

"A lot of stuff, Terri. I'm just…"

"Go on! Just what?" she urged.

"I don't know. Guess I'm thinking a lot about our conversation and the stuff the guys – the posse – laid on me after I got back."

"Really? Any conclusions?"

"Just one."

"What's that?" Terri asked, a twinge of anticipation in her voice.

"That I've been a real ass! That maybe I've had stuff all backwards. I don't know…. Let's just say I'm open to options."

Fr. Ted's mouth fell open; so did Terri's. Neither of them knew exactly what to say or do next.

"Options, James?" Fr. Ted broke in. "What kind of options are you anticipating?" Fr. Ted's question came from two places at once – hope and the bitter remembrance of another young man who exercised his options by hanging himself.

"That maybe there is a God." James couldn't believe these words fell so easily out of his mouth. He'd never heard them in his own voice before. For an instant he wondered if he'd actually said them.

Terri's eyes widened, "Really? Seriously? Are you faking it? Or are you really thinking that?"

"What other options do I have? Look where I am, Terri! Just a few days ago I was bleeding to death because some goon knifed me."

Terri and the priest stared blankly at James waiting for more.

"Look, I don't know what I think yet. I just know there's got to be more. This Chesterton guy has really messed with me. Something he said has been eating at me all day."

"Like what?" Terri asked.

"He made this weird comment. 'Every act of will is an act of self-limitation.'"

"Remember what he said next?" Fr. Ted added.

"Yeah, whatever I choose is final."

"So how does that strike you?" Fr. Ted probed. Terri sat quietly attentive; her hands clasped together, her arms resting on the table.

"You really want to know?"

"Yes, of course," Fr. Ted replied.

"It scared the hell out of me! That's how it struck me." James gathered himself, took a quick glance at the floor then stared the priest directly in the eyes. "Fr. Ted, either God is the answer or he's the problem. I've screwed up my life, but where was God? Why didn't he stop me? Why the hell did I have to end up here?" James dropped an angry fist on the table, his eyes filled. Terri reached across the table and put her hand on his arm. Fr. Ted's eyes moistened.

"James God didn't stand in Adam and Eve's way either. Look where that left us. So, was it his fault…God's I mean?"

"Yeah, well…" James' voice trailed off. He inhaled deeply, "So what's the answer? Or is there an answer?"

"There is," Fr. Ted said assuredly. "But you might not like it."

"The Jesus thing?" James snarled.

"Yeah, the Jesus thing."

James caught Terri signally agreement. "You really buy this don't you?" he sneered.

"I do…all of it." Terri answered matter-of-factly.

A long silence ensued. Moist eyes looked into moist eyes. Nobody said a thing…just waited.

James broke the silence, "I'm not there…not yet. How can a loving God be the answer when I needed one and He wasn't there?"

"I get that, James. I truly do," Terri said through a soft smile. She gently squeezed his arm. "I know."

"Yeah, whatever" James replied.

"Look, kid," Fr. Ted interjected. "It's a journey…all of life is a journey. Walk at your own pace." Motioning toward Terri, he said, "And we'll walk with you…all of us will."

That last comment and the earnestness in Fr. Ted's face as he made it sent an unexpected sense of assurance through James' body. He knew he wasn't alone, but would it last?

"One thing you've got to accept, James," Fr. Ted added, "Your fate is not sealed. You have options, options that don't all lead to dead ends like prison. Look at us, son. We've screwed up somewhere and had to find our way out. You're not alone. You just think you are. Wake up and look around you."

"Yeah!" Terri exclaimed. "Wake up! Like Fr. Ted said. I'll be here, and so will the rest."

What could he say? James was surrounded by what had been missing all his life – people who cared. Sure, no one seemed to notice him until he made a mess of his life. But here they were, sitting across from him, gathering in a chapel every night to pray for him, surrounding him like big brothers, father-figures and a sweet sister. As awkward as this newfound attention felt, he couldn't deny that by some unseen means he was on a different track and it wasn't a solo act; he had friends. Maybe this was the real deal.

"I think I'm beginning to get the message. Thanks."

"Sure, kid. You're more than welcome," Fr. Ted confirmed.

Looking over the rim of his glasses Fr. Ted commented, "You may not have gotten that far yet, but Chesterton said something else you might want to pay attention to. Citing Lord Tennyson, somebody I think you recognize, he remarked, '…there is faith in honest doubt.'"

James cocked his head as if unsure of what the priest was getting at. "What's that mean?" he asked.

"It means James, that despite all your resistance there is this spark of belief…even the desire for it. No one who truly doubts does so absent this spark of faith. It's the hope that keeps us asking for answers. We want the answers. And we want them to be true. We want them to be reliable."

"Okay," James shrugged. "I see your point."

"Chesterton seems to get it," Fr. Ted said with a thoughtful wink.

"You seem to know Chesterton pretty good," James replied.

"He's like a friend, James. It was while reading Chesterton I stopped being a bitterly disappointed agnostic. His logic painted me into a corner where I had to come to terms with my own personal anger, doubt and dare say regret."

"You doubted? But you're a priest," James scoffed incredulously.

"I wasn't always a priest young man. Like you I was kind of forgotten, thought of as a bookish nerd who never fit in with any group. So I drifted into myself. No, I didn't fall into the trap you fell into, but I fell into a dark hole that was a trap. You see, James, I had attempted suicide and was handed this book while in the hospital recovering from a drug overdose."

"I had no idea," James said almost apologetically." Terri's mouth fell open; she gaped inquisitively at the priest.

"Well, I came to terms with God. And he brought me to terms with myself, James. You see, kids, you're never the only one. You're just one. All of us have a story."

"So Chesterton saved your life," James remarked.

"No, James, Chesterton introduced me to the one who saved my life. But to his credit, he led me there. He led me face to face with God in the person of Jesus Christ."

"I see," James replied in a near whisper. "I think I have more to read."

"Indeed you do young man," Fr. Ted assured. "And by the way," he continued, "who do you think gave Warden Rowland the book?"

"Why am I not surprised?" James sniped while rolling his eyes in mock defiance.

Terri laughed. "Yeah, why would we be surprised?"

Fr. Ted joined the laugher. "But don't forget, James, this story may be about you, but it's not only about you. Got it?"

"I think I'm getting it."

"Good."

The guard stepped in, "Sounds like a good time. But time's up," and he motioned for the guests to leave.

"Thanks for coming," James said politely. "It really means a lot."

Terri smiled, stepped over and gave James a tender hug. "You're welcome."

Just before they got out of the room and the guard had him back in cuffs, James turned toward Terri, "By the way, do you have a last name?"

Terri grinned, "Sure do."

"And…?" James pried.

"Same as yours without the 'e'."

"No way!"

"Yep, I'm a Myers but not an M-e-y-e-r-s Meyers."

"Did you know this?" James fired at Fr. Ted.

"Have a nice day, kid," he chortled taking Terri by the arm while laughing to himself as they ambled down the corridor.

Another irony James thought to himself – another weird irony.

Back in his cell James grabbed his yellow pad and furiously scribbled more notes. First he hastily scribbled a question, "What the hell is going on?" Then another question, "What's this all about?" His questions, while having a severe edge to them, really meant something other than they had before. They still smacked of skepticism, but it was different. Not only had his cell taken on a different aura but so did this whole prison thing. Maybe it was for a purpose. It seemed so perplexing that since the stabbing his outlook had begun to change. Why? He wondered. Could it be that he'd truly reached bottom and when he looked up found himself amid people who genuinely cared about him? He jotted another note; this one to Fr. Ted. "I would like to meet with you and Terrance. Can that be arranged?" He folded it and put in the slot for the guard to deliver.

FORTY-SIX

Tapping her pen on the pile of papers strewn across her desk, Anne pondered the options. Hastily she grabbed the legal pad already filled with pages of notes, and began writing. "No priors. At risk. Precedence." She paced her office wondering, "What am I missing?" Spread across the credenza behind her desk open case files caught her eye. "Precedence" she whispered to herself. "Of course!" While she could not find precedent that would commute James' sentence or place him under extended parole, the possibility of minimum security incarceration might be. Perhaps it would allow for supervised leaves and more visitations. And there were those exceptional cases. Would one open the door? She reached for the phone.

"Warden Rowland," Rowland said almost mindlessly answering his phone. In front of him was a stack of files he was perusing, files for inmates due for release.

"Daddy, do you have a minute," Anne asked not even saying Hi.

"Sure. What's on your mind?" Rowland slipped his glasses off onto an open file, and swung his chair around so he could face out the window onto the drab surroundings outside. "You sound perplexed."

"No, not at all. Actually, I think I found another possibility for James. You remember those cases I told you about? I found out some more stuff about one in particular that I think you'll want to hear."

"Let's hear it," he replied.

"Well, I don't think we can commute James' sentence, but we might be able to appeal to his at-risk situation, his behavior to this point and the posse's willingness to assume responsibility for him in order to move him to minimum security, maybe with supervised leave. What to do think? Is it worth a shot?"

"Anne, off the top of my head I'd say it sounds credible. Maybe a tough sell but worth the effort. By the way, I heard from Parker today."

"Okay, fine. But what has he got to do with this?"

"The Inquiry's conclusion in addition to naming a likely perp felt strongly that James is still a target. Inmate testimonies compelled him to call and warn me on James' behalf. Anne, we need an answer."

"What does Tony think?"

"He called Parker. His County Gang squad informed him that James is in deeper trouble than before. He's convinced they'll get him."

"The Lobos?"

"Apparently not just the Lobos," Rowland answered rubbing his forehead. "Sweetheart, I don't think I've ever been more afraid for a young man in my life. James has enemies."

"Oh my," Anne's voice trailed. "Look, I'm going to consult with my trial colleagues. Let me get back to you. It might not be until tomorrow."

"Good," Rowland acknowledged. "I'll float your idea past Parker too. James will need a legal advocate on the bench. Maybe he can offer some guidance."

"That sounds good, Daddy. Check in with you later." Anne paused. "Hey, God knows," she encouraged her dad. "He knows."

"Thanks, sweetheart. I know he knows. Talk to you soon."

*****

"So what's the big hubbub about?" Scanlon grumbled as he fell into the seat in Fr. Ted's spacious office-library.

"Yeah," Terrance agreed, slipping the book he perused back into its place on the tall shelf beside Fr. Ted's massive mahogany desk. "What's going down?"

"Going down, you ask my dear Terrance?" the priest answered as if he were Sherlock Holmes responding to Dr. Watson. "What's going down is the reason we are here. Tom will fill us in when he arrives."

"So there is a buzz, eh?" Scanlon pressed.

"Perhaps, Mike. We'll know soon enough," Fr. Ted assured.

"You didn't call this get-together?" Terrance pursued.

"Your daddy-in-law did. And your wife," Fr. Ted answered offering nothing more.

"Anne?" Terrance inquired as if dumbstruck.

Immediately the office door opened and in stepped Terrance's bride who caught the bewildered expression spread across her man's face. "Hi honey," she said while giving him a wifely hug. "You seem surprised."

"Well, dear, from what I gather you've been holding secrets from me."

"Oh, not really. The Warden and I came up with something this afternoon and we just didn't have time to inform everybody."

"Ah, I see," Terrance replied. "So that's why we're here. You and *The Warden* hatched something?" Terrance remarked, a twinge of derision in his tone.

Anne smiled that Cheshire cat kind of smile and took a seat on the couch beside the door.

About then Rowland entered the anticipation-filled room.

"Well, it appears *The Warden* has arrived," Fr. Ted inflected his voice for effect. "So let's begin. Tom, what have you got for us?"

"I'm going to defer to Anne," Rowland said taking a seat beside his daughter. "Before I do, however, let me tell you what I just learned from Judge Parker."

"Parker returned your call?" Anne inquired.

"He did. That's why I'm a bit tardy." Rowland folded his hands and looked at each one of his anxious friends, who sat pensively staring at him, awaiting his report. "Parker advised me to get James out of the State House."

Expressions grew serious. No one said a word, waiting for the rest of the news.

"He went so far as to consult with Judge Abrams, the judge who sentenced James. It is their collective opinion that James needs to be moved – and soon."

"Okay, but where?" Scanlon asked insistently.

"That's the rub, Mike. Abrams hasn't bought off on minimum security, the idea Anne wants to advance. Parker disagrees. Ironically, Parker changed course mid-stream after delving more deeply into the Inquiry. He was originally convinced of James' guilt. Now he's not only convinced of his innocence but that his sentence is too severe. Worse, like us he worries for James' safety."

"Minimum security?" Terrance interrupted.

"Yes. That's what Anne's exploring." Turning to Anne, Rowland directed, "Why don't you fill us in. Give us your discovery and conclusion."

"Well," Anne began, "My discovery doesn't support any firm conclusions as yet. It does, however, make a case for moving James from the State House to a lower security unit in either a different facility or to what I'm aiming for – a minimum security facility. Judge Abrams is the wildcard." She flipped open her notepad and read her staccato jots: "Tough on drug thugs! Tough on illicit drug activities, period!" She dropped her pad into her attaché. "He earned his judgeship largely due to his zero tolerance on the drug trade. That's why he pretty much threw the book at James, handing him a stiff sentence for a first time offender. But…"

"Just a moment, Anne," Rowland interrupted raising his hand to stop her. "Let me interject some relevant background about Abrams. I've known him for several years – not as well as Judge Parker but enough to address his rationale." Looking at Anne, he continued, "Judge Abrams lost his youngest son to drugs – an overdose. It caught him and his family quite by surprise. They had no idea he was using."

"Christian family, Tom?" Fr. Ted asked.

"No, Ted, Jewish. A devout Jewish family originally from New York. Abrams was educated at Columbia University and City College."

Fr. Ted nodded and stroked his beard. Rowland continued, "Before his judgeship, Abrams prosecuted heads of drug organizations throughout the Midwest, including two prominent crime families in Chicago. He was successful, enough so that when the bench came open, he got the call."

"That explains a lot, Tom," Fr. Ted replied. "So what does that all mean for James?"

Anne answered, "It means Abrams has to be convinced that James no longer presents a problem, and that the high-risk nature of his incarceration is priority number one. Would you agree?" she asked looking to her father for guidance.

"I would, Anne. And I think this is where we lean on Judge Parker for some help; as well as Tony and his guys at County Gang." Rowland paused a moment and then added, "I've taken the liberty of consulting with Judge Parker who agreed to intervene."

"When might you expect an answer?" Terrance queried.

"Maybe as early as tomorrow but within the week."

Terrance threw his arms in the air as if begging for a better answer, "A week!" He pleaded! "So where do we go from here?"

"To prayer!" Fr. Ted fired back. "We go to prayer."

The clamor of people entering the church distracted the group.

"From the sound of things in the foyer, I'd say the warriors have massed," Fr. Ted said with a wry wink.

"Warriors?" Scanlon asked suspiciously.

"Prayer warriors big guy!" Terrance answered slapping his friend's thick thigh.

"Let's join them," Fr. Ted said, rising from his chair and heading for the door.

FORTY-SEVEN

"Meyers, you're a popular guy!"

Startled out of his thoughts, James snapped his head toward the door slit. Familiar eyes met his. This whole thing of having a guard show up at random times was becoming a ritual.

"Huh?" he asked awkwardly as if caught in a dream.

"You're a popular guy. C'mon, get up. You've got another guest."

"Another guest?" James asked puzzled by the sudden notice as he presented his wrists to the cuffs.

"A guest. Let's go."

This time the guard led him to the secured cages and sat him on one of the stools behind the thick bulletproof window. A moment later, Terri walked in and took a seat across the glass from him.

"Hey, so soon? I didn't expect to see you again for awhile," James said surprised by Terri's unexpected entrance.

"Ah, well, a friend thought I should check on you," Terri said cradling her chin in her hands, her elbows resting on the short ledge in front of the window.

"A friend huh? That friend wouldn't be a pesky priest would he?"

"Sure would be! He pulled a few strings and here I am." Terri coyly remarked.

"Pulled a few strings, eh?"

"Well, you know. He has an in with the big guy."

"You mean God?"

"No silly, with the Warden!" Terri said wrinkling her nose and giggling at her dense friend.

James rolled his eyes. "That big guy."

"Yeah, that big guy."

"Okay, so what's on his mind?" James asked sarcastically.

"You are, goofy! You're on all of our minds. It's like we have nothing else to think about." She wrinkled her nose again, "I'd say pray too but that would just piss you off."

"Well, honestly, I don't think it would piss me off."

"Oh?"Terri replied somewhat taken aback. "What's that about?"

"Been doing some more thinking"

"You've been doing a lot of that lately? What about this time?" Terri pried.

"About your story and about Fr. Ted, Terrance, Scanlon, stuff."

"What about them?" Terri dug a little deeper. "Are they starting to make sense?"

"Maybe. But it's more than that."

"Soooo…" Terri leaned a little harder on her elbows.

212

"Damn it, Terri, you're pushy as hell."

"Hey, don't swear at me James Meyers! You brought 'em up!" Terri snapped.

"Guess so. Sorry," James apologized. "What'd Fr. Ted have in mind?"

"Nothing really," Terri hesitated. "Well he really never said, but I think he thought we might have dumped quite a load on you the other day."

"That's an understatement," James agreed as if annoyed.

"You said there's more. What more?" Terri pursued.

"You are pushy," James recoiled, but with a tinge of humor this time.

"I want to know."

"Oh, wow, Terri, I don't know," James felt his heart race. Was he really ready to divulge his latest musings? He wasn't sure of them himself.

"If it'll make it any easier, remember how tough it was for me to spill my guts to you? And I barely knew you. Please trust me with this one, James. We're friends now."

"Friends, huh?"

"Yeah, friends! Do you doubt that?" Terri waited.

"Well, you're the only person I've ever said this stuff to. Honestly, other than Fr. Ted and the guys, you're the only person who seemed to give a damn." James looked into Terri's intently focused eyes. She never blinked. "I guess that does make us friends."

Terri smiled. James continued, "I feel like I can trust you, Terri. Thanks."

"You listened to me. And it wasn't easy to say those things to you. I worried you'd hate me for what I did."

"How could I? Like I said then, I'm no better off. Your story mattered to me. It matters to me now."

"About the more stuff. What'd you mean?"

James looked down at his hands, which lied folded on the window ledge in front of him. "I want to believe, Terri."

"What do you mean?"

"Oh, I think you know what I mean," James said while raising his head to look into Terri's eyes.

"Let me hear you say it." Terri waited again. James stared back at her as if unsure of what to say.

Finally he gave in, "I want to believe in God. I want to believe in your God, Terri." He felt his face flush. Did he just say what he heard come out of his mouth? Tears flooded his eyes, coursed down his face and spilled onto his gray drab prison shirt.

Terri's eyes filled, her chin quivered.

"Oh James, I want you to know him like I know him." She hesitated, wondering if she should ask him the big question. She drew a breath, "Are you ready? Do you want to receive him now?"

James bit his lip. "I do, but I'm still worried."

"Worried? About what?"

"I'm afraid that it's not real. That it's just a way of coping with life." James grimaced, "But then I see you and hear your story. And Fr. Ted – his story. And Terrance, and Mike their stories. I want God, Terri. But I still have doubt."

"Okay, James, I get it. I truly, truly get it. It took me months with the nurses before I could even say what you just said to me. But trust me please! God is real. Jesus is real. He came to save us and change us into something more than we ever dreamed we could be." Terri put her hand over her heart, "I'm living proof."

James nodded his head, "Yes you are."

"Listen James, you are my friend and I care so very much about you. Will you let me pray for you?"

"Here? Now?" James' retorted somewhat bewildered. Did he really want Terri to do that?

"Yes – here and now. I just want to…" She drew a breath. "I just want to put our conversation in God's hands, and ask for his help."

James felt his head nod. Terri wiped tears out of her eyes. "Okay then, I'll make it brief."

"Alright."

Terri began, "Dear Jesus, you heard our words. You know James better than anyone. And you love him. Please help him to trust you, and to let you into his life. Thank you. Amen."

"Thank you," James said beneath his breath.

"My pleasure," Terri replied again swishing tears out of her eyes.

"I can't remember anyone ever praying for me," James confessed.

"Yeah, well, you just did. And I meant every word."

"I know."

"Okay Meyers, time to go." The guard's sudden presence jolted the kids.

"I guess that means we're done for now," Terri said with a shrug.

"Guess so," James replied. "Hey, thanks for coming." He paused, "Thanks for being my friend."

"You're welcome," Terri said with a sweet bob of her head. "And, thanks for being my friend." She bit her lip, "And for letting me pray for you."

James didn't seem to mind the cuffs this time. He didn't notice them until Terri's face disappeared behind the door. He felt a quiver of fear when he first arrived at the State House. He felt it again. This time it wasn't the fear of incarceration, it was the uncertainty of facing God. Was he really prepared for that confrontation? It seemed inevitable…frighteningly inevitable.

FORTY-EIGHT

Rowland slid his coffee cup to the side and quelled the hubbub, "Thank you all for agreeing to meet. Your guidance will have significant affect on how we proceed in the matter of James Taylor Meyers." Thus he opened a different inquiry convoked at his urging to decide the fate of Meyer's incarceration. Around the large conference table situated in the wood paneled law office of Parker & Fulbright sat Judge William Parker, Judge Amos Abrams, Tony Harrison of County Gang, Anne Hall, Harold Raynor and Warden Thomas Rowland, an august assemblage of jurists in company with the State House head guard and the principal advisor of local and regional gang activity.

The gravity of the matter and the unusual nature of the case cast a pall across the room. Sternly sober faces concentrated in Rowland's direction at the head of the long, dark wood table. Before Rowland could continue his remarks, the door opened revealing Fr. Ted's somewhat welcome intrusion, unusually irreverent as it might seem to those for whom punctuality was as much a virtue as Sabbath keeping. Though not formally invited, Fr. Ted nonetheless insinuated himself into the meeting. From the welcoming smiles emanating from most of those gathered, no one appeared the least perturbed to see him take a seat opposite Rowland at the far end of the table. Instead his presence appeared to soften the thick atmosphere hanging like a Dickens ghost of Christmas past. They were – after all – gathered in caucus for one reason, perhaps two – the fate of James Meyers and justice. Could both matters be settled without compromise for either? That was the matter at hand. It was here among these people, colleagues for the most part, Rowland's own philosophy of humane justice would be tested.

Rowland leaned forward, his arms crossed on the table in front of him, "Since the tragic suicide of Mark Dempsey which occurred shortly after his imprisonment, we at the State House have paid much more attention to the mental, emotional and physical safety of our inmates, the younger, more vulnerable ones especially." Rowland halted allowing the weight of his comments to penetrate into the minds of his colleagues and advisors – and hopefully into their souls too. "It is not my contention alone but that of many assembled here today that James Taylor Meyers faces similarly serious, even potentially lethal threats to his life as evidenced by his recent stabbing incident." Looking toward Judge Parker; "Bill, you made this same observation with me the other day. I think the panel would benefit from your conclusions. Would you mind briefing us?"

Parker furrowed his brow, hesitating long enough to survey those seated around him as well as gather his thoughts. "Tom is right. It was the determination of the members of the Inquiry involving the death of Nathaniel Chalmers, in which James Meyers was implicated, that Meyers is at extreme risk." Motioning to his right, "We consulted with Tony Harrison, whose undercover officers corroborated that no less than two major gang factions have marked Meyers with the intent to kill him."

"Judge if I may break in." All eyes now concentrated toward Tony Harrison, who sat forward in his chair clutching his coffee cup firmly between his hands, "As late as this morning we have further ascertained that a plot to murder Meyers was foiled shortly before he met with his latest visitor." The visitor he spoke of was Terri, though her name never came up.

"That was just two days ago." Harold Raynor remarked. "Two of our guards caught wind of the plot Tony just cited and were able to quash it."

"That's right," Tony went on. "Harold's guards working closely with our embedded officers caught wind of the hit; stepped in and eradicated the threat. What's unique about this threat was that rival gangs cooperated in the plot. They want Meyers eliminated."

"Why?" Judge Abrams broke in dumbstruck by the absurdity of such a threat. "What does Meyers have on these guys?"

"Judge, it's not that Meyers has anything on them. He simply interfered. He got in the way. So now they want him out of the way. Simple as that," Tony answered. He shook his head and squeezed his coffee cup more tightly, "Look people, the kid's in a hell-of-a lot of trouble." He looked around the table into the faces staring back at him. "He's marked and these goons will stop at nothing 'til he's dead. Bottom line…Meyers' has got to be moved… immediately."

"Tony what you're saying now contradicts your earlier advice to leave him at the State House," Raynor stated.

"I know, Harold. But circumstances have changed. The kid can't stay at the State House. He's as good as dead if he does."

"What about other penitentiaries?" Abrams asked.

"No, judge. Like Tom said news travels fast. We've got to entertain another alternative. If we don't….Well, like I said, Meyers is as good as dead."

"I'm persuaded you're right, Tony," Parker agreed, rising from his seat and striding toward the gurgling coffee urn near the massive double doors. Turning to Judge Abrams whose thick, black eyebrows seemed knit into his deeply furrowed brow, "Amos we need your help." Abrams raised his head to look into Parker's face, the expression from which was more corroborating than his words. "We need you to agree to a reduction of sentence that permits Meyers to do his time in a *minimum* security facility."

"Bill, I can't make that case!" Abrams roared in defiance of Parker's seemingly outlandish demand. "The kid's not been in the system long enough to honor something that ridiculous."

"Despite the risk to his safety? Threats on his life?" Rowland demanded.

Abrams swept an arm through the air as if dismissing the matter as entirely out of reason. "Tom, the kid was convicted of abetting a known drug dealer…one of the worst. That has consequences under the law."

"Yes, but those consequences do not include exposing Meyers to mortal danger!" Rowland shot back in rebuttal, his voice rising, his face tensing. Anne reached over placing a hand on her dad's arm hoping to disarm his mood.

"Indeed not, Tom," Abrams huffed. "But what you're asking is unprecedented if not absurd."

"Not so, Your Honor." Anne entered the conversation. "Two cases, one recent, did make exception for a prisoner who came under similar threat as James Meyers."

"And…" Abrams asked in a petulant tone.

Anne addressed Abrams directly, and in impressive lawyerly demeanor cited, "In Rawlins v. Virginia, the magistrate upon review of reports corroborated by prison officials saw fit to move the endangered prisoner to a lesser secured facility, with the proviso that the prisoner would come under the supervision of a court appointed guardian."

"When was that case tried, Mrs. Hall?"

"Last year, your honor." Anne reached into her attaché retrieving a copy of the court document. "It was perfected only four months ago. Presently the prisoner is assigned to the minimum correctional institution associated with the Virginia State Penitentiary."

"And who was assigned guardianship?" Abrams demanded.

"The prison chaplain, sir."

Abrams rocked back in his thick padded leather chair, resting his elbows on the armrests, his hands folded in front of him. "Can I assume, Tom, you are prepared to make a like-kind proposal?"

"I am, Amos."

"And who would you appoint if I were to consider your proposal?"

"Specifically, Chaplain Fr. Ted Harding along with myself and two other men."

"You, Tom? Doesn't' that risk conflict of interest on your part?" Parker asked on behalf of Judge Abrams as well as normal legal protocol.

"I would not be appointed in any official capacity, nor would the other two men. The guardianship would be served strictly and entirely by Fr. Ted."

"But you did name yourself and these men." Abrams noted. "Of consequence I presume you intend some role for yourself official or not."

"Indeed you are correct. Our unofficial role would be what it already has been – to provide support for Meyers, and offer him guidance toward a radical change in direction and behavior befitting a prisoner suitably reformed to reenter society."

"I see," Abrams said tugging awkwardly on his suit vest.

"Let me add something here if I might," Fr. Ted broke in. "The circumstances, while unusual, are not without merit. Serving justice under the law clearly demands punishment for the offender. I'm confident we all agree on this point." The priest took a sip of tea, returning the cup to its place on the table with considerable deliberation. Speaking as if lecturing graduate students at Loyola, he continued, "In this case James Meyers deserves to be in prison for his actions." He once again halted his words, cocked his head to the side as if questioning his own comments. "I wonder, however, if imprisoning him among men whose heinous crimes and whose hardened attitudes won't likely persuade him in an unintended direction. Perhaps he stands to gain more if placed in an environment where punishment leads also to something more conducive to a change of life, where he is held accountable not solely for his crime but for change..for discernible change in attitude and behavior."

"You make you point well, Father," Abrams conceded. "But you're not a lawyer."

"You're correct, Judge Abrams, I'm not a lawyer. As a professor of ethics and moral theology, however, I've had more than ample opportunity to study the effects of incarceration quite intimately."

"Explain your comment, Father" Abrams insisted.

Folding his hands on the table and leaning toward Judge Abrams, Fr. Ted extended his *lecture*, "James Meyers is young and impressionable. He's not a thug. He's not a drug lord. He's a frightened, disillusioned young man who stepped off the right path onto a path he genuinely regrets."

"Regrets?" Abrams asked unconvinced.

"Yes, regrets," Fr. Ted confirmed. "He doesn't regret it because he got caught. He regrets it because it was wrong. But as it stands, he has little chance to honestly atone for his crime, and even less chance to learn and change his life's direction. Instead he's terrified – so terrified his only concentration is survival."

"I see," Abrams replied. "Am I to understand that this consortium agrees with Fr. Ted's assessment?"

Rowland spoke for the group, "It is, Amos." Straightening his back and pushing out onto the edge of his chair, Rowland added; "I cannot possibly overstate the consequential nature of our advocacy for this young man...and ultimately others like him."

He cast his eyes around the room, "Each of us sitting here, including you yourself, Judge Abrams, represents an important contributor to what becomes of James Meyers." Thoughtful eyes stared back at Rowland as he continued, "What good is incarceration – even as punishment – if it fails to produce a better man? Or worse, if instead it produces an embittered young man confirmed in his suspicion that life is stacked against him?"

In a conciliatory gesture, Rowland addressed Abrams; "Amos, I didn't call this meeting in order to leverage you into amending Meyers' confinement. It was and is my hope that we together can come to an acceptable alternative that serves both justice and the best interest of this young man. I agree with Fr. Ted. Meyer's is no criminal. He's the kid who threw a large rock through a window for one purpose – to let the world know he exists and he matters." He hesitated before adding, "I concede drug dealing is far more than a rock – deserving severe punishment. Like others have already judged, I too agree Meyers' deserves prison. But he does not deserve to be the prey of gangland predators. And that is what he risks if he's kept at the State House…or sent to another maximum-security prison."

"Apparently you agree, Bill," Abrams asked of Parker.

"I do, Amos. I think Tom's spot on."

"But minimum security? How can you honestly justify minimum security?" Spreading his arms as if pleading, Abrams argued, "What kind of precedent does that establish for future cases? You know how the law works. Once a case is re-adjudicated it becomes *stare decisis*…precedent…affecting the outcomes of future cases." Gesturing as if pleading a case, Abrams concluded, "If we…If *I* commute Meyers' sentence, haven't I materially established unfair precedence?"

"I concur, Amos, that indeed you will have established precedence. But I take umbrage that you insist it would be *unfair* precedence" Judge Parker rebutted. "That, however, doesn't mitigate the larger problem…There's a young man's life at stake, Amos!" Avoiding Abrams' attempt to butt in, Parker waged ahead, "And the precedence you will have established will carry the weight of court records and rebuttal argument that explicitly defines the conditions under which this precedence was created." Parker's voice rose and remained forceful, "As you well know, Amos, applying the law is not merely – nor is it ever merely – a matter of rendering judgment. Judgment stands on evidence, results from arguments made pro and con on the strength of that evidence, and is entered into the record accordingly. It is never merely naked judgment. It is *trial* judgment."

"But it is precedence made from an exception to explicit statutes pertaining to cases like Meyers'!" Judge Abrams bellowed dropping a clenched fist on the table as if to punctuate his point.

"Amos, this *is* an exceptional circumstance!" Roland insisted. "Let me remind you again, a young man's life hangs on the wisdom of our judgment."

He must have felt ganged up on – or at least as if the argument was lost; because Abrams dropped his hands onto his lap and sighed; lowered his voice and became reflective. "How do we ever make truly wise and profitable judgments? At best we make compromises that are neither entirely fair nor entirely right." Taking a moment to think, Abrams sat as if alone, lost in the cavern of his own conflicted thoughts. Calmly in measured tones he continued, "We do our best. We study; we argue; we ponder; we consult God or our own conscience, and then with all the fortitude of will we can muster we render our conclusions. Never perfect. Always and painfully a compromise with the perfect."

"Sadly so, my friend," Parker groaned. "I can't say I have ever rendered a judgment where I was fully persuaded it was without incident of mistake." Looking up at the ceiling as if appealing to the heavens, he confessed, "I've paced the floor at night wondering what I overlooked; what bias clouded my objectivity. In the end, Amos, we do our humanly best to interpret something so complex as the law."

"And human nature," Fr. Ted added.

"Yes indeed, and human nature," Parker conceded.

"So where do we stand, Tom? Where do we go from here?" Parker inquired as if pleading for a rational answer to an improbable set of circumstances.

Seated deeply into his chair, elbows resting on its arms, his fingers laced, Rowland surveyed the strained and serious faces as he weighed Parker's question. His eyes paused at the far end of the table where sat his closest ally and dearest friend, "Ted are you up to taking accountability as James Meyers' guardian?"

"Yes, and eagerly so, Tom," came Fr. Ted's response with a reassuring smile.

Then the wise priest turned the tables, "Are you?" Fr. Ted asked in return, "Are you ready to stand with me?" Gesturing to those seated around what was now a table of inquisition, "Are all of you ready to stand with this young man?"

"I am," Rowland solemnly assured.

"As am I, Father," Parker joined.

Others quietly acknowledged their support. No one dissented.

"Judge Abrams, I'd say the ball is in your court. Will you help us help this young man?" Rowland calmly asked.

Still troubled by what he regarded as an unorthodox – and perhaps unmerited request, Abrams tacitly replied, "Reluctantly I'll agree to review Meyer's case, Tom."

"Reluctantly? Why the reluctance? What's bothering you, Amos?" Rowland asked not masking his annoyance at Abram's less than full concurrence.

"I've never commuted a sentence where I felt strongly the evidence supported the judgment, Tom." Abrams took a moment before continuing. No one interrupted. "In this case, however, I may have overlooked something of graver consequence. I may have not taken into serious consideration the young man himself." Abram's stared blankly into space.

"In fact at his sentencing I distinctly remember asking Meyers what went wrong. Where and why did life stop meaning something precious and vital to him?" Once again he paused. Pensively rubbing his deeply furrowed brow, he went on: "From every perspective worth considering, he had far more going for him than against him. He simply didn't fit the profile of a drug dealer." Looking now at Rowland, he concluded, "And yet as the man presiding from the bench, I felt constrained by my oath to uphold the law. I chose to overlook what might be construed as paternal concern for a troubled young man in order to objectively…and justly…enforce the law to the letter."

With a pained look of confusion etched across his face, Abrams fairly begged Rowland, "What would you do, Tom? If you were me, sitting in the seat of judgment, sworn by oath to uphold the law, what would you do differently? I'm truly torn." Looking across the table at those advocating for James Meyers, he concluded, "Each member present has made a clear unambiguous case for this young man. I'm persuaded by the compassion and conviction each of you has demonstrated. I am also persuaded by this sworn duty that constrains me."

"Tom if I may," Judge Parker interceded. "Like you, Amos, I sit on the bench and make judgments from evidence. Like you I find myself in difficult, at times seemingly irreconcilable, conflict with my duty and my heart. And like you, Amos, I'm a father." Parker halted. An anguished expression spread across his face. "Unlike you, my friend, I have not lost a son."

"I think I might be getting your drift, Bill," Abrams said in a tone of careful deliberation.

"I think you might too, Amos. If I were where you find yourself right now, even in light of all the arguments we've made, I can't honestly say what I'd do or how I'd render judgment. But I've had the advantage of watching Tom, Fr. Ted and a couple other men…one a former convict who served his time at the State House."

"I'm certain you're speaking of Anne's husband," Abrams acknowledged.

"I am. These men, Amos, haven't set aside the fact that Meyers' committed a crime deserving the punishment you meted out. They have, however, looked past it into the soul of the young man and advocated for him. It's this kind of accountability – men assuming the responsibility of mentoring a younger man – that compels me to look not only to the letter of the law but its spirit." Parker sat forward in his chair, leaning toward his longtime friend and colleague, "You know as well as any of us that spirit…the *spirit* of the law…seeks the reformation and restoration of the prisoner every bit as much as it applies just punishment for the crime committed."

Abrams turned toward Rowland, "You truly believe you can help this young man?"

"Yes, Amos, I do. And so do the men and many other people who have stood with us."

"Others?" Abrams remarked inquisitively.

"Our spouses and a group of kids who've united with us every night at Ted's parish to pray for James."

"I see," Abrams replied. "It appears Meyers has a small army looking out for him."

"Oh, it's an army made in Heaven," Fr. Ted said through a wry smile and twinkle in his eye.

Abrams laughed out loud, and those around the table shared the laugher with him.

"So, dear priest, you're advising me that I'm taking on Heaven itself if I were to uphold Meyers' sentence?" Abrams responded adding his own twist of humor.

"Your honor might be doing precisely that," Fr. Ted playfully rejoined.

Again pleasant laughter swept the room.

"Well," Abrams said regaining his decorum, "I think, Tom and members, I would like to see your proposal. And I assure you I will entertain it, which is to say take it seriously." Gesturing politely toward the panel members he added, "In all candor, people, I'm moved by your commitment to this young man's well being, especially by the force of your convictions. I'm also persuaded in light of his circumstances to reconsider his incarceration. How soon can you produce your proposal?"

Rowland looked at Anne, who was already reaching into her attaché. "Immediately, your honor," Anne answered, sliding a bound document toward Judge Abrams.

"Impressive," Abrams remarked with a chuckle. "Thank you, Mrs. Hall." Addressing Rowland, "I'll render opinion by ten o'clock tomorrow morning. Will that be soon enough?"

"It would, Judge Abrams. You have our gratitude," Rowland answered.

FORTY-NINE

Rowland sat perched at his desk fidgeting with his glasses. Fr. Ted occupied a spot on the leather couch with a cup of Earl Grey. Scanlon straddled backwards on one of the side chairs, while Terrance browsed Rowland's library. Twenty minutes after ten and no word yet from Judge Abrams. Each man, somewhat bleary-eyed from the late-night prayer gathering at Fr. Ted's parish, barely said a word. Scanlon mustered monosyllabic grunts when addressed. Fr. Ted, usually open to conversation, distilled his thoughts in quiet solitude. Only the sound of Terrance flipping pages disturbed the silence. For all the look of it, one might have thought a funeral procession was about to break out.

Anne waited patiently in her office, doodling away on a brief that really needed no attention. She promised not to call but wait – prayerfully wait. Mary Rowland and Stephanie Raynor sat pensively by the phone at the Rowland residence stirring their coffee, muttering quick prayers, anxious as anyone for hopeful news. James, on the other hand, was entirely oblivious to any of this, sitting idly in his cell pondering his meeting with Terri – her prayer, his admission and wondering – still wondering – what lie in store.

"Rowland here," Tom Rowland answered barely before anyone else heard the phone ring. Terrance closed the book in his hands, grasping it like was a life preserver. Fr. Ted, caught mid sip, held his cup an inch from his open mouth. Scanlon sat erect in his chair. All waited, listening for the slightest meaningful word, any inflection or gesture from Rowland.

"Yes, I see, Amos. I understand," Rowland said giving away nothing. For the sound of it, the news wasn't favorable. "I'll convey your conclusions to the team. They're here with me," he remarked. Rowland rubbed his forehead, his eyes riveted to a spot on his desk. "I appreciate your call. Thank you, Amos. Good day."

Rowland held the receiver close to his face before returning it to its cradle. Finally he raised his eyes; three pairs of eyes were riveted on his. "Gentlemen," he began. "It appears God has heard our prayer." Fr. Ted sat his cup on its saucer and placed it on the coffee table in front of him. Scanlon stood, still straddling the chair. Terrance took a step toward Rowland's desk, "Tell us, Tom."

Rowland could hardly hold his composure. A slight tremor in his voice betrayed the deep emotion surging through his entire body. "Judge Abrams has agreed to our proposal...as submitted." Looking directly into the men's faces, he announced, "James will be reassigned to the minimum correctional facility. Ted, you're his court appointed guardian. Mike and Terrance, you are assistant guardians under Ted's authority. Men, James doesn't know it, but the world just changed for him. It has changed and so must he."

Terrance and Mike pumped their fists in the air shouting like warriors who vanquished the enemy. Fr. Ted could hardly contain himself. He rose to his feet and embraced his trusted friend as Rowland came from behind his desk to join in the celebration.

Betty burst through the door with a stunned look of bewilderment spread across her face. Rowland hadn't told her anything. "What is going on in here?" she demanded.

"Betty, great news!" Rowland announced.

"What great news?" Betty begged thoroughly bewildered by the scene.

"James Meyers, Betty."

"What about James Meyers?" She insisted, spreading her arms palms up as if entirely lost at sea.

"He caught the most important break of his young life," Rowland enthused.

"Okay! Tell me," she pleaded.

"Oh, I wish I could. Bear with me for now. I'll get you up to date later today."

"Okay, but…"

"Yes, I'm sure we look like lunatics right now. But I assure you, we're quite within our minds despite any appearance to the contrary."

"Lunatics? Yes, that pretty much sizes it up," She said shaking her head as she closed the door behind her. The "lunatics" continued their celebration. Finally Rowland raised his hand and the loud reveling ceased. "We've got to thank God right now, men. He has answered!" Together the men huddled up as if gathering in the end zone after a game-winning touchdown. "Ted, lead us," Rowland directed.

"Gladly, Tom. Most gladly," Fr. Ted replied, bowing his head.

As Fr. Ted's prayer concluded Rowland's phone rang again. It was Judge Parker extending hearty congratulations and encouragement to the posse and most ingenuously to the young man he once suspected of the Chalmers murder – James Meyers.

"Tom," Fr. Ted inquired, "What else can you tell us?" The men took their seats, Rowland leaning against the front of his desk, arms folded across his chest.

"I'll advise Raynor in a moment and summon James to my office this afternoon. Can you men join me say two o'clock?"

"Count on it," Terrance confirmed for himself.

"My calendar's clear, Tom," Fr. Ted added.

"Me too," Mike chimed in.

"Okay, two o'clock it is, here in my office."

Rowland then spelled out the few available details. "I'll get a call likely later today from the facility formally advising me of their acceptance and probable move date, which I'm assuming will be tomorrow sometime."

"That soon?" Scanlon interrupted pleasantly surprised by the timeframe.

"Yes, Mike. The sooner the better. Between now and then I'll be directing Raynor to increase security around James." Turning to his friend he asked, "Ted, can you meet James at the new facility?"

"I'll go one better. I'd like to ride along from here if that can be arranged."

"I'll see to it," Rowland said, jotting a note and dropping it on his desk planner.

Terrance wanted more. "Aside from his protection, what else does this move really mean for James, Tom?"

Rowland pursed his lips before answering, "That's a great question, Terrance. What I envision is more face time for you guys with James."

"I'm of the opinion from past experience it should ease James' tension, give him some breathing room...and a sense of hope that he hasn't had in sometime," Fr. Ted added. "And another thing," Thinking further out loud, he extended his comments, "And perhaps Terri, his young nurse friend, can play a larger role in his life. At least I hope so," he finished with a wistful smile stretching his beard.

"Matchmaker Fr. Ted," Scanlon scoffed. "You old..."

"Watch yourself, Michael. I am a priest," Fr. Ted cautioned pointing a finger upward to the sky. "God is listening."

"Yeah, yeah, yeah," Scanlon scoffed. "Seriously, guys, don't you get the feeling the kid is finally out of purgatory?" Once again Scanlon set himself up like a lobbed softball for Fr. Ted's sharp wit.

"Purgatory you say, Michael. Well perhaps he is, but I dare say you aren't."

The room roared with laughter. Betty rose from her desk but resisted the urge to disturb the "lunatics." Scanlon just dropped his head in mock dejection.

Terrance threw an arm around his pal's massive shoulders. "I'm with Scans," he announced. "If the kid's not out of purgatory, he's sure as sunrise out of hell."

Scanlon shoved an elbow in Terrance's ribs, "I'll take that, T. You and I've been there – hell and back. Now it's the kid's turn." Running a hand over his head, "He knows hell. Let's give him heaven!"

"Amen! Big guy. Amen!" Terrance affirmed pumping his free fist into the air.

Rowland rested against his desk, enthralled by the morning's events. Drained but exhilarated, he reached for the phone.

"Who you calling, Tom?" Terrance asked; a massive smile plastered across his face.

"You're bride, Terrance. I'm calling Anne."

Terrance nodded. "She'll be thrilled. Matter of fact, I think I'll dash over there now."

"I'm heading for home," Scanlon announced. "Sally's got to hear this first hand."

For Fr. Ted, it was time to make his way to the church, to its altar where a meeting with God awaited. He knew better than everybody that step one of a long catechetical journey – a journey of transformation – was still unfinished. James needed further intercession. As a priest, he knew his job was to present James to Christ. Like Abraham offered Isaac so must this father offer his godson to God.

*****

One more bewildering walk to the administration building with a guard who revealed nothing, James strode gingerly still compromised by lingering fatigue and pain as the guard held firmly onto his arm. Not a word passed between either of them; James certain the guard, if he knew anything, wouldn't reveal it. Then too, he caught the vibe that security might still be part of the motivation to move as expeditiously as his wounded body would allow.

"Go on in, James," Betty directed. "They're waiting for you."

"They're waiting? Who's they?" James asked somewhat timidly.

"Oh, yes. You'll see," Betty teased with a coy lilt to her voice.

The guard unlocked the cuffs. As they fell from James' wrists, the door to Rowland's office opened. He stepped in and was suddenly subsumed by a room full of familiar faces, all of which seemed apparently pleased by more than his presence. Dumbfounded by the scene, he wasn't certain how to react. Immediately his eyes locked on his dad, who rose from the leather couch and moved across the room to embrace his son.

"Dad?" James asked awkwardly. "Mom?" He asked, again struck by the unexpected sight of his parents. By now his mom had joined James and her husband in a family embrace, while the others nestled in Rowland's office were warmed by the spectacle.

Motioning to James, Rowland said, "Have a seat, young man. We have some things to discuss with you."

Mom and dad returned to their place on the couch, as James, thoroughly caught off guard, slipped into the only open chair in the office, obviously quite taken aback by the sight of his parents and the posse – Anne among them. He scanned the room, taking note of those in attendance. Fr. Ted stood behind the couch, resting a reassuring hand on the shoulder of each of James' parents, sporting that wise grin that stretched his thick salty beard. Anne had taken a seat in the large leather chair to the left of the coffee table, with Terrance perched on one of the armrests beside her, an arm affectionately draped over her shoulders. Scanlon, ball cap pushed back on his head, parked on the far corner of Rowland's desk, while Rowland reposed in his high-backed leather desk chair, arms crossed – a full house for sure. He felt like he was on exhibit, like a fish in the fishbowl. His mind raced: "What the heck was going on?" While he was tensed and on edge, everyone else seemed quite relaxed, like cousins gathering for a family photo. Even his mom appeared unusually poised, maybe even radiant. The broad grin on his dad's face seemed out of context for a meeting at the prison. For a flickering second, he expected the door to open and Terri to step in. She didn't. Right now, he'd have felt more comfortable if she had shown up. She'd become the shoulder he could lean on; the one person he trusted most, whom he believed understood him best.

"You appear somewhat uncomfortable, James;" an apparent rhetorical observation on Rowland's part, or so it seemed to James.

"That's an understatement, sir," James answered, his voice tinged with a note of sarcasm.

Rowland rocked comfortably in his chair, "I'm guessing you would like to know what all this hubbub is about?'

James said nothing, just shrugged his shoulders as if the answer were self-evident.

"You recall me asking if you'd read a certain phrase in that book?" Rowland asked, referring to Chesterton.

"Yeah. Sure. Why?"

"Do you recall the phrase?"

"You mean the one about finding an angle that won't let me down?"

"That's the one," Rowland confirmed.

"Okay, but what about it?"

Rowland leaned forward in his chair, resting his crossed arms on his desk. "You might also recall my comments. That perhaps given the people surrounding you that day, you might consider a new possibility – an angle against which you could lean without worry that it would fall out from under you."

James surveyed the room again. He couldn't deny the support he'd received from each person seated in front of him, including his parents. "So? What are you telling me?" he asked, returning his attention to Rowland.

"What one thing do these people have in common, James?"

Once more James' eyes roamed the room, at times catching his own reflection in the eyes of those seated only feet away. Terri came to mind, as did the nurse in the dispensary, even Mr. Raynor, the head guard. Each one had offered him a ray of hope then backed it up with their actions. He bit his lower lip, perhaps to disguise welling emotion he couldn't fully stifle. "They have me in common," he answered. "I'm what they have in common."

"That's right, son," Rowland affirmed, speaking like a father and not the warden. "They are an important part of that wall, James. They've stood for you when you couldn't stand for yourself." Rowland rose from his chair and leaned against the near corner of his desk. "Young man, these people, and many others, have carried you since you arrived in prison. They've listened to you; prayed for you; advocated for you; and offered you hope for a better, more satisfying life. They are pillars planted by God in that wall, James. With God, they are that wall."

Rowland's phone buzzed. "Send her in, Betty."

As the door opened behind him, James turned to see who was entering the room. "Terri!" he exclaimed, rising to his feet to meet her.

The two kids exchanged a brief hug, as James' mom slid closer to her husband to make room for Terri beside them on the couch.

"You know my folks?" James was taken aback by the obvious familiarity between Terri and his family.

"Oh, sure," Kathleen, James' mom, said. "We've been praying together for you." She added, giving Terri a pat on the knee.

"Well, now that we're all here," Rowland broke in. "About that wall, James – it's here…and it's been working on your behalf."

Rowland pointed at Anne, who lifted a neatly bound document from her lap. "James, I'm not sure we've ever been formally introduced. I'm Anne, Terrance's wife and *the Warden's* daughter." Her emphasis on the Warden drew a mawkish groan from the posse.

"Inside joke," Fr. Ted explained with his customary wink.

"I've been working on your legal file, attempting to find ways we can help you while also upholding appropriate justice. That might not all make sense, but there's a reason behind it." Anne looked at her dad for concurrence.

"That's right." Addressing James directly, "While the Inquiry exonerated you of any culpability for Nate Chalmers' death, it raised attention to your at-risk status here in the State House. Anne, and certain of her firm's colleagues, have undertaken on their own time, and at their own expense, to research court records pertaining to similar situations in other penitentiaries. She presented her discovery to me and a panel that included your sentencing judge for consideration."

Rowland walked across the room and retrieved the document Anne was holding out to him. Returning to his desk, he pulled his glasses from his shirt pocket and opened it to the relevant page that described the revised court orders.

James sat anxiously in his seat, wondering what this all meant. Expressions hadn't changed. Smiles still dominated. Eyes focused on

Rowland, who stood statuesque beside his desk, intently surveying every page. He, now, was the judge. And James was his subject.

The scene set James on edge. He felt himself brace. Unwelcome memories flooded his mind, memories of Judge Abrams studying the document from which, while leering down from his high perch on the bench, he would pronounce sentence – "James Taylor Meyers the court has found you guilty…you are hereby sentenced…" And then that thundering echo of the gavel's fall that punctuated the verdict and sent a shockwave of soul killing dread through his body; like then, James found himself involuntarily quiver awaiting Rowland's *verdict*. Terri noticed and shot James a soft smile, mouthing the words, "It'll be okay." He drew a deep breath and waited.

Rowland peered over his glasses and looked James directly in the eyes. James squirmed and straightened to face him.

"James, the court has come to the conclusion in the matter of your sentencing to move you from maximum security here at the State House, to minimum security at the Marysville Correctional Institution a short distance from here."

James' eyes widened. His heart raced. Was this a dream? Had he heard Rowland correctly? Minimum security? What did it mean? He waited for more.

"Sir? Minimum security? I don't understand. Why?"

"It has been determined that the State House presents a substantial risk to your safety. It was the opinion of the panel I mentioned earlier that you need to be moved…immediately. It also means a change of status but not a change of sentence. You will serve out the remaining portion of your six year sentence, but you will be housed in a safer environment, and one we're persuaded is more suitable to your situation."

"I'm…I don't know what to say." James ran his hands through his hair.

"You needn't say anything, James," Rowland's reply was terse. "What you need to do, son, is continue the behavior you've exhibited so far here. Can you do that?"

"Yes, of course, sir. I can do that."

"That's all we ask of you for now." Rowland crossed his arms as he stood over James, the file still in his hand. "You might also recall something else I said to you when you first arrived. I cautioned you to toe the line."

"Yes you did, sir. Have I?"

"This move would not have occurred, regardless of your circumstances, if you hadn't. The most compelling action you took in your favor, James, was helping a fellow inmate in crisis…even though it eventually cost you something too. You may have acted naively in terms of prison culture. But you acted out of concern as a human being for another human being. That has merit, son."

James dropped his head, "But he died anyway."

"He died with an advocate," Fr. Ted offered. "He died with a friend."

James lifted his head to see approving nods and proud parents looking back at him.

"You seem troubled, James" Fr. Ted observed.

"Oh, not really, Fr. Ted. It's just that I wonder…" James' voice trailed off.

"Wonder what?" Rowland urged.

"Can you tell me what it means for us…for our conversations?" Looking at Fr. Ted, "I just sent a note asking to meet with Fr. Ted…and with Terrance."

"Listen to me, James," Rowland demanded. "You needn't worry about that. We're not abandoning you, son. Actually, those matters will improve. One of the advantages to minimum security is more visits and more frequent visits. It also means that you'll be assigned a guardian, someone who will take accountability for you under the court's jurisdiction."

"A guardian?" James asked pensively.

"Yes, a guardian," Rowland confirmed.

"Do you know who, sir?"

"Someone I think you'll approve of," Rowland said letting his eyes drift in the direction of a broadly beaming Fr. Ted.

"Fr. Ted?" James asked, his voice rising with anticipation.

"Fr. Ted, James." Rowland raised an open hand, halting James' effort to comment, "And it gets worse."

"How so?"

"Terrance and Mike have been appointed assistant or associate guardians under Fr. Ted."

Terri couldn't hold back, "And I get to come by more often."

"And so do we, son," James' dad, Don, said with a father's pride.

James could hardly believe his ears. Was this truly the angle Rowland foresaw against which he would not fall? Was this the unfailing wall he spoke of moments ago? Suddenly he broke down, fell from his chair onto his knees weeping as if he'd been pardoned from a fate worse than death itself. His shoulders heaved; heavy waves of emotion poured out of him with the force of a breached dike. All of the pent up emotion bottled inside, all the fear and doubt gushed from the subterranean depths of his soul. His mom and dad dropped to their knees beside him. Terri fell to her knees, wrapping her arms around his shoulders, sobbing tears of delight. Fr. Ted made the sign of the cross, whispering a prayer as he swept his hand across his chest. Scanlon bent over still seated on Rowland's desk, earnestly yet quietly praying. Terrance and Anne, clasped hands as they, too, prayed quietly between themselves. Rowland stood stalwartly over them, watching and praying.

"James," Rowland interrupted, his voice affecting quiet authority. James rose, still kneeling on the carpeted floor, his occasional snarky attitude gone. Brushing tears from his swollen eyes he looked at the figure of the man he once feared, the Iron Czar as he was known throughout the cell blocks. But now, the man was like the father he'd hoped his father would be. "There's more."

Pulling himself back onto his chair, James regained his composure.

"You will be required to write a letter to the two judges whose advocacy made this day possible. You will express your appreciation to Judge Abrams and Judge Parker. Both men took a huge risk releasing you to the custody of members present with you in this office. Have I made myself clear?"

"You have sir. But why…why did they change their minds?"

"They changed their minds, James, because we…those of us here…convinced them that we would take accountability for you, and that you would present no threat to their good judgment or our good faith." Rowland stiffened, "Am I right?"

"Yeah…yes…certainly sir. I won't do anything to make them…or any of you…regret what you've done for me." James' eyes went vacant as he pondered what had transpired. Looking at the floor, still shaking his head as if in a fog, he said, "I can't tell you what this means. I hardly know how to thank you…all of you." An image came to mind he had never considered until now. "You've become like family to me and to my folks. You are my family," he said through tears coursing down his face. Looking up at Rowland whose expression had not changed, "Sir, does this mean you'll honor my request to meet with Terrance and Fr. Ted?"

"Tomorrow morning…nine o'clock…at your new residence." Rowland glowered.

"Sir: Something wrong?" James asked.

"Just this young man. Why wasn't I invited?"

"Oh my gosh, sir. I didn't mean…"

"No worries, son," Rowland interrupted with wave of the hand. "You'll get your date with the priest and the ex-con."

Laughter began to roll through the office and this time Betty joined the crowd. Rowland waved her through the door. "Well, Betty, we're saying goodbye to James this afternoon. He's heading for Marysville."

"Well, I'll be," she cried. "What a wonderful surprise!" She gave James a motherly squeeze, "I'm so happy for you! You'll be missed…by me at least," a playful twist of humor rising in her voice and expression.

"I'll miss you too, ma`am. You've been kind to me. I appreciate it. Thanks!"

"Oh, you are quite welcome, Mr. James Meyers. I can't wait to see what you make of yourself." She barely took a breath before wagging her finger in his face, "You know, Mr. Meyers, you have possibilities. Don't you let anybody tell you otherwise!" A motherly scowl came across her face, "You'd better agree with me on this, Mr. Meyers. I'll chase you down if you don't!"

"I do! Honestly, ma`am...I do!" All the others got quite a kick out Betty's insistence. James was no match for this feisty, motherly lady who cared so very much for the young man.

"Good! You see to it that you behave yourself; get straight and stay straight!" She snapped, her finger wagging ever furiously under James' nose. "I want to hear only good things about you. And I *will* be listening!" With that last jab, Betty embraced James once more, turned and walked back out the door, wiping tears from her eyes.

FIFTY

A bracing rush of early spring air, vibrant and fresh sent an exhilarating charge through James' slender body, a body that had become even more slender with recent events. It had been some time since he last tasted the out of doors; caught the fragrance of freshly mowed grass or the pungent aroma of blooming jasmine. It had been longer still since he rode in a windowed vehicle and saw the countryside pass by. His imagination seemed to awaken, and Fr. Ted observed a spark of enthusiasm in his young charge.

"Beautiful day," Fr. Ted mused.

"Yeah!" James offered in one word.

Fr. Ted chuckled. James' eyes never left the scenery racing past. He seemed like a boy who'd never seen the wide open spaces, the lush spring farmland or sunlight bursting through breaks in the brilliant white clouds.

"What's so funny?" James snarled.

"You are, my young friend. You are," Fr. Ted didn't hold back his laughter.

"Huh?"

"You remind me of a new pup on its first car ride; taking in everything as if amazed by it all."

"I kinda am amazed, Father." James said; his voice softening. "It's been a long time. I didn't think I'd ever see this stuff again."

"New life, son – Spring is about new life."

The van pulled through the open gate. Tall elms, limbs still in their naked winter dormancy, lined the long driveway into Marysville Correctional Institution, James' new home. Coming to a stop in front of the red-brick, colonial styled single-story building, a guard stepped from the large white-washed front doors, strode authoritatively toward the van, and opened the sliding door. "James Meyers?" He asked plaintively.

"Yes, sir," James replied.

"Please step out and follow me."

James stepped out onto the curving sidewalk, Fr. Ted immediately behind him. Nothing drab about this place, James thought quietly to himself. Gray-stone walls overwhelmed by parasitic ivy; rows of coiled razor wire; guards over-lurking a stubble grass yard – no more. In contrast this was Eden. Early spring crocus and daffodils rested comfortably in neatly groomed beds, with manicured boxwoods flanking them. Birds flitting about from tree to tree trilled their greeting. Only the shackles binding his wrists and ankles reminded him of his status – a felon.

"This way, men," the guard ordered, turning a corner inside the open entrance, and striding down a long hallway. He stopped in front of a glass-paned door, opened it, stepped aside and ushered the men into the comfortably appointed outer office. A closed door opposite the room announced its occupant – Bramford Thomas Hollinswood, Warden.

The entrance door opened again. A short, rather officious behaving woman, primly clad in a brownish wool suit burst in. All five feet of her petite frame strutted by the men as if they were invisible. "Must be the house governess," Fr. Ted mused snidely to himself; a noticeable curl to his lip. She properly sat down behind the oak desk situated to the right of the warden's office door, slid her glasses onto her nose, which hung pendant on a chain around her neck, and picked up the phone. "Yes, Mr. Rowland, I believe the men standing in front of me are the ones to whom you refer. They apparently just arrived." She waited a moment, evidently getting instructions from Rowland. "Yes, sir, I will pass your message along," she replied in feigned congeniality, and dropped the receiver onto its cradle.

"You must be Fr. Ted," she said with an air of diffidence, as if indicting him for being a priest. "And *you*...you must be James Meyers...our *new* prisoner," as if greeting a boarding school arrival – or a rodent.

"We are, madam," Fr. Ted replied. "And who might you be?"

"Mrs. Washburn, sir. I am the Warden's private secretary," she added twisting her nose skyward. The cosmetic southern inflection, however, was what really amused Fr. Ted.

"What part of the south, Mrs. Washburn, do you hail from?"

"South, sir? You think I'm from the South?"

"Your accent, madam."

"I am from Manchester, New Hampshire, from a long, proud line of New Hampshireites," she answered, her voice swollen with pride.

Though he stifled it, Fr. Ted's first impression went something like, "No wonder it's called the Granite State – cold and rigid." As for the affected accent, discretion coaxed him into leaving it alone, though it took every ounce of restraint to bite his tongue.

James, on the other hand, had a slightly different impression, which he, too, kept to himself. It rhymed with itch.

"You told Warden Rowland you'd pass along his message," Fr. Ted nudged.

"Oh yes!" Adjusting her glasses, "He wanted to let you know, Betty already misses James."

"I'm certain she does, Mrs. Washburn," Fr. Ted confirmed, rocking on his toes. In an affected tone of his own, he went on, "James made quite the impression. I'm truly certain, my dear lady, the two of you will get along quite nicely." Mrs. Washburn's mouth fell open, and she huffed a bit, obviously not the least amused by the priest's false pretentiousness.

Gripping the lapels of his tweed jacket, Fr. Ted asked, "When might we see Warden Hollinswood? He is expecting us isn't he?"

"Yes, quite right, sir, I mean Father," she replied, somewhat flustered by her lack of decorum. Fr. Ted had caught her off her game, which obviously somewhat unhinged poor Mrs. Washburn. James hadn't been this entertained in months. He felt like kicking his impertinent guardian, but at the same time really enjoyed the act.

"Warden Hollinswood will see you now," Mrs. Washburn said while rising to open the door into his office. "Go right in," she said through a strained smile, her hair bun bobbing awkwardly atop her head.

"Father Theodore Harding, how the world are you my good friend?" From behind the large oak desk that sat in front of barred windows, a long, lanky frame unfolded rising to his feet, all six feet six inches of him, his mostly silver short-cropped afro gleaming in the streaming daylight through the window panes, "C'mon in here. Good to see you again. It's been awhile."

Fr. Ted reached across the desk to shake Hollinswood's outstretched hand. "It has been awhile, Bram." The two old friends greeted one another like brothers.

"Well, have a seat gentlemen. Let's talk," Hollinswood said gesturing to the two wood chairs in front of his desk. Crossing his hands in front of his chest, while leaning into the back of his own tall executive chair, Hollinswood took a moment to silently appraise his new tenant. Studying him as if staring into a curious piece of art or diagnosing a wart, he'd occasionally mutter "Hmmm...I see." The ordeal put James' teeth on edge, but he said nothing. Satisfied he had a bead on his subject Hollinswood glided a hand over his face, rocked forward in his chair and leaned imposingly over his desk.

"James Meyers," tumbled like thunder from his mouth, drawing out James' name as it if were a line of poetry, his basso voice strong, resonate.

James snapped to attention, "Yes, sir."

"I'm told you've had a spot of trouble come your way."

Again James answered briefly, "Yes sir."

"Care to inform me about it?"

James shot a glance at Fr. Ted, who merely nodded while training his eyes on Hollinswood.

"I was knifed, sir."

"Yes, I know, young man. But why are you in prison?"

James' head fell to his chest, "I broke the law, sir."

"How?" Hollinswood pressed.

"I got caught dealing drugs."

"Indeed you did, son." Hollinswood glowered over his black-rimmed glasses, "Was it worth it?"

James' shoulders slumped, "No." Raising his head, he addressed Warden Hollinswood straightforwardly, "It definitely wasn't."

Hollinswood let out a long sigh, "So here you are." With that, Warden Hollinswood reached across his desk, presenting his hand to James. James had to stand in order to shake the warden's hand. Hollinswood didn't let go. "James, I know your story. The good father here and Warden Rowland filled me in quite well. We'll talk about that more later."

Returning to his chair, Hollinswood's long, creased face grew serious. "There's just a few things you need to know about Marysville."

James sat up.

"It's still prison, son. Don't let the flowers outside fool you. You're still in prison."

James' eyes clamped shut as the weight of Hollinswood's words washed over him.

"You have most of five years remaining to your sentence. And, barring any behavioral issues from you, this is where you'll spend them. That clear?"

"Yes, sir. It's clear."

"That said, there are some differences between here and where you came from. One thing, however, remains as it was – discipline. You will behave or you will return to the State House. Again, have I made myself clear?"

Hollinswood's commanding voice needn't be repeated. The sounds it made were as clear as the words it spoke.

James nodded his understanding, "You have, sir."

"Good." The tension released from Hollinswood's face. "So here's the difference – Security. There are guards, alarms and the like, but there's no high walls, no razor wire, nobody standing guard in a tower. Your room has a bed in it, and we do call it a room...not a cell. You have privacy, although there's a narrow window beside the door. And the door...it's locked. But it's wood not steel. You have a water basin and john. If you want books, you can have all the books your room will hold. They will be inspected before being delivered to you. But I encourage the men to read – to learn – to educate themselves. From what I've read and what Fr. Ted has told me, you're quite the reader." A silly smirk came over his face, "Tell me. Do you really dig Foucault?"

"You know Foucault, sir?" James asked, eyes widening.

"Well we've never met, if that's what you mean. But, yeah, I've read some of his stuff."

"Wow," James said before he thought. "I mean, that's something."

"What? You think you're the only scholar in the room?" Hollinswood boomed in mock rebuke.

James stammered, "No...I guess not. No, of course not."

Hollinswood threw his head back and roared in sonorous peals of laughter. Fr. Ted joined him.

James hardly knew what to think. Once again he found himself the butt of an awkward joke.

"Well, my dear young Meyers, I'll have you know I went to school too!" Hollinswood sneered, still laughing.

"I'm sure you did, sir. I didn't mean to…"

"Oh forget it, son! I was jerking your chain." Gawking over at a chortling Fr. Ted, he remarked, "Looks like it worked."

"Indeed it did!" Fr. Ted blurted. "Indeed it did!"

James regained his composure, somewhat relieved by the humor even at his expense. It made him feel at home, like Rowland's office had come to mean to him.

"If I may ask, where did you attend college, sir?" James inquired.

Pointing to the diplomas hanging in frames on the opposite wall, alongside the door they entered, Hollinswood answered, "Howard University for my undergrad, James." Then pointing a little to the right, "And another H-word college for law school."

"H-word school? You must not mean Yale then?" James asked innocently enough.

"Yale!" Hollinswood boomed. "Yale?' He glared over his glasses at James, who was now convinced he'd committed the unpardonable sin and was doomed to the netherworld.

"Yale is not Harvard, son! I went to Harvard! Go look at that diploma."

"Now sir?" James was still reeling.

"Yes, now!"

Fr. Ted was thoroughly entertained.

James rose from his chair and waddled over to the wall where the diplomas hung proudly in place. "Did you practice law too, sir?"

"I did. I did indeed."

"Were you a prosecutor?"

"Defense attorney, son. Like your Mr. Rowland, I defended clients."

"I don't mean any disrespect, sir. But why give up it all up to work in a prison?"

"Good question, Mr. Meyers! I'll answer it." Hollinswood flopped both of his long feet on his desk and rocked back in his chair. "I was asked to."

"The governor?" James probed.

"Yes, the governor, but someone else…someone higher up."

"Higher than the governor? You mean like the president?" James asked incredulously.

Hollinswood laughed again and winked at Fr. Ted. "No son, not the president. The president isn't high enough."

"Who then?" James asked shrugging his shoulders.

"God, son! God asked!"

"No!" James thought to himself. "Not another one!" He didn't mask his displeasure. His face projected his dissatisfaction without a word said.

Hollinswood read him. "That trouble you, James? Does my saying, God asked me, mess with you?" he asked like he was James' confessor.

"I guess I'm getting used to being the only pagan in the room," James mocked.

"Dangerous place to be, James Meyers."

"You mean hanging around so many Christians?"

"Oh no, son. It's not the Christians who'll get you. It's the pagans! How many Christians tried to stab you in that prison?"

"I see your point."

"Well, enough of that for now. Want to see your new space?" Hollinswood rose from his chair, and started for the door. "By the way, son, your first leave is a couple days from now."

"Leave?" James asked unsure of what he heard.

"Yes, leave. Fr. Ted'll fill you in when you guys meet tomorrow." Addressing Fr. Ted, "Terrance still joining you?"

"That he is, Bram."

"Ah, fine! That's just fine," Hollinswood gleamed. "Follow me gentlemen."

*****

Roomier and far more comfortable, James surveyed his new home. He couldn't prevent an approving smile.

"Like it, do you?" Hollinswood drawled. "A little homier than the State House, I'd wager."

"I do like it. And, yes, it is much more like home."

"Well, make yourself at home then, James. It's yours for a good while."

A springy bed, wood desk and white porcelain fixtures, it did remind him of home. And there it was, prominently displayed on the desk top – the Blue Book as he called it.

"So, James, here's the rest of the deal. Three meals everyday in the cafeteria. You'll see it a little later. An hour a day in the yard, and four hours a day with a work crew – manual labor mostly. Grounds keeping, laundry, library work, cafeteria, that sort of thing. Then I want you to spend time in the books. We promote a directed-studies program here – college credits. The local Community College affiliates with us – sometimes brings a professor right onto our campus. Mostly, though, you'll take your courses online."

James could hardly believe his ears. School! College! It was almost too good to believe.

"And, you are granted one two hour off site supervised leave per week, which you'll work out with Fr. Ted, your court appointed guardian. Other than that, you can have visitors as often as you wish. You must register them at least two days in advance, and receive clearance from security." Hollinswood, swept his suit coat back, placed his hands on his hips, sauntered out of the room and leaned against the door jamb. With his head tilted and his hands now jammed into this trouser pockets, he advised his young new tenant, "The rest, as we say, is up to you. Learn. Grow. Get a handle on a new start. How's that sound to you?"

"It's a deal, sir!"

"A deal, you say?" Hollinswood retorted through a smug smile. "Well deal it is, James Meyers." He turned serious, "Listen, son. My door is open. I'd rather you approach me directly than find yourself in a mess. Come see me. I'm here to help."

What a change in atmosphere. It might be prison, but it felt more like a new beginning.

"Hey, is there a James Meyers around here?" a voice shouted from down the hall.

James rose from the bed and shuffled into the hall. "Right here," he said with a restrained wave.

"Phone call."

"Go ahead," Hollinswood directed. "Go get your call." James started to waddle down the hall. "Just a minute," Hollinswood said, reaching into his suit coat. "Let's get those irons off you." With a twist of the key, the hand cuffs dropped off. A second later, his ankle irons fell to the floor. "You won't be needing those here. If you do, it's because you're headed back to the State House." Hollinswood stretched to his full height. "I'll guess that won't happen with you, will it?"

"No sir!" James affirmed. "I don't ever want those things on me again."

"That's my boy," Hollinswood said with a quick nod of the head. "Now go get your call."

*****

"Hello," James said after picking up the dangling receiver.

"Hi!" came the reply.

"Hey, it's you," he said with a note of excitement to his voice.

"Yep, it's me. It's Terri," the familiarly perky voice responded. "Just wanted to see what you thought of the new place. How are you?"

As the kids chatted, Hollinswood took occasion to consult with Fr. Ted. "That kid doesn't belong in prison, Ted. What a tragedy."

"You're right of course, Bram. But you know; it might turn out to be the best thing that's happened to him."

"You might be right, good Father. He's kind of a captive audience. No place to run. No way to escape his past. Plenty of time to deal with it."

"Well, you should know," Fr. Ted said, titling his head back to look his charming, southern friend in the eye.

Hollinswood sorrowfully shook his head, "Ahhh, you had to bring that up, didn't you?"

Fr. Ted just offered him a knowing smile in reply.

"Yeah, I remember those days," he began through a long sad sigh. "Montgomery. Selma. Birmingham. They were heady…and they were ugly, Ted. So much hatred. So much hatred," he sighed again, his eyes tight closed as if in a bad dream. "God knows, my dear friend, I almost died in those places." A brooding chuckle escaped his lips, "I think my soul did die for a spell. Violence! Anger! I watched three friends of mine practically stripped bare from those infernal fire hoses. Darn near drown them…I'm not joking. Two other guys hit the ground so hard their heads struck the pavement knocking them stone cold out." Pausing to rub his chin, "At least they didn't have to hear the N-word for the millionth time."

"How did you survive it, Bram? I don't think I've heard you say.

"Grace of God, Father Theodore! Grace of God."

"But for that grace, Bram. But for that grace, we're all doomed to hopelessness."

"Ahhh, indeed, Father." A broad smile spread across his face, "I found Him looking for me. Of course he knew where I was all the time. It was me who was lost. After getting out of jail for the umpteenth time – Birmingham this time – I got accepted at Howard. Met some good men there – white and black. They loved me, Ted. They threw their arms around me and didn't care how black I was. And I was blacker than my skin color, if you get my meaning."

"Oh I get your meaning, Bram. I thoroughly get your meaning."

"They showed me Jesus. That's where I met him." Hollinswood's face fairly glowed, "I've never looked back."

About then James reappeared with a silly grin on his face.

"So, you have good chat with your girlfriend?" Hollinswood jabbed.

"Yes, sir. I did," James confirmed, uncharacteristically letting his guard down. To Fr. Ted, those words sounded like sic 'em to a dog.

"Oh, so you finally acknowledge it?" Fr. Ted coyly asked.

"Acknowledge what?" James fired back.

"Terri! You finally acknowledge what everybody else already knows!" Fr. Ted remarked tapping a finger to his head. "We all know! Am I right?" he pressed, his hands raised palms up and his shoulders hunched.

"You aren't going to give up, are you?" James carped.

"You didn't answer my question."

Looking at a bemused Hollinswood, James asked in feigned sincerity, "Would you please lock me in my room now, sir?"

Hollinswood placed one of his large hands on James' shoulder, "Now son, there's not a thing wrong with you havin' a girlfriend. Lot's of the guys in here have a girlfriend."

"Just give me the keys. I'll lock myself in," James snorted. The men filled the halls with loud laughter. James groaned.

Still chortling, Hollinswood turned on his heel, "Follow me to the library. You too, Father Theodore. I'll show young James here where you guys'll meet tomorrow."

Hollinswood shoved the two wood window-paned doors open like a linebacker splitting the line. "This is the library, James," Hollinswood announced quite proudly, sweeping his long arm and large hand through the air. "I want to see you in here a lot, son. I want to see you puttin' that fine mind of yours to use, right here, in this room with these books."

James found himself immediately mesmerized by the long stacks so neatly rowed, the large oak tables and study carrels that lined the perimeter of the room.

"Impressed?" Hollinswood asked rather smugly. "You should be. Took me more than a decade to convince the state administrators that cons have brains worth educating. Finally, after a long battle, my convictions prevailed. This, son…this library," Hollinswood said again with a large arcing sweep of his hand, "is the envy of the prison system nationwide."

James walked over to one of the tables and ran his hand over one of the chairs.

"Go ahead, sit down. Gonna reserve that spot for you, Terrance and Father Theodore. That's where you guys'll hold your conversation. How's that?"

"I don't know what to say, Mr. Hollinswood. It all seems so unreal. I've dreamed of a place like this. Never thought I'd find it here…in prison."

Hollinswood strode to the other side of the table, placed his massive palms in the middle of it as he leaned over James. "Well, son, like I said. I want to see you here every day," punctuating his statement by driving one of his long fingers into the table top. "Right here. What do you say?"

James looked directly into Hollinswood's face, "You've made a dream come true. How can I say no?"

"Yeah, that's my boy." Turning to Fr. Ted, "I think we have a scholar in the making, Ted. I truly do."

"I couldn't agree more."

"So gentlemen, I'll leave you here for now. Ted, I'm sure you can find your way out of here. And James, welcome. I look forward to watching you grow."

Fr. Ted and James watched Hollinswood disappear through the library doors and down the hall to his office. The stage had been set. Tomorrow would be an important day – one of the most important days in James' young life.

FIFTY-ONE

"It all just seems so illogical to me," James answered in reply to Father Ted's question. "You asked me where I am with all this stuff. That's where I am." He ran his fingers through his now longish brown hair. "I want to believe. I just can't seem to get past this…"

"Dark hole of unbelief?" Fr. Ted interrupted, completing James' sentence for him.

"Yeah, dark hole."

"How large would God be, James, if you could hold him in your hand?" Fr. Ted asked.

"Well, not very large at all? Where you going with this?"

"If you could reason yourself into belief in God, wouldn't that make for a small god?"

James quietly mulled Fr. Ted's question.

"Let's bring Chesterton into the conversation again." Pulling the worn text from his jacket pocket, Fr. Ted opened it to a marked passage and began reading.

"A man cannot think himself out of mental evil; for it is actually the organ of thought that has become diseased, ungovernable, and as it were, independent." Looking up from the open book, he asked James, "How does that strike you?"

"Sounds like I have a diseased mind," he shrugged.

"We all do, James. Not one of us has a complete, uncorrupted, untwisted grasp of certainty…or reality, because we all inherited the same ego – Adam's ego." Lying the book face down on the library table, open to the page from which he read, he probed James' spinning mind, "You recall the story in the Garden of Eden, don't you?"

"Yeah. So?"

"What was their downfall? Adam and Eve I mean. What brought them down?"

James warily cocked his head like he was about to walk into a 'gotcha', "The apple."

"Not at all my young scholar – the apple was the opportunity that the ego latched onto. The devil had the unsuspecting couple thinking the apple held the mystery of knowledge – knowledge that would make them equal with God."

"So it *was* their ego that did them in?"

"Quite right my dear Watson. You've solved it again," Fr. Ted enthused in his best Sherlock Holmes imitation. Returning to his priestly self, he continued. "Every man since our original parents has sought in his own way to ignore or…worse…delete the existence of God in order to be a god." Picking the book up from the table, Fr. Ted resumed reading.

"He…man…can only be saved by will or faith. The moment his mere reason moves, it moves in the old circular rut; he will go round and round his logical circle, just as a man in a third-class carriage on the Inner Circle will go round the Inner Circle unless he performs the voluntary, vigorous, and mystical act of getting out at Gower Street. Decision is the whole business here; a door must be shut for ever." Fr. Ted once more laid the book on the table. "A door must be shut *for ever*," he recited, staring straight into James' face. "It must be shut, James, by a voluntary, vigorous, mystical – and I add, courageous – act of will."

"But what about opening a door you don't quite believe is real?"

"How has the one you've been roaming around in worked so far? Are you satisfied it's furnished the answers? Or has it raised more questions…or more doubt?"

"I think we know the answer to that," James conceded.

"So why do you think you've left that one door, the God door shut? Why do you so angrily avoid it?"

James sat a moment contemplating Fr. Ted's question. "Fear, I suppose."

"About what?"

"That maybe it'll let me down. Maybe it'll…" James hesitated. A sickening qualm overcame him.

"James, I think I know that answer."

"Okay. What is it?"

"That maybe it is real."

James remained quiet, saying nothing. Fr. Ted, he thought, knew best what he – James Taylor Meyers – feared most. If what lies behind that un-open door is true, it would mean truly confronting his demons, the very dark predators that had diseased his mind and brought him to the conviction that it was God who was the evil one. Because it was God who failed him in the first place and in his present place. It would mean a complete change of mind, of heart and of life. Could he muster it? Could he accept it? "You're right," James finally consented. "I am more afraid that it might be true…be real. I'm petrified by the thought that I might reach for it but it won't open for me." James squeezed his lips tight together, temper rising. "But, damn it, where was he when I need him? It might be real…this kind of truth you're shoving at me, but I haven't seen it. So what's the combination? Where's the key?"

"Oh you're ever so right, James – It *is* real. But I understand that reaching for the knob…well that's another matter. The door will open – for certain it will open. But you are correct to assume that you do have to know the combination…and possess the courage to enter it." The wise priest then waited a moment before adding, "And be willing to shut forever the door inside of which you've been standing…the one you've falsely trusted."

James swallowed hard; his mouth had turned to cotton. "Combination? Okay, so what is it?"

"One word, son. It's a one word combination."

"Faith?" James defiantly replied.

"Yes…faith," Fr. Ted confirmed. "Faith, James, is the most intentional act any person will ever take. Delicate yet powerful, faith has within it the potency of creation itself. It unlocks the power of God for us, the very same power of God that spoke creation into existence. And the power to change your life…change it for good and forever."

James wanted corroboration. He really wanted an out. He looked at Terrance, who was seated at the end of the table between him and Fr. Ted. "Was it that way for you?"

"Absolutely! I don't have your intellect, kid. But I had your doubts…all of them. I hated God! Man I hated him!" Terrance's eyes went steely gray, "I knew he was around. It just didn't seem he was around for me. So I hated him."

"That's it? You never wondered if he even was…*around?*"

"There's more to the story. Things didn't go so well as a kid. So I decided it was God's fault."

"But you still entered the combination? You opened the door?"

"Where else was I going to go kid? You tell me, if you're already standing in Hell where else are you going to go?" Terrance's comments dug deep.

"Just like that?"

"It's never just like that, James. All of us resist letting go and trusting God." Terrance took a second to study his combatant. "Look, no one wants to stop playing god, even while we're standing in Hell itself. Sure I had questions. Sure I had doubts. Man, I still have questions. But I know where the answers are now. And I'll tell you, James, I've not been disappointed. They've held up…the answers that come from knowing God…and from letting him know me."

"James, I wonder if some of your issues of logic aren't more issues something like Terrance's issues of disappointment and contempt," Fr. Ted suggested.

James thought for a moment. "Maybe. But as things went along, it seemed if my folks ignored me why would God care if I existed?"

"So you started looking elsewhere for answers?" Terrance asked.

"Yeah, I did. It didn't make any sense," James remarked.

"What make sense?" Fr. Ted pursued.

"Why!" James responded with a shrug. "Why we're here! What's the point? What's the end game?"

"Foucault became your go to, then?" Fr. Ted proposed.

"Not entirely. What he said about defining life made some sense to me."

"In other words, if we define anything we do violence to everything. That's what you mean?"

"Yeah! After all, aren't we making it up as we go? Isn't there more than one way to truth…to why?" James posited.

"So we're back to logic even if it's an existential logic?" Fr. Ted conjectured.

"Sort of, I think. It just seemed to me that even if we defined stuff, at some point those definitions would mean something to us…to me. It would give me that wall Mr. Rowland talked about. Something to lean on that wouldn't fall out from under me."

"In other words a god made in your own image?"

"I suppose."

"So what's the answer?" Fr. Ted persisted. "What's the grand story?"

"There is no grand story!" James fired back. "That's the point! There is no grand story! It's just us…time…death! We make our own story! Maybe it's like you said; we make our own god!"

"Oh, I beg to disagree, young man! There is a grand story! It's the metanarrative…the underlying story…from which every narrative, including our own, takes its story. It's the story you fear the most, because you fear that it might indeed be true. It opens with the words, 'In the beginning God created.' It winds through history coming to the words, 'In this way God gave us his only and uniquely begotten son.' It continues with the Son's pronouncement, 'I am the way and the truth and the life,' climaxing in the promise of his sudden, exalted return. Whether we accept it or reject it, it's still the story that begins every other story."

"Explain," James demanded.

"Think of it this way. It's like Chesterton describes truth and logic. Illogical truth – rational because it is truth, but truth that stands beyond logic…beyond our ability to define it – is, indeed, larger than logical truth, simply because it cannot be reduced. It is revealed truth; truth that comes to us, from outside of us. Truth we know intrinsically to be truth. It can no more be found by human reason alone than a politician can tell the truth." Fr. Ted held out his hand. "It can no more be held in our mind than air can be held in our hand. If it could be held in our minds, it would have no power of authority. We would have reduced it to something smaller than ourselves. Truth must be living, large and authoritative, and dare say personal, to be meaningful…indeed, to be truth. And it must have a guiding premise, a story or it is nothing at all."

"But hasn't science pretty much done away with that myth?"

"The myth of metanarrative…God's story?"

"Yes! Hasn't it proven that there is no overseer…no final truth beyond the physical universe?"

"Actually, James, it has done precisely the opposite. First of all, science…honest science…is not opposed to theistic faith. Neither is theism opposed to science. In many ways science by opening up the immensity of the universe has also pointed to the plausibility of an ever larger causal force. If science is listening, it will recognize that theism responds to the other great questions – it answers rationally and intrinsically what the limitations of human reason cannot comprehend."

"Like?"

"The same things you asked. Where we and the cosmos came from; the point of it all; the vitally important matter of morality; and what's the end game when it's all over."

James' face looked as if he'd sucked on a lemon.

"I take it you don't buy that reasoning," Fr. Ted presumed.

"But won't science ultimately answer those things too?"

"Not scientifically. Science depends on data – hard physical, objective, measurable evidence. What it can't answer are those other philosophical matters."

"But isn't the cosmos ultimately material – just stuff?" James argued.

"Only since the Enlightenment has the assumption been made that the physical universe is the only reality – the only truth," Fr. Ted asserted. Waving his hand in a grand arc for emphasis, he asserted, "From the beginning of mankind the cosmos consisted not only of the physical universe but the metaphysical universe also – the universe beyond the physical. That was the debate between Plato and Aristotle. One pointed to the sky the other to the ground, when in truth they were both right. Just because the metaphysical part of the cosmos is not seen or sensed or objectively explicable does not render it irrational or devoid of existence." Pausing for a moment, he let James think about what he had said. "James, let me ask you this. What is science's answer for what it cannot explain?"

"That someday it'll be able to explain it."

"Scientifically or philosophically?"

Unsure of how to answer, James' mind went idle. "I don't know."

"When a scientist hits the wall…runs up against a question he can't answer…a philosophical question like meaning, morality, destiny, even origins, but attempts to answer it absent the hard physical data which he has objectively evaluated. What then, James? What then is the scientist but a philosopher without an answer? By denying the metaphysical hasn't he leaped into the world of the philosopher, offering a philosopher's perspective to those niggling questions?"

"Maybe, but…"

Terrance interrupted, "Just a moment, James? What is it really that makes God so hard for you to accept? Logic or disappointment? Are you convinced there is no God, or are you pissed off he let you down?"

Terrance's question had the force of a sucker punch. It cut to the crux of James' argument and brought him full circle right up against the door he refused to reach for…to open. Nonetheless, he let his guard down and let Terrance in. "Some of both. I can't accept a god who let's bad stuff happen. And I can't accept Fr. Ted's idea of illogical truth."

"So you want proof for God? And you want a God who comes to your rescue…at least a God who shows up?" Terrance clarified.

"I guess."

"I wonder, James, if it's less a matter of proof and more a matter of preference," Fr. Ted added.

A perplexed look came over James' face, "What do you mean?"

"In the end, James, finite beings like us can't prove or disprove the existence of God. It's absurd…logically absurd…to think the finite can comprehend the infinite. For some – I sincerely hope not you – it becomes a matter of preferring God's non-existence. Stuff happens, things go wrong and suddenly it's God's fault. " Pointing at Terrance, "Maybe what hangs you up is like what Terrance suggested – a matter of anger…of disappointment. I'd even go so far as to say it's a sense of betrayal that has you clenching your fists at God and doing your best to deny his existence. In the end, you just don't want him to exist – certainly not if he's the God you think he is."

"So that's where you think I'm 'hung up' huh?" James asked defiantly.

Terrance answered, "I do."

"So do I James," Fr. Ted echoed.

The Marysville library went suddenly quite. Stacks of books seemed to glare down at James as if a gallery of the unconvinced. It was as if his effort to put God on trial – as he once called it – had been foiled, and his arguments were mere hollow echoes that throbbed in his ears. He had to admit to himself, all the logic in the universe would not help him in his quest to deny the obvious. Fr. Ted was right. He felt betrayed – so betrayed he wanted to reason God out of existence – his own existence if none other. But there was one matter he could not resolve.

"Illogical truth?" he asked as if thinking aloud, his voice still snarling. "Is there really such a thing?"

"There is," Fr. Ted strongly affirmed. "Want an example?"

"Is there one?" James asked doubtfully.

"Love!"

"Love?" James responded unconvinced.

Fr. Ted waved a finger past his face as if to signal an important point was coming. "Well, you answer this question," he began. "What kind of logic would it be for God to send his son, Jesus, to die for the sins of mankind? What, pray tell, is logical about that?"

James' eyes narrowed in thought. "I'm not certain I could call such a thing logical. It sounds awfully inhumane to me."

"Or was it an act of the most selfless kind – an act of unsurpassed love?" Fr. Ted contended.

James sat quietly mulling these words. He had no response. They struck him with an odd force of persuasion. Christ's passion – if true – was undeniably an act that defied logic. And how could he deny it as a supreme act of an uncommon love? Who would do such an absurd thing – and, for people who neither deserved such unmerited love, nor for people who, like him, doubted Jesus' very existence?

"If it were true," James responded. "It would be illogical – and quite undeserved."

"Now you're on to something, James!" Fr. Ted exclaimed, slapping the table with the palm of his hand. "Now you're on to something!"

James braced but said nothing.

"So let me ask you something else that may lead to an *illogical* truth. How has it worked out so far for you to be god – the final arbiter – of your own universe? Or how well have the alternatives to God served you?" Fr. Ted sat poised in his chair, who with Terrance awaited James' answer.

Suddenly anxious, James shot a quick glance toward the exit sign. Fr. Ted could have asked any question but this one. All of his reasoning – every scheme of mind – had not produced answers – just more questions, and more disappointments. They left him vacuous, searching and increasingly skeptical that any combination of pursuits would result in that enduring peace and confirmation of meaning he so desperately sought. More, though, his belligerent determination to avoid the God alternative kept returning to the same dead end. Fr. Ted – and Chesterton – was right; every road away from God led inextricably back to God. No matter how hard he ran from him, he inevitably crashed into him as if crashing into the cross and feeling its splinters pierce his own flesh. That door kept staring at him. But could he reach for it? Could he muster the combination…the faith? He had finally reached bottom. He finally ran out of answers.

His heart began to race. An inexplicably painful yet summoning sense began to surge through his soul, as if an inaudible voice were calling him. Trapped! Locked at a crossroads – he shot another furtive glace toward the exit sign. No escape! In his cell at the State House, though forced to face his failure, he was nonetheless free to exert his godlike prerogatives to avoid the encounter that now stared him squarely in the face. He'd asked for this meeting, somehow hoping to resolve the quandaries prowling his mind and tormenting his soul. Somehow he might have even accepted the possibility of a show down – of having to come to terms with himself once for all. What he hadn't counted on was the restless turbid conflict surging through him at this moment.

The bottom had been reached. The arguments waged. The witching hour had arrived. Which road? Which road would it be? God...or god? He took note of the men who sat with him. Their lives genuinely reflected everything he wished for. He recalled Scanlon's story – obvious transformation. Terri's too. His heart beat harder. His face felt flushed. His mind raced. Without the slightest thought that today might come to this kind of crisis – an encounter with God – here he was.

"What's going through your head, kid?" Terrance asked.

James said nothing. He stared blankly into the table much like he stared into the carpet the first time he was ushered into Rowland's office. That day he was crushed by hopelessness. Today was different – and more frightening.

"James," Fr. Ted broke in. "Did you hear Terrance's question?"

James lifted his eyes, peered anxiously across the table at Fr. Ted, his chest heaving. "I want to believe." He gulped another breath, "Help me."

Fr. Ted dropped his chair onto its front two legs, reached across the table placing a hand on James' arm. "I've never wanted to hear those words more. I've never wanted to help someone find his way home more."

Terrance reached from his seat, laying a hand on James' shoulder, "That goes for me, too."

Tears coursed down James' face, spilling onto his dull white shirt. "What do I have to do?"

Fr. Ted looked deeply into the young man's eyes, noting the seriousness and vulnerability reflected in them. "James, the work has been done. Jesus paid the price. Your role? Ask him to forgive you of your sins and to enter your life. Is that what you want? Are you ready to let him change you and restore your life?"

James had come to trust this priest, this fatherly figure who, with Warden Rowland, seemed like fathers to him. Still, he felt the need to ask, "If I say yes, will you guys be there with me? Will you help me?"

Terrance slid his chair beside James and wrapped his arm around the kid's shoulders, "They have never left me, James. And I was right where you are now. We'll be there...not only for you, but with you."

James closed his eyes and nodded, "Yes, I am ready."

Terrance held James like a brother as Fr. Ted guided him. "I'm going to ask you some very important questions, James. I want you to answer them honestly...from your heart. Will you?"

"Yes, sir...I will."

"James do you confess you are a sinner separated by your sins from God?"

"Yes, I do," James began to sob.

"Son, do you ask Jesus Christ to forgive you of your sins and cleanse you from all unrighteousness?"

Through now convulsive sobs James whispered, "I do. I truly do!"

"Do you accept Jesus Christ as your savior?"

"Yes!" He exclaimed, pounding a fist on the table. "I need him to be my savior!"

"Will you let him transform you, change your life and make you new?"

"Yes! Please, please change me!" Again he struck the table with his fist, deep sorrow resonate in his quaking voice.

"Will you thank him, James, for saving you and for giving you new life?"

James looked up, "You mean he has already done it? I'm saved?"

"James," Fr. Ted began, "He has indeed heard your prayer. He's been waiting for you. There is nothing he wants more than to answer your prayer; to give you that new life and make you his child."

"Yes, yes, yes, I thank him!" James fairly shouted.

"Then, son, as a priest I say what Christ himself says to you. In the name of the Father, the Son and the Holy Spirit you are absolved of your sins, made new in Christ and are a citizen of His Kingdom." Fr. Ted traced the sign of the cross over James; then reached out his hand to him. As James took his hand, Fr. Ted said, "Welcome home, son. Welcome home."

Terrance embraced James, "Welcome to the family, kid!"

As the men sat back in their seats, a hush seemed to hover over the library table that had quite honestly served as an altar. An old life died on it. A new life rose from it.

"How do you feel, son?" Fr. Ted asked; that warm smile spread broadly across his face.

James calmly comported himself, his eyebrows knitted in thought. "I feel reborn."

"You are reborn, kid," Terrance assured. "Exactly how I felt! Reborn!"

James exhaled as he looked at each of these men beside and in front of him, "I don't know how to thank you guys. You've put up with a lot."

"James," Fr. Ted answered, "We – the posse – made a pact when you showed up at the State House, that we would commit ourselves to you. We'd endure with you and hope for this day."

"But you didn't even know me."

"True," Terrance affirmed. "But God did. He knew you long before we did and set the wheels in motion."

"Prison? You think he intended me to go to prison?" James asked unsure if that's what Terrance was implying.

"Well, you set those wheels in motion on your own. God just made sure you landed where somebody would show up to help you," Terrance answered, giving the kid a brotherly whack on the shoulder.

"Yeah," James said with a shrug. "Guess I did."

"James, prison made you a captive audience. You couldn't run from yourself any longer. In a sense, God used prison to save your life," Fr. Ted offered.

"I suppose," James said. Wiping a sleeve over his tear-soaked face, he let out a heavy sigh, "I've never felt so free...or so loved."

"I know exactly what you mean, bro. Been there," Terrance assured. "But you are home now, kid. And we'll work even harder to keep you home."

"I'd take the ex-gang leader seriously, son," Fr. Ted joked. "He doesn't accept no for an answer."

James smiled, "I'm glad. I need you guys."

"Hey kid, we need you too. It cuts both ways."

James didn't quite know how to respond to Terrance's comment. Somehow, though, he knew he'd find out.

"Okay, James, now the real work begins," Fr. Ted said, sitting back and shoving Chesterton into his jacket pocket from which he'd pulled it earlier in the conversation.

"How so?" James asked.

"You didn't just make a transaction with God. You entered into a relationship with him. That takes time to develop. It takes work. You'll be distracted...challenged. Doubts will crop up. The enemy will use every trick in the book to attempt to deceive you. That's why we need each other – all of us! We'll help you grow in this new relationship. And we'll grow together – you and us. Together we'll learn what it means to follow Christ." Fr. Ted's face tightened, "You up for it?"

"I've never been more up for anything, sir," James exclaimed. "Bring it on!"

"That's my boy!" Fr. Ted gleamed. A silly expression came over his face, "You know that *Blue Book* I believe you call it? The one lying on the table in your room."

"How'd you know I called it a Blue Book?"

"I picked up a pile of yellow paper you threw on your floor just before one of my visits. You'd scrawled it on one of those pages."

"Oh! That was then."

"You mean back when you hated the God who just saved you?" Fr. Ted asked with a wry smile.

"Yeah...back then." James anticipated Fr. Ted's next *suggestion*. "I suppose you want me to get friendly with it. Right?"

"Indeed I do. I want you to read the first chapter in John before our little outing tomorrow evening."

"Outing? Tomorrow evening?"

"You tell him, Terrance," Fr. Ted said, winking at his posse mate.

"Well, James, you're going to get to meet some important people, including a couple of my guys."

"You mean your hoodlums," Fr. Ted dug.

"Ex-hoodlums, Father! *Ex*-hoodlums!" Terrance fired back with a scowl.

James was confused. "What are you guys talking about?"

"The kids that hang out at my café," Terrance replied. "Fr. Ted calls them my *hoodlums*."

"Oh," James said somewhat mystified. "I've met some of those *hoodlums*."

"Yeah, well, those kids are lot like you and me, James. They've come to the same place we've come, and a lot of 'em through the same tough stuff." Terrance, continued, "I want to introduce you to two of the guys. They were members of the gang."

"The Lobos!" James exclaimed. "Aren't those the dudes that tried to kill me?"

"Actually, yes and no," Terrance answered. "The guys that went after you were Lobo infiltrators and rival gang members who wanted you out of the picture. But these guys, Dirk and Tag, they were my lieutenants. They got busted; went to jail and found Christ just like you and me."

"You'll want to know these boys, James," Fr. Ted volunteered. "They're redeemed hoodlums. Great guys, really."

"Thanks for the endorsement, Father. Wasn't sure you had it in you," Terrance sniped. Fr. Ted just smiled.

Terrance got the conversation back on track. "Anyway, Fr. Ted and I've arranged to bust you out of here tomorrow evening so you can meet the people who've hung in there for you the last few weeks."

"That's right, James," Fr. Ted broke in. "While you were recovering in the hospital the posse, their spouses, members of Terrance's café, your parents and another interested person have met nightly to pray for you."

"Nightly?" James asked.

"Without fail! They've met every night at my parish just to pray for you," Fr. Ted replied.

"Oh, wow! I don't know what to say." James was taken aback by this news. He'd heard that people met to pray for him, but he had no idea how many or how often.

"Just say thanks when you see them tomorrow night," Terrance advised.

"For real, I'll thank them. I'm just amazed." A quizzical expression came over James' face, "Who was the *interested* person?"

"Terri, of course," Fr. Ted announced.

"She's attended...every night?"

"She has, James," Terrance said. "That girl really cares about you."

Fr. Ted folded his arms on the table, "I think we should pray. And this time, James, I want you to speak to God. Thank him for forgiving you and entering your life. Can you do that?"

Through his obvious awkwardness, James managed a simple but profoundly sincere prayer: "I don't hate you anymore." Tears welled in his eyes once again. "I don't even know how to say thanks. It just doesn't seem like enough. And thank you for these guys. I need them. Help me, please. Jesus, help me."

"Amen," Fr. Ted concluded the prayer. Terrance echoed the same.

FIFTY-TWO

"Tom, he arrived."

"Who arrived where, Ted?" Rowland asked puzzled by the vagueness.

"Tom, James accepted Christ not a half hour ago. Terrance and I just left him."

Rowland dropped the papers in his hand and pushed away from his desk. "Our James? He's a Christian?" Rowland sounded shocked by the news.

"Tom, where's your faith?"

"My faith's fine, Ted. It's just been such an ordeal. To hear these words seems almost otherworldly."

"Remind you of Terrance? His surprise breakdown and confession?"

"Somewhat – Yes, in many ways it does. I'm so overwhelmed, I hardly know how to react."

"You could start by thanking God, Tom. He definitely heard our prayers."

"Without doubt he did – he clearly did. And, yes, my soul is praising him right now. What truly great news!" Rowland rubbed his brow. "I guess now, the hard work begins. Right?"

"Oh, I wouldn't characterize it so harshly, Tom. I would say the journey has just taken shape. The good stuff is in front of us, including our boy."

"It's been quite a process, hasn't it?"

"Properly so my friend. Process is an excellent way to think of it. Step one – we've taken step one. Now on to the next step in that process as you so well put it."

"What would that look like, Ted? What's the word you use?"

"Catechumenate, Tom. You know – helping our boy get a firm grasp on his faith; how it will change his life; how it will bring him into a new and healthy community of people on the same road as him. And prepare him for the ultimate coronation – his baptism."

"Catechumenate – that's quite a word."

"Well, think of it as initiation, Tom. The kid's entered into a season of initiation." Fr. Ted paused. "Tom, I won't lie to you. As you already anticipated, this is a dangerous season just like the last one. But I assured our boy, we'd all be there for him."

"Absolutely right! We will be there for him…and each other." Rowland took a quick glance at his watch. "We're meeting at your parish again tonight? Seven o'clock?"

"We are indeed."

"I'm going to dash home right now. Mary's got to hear this face-to-face. I'm sure the phone lines will buzz once she hears this news."

"You might want to call Anne first."

"Looks like she beat me to the punch. I have a message she has already phoned my office."

"It's a great day, Tom!"

"Never better my friend! This will be one special evening."

"Prayers rising! See you then."

Rowland grabbed his suit jacket, packed a few papers into his brief case and headed for the door. Just as he swung the outer door open in stepped Harold Raynor.

"Right on cue, Harold."

"Oh? What's up?"

"Harold, our boy gave his life to Christ this afternoon."

"Praise be!" Raynor exclaimed. "Tom, that's wonderful news. Does Mary know?"

"I'm heading home right now to tell her."

"I think I'll call Stephanie."

"She'll be thrilled, Harold." Rowland drew Raynor into the office and shut the door. He didn't want to give away James' location. "That's not all. James will be at the church tonight. Ted and Terrance are bringing him over."

"That'll be something special!" Raynor beamed. "Wouldn't miss that for the world."

Raynor's expression changed. "Tom, I'm afraid I've got other news...not so good."

"Let's have it."

"Tony's identified up to a dozen infiltrators who are getting intel from the outside. Nothing to do with James. But he's convinced trouble is brewing."

"Okay, what does he advise?"

"Move them out – way out. He's confirming IDs and will get a report to us as early as tomorrow morning. I've called in reserves for the night and upgraded security to orange. Are you good with that?"

Rowland bit his lower lip. "Good news never lasts for long, does it?"

Raynor rocked his head. "No...it doesn't. But Tom, evil may pursue us. It will not overpower us. Look how God protected James."

Rowland put his hand on Raynor's shoulder. "Harold, I've never been more convinced. If I ever doubted God's oversight, that was dealt with today. He has everything, and I mean everything under control, even this big house. I agree with your assessment and actions. Good job! I appreciate it."

"On that note, Tom, let's celebrate! Our boy's safe. God has clearly taken care of him."

"Walk me to my car, Harold. I could use the company."

FIFTY-THREE

"Anxious?" Fr. Ted asked looking through the rearview mirror into the back seat of his cluttered compact car. James never heard him; his mind busily fretted over what to expect once inside the church. He bounced his legs like he was overcome by a nervous tic. Who would be there? How would they react to him? What would he say?

"Hey, kid! Fr. Ted asked if you were anxious," Terrance chided.

"Anxious? You've got to be kidding. Dude, I'm terrified!"

"Worse than day one at the State House?"

"I wouldn't rule it out."

Terrance and Fr. Ted nearly doubled over with laughter. Their apparent insensitivity to James' situation, albeit impertinent, kept the mood somewhat light.

"So," Terrance asked again, "Would you have preferred to stay on schedule – showed up tomorrow night instead?"

"No! I'd have been a mess! I feel like I'm being set up for the firing squad as it is!"

"Cool your jets, kid. You'll be fine," Terrance encouraged. "You think you've got it tough? I had to face the warden's family right after I was released. I survived. You will too," he added for good measure.

James didn't seem the least reassured as the car came to a stop in the church parking lot. Several cars had already arrived. "Looks like a full house," he remarked.

"Could be," Fr. Ted agreed. "Let's go see."

Terrance pulled the tall, heavy wood door open. Fr. Ted led the trio inside. Not a soul. "Must be back in the chapel," Fr. Ted mused as he led the guys down the aisle of the nave, illuminated only by the light behind the crucifix above the altar, and waning daylight that burnt life size images of biblical scenes through the massive stained glass windows.

Happily for James he was permitted street clothes for this outing. Fr. Ted made those arrangements with Warden Hollinswood. It didn't seem, however, to make him any less ill-at-ease. Enthralled by the cathedral-like structure, its massive vault, and brilliant windows that colorfully depicted the Christ-story, James was momentarily distracted from the anxiety that plagued him. He knew it wasn't death row to which he was being led, certainly not within such a grand hall of worship. Still, before entering this holy space, his nerves hadn't gotten the message.

Oddly, he felt at home in this place. The beckoning eyes of the saints painted into the glass, the exquisite Pieta situated in the north transept, the anguished face of Christ staring from the crucifix weren't the least off putting to him. Ironically they left the opposite impression, a calming and assuring sense of presence. They were the witnesses he read about the night before while thumbing through the Blue Book. He'd stumbled onto the pages in Hebrews that described these martyrs and exemplars of faith – men, women, even Christ himself, who witnessed to the undying, enduring hope into which he'd just prayed.

He felt Terrance's hand drop onto his shoulder. "Hey kid, pretty cool isn't it?"

"Yeah! I like this place."

Terrance gave James' shoulder a squeeze as they walked toward the chapel. Fr. Ted pressed open the chapel door. Applause and hoots from the hoodlums poured out as the men entered the room. Fr. Ted hoisted an open hand high over his head to silence the crowd, all of whom came to meet the young man they've spent endless nights praying for, hoping for and now welcoming into their family. Motioning for James and Terrance to join him at the ambo surrounded by kids who couldn't find room in the few packed pews, he opened, "My goodness you'd think something really big happened today." The room erupted in laughter and more hoots. "What happened, did your houses burn down? Do you need food and shelter so you came here? What's the big deal?"

Terrance's hoodlums, those packed around on the floor and standing along the walls hollered in unison, "James!" James could hardly hold his composure. All these people here – for him. Like the silent witnesses etched in glass, painted in icons and resting in statuary in the nave, these *noisier* witnesses communicated solidarity and welcome unlike any moment in his life. They knew God and now so did he. They were bonded – a brotherhood of former gang bangers, druggies, prison authorities, parents and a priest.

"So that's the big deal!" Fr. Ted shouted in reply and the kids roared. Once more he raised his hand and the room faded to silence. Don and Kathleen along with the Rowlands, Anne and the Raynors were plainly enjoying the kids' energy and enthusiasm. "Family and friends, it is a big deal that James is with us tonight." Again the kids raised a roar.

"Hold it guys!" Terrance intervened. We're all excited! But let's get the scoop together. Okay?" A few "Right on Pastor T's" filtered around the group. "It's yours now, Father."

"So you guys listen when the big dog speaks, eh?" Fr. Ted joked. Polite laughter sprinkled around the room.

"James, here is your family new and old. As you can probably sense, they love you, son, and are so very excited for you. You didn't join a religion, or a club or any other organization. You, like all of them and me, were reborn into the family of God."

"Amens," echoed across the room. Heads nodded. Eyes moistened. James looked intently into the faces of his family. Their smiles were brighter than the day he was released from maximum security and sent to a safer place.

His mom mouthed, "Love you." He mouthed the same to her. Terri, eyes swimming, stood and gave him a gentle hug. "I'm so happy for you, James."

He hugged her back, "Thanks for caring, Terri. You're the best friend I've ever had."

"And you're mine," she said before taking her seat beside his mom.

"James, will you allow me to ask you some important questions?" Fr. Ted let James know earlier that day that he would ask him the same questions he did the day before in the library – and a few others.

"Yes sir. I'm ready."

"I'd like Don and Kathleen along with the posse and Terri to join James and me here." As they stood, kids scrunched themselves against the wall or stood snugly beside one another forming a rimming wall of witnesses around them.

"I don't intend to make this overly formal, but the moment is holy and merits thoughtful and conscious intention," Fr. Ted instructed.

Facing James with a book of rites in his hand, he began to read, "James, God gives light to everyone who comes into this world; though unseen, he reveals himself through the works of his hand, so that all people may learn to give thanks to their Creator."[2] Looking up he asked, "James Do you accept those words as true for yourself?"

James nodded his head, "I do, sir."

Fr. Ted nodded in return and continued to read, "James, you have followed God's light and the way of the Gospel now lies open before you. Set your feet firmly on that path and acknowledge the living God, who truly speaks to everyone."

Once again, Fr. Ted asked, "James, are you willing to set your feet on that path?"

"I am, sir."

As Fr. Ted instructed them, Don, Tom, Terrance, Mike and Harold placed their hands on James shoulders.

"James, I am now going to ask some more very important questions." Fr. Ted began again from the book of rites, "Are you, James Meyers, willing to walk in the light of Christ and learn to trust in his wisdom; commit your life daily to his care, so that you may come to believe in him with all your heart?"

James felt his heart warm, "I am, sir. I am."

"This is the way of faith along which Christ will lead in love toward eternal life. Are you prepared to begin this journey today under the guidance of Christ?"

---

[2] Taken from *Rite of Christian Initiation of Adults: Study Edition*. Chicago, IL.: Liturgy Training Publications, 1988.

A broad smile spread across his face, and his eyes brightened. His mind returned to a dark scene when he was ushered handcuffed and shackled from the courtroom to the prison van. In that moment he uttered to himself, "I'm a felon." In this room, at this time the men holding his shoulders were ushering him into eternal life. He was no longer a felon before God. He was his child and his heart glowed. "I am sir. I truly am."

"James, you have the look of a new man," Fr. Ted observed.

"I feel like a new man, Father."

"And so you are!"

"Gentlemen," Fr. Ted said turning his attention to the men standing with James. "I have a question for you. You see guys, our journey together with his young man has just begun. He'll need men to walk the long journey with him. It will require each and every one of you, including myself. As you can attest, it's a dangerous journey but one with remarkable blessings that come with it. So, I ask you, are you – each of you – present with James ready to help him follow Christ? Will you journey with him? Will you pledge yourself to his safekeeping? Will you hold him and yourselves accountable before God for the life of this young man? "

Strong male voices sang out, "We will."

Turning to the rest of those gathered, "The same goes for you. Are you willing to share your lives with James and offer your support for his growth and safekeeping in Christ?"

The room reverberated with "We will!"

"James, your Christian family has spoken. Will you accept their help? Will you offer them yours? Will you let them pray for you? Will you pray for them?"

"Gladly, sir. Yes!" James looked across the chapel, "Thank you! Thank you all!"

"Then, James, here is your family of faith," Fr. Ted pronounced. "How about saying a few words to them? Let them hear from your heart."

James drew in a deep breath. "I hardly know where to start. I'm so overwhelmed...so totally overwhelmed." He looked down at Terri.

"Go ahead," she whispered. He reached for her hand.

"I was such a loser. I thought God hated me. So I hated him back...even to the point of denying he existed." Spying his mom and dad, "I'm so sorry for the grief I caused you." He broke down. Terri rose and stood beside him. Don put his arm around James' shoulders. Kathleen reached out and took his other hand.

"We forgive you, son," Don said. "Will you forgive us?"

James looked his dad directly in the eyes. He could see the depth of conviction they held. "Oh, dad, how could I not forgive you? You're my dad and I love you." The men threw their arms around each other, the first embrace either could ever recall. Broken yet healed, abandoned but reconciled, lost and now found, more ironies – ironies that needed no explanation. In that instant James discovered for himself the most illogical, albeit rational truth of all – God's Love.

FIFTY-FOUR

Under the dim light of a small reading lamp his parents furnished for his new room, James made vain attempts to summarize this life altering day. Finally only these few simple words fell onto the yellow page, "I met God and everything changed. I'm different and I can't explain it. I'm home and never expected to be. I'm at peace." With that he snapped off the light and sat alone in the darkness at the small wooden desk. There was no risk of nightmares tonight. No fear of the dark. Even in the black of his unlit room he felt the warmth of a new light, a light that burnt deep inside him, and something he'd never felt – peace and contentment. He wanted to pray but stumbled at the effort. "Jesus, I've never spoken to you. But it's like you've been speaking to me my entire life. I don't know what to say. I've stopped running. I belong to you now – and I want to. Thank you." His hand glided over the cover of the Blue Book. He didn't shove it away. Instead he recited in a whisper, "For the Lord God is a sun and shield. The Lord gives grace and glory. No good thing will he withhold from those who walk uprightly." Fr. Ted's verse from the Psalms had taken root. What James couldn't yet fathom was how deeply it would fasten into his soul. He caught a glimpse the next morning after a comfortable night of sleep that for the first time in a very long time gave him rest.

*****

"Quite a day and quite a night, wasn't it?" Fr. Ted remarked, seated comfortably across the library table from James, the very table that served as an altar the day before.

"Oh man, I have no words," James answered shaking his head. Fastening his gaze on the bemused priest as if abruptly shaken by the sudden reality of all that happened, he asked, "Where do I go from here? What's next?"

"You mean where do *we* go from here?" Fr. Ted had been rocked back on the hind legs of the oak chair. Now he sat it firmly on all fours and dropped his folded arms on the table so he could square up to his young charge. "Remember, you're not alone. We promised to walk with you – together. That promise, James, means we walk together – all of us."

"Yes sir. I do remember. So where do *we* go from here?"

"Becoming a Christian, son, above all is living in relationship with Jesus Christ. It requires time – and willingness to let it change us, transform us. I like that you're experiencing peace and a sense of belonging. You know what that indicates?"

"I suppose that God has taken charge."

"Yes and more: It means that the Holy Spirit is bearing witness with your spirit that you are a child of God." Pulling a thinly padded leather New Testament from his vest pocket he opened it, cleared his throat and read, "Therefore, if anyone is in Christ, he is a new creation; the old has passed away, behold, the new has come." Peering over the text at James he asked, "Have you ever heard those words before?"

"I might have. But honestly, until now they meant nothing to me."

"But they do now?"

"Yes they do. I feel new. I want to be new." A rather quixotic smile broke across his face. "New creation huh? I suppose that means the old James has died."

"I couldn't have said it better," Fr. Ted thoughtfully affirmed. "St. Paul who wrote these words also spoke about laying down the old man and putting on the new man – a new man made in the image of God."

"Why did I hate him – God I mean?"

"You were deceived, James. We've all been deceived. Now it's time to live in the truth – to live in the light of true reason and honest hope."

"So, where do *we* go next?"

Fr. Ted chuckled, "Are you up for some coaching?"

"Yeah, I suppose I am. What kind of coaching?"

"There's a process that's as old as our faith where newcomers learn, and where people accountable for their progress both teach and join them on the journey. I'd like to apply for the job of your teacher. And I'd like the other guys in the posse to be your mentors. Are you up for that?"

"Really? Yeah, that would be great!"

"Okay then, that's how we'll roll."

James broke out laughing.

"What's so funny?"

"You are," James said sarcastically. "That's how we'll roll? Now you're sounding like one of the hoodlums."

They both broke into loud laughter. They laughed so hard tears began rolling down Fr. Ted's cheeks. He pulled off his glasses and wiped a handkerchief across his face. Waving his other hand in the air mostly to quell the riot of laughter and get things back on track he said, "Well okay, now let's get down to business."

Stuffing the kerchief back into his breast pocket, he continued, "I had a long talk with your folks last night after Terrance and Anne drove you back here. They wanted to know what's next. I suggested that you enroll in a cohort group of people who, like you, have just come to faith in Christ, and who are on a formational track to become Christ's disciples. We call it the Rite of Christian Initiation of Adults – RCIA for short. It meets weekly with the goal of preparing members for the rite of baptism, confirmation and first communion."

"What'd they think?"

"Honestly, it struck them as being a little too Catholic sounding. But when I explained that this process bears the Apostles' fingerprints they kind of relaxed their concern."

"So it is Catholic?"

"The RCIA is Catholic, but the process was originally known as initiation and formally named the Apostolic Tradition in the early third century. It was given a strange sounding name before that in the late second century."

"Okay, what was that?"

"The Catechumenate."

"The cat-ate-what-a-ment?" James repeated his eyes bugging out at the strange sounding term. "What the…"

Fr. Ted burst into laughter again. "Now you know why we just call it the RCIA." Again he wiped briny water from his face while still sputtering with laughter at his bewildered charge.

"Yeah okay, but what does it mean?"

"It simply implies both learning and teaching. The intention was that the entire church community would walk together to assist new believers on their journey. It was risky business in those days to come out for Christ. It took courage. So this process was kind of like boot camp – a rather rigorous process guided by people who'd already survived the wars so to speak."

"And it's still the thing today huh?"

"It kind of got forgotten through the Middle Ages but has enjoyed a revival since the late twentieth century."

"How long will it take – this cate-ate-what-a-ment?"

Fr. Ted shook his head at James' sorry attempt at this strange sounding word. "How long will it take? That's up to you, James. It goes as you go. The goal, if that's what we should call it, is your baptism, your first communion and your confirmation into the Body of Christ. But all that happens only when you demonstrate surrender to God, growth in your understanding and behavior and feel in your own heart you are ready to step into those waters."

"Baptism. Really? Is that necessary?"

"What's your hesitation?"

"I don't know. I'm not very good with public stuff."

"You mean with public humiliation?"

"That especially!"

"How'd it go for you last night? That couldn't have been easy."

"It wasn't – certainly not at first. But when everybody supported me like they did, I didn't feel out of place at all."

"Your baptism will go just the same. In fact this whole process will."

"Yeah well." James' expression remained unconvinced.

"What's bothering you, son?"

"Can I be honest with you Fr. Ted?"

"Yes, of course."

"Are you expecting me to become Catholic?"

"So that's your worry!" he answered with a chuckle. "No I am not expecting that. Whether you become Catholic or remain Protestant is entirely your call. You have to know your own heart on that matter, and follow God as closely as you are able."

"What if I decide I want to be Catholic?"

"What do you mean?"

"I don't know how my folks will take it. Like how would I break that news to them?"

Fr. Ted could tell James was unsettled about a lot of things, and definitely getting the cart ahead of the horse on many of them. "James we'll deal with that as it arises. The big thing, son, is proceed on the journey with Jesus that began here yesterday afternoon. Will you trust me with that? Will you trust me that as we approach a variety of crossroads we will deal with them wisely and with consideration for everyone affected by whatever decisions you make?"

"I guess I am moving kinda fast. Yeah, I can trust you. But will you let me get things off my chest, or ask stupid questions or even disagree with you?"

"Of course I will, James. The entire point of this season in your journey is to confront those issues. For now they precede all these other worries. First get to know God. Learn to trust him. Learn to obey him. Learn to care about someone other than yourself. Prepare for the moment when you will be asked to live in your baptismal covenant. That last part won't make much sense for awhile. But ultimately it will." Fr. Ted clapped his hands tightly in front of him. "Look, Paul told the Christians in Rome come and die. That's where we begin. We die. The old man – the old James if you will – is buried in the waters of baptism and reborn into a new creation in those same waters. That's the beginning, James. And that is what is meant by covenant – the death of an old way, the birth of a new one through the mercies of God and his gift of Jesus. The rest will get solved in due season." For good measure, Fr. Ted repeated, "Get to know God and let him know you. Nothing else matters for now."

"It really is a relationship isn't it: Like getting to know someone?"

"Absolutely my young son – It is the relationship that starts all other relationships."

"Terri told me the same thing. At first I didn't get what she meant. God was always an abstraction to me – just another philosophy. I never took him personally other than to blame him for all my junk."

"You're in for quite a ride young James. Strap in and hang on."

"Can I ask you something, though?"

"Sure. Shoot!?"

"What will my baptism be like?"

"Like a milestone. Like a moment in time you will always remember. A time that will anchor you in your faith and bring you back to the covenant you made with God when things get tough. It will be a coronation." A blissful look fell over Fr. Ted's face. "I remember mine like it was yesterday."

"How long ago was it?" James asked.

"It will be twenty-five years this Easter, James. I'll never forget it. Not ever!"

"It really changed you didn't it?"

"Oh my goodness, that's quite an understatement. But then again, it's still changing me."

Fr. Ted looked at James, who was now warming to the conversation. "Do you remember the story in the Old Testament when the Israelites crossed the Jordan River?"

James replied, "I can't say that I do."

Fr. Ted swept his hand across the table like it was a map. "When the Israelites had reached the Jordan River the Levites carried the Ark of the Covenant on long poles into the water. The river backed up allowing the Ark and the people to cross on dry ground. Once they crossed, God instructed them to remove twelve stones from the riverbed and pile them on the new shore. Any idea why he asked them to do that?"

"Not a clue."

"It was so that when their children and grandchildren asked them why these smooth stones, polished by years of water washing over them were placed as they were; their fathers and grandfathers would remind them that this is the place where God fulfilled his promise – the promise of a new land. The cross is another such symbol. And so is our baptism, James. It will always remind us that God has fulfilled his promise. When Jesus arose from the grave he defeated death! Defeated it, James! He destroyed evil and won our salvation. Baptism is our participation in that victory – His victory!"

"That's cool! Does the New Testament say anything like that?"

"Oh most certainly it does. The Apostle Paul spoke of baptism in these terms." Flipping the pages of his New Testament, he said, "Listen to this. 'Do you not know that all of us who have been baptized into Christ Jesus were baptized into his death? We were buried therefore with him by baptism into death, so that as Christ was raised from the dead by the glory of the Father, we too might walk in newness of life.' How does that strike you?"

"Oh wow, that's pretty vivid. I never got why baptism was such a big deal. It just seemed like something the church did but never really took seriously."

"Yeah, well, sadly we tend to read other people's opinions with greater trust than what the Bible itself has to tell us. Even among Catholics the message can get missed. But to the earliest Christians, those who followed the Apostles, baptism was salvation."

James bit his lower lip, his eyes narrowed. "Salvation…" he said in a near whisper. "So that's what the first Christians thought it was?"

"They did." Fr. Ted sat back in his chair and got that professorial look on his face. "Even Peter said as much in his letter. He compared baptism to Noah's flood that destroyed the world but also spread the seed for the new earth. The Fathers who came after the Apostles rather humorously called baptism both tomb and womb – death and new birth."

James' eyes widened. "That's huge! Hearing this makes me want to be baptized now."

"And you will be sooner than you think. Easter is just weeks away. Right now, we're in the season of Lent, a time of patient waiting, as well as a time of preparation and repentance."

"Sounds like where I am – waiting and repenting," James confessed.

"It is precisely where you are my young catechumen," Fr. Ted affirmed with his classic wink and broad smile.

"So what does a cat-uh…"

"Cat-eh-que-men," Fr. Ted sounded out slowly.

"Cat-eh-que-men?" James tried again.

"Exactly!"

"Okay so what does one of these dudes do?" James asked raising his palms as if unsure of himself.

"You ready for this?" Fr. Ted asked baiting his young friend.

"I suppose."

"Kneel – that's what you're supposed to do."

"Kneel?" James snarked.

"And listen," Fr. Ted added.

"Man you lost me," James said with a note of frustration in his voice.

"Fair enough," Fr. Ted replied. "By kneeling you learn to pray. In praying you learn to confess, offer thanks and listen. You will come to a time in your Christian life, James, where you'll regard all of life as prayer, a constant conversation with God whether you're speaking or listening. Because ultimately, prayer is living in the presence of God and wanting what he wants. It's unlike any relationship you've ever known."

James sat a moment before responding. "I've no idea what that must be like. But it sounds like something I need. I just don't know if I can handle that much trust."

"That's why, James, we walk slowly. We listen intently. And we trust as deeply as we are able. In time you'll find your trust has grown as your relationship with God grows. It's a mystery that only walking the journey will reveal."

"You really know God don't you? You really trust him."

"I do, James. Who I am right now is a product of many years of obeying God; screwing up and getting back up; and finding out through the thick and thin that he's always present even when I don't feel his presence."

"I see. So how do I begin? Where do I start?"

"I'm going to give you a simple prayer to recite before drifting off to sleep at night. It's an ancient prayer, sometimes called the Jesus prayer. It goes like this. 'Lord Jesus Christ, son of the Living God have mercy on me a sinner.' Can you remember that?"

"Yeah sure."

"Let me hear you recite it."

James recited the words of the prayer finding himself struck like a sucker punch that caught him completely off guard.

"What's wrong?" Fr. Ted gently asked.

"Nothing. It's just that I feel so…I don't know."

"Vulnerable? Unworthy? Like maybe this prayer is looking right through you?"

"No joke!"

"Good," Fr. Ted nodded. "I pray this prayer every night and often many times each day. It's the attitude of someone who's dying to his sinful self, his sinful past and presenting himself to God. Asking for mercy, James, is admitting we're guilty of breaking relationship and trust with him. You see, trust is a two-way street. You want trust? What are you willing to pay for it? Are you willing to allow God to examine you – your motives, behaviors, thoughts?"

James slowly nodded his head. He looked away for a moment; quietly contemplating Fr. Ted's probing questions. "This isn't going to be easy, is it?"

Fr. Ted let out a soft chuckle, "No, it won't be easy. But here's the rub, James. It wasn't easy for Jesus. Remember what it cost him to win us – to win our salvation?" Fr. Ted took a moment to reflect. "Bonhoeffer, a remarkable Christian writer of the last century, said it well. I'm paraphrasing but it went something like this: What cost God much cannot be cheap to us."

"That's huge!"

"Indeed it is. That's why my son we need each other."

"I'm trying to wrap my head around the idea that you or any of the guys need me."

"Still wrestling with that huh?"

"What do I have to offer?"

"Friendship: Your willingness to step outside yourself and pray for each one of us. Your willingness to stick with the journey as you appropriately called it. Your willingness to support us when we're in a tough spot. No one expects you to be anything or anyone other than who you are. You've already given us plenty. When you gave your life to Christ yesterday, you affirmed our faith in him as well. Do you see?"

"I suppose. I've just never felt like I had anything that anyone would want."

"Well, James, that's simply not true. You are valuable. You are needed. And we love you, son."

Deep emotion rose and filled James' eyes. Fr. Ted had never seemed more like a father and not just like a fatherly-priest than he did just now – his words never as gentle and yet as thunderously potent. "I hardly know what to think, Father. I have no words. I'll do my best."

"I know you will, James. I have no doubt of it."

"What if I screw up?"

"Welcome to the club. What you'll do is what I and the other guys do, James. Don't hide your failure. Confess it to God. Ask his forgiveness. And thank him for it. John wrote, 'If we confess our sins he is faithful and just to forgive us our sins and to cleanse us from all unrighteousness.' That's what we do. We do it privately and we do it together like brothers."

"So he doesn't just throw us out when we fail?"

"No he doesn't. He reaches down to lift us up, but he doesn't throw us away."

"This is all so weird."

Fr. Ted laughed. "Weird you say? Well you're in for some intense weirdness my son. Like I said awhile ago – strap in. You're in for the ride of your life."

"Yes sir!" James heaved a long sigh, "I'm ready."

"I'm going to give you something I want you to memorize. It's called the Apostles' Creed. It's quite old. We'll discuss it together and with the other catechumens when we meet. I also want you to memorize the Our Father. You'll find it in Matthew chapter six."

"You mean in the Blue Book?" James asked somewhat sarcastically.

"We'll start calling it the Bible," Fr. Ted answered with a twist of his head and a wry smile.

James knew he meant business. "Yes sir. I suppose we'll discuss it too?"

"And memorize it," Fr. Ted confirmed.

"Ugh, my head'll explode with all this memorizing junk," James sighed combing his shaggy hair with his fingers.

"Not really. Not for a bright mind like yours. But here's how you'll memorize it. You'll memorize by meditating on each portion of these passages. You will learn to reflect on their meaning and ask God to form your mind and life around them. Before long they won't just be in your memory. They will have become part of who you are – the new James."

"Kind of like re-programming the computer, eh?"

"Precisely! Like the old cliché, garbage in, garbage out. You've been feeding yourself a bunch of bad stuff. Now you're on a new diet, one that will restore you to spiritual health." Fr. Ted rocked back on the back legs of his chair again, "So, are you still up for it?"

"Yeah I am. Actually, it scares the crap out of me, but I know it's all good. Yeah, I'm up for it."

"That's my boy!" Locking his hands behind his head, Fr. Ted laid out the game plan. "Warden Hollinswood is willing to cut me a little slack that will allow you to attend important masses over the next few weeks, as well as spend your weekly outings attending RCIA sessions beginning next week – Tuesday night to be exact." He reached into another coat pocket and pulled out a book. "Altogether, there are twelve catechumens – including you – who will be in attendance. We're reading this." Fr. Ted slid the book across the table toward James.

"This is Our Faith: A Catholic Catechism for Adults," James read. "I thought you weren't going to push me toward the Catholic Church?"

"I'm not," Fr. Ted said still reposed on the hind legs of his chair, his hands still locked behind his head.

"Okay, but what's this? It sure looks like Catholic stuff to me," James said holding it up to Fr. Ted.

"It is."

"I don't get it! Are you screwing with me?" James snorted, obviously perturbed.

"No, I'm not, and you know I'm not. That book follows the creed you'll memorize. Long before there was a Roman Catholic Church or an Orthodox Catholic Church, and longer still before there were Protestant churches there was the creed and the scriptures. Everything any of these large church bodies believes comes from these sources. The creeds conveniently summarize the Gospel. The word credo is Latin. It means 'I believe.' As you read and memorize the creed, ask yourself: Do I believe these statements? And to be fair, yes you'll learn a bit about Catholicism. But you'll learn more about what every Christian who loves God should know."

"Okay. Sorry for being a jerk."

"Te absolvo."

"What!?"

"You're forgiven," Fr. Ted said through another chuckle.

"Can't you just say that?" James snarked.

"I did – as a priest," Fr. Ted answered playfully. James rolled his eyes.

"So here's your reading assignment for the week. Read Part One, the Profession of Faith. You'll find the creed toward the back. I flagged it for you. Memorize the Our Father and read the Creed daily. We'll chat about each of these during our visits together and with other RCIA folks. How's that?"

"You sure don't expect much do you?" James said with a cocky snort.

"Well, would you prefer to hang out at the State House?"

"Absolutely not!" James fairly shouted.

"So the assignment isn't all that bad then is it?" Fr. Ted said with a chuckle and wink.

"Guess not," James conceded. "Besides, I think I'm gonna like this stuff, especially our discussions."

"Oh, I'm sure you will, James. In contrast to all that you've dealt with in our young life, I'm confident these assignments will seem like fresh air."

"Oh man! I could use a bunch of that."

Fr. Ted merely nodded with a knowing smile creasing his face.

"Will the other guys – the posse – participate in any of these things?"

"Yes they will, especially Terrance and Mike. And someone else."

"You wouldn't mean Terri would you?"

"Indeed I would." A silly expression came over Fr. Ted's face, "I'm assuming that would meet your approval."

"What can I say? We're friends," James shrugged.

"Hmmm…just friends huh?"

"Don't you have someone else to torture?" James said with a mock snarl.

Fr. Ted broke out in that infectious laughter. About then Warden Hollinswood appeared in the doorway. "What's goin' on in here with you guys? Don't you know this is prison? Nobody laughs in prison." Hollinswood caught sight of James' expression. "Oh I see; looks like the good Father here is tormenting you about that girlfriend of yours isn't he?"

James' shoulders sagged, "You guys make prison look good."

At that both men burst into laughter at James' expense.

"Well Master James," Hollinswood began, "What I really came in here to say was welcome home son. I'm so proud of you and so happy for you."

James' visage changed, his heart warmed as Warden Hollinswood's deep southern drawl dropped these embracing words into his ears. This man whom he'd only met a few days ago had already grown comfortable to him – another father type he thought.

"Thank you sir, that means a lot. It really does."

"Well you're quite welcome. And," he said stroking his chin, "you're not alone. We've got other boys in here who've come to the same place – given their lives to God."

James cocked his head.

"That's right son, you're far from alone. Just thought you'd like to know that."

"That's cool. When will I get to meet them?"

"Next Sunday if Fr. Theodore doesn't make you attend that starchy church of his – all that bowin' and incense and muttering." Hollinswood shot Fr. Ted a broad mawkish smile. "Otherwise I'll introduce them to you. How's that sound?"

"It sounds great!"

"Besides you'll bump into a few of the guys in the cafeteria or the yard or right here. Got a couple more Christian scholars like yourself taking courses. You'll meet them. In fact they'll likely find you. Stories travel fast inside these walls."

"Stories sir? They know about me?"

"Know about you? Are you kidding! They saw you guys in here the other day. They heard a new brother arrived and I don't mean just to this place. Yeah, they know your story and they'll be excited to hear about it."

"Wow, news does travel fast," James remarked with a bewildered expression on his face.

"Indeed it does young Master James." Hollinswood gave James' shoulder a firm squeeze, "Well I got to be getting back to my office – infernal, endless paper work. Makes me feel like I'm doin' time. See you gentlemen later." With that the guys watched Hollinswood disappear through the doors like they did the day James' arrived.

"He's something, isn't he?" James observed.

"That man, James, has been through a lot, seen a lot and lived a lot. He's well into retirement age, but the State just can't force him to quit."

"Why not? But why would they want him to quit?"

"He's been a pain in their backsides for a few decades, James. They think he's too progressive. Like this library, they bucked him for a long time. But when it worked, they took the credit. They just think a man of his age ought to head out to pasture. That would kill Bram though. He sees this place and these men as his home – his calling if you will. He'll leave when they find him dead at his desk."

"Is he married? Got kids?"

"Was married. His wife died a few years ago – pancreatic cancer. Bram took it hard for a long time. But he held faith and has come through it with remarkable resolve."

"Kids?"

"No kids. They had a stream of foster children run through their home over the years, but no kids of their own."

Fr. Ted noticed James staring into the table. "What are you thinking?" he asked.

"I've been a real ass. All I've thought about is me and my mess. Then I meet someone like Mr. Hollinswood and…"

"And what?" Fr. Ted prodded.

"And I realize we all have a story and it wasn't cheap."

"Yes. Every one of us has a story. Isn't it good to know, though, our stories have chapters – even chapters that lead somewhere and not dead ends?"

"Like the new chapter I'm on, right?"

"Yes! Just like the fresh page you're writing."

Fr. Ted leaned back down in his chair, his arms crossed over his chest. "James, I want you to learn how to communicate with God – to pray. Start by thanking him for your new chapter – your new story. Ask him to forgive you of all you've thought, done or failed to do that put tension in your relationship with him. Then ask him for guidance. Pray for others, including your friendly priest-friend. And then listen. Just sit in his presence and do as the Psalmist said – 'Be still and know that I am God.'"

"I started that conversation last night," James affirmed. "I won't stop."

Fr. Ted beamed but said nothing. The men just sat quietly for a moment.

"Father Ted, may I ask you something personal?"

"Sure. What's on your mind?"

"What did you mean when you said you haven't always been Catholic?"

"Oh, that's a long story, James."

"Got a Readers' Digest version?"

Fr. Ted chuckled, "I suppose I do." He looked past James as if crawling back into his memory. Finally he drew a deep breath, "I was raised in a nominally Christian family – attended church once in a while but nothing more. We were Protestant – Methodist. My dad saw his role as wage earner, but had no spiritual inclinations. He pretty much left my mom in charge of raising me, my younger brother and sister. I was a bookish sort, so when things got rough between him and mom, I hid in a book.

At college I fell in with a group hooked on the Dead Poets Society, kind of a macabre bunch who liked reading poetry in a dark room by flashlight or hanging out in a smoky bar."

Fr. Ted doffed his glasses wiping the lenses with a handkerchief he pulled from his pocket. "Well, I had my episode of despair I mentioned to you and Terri the other day while hanging out with these dark intellectuals.

While recuperating, a few guys from Campus Crusade for Christ befriended me. They led me to Jesus.

I began attending church with them – an active independent Protestant community that took in college kids. One of the leaders, a man in his early forties and college prof handed me a book one evening. He said that given my penchant for intellectual stimulation I might benefit from the formational message of this book. It was titled *Celebration of Discipline* and written by a Quaker pastor. It introduced me to an intimacy with Christ that I had come to crave. What caught my attention, though, was how many of these devotional masters as they were called were Catholic, many of whom lived during a very dark period in the Church's history. I began accumulating their writings, studying their teachings and imbibing their content. They led me to the Church Fathers, James; the men – and women – who followed the apostles. I began devouring their commentaries on scripture. It was like I fell under their spell – utterly enthralled by their theological depth and their passionate heart for God. These were people for whom being Christian was dangerous – often fatal. Their faith was not easy but costly."

Fr. Ted placed a finger thoughtfully across his lips. "It wasn't long before I felt a strong urge toward ministry but wondered how it would take shape. I was living among deeply devoted Protestants whose devotion to God was quite compelling to me. Though they didn't understand my bent toward the Catholic Church they nonetheless supported me. None of them had read the Fathers, the desert monks the early theologians, the Scholastics or any such scholars. That didn't, however, deter them from their opinions, which they shared out of what I took to be genuine love. But for me," he said biting his lower lip, "it was like finding a great masterpiece left covered out of sight that held within it not only the kernels of faith I had come to accept, but the entire body of Christian heritage – the fullness of the Church if you will."

With a blink he continued, "I went off campus and sought out a Catholic priest, a man esteemed for his work among the poor as well as a distinguished scholar. At no time did he attempt to convert me. Instead, he implored me to listen to the Holy Spirit and follow him explicitly. I began to attend mass at his parish. We met frequently, me with my pad of questions and him with patient, fatherly guidance. I say guidance, James, because though he answered me directly, he almost always sent me off to research my own answers, often sending me from his study with an arm load of books loaned from his library.

What transpired I can only attribute to the uncanny will of God who with humor as well as obvious intention opened a door and invited me to join him there – it happened to be a Catholic university – Loyola. During my studies, I came to a deep inner conflict that I can only describe as the Holy Spirit convicting me – calling me. I approached my priest-mentor who discerned that perhaps God was calling me into the priesthood. How could this be? I argued. I'm not Catholic. More, I had absolutely no intention of becoming Catholic." A quizzical expression came over Fr. Ted's face, "Funny really."

"What's funny?" James broke in.

"Funny how God uses our prejudices against us. You see he birthed the Church and called it the Body of Christ – all of it, James, not just portions of it. But for us finite, fickle humans it's like looking into a prism but only seeing the facet that emits the color of our chosen prejudices. We tend to develop opinions and fortify them over time. They become for us the traditions of belief that too often form traditions of exclusion instead of traditions of embrace. I took that analogy from someone who suffered religious persecution as a kid growing up in Eastern Europe, but who became one of the leading theologians of our time."

"I take it he's Catholic?" James interrupted to ask.

"No actually he's not; he's Protestant, but he gets it."

"So how did you get from where you were to becoming a priest?"

"By being confronted with my prejudices. Monsignor Rosen – that's his name – put his finger under my nose and asked me point blank what I had against the Church. I listed the typical hurdles – Mary, papal infallibility, works righteousness and sundry other issues. Before I could get too far Monsignor Rosen stopped me and asked me where I came by these opinions. I hadn't a very good answer. I told him from respected church leaders. He then asked if I'd ever read the Church Fathers, or studied the Catechism of the Church, or the Vatican Two documents, or the Joint Declaration on the Doctrine of Justification. Of course I hadn't and he knew it. He never embarrassed me with my ignorance, James. But he never let me get away with poor research either. That's when he loaded my arms with books and sent me out to do honest research. At the top of the list was the Bible. He called my attention to several passages I had read from only my facet of the prism. He challenged me to add another facet – one that I ultimately learned brought all the colors into clarity."

"Sounds like he treated you like you're treating me," James chided.

"I guess you could draw that conclusion. I dare say, however, he was a lot tougher on me than I've been on you – so far," Fr. Ted replied while looking at his charge over the rims of his glasses like the sagacious mentor-scholar-priest that he was.

James sat a little straighter. In these brief moments he learned more about the man across from him than he'd expected; his admiration and respect for him growing with each new disclosure. James saw in his mentor unforced and unfeigned candor, a transparency that allowed him to reveal his flaws and failures with equal relish as his successes, which he spoke of modestly as if they were more gifts than achievements, gifts that came from someone or somewhere other than his own exertions. This was a man who was more, much more, than the sum of his resume. He evoked the kind of peace, the quiet certitude and contentment that seemed so real and so very desirable, James found himself aching for its source and its stream within his own soul. Fr. Ted made no pretensions of its source – the grace, mercy and love of Jesus Christ.

"Was that when you became a priest; I mean after you read all those books?"

"No, it took a few restless years, struggling with my apprehensions, misgivings, distorted biases, and the sheer determination to avoid becoming something about which I was certain I did not want to become."

"But you did – you finally caved. After all, you're a priest. So when did it happen?"

"As I said, Monsignor Rosen loaded my mind not so much with sources advocating Catholicism, but sources deeply persuaded by early, hard fought and hard won truths that have survived millennia despite the at times harsh environments that threatened them. The truth looming over them all dealt with the vexing question Jesus asked his disciples; 'Who do you say that I am?' The ensuing councils, the miracle of scripture itself, the traditions that have sustained our faith assiduously and emphatically answered, 'You are the Christ of God.'

James, all of those voices – all of them – follow from the apostles through the fathers, the early theologians to us, and all of them were catholic long before the word catholic was described as either Orthodox or Roman. In so many words, the further I read the more I painted myself into a corner."

Fr. Ted's face tensed, "One day it all came crashing down on me. I was especially overwrought at the time about something; it seems like it was over papal infallibility or transubstantiation – well anyway. Those topics always bugged me – still do at times but for different reasons.

Anyway, I digress. In his unique wisdom, Monsignor flipped the table on me. Instead of confronting my arguments directly or sending me off with another pile books, he sent me to the retreat house administrator, a kindly woman old enough at the time to be my mother, and said chat with Katrina. What about, I asked? He said just let her tell you her story. So I did – that day. As I listened, I heard in her heart more than her words a settled contentment and deep conviction so authentic it could only have come from God. In that instant it was as if God spoke from heaven itself, 'What will you do with all I have shown you?' I'm not a stoic but neither am I a cry baby. But James, the dam broke and I knew that God had spoken and the only answer available was to obey his calling."

"I guess that's when you made the decision – when you turned Catholic?"

"Yes, it was James. I immediately returned to Monsignor's Rosen's office. He saw me coming and knew from the expression on my face that I'd had the encounter he'd expected I would one day have. 'So did Katrina help you?' he asked. All I could do was nod my head. Monsignor put his hand on my shoulder and said to me what I said to you yesterday James, 'welcome home my son.'"

James sat silently watching his mentor's face assume the pathos it must have had on that defining day so many years ago. He again realized how vital one's story is to the unfolding of one's life. "I don't know what to say, Father Ted. I wonder if God might be leading me there too."

"Time will tell, James. As I said earlier, the first order of business is to know God and let him know you."

"I understand. Can I ask you another question?"

"Sure."

"Monsignor Rosen – was he always Catholic? Or did he have a story kinda like yours?"

"No, Monsignor wasn't always Catholic. His name tends to give him away. He was Jewish, James. His parents survived the Holocaust; moved to New York when Rosen was a boy and then moved to the Midwest. Rosen had his epiphany, if you want to call it that, while in Rabbi school. One of his friends – a fellow scholar and Catholic – handed him an open New Testament one afternoon as he tells the story, and dared him to read the passage."

"So he took the dare, eh?"

"That's putting it mildly. Rosen was so incensed by his friend's impertinence he set out not only to read but use the passage to refute Jesus as Messiah. The passage was the Book of Hebrews – the one book in the New Testament that a Jewish kid would least want to read. It's all about Jesus as Messiah, the fulfillment of ancient prophecy.

As such things happen, the angrier Rosen got the harder he dug into the book. But just like you my young friend, the good Jewish boy found himself squarely confronted by the very person he fought to deny. You see, putting a New Testament into a Jew's hands is like feeding him pork – it's verboten in the extreme. But daring him to read an apologetic treatment for the Messiahship of Jesus was like desecrating the Temple itself. Though Jewish people do not deny the historic figure of Jesus, they cannot abide the notion that he truly became our Messiah. But that was the point at which Rosen met his doom as a rabbinical scholar. Suddenly it was like the veil of heaven parted for him; like Paul's confrontation with Christ while storming on his way to persecute Christians in Damascus.

'What will you do with all I have shown you?' My Lord, James, we all hear that question sometime in our lives. For Rosen it happened on of all days a Saturday – a Sabbath day. He was poring over portions of the book most difficult for a Jewish mind to grapple away, and was immediately struck by all the parts that spoke of Jesus as fulfillment of God's covenant made with Abraham. As Rosen tells it, 'I came to a painful crossroads. If they were true, then Jesus must be seen in new light.' That afternoon, Rosen says, 'the light went on and I was reborn. Suddenly I was no longer searching for the Messiah, I had met him and he is Jesus.'"

James sat mesmerized. Fr. Ted concluded, "You see my dear young friend, Jesus finds us. When he does – when he calls our name – we know it is him."

"It's like he's just waiting for us to wake up or something."

"That's a good way to put it. But we tend to prefer blindness until the light is just too bright to ignore."

"Yeah, I know. Like you said, we've all got to face our prejudices sometime."

"Yes we do. That's why I sometimes say to my Protestant friends who still catch a few Protestant tendencies in me, I hope I'm never so Roman I can't be catholic. In other words, I hope I can embrace the entire Church – and I hope they can too."

"Fr. Ted, call for you." Fr. Ted turned toward the door to see a young guard holding the door open.

"Looks like we'll have to continue our chat tomorrow."

"And Meyers," the guard announced, "It's time for you to join the yard crew."

While pushing a lawnmower across the tall, rain wetted grass, James' ruminated over the last twenty-four hours. It struck him how different yet how similar each story was. He couldn't wait to chat with Fr. Ted again. But first the homework, and a call to Terri.

FIFTY-FIVE

"Tom, do you have a minute?"

"Yeah, Harold; what's up?"

"Let's step into your office."

Rowland noticed the strained look in Raynor's face as he followed him through the door.

"Tom, Tony got some names. He red flagged one in particular. He's not in the State House, but has a tie to Chavez."

"Okay. What does that mean for us?"

"They know that James isn't here anymore."

"You mean the Lobos?"

"Yes, the Lobos and the Nuevo version of the Lobos. They all know he's been moved. They just don't know where."

Rowland's face went ashen. It was like he aged a decade. "Good Lord! So they're after him? They're after James?"

"Tony's convinced they are. And…Tom, they might be after Terrance too."

"Terrance!? I thought they'd given up on him."

"Tony thinks they can get to Meyers if they get to Terrance. Somehow they've made the connection."

Rowland dropped onto the sofa as if shot. His eyes searched the room, but it wasn't for anything in it. "Harold did we…did I…"

Raynor cut him off: "Don't go there, Tom. No, we didn't err in sending James out of here. Look, you know we took every precaution right down to secreting him out under cover. We even broke the rules for once, sending him with Fr. Ted instead of an armed guard; and sending a bogus van with one of Tony's guys in shackles. That took guts, Tom. From Tony's intel, the ruse worked."

"Harold, I'm not worried about our tactics, I'm worried that we can't seem to get ahead of these thugs."

"I know. According to Tony, the FBI and local gang cops have intel on a meet between the two alphas and their lieutenants."

"How'd he get that?"

"Through a plant – one of his guys."

"What's the plan?"

"A bust. They've got these guys on a boatload of recent activity – racketeering, drug smuggling, human-trafficking to name just the big stuff."

"Did Tony give you the details?"

"No, of course not; he's not even sure about the when and how. But he says it's imminent – real soon."

"But what does Tony's intel mean for our boys – Terrance and James?"

"Not sure. He advises Terrance to keep a low profile. For one, stay clear of Marysville. Tell Mike to do the same. We're not sure if they're on to him, but it's not worth taking chances."

"Okay, I'll tell them. What's the fallout here?"

"It's gone suddenly quiet again. Tony's take is that all the focus has gone elsewhere – but where he's not sure yet. But he thinks we'd better get Chavez out of the State House."

"Actually, I'm a little ahead of you guys there," Rowland offered. "I've petitioned the courts for a transfer. I should have it later today."

"Excellent! Where'd you recommend."

"Rikers in New York."

"Well, that should disconnect the pipeline for awhile."

"Let's hope so. To be safe, I'm going to fill Ted in too."

"That's a good idea. Hey, for what it's worth, Tom, I think you've done a heck of a job with all of this. I'm grateful to work with you."

"Thanks, Harold. That goes for me too. I'm quite glad to have you alongside. "

"Are you going to say anything to the kid?"

"James? No, I don't think so. He doesn't need another fuse to fret over. Ted called and told me they had quite a discussion this morning. James seems unusually composed, he said. Let's keep him that way. We'll do the worrying for him."

"And the praying."

"Mostly that."

FIFTY-SIX

"Tom I want to bring James to the posse. Bram will okay it."

Rowland wasn't sure. "You know the risks, Ted. You know the kid's still marked."

"Yes, I heard what you said. But I can't help it. I'm still convinced that God's got our kid marked too."

"You certainly push the limits, Ted."

"Tom, I refuse to give into the bullies. Look how far God has brought James – and us. Do you honestly believe he has stopped guarding him?"

"Of course not!" Rowland barked. "I'm just cautious."

"No fault in that, my friend. I would urge us all to keep faith as well as sound reason intact. What's Terrance think?"

"He would agree with you."

"Well then, how do you want to proceed?"

Just like the wily priest to lob the ball back into his friend's court. Rowland conceded, "I think James should fill that chair."

Fr. Ted clearly understood the inference, and beamed his appreciation without a word.

"I want to invite Terri also. Will you agree?" Fr. Ted asserted.

"Wholeheartedly! That young lady has won us all, Ted. She's courage in a pint-size package. I think she offers our boy the right dose of encouragement and accountability."

"I couldn't agree more. I admit I've grown very fond of this vivacious nurse. She doesn't let James get away with anything."

"Alright then. Seven at your place?"

"I'll have the coffee percolating."

*****

"Hi Terri," Anne rose to greet Terri as she came through the rectory door. Terrance entered the room with Fr. Ted, each with their coffee, Fr. Ted with a bagel and nattering about something that had each of them gently jabbing the other – coffee sloshing carelessly out of their cups and onto their sleeves. Tom Rowland entered behind Terri as Scanlon pulled into the driveway in his rattling diesel pickup. Soon the entire room was filled with the posse now with two females among them. Fr. Ted took his usual seat in the overstuffed armchair, setting his coffee and bagel on the lamp table beside him.

"Okay folks, let's take our seats," he said, folding his arms over his droll belly and crossing his feet, the picture of repose.

Terri noticed the empty chair. "Are we waiting for someone else?" she politely inquired pointing inquisitively at the chair.

"It's for me," a male voice answered from the kitchen. Just then James walked into the room. Terri's eyes flashed excitement, her mouth fell open, "James!" She lunged from her seat and threw her arms around his neck. "I didn't expect to see you here. How cool!"

"I didn't expect to be here. Fr. Ted pulled a few strings."

Rowland shot the plucky priest an icy stare. "Pulled a few stings huh?"

"Pulled a few strings? Not really. Bram called it house arrest."

"And I suppose you were appointed as guard?" Rowland grumped.

"More like *guardian*," Fr. Ted replied rather smugly while taking a bite out of his bagel.

"Well I think it's fantastic," Scanlon butted in. "Besides, I can handle those thugs if they come knocking." With that he put James in a headlock before giving him an approving slap on the shoulder.

"Remind me to never tick you off," James groaned while combing his hair back in place.

The rest of the room was laughing in amusement at both Fr. Ted's derring-do and Mike's big brother act.

Anne sat with a contented smile spread across her face.

"What're you thinking babe?" Terrance asked.

"James, you sat in the appropriate chair. Do you know why?"

"I don't."

"Fr. Ted placed that chair where you're sitting a few weeks ago and told us it was reserved. He reserved it for you."

James' head cocked. Terri's eyes moistened. Looking at Fr. Ted, "You were expecting me?"

"We all were, James. When we met we prayed you'd meet with us one day. Like Anne said, that chair has been yours for awhile. We've just been waiting – and hoping – you'd arrive to fill it. And here you are."

Rowland broke in, "That chair, son, comes with an expectation attached to it."

"I kind of thought it might. You never let me off that easy," James joked.

The room filled with laughter. Rowland broke into a broad grin. "So what do you think we might expect of you?" he asked.

"Fr. Ted told me you guys need me like I've needed you. I didn't know what he meant. What do I have that you need? He said friendship. And he said my prayers for all of you."

"He's right, James. That is the expectation. You might be new to the faith, but as a child of God, just like the rest of us, we need one another. We need you just like Fr. Ted said."

"I've gotta say, it feels weird to be needed, especially by folks like all of you. No one's acted like I was necessary – more like I was...I don't know..."

"Expendable?" Fr. Ted interjected.

"Yeah. Like that."

"Well, if you sit in that seat it means you're part of this family. One day, once you're out of the clink, you'll be invited to join us," Terrance added.

"You mean as part of the posse?" James asked as if dumbfounded by Terrance's rather veiled implication.

"Why not, kid?" Scanlon asked.

"You kidding me, Mr. Scanlon? I'd love to be part of this group. I owe you all more than I can ever repay you."

"It's Mike, James. Never Mr. Scanlon. And no, I'm not kidding."

Scanlon's tone sent James back in his seat. "Yes sir...Mike."

"Good. Look kid, some of us in this room have been real mess ups; you know that. You've heard our stories. But God called us and here we are. He might just be banging on your door too. So pay attention," Scanlon ordered.

"Mike's right," Terrance chimed in. "We've been here for you, but we need you too – your prayers mostly. One of the things these guys coached me to do very early in my faith was to wake up to other people around me. The story might be mine, but it's not just about me. Same for you. There's guys at Marysville that God might cross your path with – pay attention. We'll be there with you. But you might be the point guy."

"Well, I think we've given James a lot to think about for one night," Fr. Ted intervened to say. Setting his coffee cup aside on the table, and brushing bagel crumbs from his jacket, he more formally opened the evening get-to-gather. "I wanted to bring us together with James to lay out the path he'll be on if he chooses to accept it." Fr. Ted said that last bit with a nod to the kid. "Then too, it becomes our path. This posse isn't just a rescue outfit. We don't make decisions; we make disciples. We know that. The years, and our experiences, have taught us that faith exceeds mere decision. It becomes our life, and our life becomes formed by how that faith gets fed. God never made it possible for us image-bearers of his to go it alone. It's a complete fiction to assume faith to be a private matter. As a triune God, he lives in an eternal community of Father, Son and Holy Spirit. As his image-bearers, his foremost interest in us is that we join him in relationship. By extension, friends, that means we join in relationship with one another and help one another along this at times dangerous trek."

"Well spoken, Ted," Rowland offered, setting his own cup down. "What do you have in mind?"

"Tom – and group – I'd like to propose an idea. It seems to me that this group has God's intention written all over it. Terri," he said looking directly into her face. "That includes you. In all fairness, I haven't broached this with the guys. So I'm taking a chance here. But I'd like to have Terri join us as one of us and here's why." Again turning his attention to her, "Young lady, I've not seen in very many people the genuine mix of grace and grit you exhibit. You've won our hearts. You've proven your mettle as someone who truly cares about God's grace in another person's life. You might be young in your own faith, but you've learned well." Opening his arms to the group, he stated, "I'd like to propose that Terri be installed as a member of our posse. What do you think?"

"Well, you certainly put us all on the spot," Tom remarked. "But I can honestly say I have no objection whatsoever. In fact, I wholeheartedly support your nomination."

"So do I," Anne chimed in. "I'd enjoy another female in this room full of testosterone. And I couldn't think of anyone I'd prefer to join-up with."

"Me too," Scanlon affirmed. "You add a lot little sister."

"Well Terrance," Fr. Ted said to the silent member in the room. "What's your opinion?"

"No brainer," Terrance answered. "I'm totally sold."

"So James; what do you think?" Fr. Ted asked his obviously stunned charge.

"Yeah! For sure!"

Terri's face blushed bright red – embarrassed from all the unexpected attention and approval. "You look uncomfortable my dear," Fr. Ted observed. "You appear a bit unsettled by my proposal."

"I hardly know how to thank you all. You've made me feel so welcome. Fr. Ted told me I'd become a part of a God thing. He wasn't kidding!" Once more the room erupted in joyous laughter. Terri clapped her hands over her face, her eyes wide and beaming.

"So, the proposal passes. Terri has just joined the posse." Applause filled the room as the members stood in unison. Again, Terri's face burnt bright like a painful sunburn. James reached over and gave her a gentle hug. "Glad you're here," he whispered in her ear.

"Ted, you said you had a path for us. Why don't you let us in on it," Tom directed.

"I do. Easter's a little more than a month away. I've asked James to join a group at my parish that's preparing for baptism at the Easter Vigil. I'd like each of you to play an integral role in this process." Raising his hands like he was holding back a flood, Fr. Ted explained, "Now before anyone gets hives over participating in a Catholic formational process, let me help you. First, if James chooses, we can perform his baptism with just us, his folks and the hoodlums. Or, if he opts, during the Easter Vigil."

"But if he wants it here, at St. Ambrose, won't that make him Catholic?" Terrance asked with a hint of doubt in his voice.

Fr. Ted looked over his glasses at Terrance, "Yes, it would. Would that be a problem?"

"I don't know. Guess I haven't thought about it before now," Terrance replied somewhat puzzled that he even bothered to ask the question. "To be honest, I'd never really given the fact that you're Catholic any thought. So why would it matter? We all love God and each other. I'd say it's entirely James' call."

"That goes for me, too," Scanlon affirmed. "Fr. Ted has been more of a pastor – and father – to me than anyone. It never really bugged me that he was Catholic."

"James, what are you thinking?" Rowland broke in to ask. "You seem a little to yourself."

"When I walked into this place last night, it was like another world opened up to me. It was here, with all of you, the hoodlums and my folks where church made sense to me for the first time. I don't know what it means to be Catholic – or really Protestant for that matter. I just know what it means to be loved like I've never been loved before. It was Fr. Ted who confronted my screwed up mind and showed me Jesus. But so have all of you guys. I don't know where else I would go. Now that I know Jesus, I just want to get on with my new life. If I can do that here, with all of you and with Fr. Ted, I think that's what I want to do."

The room fell silent. It was like the wheels were grinding in their minds; as if for each person the Church enlarged in their vision, and became what it only pretends to be among its shattered and scattered parts – the one Body of Christ. Until this moment it had not mattered whether one was Protestant and another Catholic. It only mattered that the Gospel – the Good News – was proclaimed. So why would a divisive rift threaten to divide them now? Are they not the same people, those called by God for this singular purpose? Was not James the concentration of their shared concern; this young man whose life hung precariously by the thread of their united prayers gathered as one prayer to God? And was he not now the incarnation of what the united Body of Christ had birthed through the grace of Jesus Christ? Was he not their common possession and their common responsibility? It became exceedingly apparent that, for the first time in the life of the posse, the potential for division or the galvanizing of unity confronted them. At stake was the formation of this young man into a devoted follower of Christ. How would they handle it? Would his decision to enter the Catholic Church threaten the unity among the members?

"If I may comment," Rowland broke in to say. "James, I may not be Roman Catholic, but I pray I am catholic enough to know that God will speak to you regardless of the tradition you choose to follow." Gesturing toward

Fr. Ted, "My best friend is a Roman Catholic priest. Why wouldn't I entrust to him the spiritual formation of a young man I care so much about – you? I want you to know son, you have my total support. Speaking for myself, I eagerly look forward to attending Easter Vigil here with you and all the rest."

"Same goes for me," Scanlon stated with confidence. "Sign me on."

"Yeah, me too," Terrance added.

"I think I might be more Catholic than I realize, James," Anne offered. "I love the liturgy and the sense of holy reverence here. I think you will too. In my mind, you've made a wise decision. You have my support."

James looked at Terri who was utterly beaming, "What do you think?" he asked her.

"Wow, I'm blown away! Honestly, I was really, really hoping you'd say here. I'm so sold on Fr. Ted; gosh it's like he's my dad or something."

Terri won the room with her gushing admission. "Thank you my dear," Fr. Ted said with a wink. "I assure you, I've never had a sweeter daughter in my life." He reached across the arm of his chair to lay his hand on Rowland's arm, "And thank you my friend. We've been through a great deal together. I could not want for a better friend – or brother."

Cocking his head to the side, Fr. Ted addressed James directly, "Well young man, you're observing what Christ intended when he prayed to the Father that we all might be one. Understand this, though; if the time comes when you feel the call of God to leave the Roman Church, I will not stand in your way. Instead, I will still be your friend, your mentor and your spiritual father. How does that sound to you?"

"Why doesn't every Christian feel this way? Why don't they just agree to care about one another like you guys have cared for me?" James answered.

Fr. Ted shook his head as if unsure how to respond to so obvious a question. "Well son, let's show them how. Shall we?"

"Yes sir. I can't begin to thank you all. I know I said it before, but I can't find better words. You all mean more to me than I can say."

"Ted, you said you have a role for each of us to play in this process. What do you have in mind?" Rowland asked for the group.

"Tom, I want you to take the lead as James' godparent. That's a bit unorthodox since you're not Roman Catholic, but I'm willing to overlook that matter. Mike and Terrance, I want you to be James' god-brothers. Together you guys will pray for James, encourage him and help him remain accountable for growing in his faith. How does that sound to you?"

"Fine by me," Terrance answered.

"Yeah, good here," Scanlon agreed.

"Me, too, Ted," Rowland said. "I like where I think this might be going."

"Guys our roles will be no different than they were when James was at the State House. Now we'll direct them toward his baptism. There are some rites, however, where we'll need a Catholic as James' sponsor."

"Okay, who?" Terrance inquired with a shrug. "That's not likely going to be any of us."

"Ah, so here's my suggestion," Fr. Ted began. "I'd like to ask Harold Raynor to join us for that purpose. He will be the one who stands with James during those special times when the rites are performed. But for Easter, I want us all there. Agreed?"

"Fabulous!" Terrance blurted.

"Ted, I like the idea and I'm certain Harold would be more than willing to serve."

"Good! But there's more," Fr. Ted said with a coy smirk on his face.

"Terri," I want you to play a role too. I want you to stand with James when he takes those rites. Will you?"

"Really!? I'd love to!" she squealed. "Oh wow! Do I have to be Catholic?"

Everyone broke into good natured laughter. "No you don't," Fr. Ted answered still sputtering with laughter. "You just have to care enough for your friend to be there with him."

"I can do that!" Terri exclaimed. "I want to do that. Fr. Ted, I may even want to be in your church too someday. Would that be okay?"

"Of course, my dear. We'll discern that together as we all walk this pathway. How does that sound?"

"I love it!" Terri cried. "Thank you so much! This means so much to me to be with you all."

"Terri, you mean a lot to each of us," Anne broke in to say.

"So here's how it will go," Fr. Ted said sitting deeper in his chair, his hands folded and resting across his belly. "James has not experienced the rite of welcome that precedes the season of catechesis. I want to conduct that rite this Sunday during mass. James it consists of the kind of questions I asked you last night. Harold Raynor will stand with you along with Terri. Are you okay with that?"

"I am," James replied.

"Each week James will attend RCIA sessions at which time I want at least one of you gentlemen and Terri to attend. The Sunday before Easter we'll conduct what's called the Final Scrutiny. There are three all told, and this is the last one – the one preceding Easter. Though James missed the first two, it's important he participate in this one. It's where he publicly denounces sin and embraces Christ with his other new brothers and sisters. And then the big event – Easter Vigil. I call it coronation for all those receiving baptism, confirmation and first communion. Nothing like! It's Heaven!"

"You want us to attend all of these rites?" Anne asked.

"If you can, Anne. But Easter Vigil for certain."

"We'll be there," Terrance asserted. "I think the entire Café will be."

"I'll alert the ushers," Fr. Ted said with a chuckle.

"I don't know how to explain it, but I've never felt so united in anything we've ever done," Scanlon stated. "We are family, aren't we?"

"Indeed we are Michael," Fr. Ted confirmed.

"James, believe it or not, you've done something pretty special for this group," Rowland said through a warm smile. "We've been close, but never this close. Maybe we can show the world that watches us what it honestly means to be one."

"Thanks, Mr. Rowland. I hope so too."

"People, let's pray the Our Father as our benediction."

Together the group stood, joined hands, their voices rising as they declared in unison, "For Thine is the Kingdom and the power and the glory forever. Amen!"

FIFTY-SEVEN

An air of anticipation wafted through the congregation at St. Ambrose Catholic Church. Seeing so many unfamiliar faces, several of whom resembled the great unwashed, raised a few eyebrows among the faithful. The hoodlums gathered in the back, each one taking his or her turn at the font, dripping holy water about as they clumsily signed themselves before scrunching into the last row of pews. Oddly they seemed far less awkward about their surroundings than did the Meyers – or Rowlands for that matter. Terrance and Anne, however, appeared to be quite at home, dropping onto the kneeling rail in front of their pew, bowing hand-in-hand to pray. James and Terri took their places in the pew marked "Reserved."

Organ music filled the cavernous sanctuary and on cue the congregation rose. James and Terri stood and turned toward the center aisle with the rest of the congregation. A young girl in her early teens, robed in white, a white rope knotted around her waist proceeded toward them holding a crucifix on a tall pole. Behind her a man held an ornate book high over his head – the Gospel. As it passed, people reverently bowed as if a great presence had passed by. Following them was a woman, her hands pressed together in front of her as if in prayer. And behind her, vested in white with a red brocade stole was Fr. Ted, he, too, holding his hands in reverential piety. The sight of a vested Fr. Ted gave James a start. He was the picture of his calling, the man of spiritual priority who was at once spiritual mentor and impish tease. In the moment, he stood apart and yet near, his stature unmistakable, his authority unapproachable. He was the figure of heaven upon earth, the sight of which nearly made James tremble.

From the platform, Fr. Ted stepped forward, raising his right hand above his head he intoned, "Let us begin our prayer in the name of the Father and of the Son and of the Holy Spirit." With these words he traced the sign of the cross in broad strokes as each member followed in kind, signing themselves. James and Terri acted in kind more or less on the impulse of others standing around them.

James was immediately taken by the profound sense of awe that overshadowed the gestures, the obvious reverence; the bodily movements of bowing, kneeling, standing and the unison voice of the congregation as it recited responses to the scriptures. Everything seemed intentional – nothing haphazard or out of place. He allowed his eyes to stray around him. A few people caught his notice – affecting him by the expression of holy wonder and piety etched in their faces. Of course there appeared some, who seemed only to be going through the motions as if unaware of their significance. He recalled a poem he once heard; somewhat surprised he so vividly remembered it. "All of earth is crammed with heaven and every common bush ablaze with God. But only those who see take off their shoes. The rest sit round and pluck blackberries." It came from Elizabeth Barrett Browning, though he'd forgotten the poet's name.

As he concluded his homily, Fr. Ted strode to the center of the platform and stepped down into the nave. "I'd like to invite James Taylor Meyers to join me, along with his sponsor, Harold Raynor and his friend, Terri."

His palms sweating and his knees quaking James stood, Terri squeezed his hand. He stepped into the aisle and approached the front. Harold Raynor drew up beside him. Addressing the congregation Fr. Ted began, "Though a bit unorthodox this near Easter, I am pleased to offer the Rite of Welcome to the Catechumenate to James. Very recently, James came to faith after a long season of searching. Several of us have met in prayer nightly for this young man. I would like those of that group who are in attendance with us today to stand." A stir of wonder spread throughout the faithful who watched as the hoodlums, the family and friends stood in unison. "These dear friends are his witnesses, each one offering of himself or herself for the life of this young man. Please thank them." Applause broke out along with warm gestures of welcome. James' felt his heart glow and his anxiety release. "I am so very grateful to welcome you to this moment, James. In the spirit of Christ, 'What do you ask of God's Church?'"

As Fr. Ted had instructed him the day before, James answered, "Faith."

"And what does faith offer you?"

"Eternal life."

The acolyte stepped over in front of Fr. Ted with an open book. Raising his hands, Fr. Ted began to read from the text: "God gives light to everyone who comes into this world; though unseen, he reveals himself through the works of his hand, so that all people may learn to give thanks to their Creator." Lifting his eyes he momentarily looked at James. Returning to the text he continued, "You have followed God's light and the way of the Gospel now lies open before you. Set your feet firmly on that path and acknowledge the living God, who truly speaks to everyone."

James' mind slipped from the words to the moment this truth became his truth. How very much different his world now looked than it did merely one week ago. "James," he heard Fr. Ted say, seizing his attention back to this moment, "This is the way of faith along which Christ will lead you in love toward eternal life. Are you prepared to begin this journey today under the guidance of Christ?"

With full confidence, James answered, "I am."

Addressing Harold Raynor who stood with his hand poised on James' right shoulder, Fr. Ted asked, "Are you ready to help James find and follow Christ?"

Giving James' shoulder a firm squeeze Raynor answered, "I am."

Now to the congregation, Fr. Ted inquired, "Are all of you gathered as witnesses to this confession and rite of welcome ready to help James on his journey with Jesus Christ?"

"We are," the congregation answered as one voice.

Raynor took a position in front of James. "James," Fr. Ted said, "Receive the sign of the cross on your forehead." As he said this, Raynor placed his thumb on James' forehead and traced the sign of the cross. "It is Christ," Fr. Ted continued, "who now strengthens you with this sign of his love. Learn to know him and follow him. Will you?"

"I will," James answered sobered by the realization that it was the head guard at the State House whose thumb it was that placed the sign of the cross on his brow.

"James, turn and face the congregation." As James turned a church packed with smiling faces greeted him. "Together we affirm, 'Glory and praise to you, Lord Jesus Christ,'" Fr. Ted sang out. Voices echoed from the congregation, "Glory and praise to you, Lord Jesus Christ."

James once recited to himself, "I'm a felon." As he returned to his seat beside Terri, he whispered, "I'm a catechumen."

*****

After the dismissal following the Rite of Welcome, James took his seat among the other catechumen, sponsors and catechists (teachers) in the classroom situated in the annex across the parking lot. Harold Raynor took a seat beside him and Terri on his other side.

"Quite a ceremony wasn't it?" Raynor leaned over to ask as a few late comers filed into the room.

"Honestly, Mr. Raynor, it blew me away. This whole week has blown me away."

Raynor gave James' shoulder a friendly pat. "It's just begun, James. The good stuff has just begun," he asserted smiling reassuringly at James.

James may have been the newcomer but no one made him feel like it. Just the opposite – everyone, including fellow catechumen, went out of their way to greet and welcome their new member. He enjoyed the attention even if it seemed awkward at first. It made it easier, though, having Terri seated beside him, who, with Harold Raynor, followed as the catechumen exited through the side door at the front of the nave.

He was especially impressed, even moved, by the brief bios each member offered as they introduced themselves to him. At the urging of the catechist (teacher), each person related a profoundly personal reason for their own journey to Jesus. A middle-aged man raised as a Buddhist met a nun while he was treated in the hospital that "seemed so at peace with her God she almost glowed. I wanted that same peace," he said. A couple to his left recounted their personal conversions to faith in Christ through another church community, "but there just wasn't much depth. Our devotional lives became shallow and we knew there had to be more. We wanted to grow in our faith and found that possibility here." Two other women in their early thirties came because their kids kept pestering them with questions about bible stories they brought home from school. "I had no answers for them," one of the moms stated. "Here we sent out kids off to a Catholic school because of its educational reputation, but neither my husband nor I expected they would be immersed in Christianity. We decided I should find out more. What I didn't expect is that I would encounter God." "Me, too," the other mom quipped. "And for me it has meant an entire change of life, I'm a believer and wonder how I ever got along without God."

James felt remarkably comfortable as these people so easily recounted their stories. There were a couple folks still unsure if God and the church were for them. Still, they came searching and had not dropped out of the group. One of them, a gentleman in his mid-fifties remarked, "I've been a confirmed atheist my entire adult life. My wife, she's Catholic, thought I ought to at least investigate the faith. That's why I'm here."

Finally the catechist turned to James: "How about letting us know who you are, and a little about your faith journey?" James squirmed a bit and let out a deep sigh. "That's a long story. Just so you all know; I'm a prisoner at Marysville. Got caught in a drug bust." The room fell utterly silent, every member mesmerized by James' story. He'd pause. They'd ask for more. As he described the events leading to his own encounter with Christ, people's eyes filled, occasional groans fell almost involuntarily from someone deeply moved by a particular revelation, especially as he let them in on his conversations with Terri, Fr. Ted, Terrance and others.

"So you're really a brand new Christian?" One of the young moms observed daubing tears from her eyes.

"I am," James answered.

"And you, Terri; you're kinda new too, aren't you?" the mom asked.

"Yes," Terri replied. "Just a baby really." The gathered chuckled.

"So are you looking to become Catholic?" One of the others asked.

Terri took a second to look at James before answering. "Maybe. It's all so new to me; I'm still kind of seeing where God will lead me. But I'm open."

James reached for Terri's hand under the table. Suddenly he and his friend found themselves joined on a path of discovery together, one neither of them comprehended but openly accepted. For James it was reassuring to realize that those who led him were indeed fulfilling their promise to walk with him. For Terri, it was assurance that she, too, was embraced by God for a purpose and to an end she could not possibly anticipate.

This entire day was more than James – or Terri – could have fathomed. It was as if their world – not just James' world – expanded; as if God had gathered them both in his embrace along with many others whose journey they now shared, and assured them of his presence. It was the picture of the Body of Christ, a community formed by his passion and victory, set apart like no other to fulfill that one great commandment – to love one another as Christ had loved us. So much change in the course of a single week; the bottom not only had been reached; it was as if a seed had fallen into the ground and died – and then sprang to life – new life. And the journey had just begun.

FIFTY-EIGHT

Mike and Terrance waited impatiently for Fr. Ted to finally emerge from the rectory. Anxiously Mike kept his big diesel running, his foot on the brake but the truck in gear. Rowland's revelation from Raynor and Tony of County Gang sent quivers of anxiety through both men, whose eyes raked the grounds, searching tell tale signs of thugs on the prowl.

Without warning the side door of the truck jerked open and a figure clad in black jumped into the back seat – it was Fr. Ted. "What the…" Scanlon exclaimed nearly jumping out of his seat, the truck lurching slightly as his foot fell momentarily from the brake. Terrance spun around in his seat ready for conflict.

"Sorry guys – didn't' mean to startle you."

"You almost became an ex-priest!" Scanlon bellowed. "Don't ever do that again!"

"Look, I know we're all on tenterhooks. But nothing's happened yet and hopefully it won't," Fr. Ted rejoined. "You guys want to know why I was a bit tardy?"

"Sure – of course!" Terrance snapped.

"Terrance your father-in-law called me just before you guys rolled in. Chavez has been relocated – Rikers as Tom hoped. For now Tony thinks the atmosphere will quiet down with the head dog out of play."

"Wolf, Father," Terrance corrected. "He's the head wolf and they never quiet down. They just become more strategic."

"That's not very comforting," A nervous Scanlon reacted.

"So you think Tony's got his signals wrong, Terrance?" Fr. Ted inquired in tone of uncertainty.

"No, they'll quiet down but the risks are only temporarily postponed." Terrance swept a hand through his hair. "Look guys, we still need to watch ourselves. My take is they'll name a new alpha and their focus will change. But that doesn't mean we can get sloppy."

"Change their focus? To what?" Fr. Ted asked.

"Turf – they're on a turf grab. They may even forget James…and me…for awhile."

"Okay, well then, let's make the most of the time we've got," Fr. Ted stated.

Scanlon raced along a circuitous maze of side roads and alleys to Marysville, parking behind the facility in the employee lot. Hollinswood had given his good friend, Fr. Ted, the combination to the electrified gate. By now it seemed for the sake of safety rules were optional. "Besides," Hollinswood argued, "We need a priest around here more often. So why don't you sign on as our chaplain?" Fr. Ted liked the idea and rather uceremoniously took up his quasi official new role, which commenced with getting the posse into the asylum undetected by the thugs.

"Hey," James said as he observed the strained faces walking through the door, "You guys don't look so good. What's up?"

"Nothin' kid," Terrance said wrapping an arm around James's shoulder. "Where you taking us?"

"The library," James answered. But he wasn't buying Terrance's feigned attempt to disarm his suspicions. "Look, you're hiding something. Out with it," he snapped.

The guys pushed open the library doors. Two residents were seated at the table and two others were roaming the stacks. "Is there a private place other than here?" Terrance asked not masking his tension.

"Yeah, the lounge. I didn't see anybody there," James answered.

Without a word, Terrance took James by the arm; Scanlon and Fr. Ted trailed. The lounge was clear. Terrance pointed at the sofa. James and Fr. Ted dropped into it. Terrance swung the two lounge chairs around in front of them. He and Scanlon took them. Glancing around the room verifying it was clear of listening ears, Terrance then looked at Fr. Ted as much as to say, "You tell him."

Fr. Ted had taken his glasses off to wipe perspiration from his brow. "Tom – Mr. Rowland – thought we shouldn't break this to you. But things have changed overnight. He might join us later. Look, James, we got word from Tony that the Lobos have figured out you're no longer at the State House. They've put out a hit for you…and Terrance."

James slumped in his seat, his face pale as the white T-shirt he wore. "Will it ever end?" he begged in a near whisper.

About then Hollinswood caught up to the men. "Gentlemen, I just heard from Tom. He informed me he won't be coming."

"Why? Is he worried he might get tailed?"

"I think that's exactly his concern, Mike," Hollinswood answered.

"So how bad is it?" James asked still slouched in his seat, his arms dangling limp at his sides.

"Dunno," Terrance responded. "Here's what we do know and what I think it means." Leaning closer to the men, he said in a near whisper, "Tom and the admin at the State House have moved Chavez out. He's on his way to Rikers in New York. That means the Nuevo Lobos don't have an alpha for now. That will change. When, I don't know. There'll be a power struggle for awhile but these guys know how to settle those things. It won't be long and they'll be back in business." Terrance leaned even closer to James. "Look kid, from my experience with these jerks, they'll be preoccupied with naming a new alpha. While they're distracted with that they'll forget you and me – at least for now. Once they get that matter settled, they'll be back to staking out new turf and recruiting members. That doesn't mean we're off the hook. But I think we're okay for now."

James cocked his head to the side, his mouth open. "Not real assuring."

"Kid, it's been like this for me since I got out of the joint and dropped out of the gang. Somehow God has kept me protected. I'm convinced he's got us both covered. Go with me on this. We're not going to let this threat beat us, James. I'll level with you. It scares the hell out of me, but these guys are not going to beat us. Do you understand?"

James shook his head, "Aren't you worried man? Aren't you afraid they'll get you someday?"

"Weren't you listening? Yeah it digs me at times. But man I've seen God work. It doesn't bother me like it used to."

"Not now huh?"

"Look, what you're gonna find out as you grow in your faith is that circumstances may not change, but how you see them will. You see, he changes us! And that definitely changes how we see things. Yeah, it scares me that these asses want to kill me. Scares Anne, too. Shoot, kid, it scares us all. But that's not the big deal. The big deal is to let God take charge. Step out and let him work! He is greater than anything we face."

Terrance's words, the pathos etched in his face struck James. He straightened himself, swallowed hard and said, "You would know. Of all of us, you would know."

Hollinswood hadn't left. He remained standing off to the side. Fr. Ted pointed his direction. "This man wears the scars, James."

"What do you mean wears the scars?"

"Bram," Fr. Ted said now craning his neck to look up into Hollinswood's face.

Hollinswood swept his coattails back and pulled out his shirt. Lifting it James caught sight of long, welted scars across Hollinswood's chest and abdomen. "Got these during the riots, son. Peace was nearly deadly."

"Oh my gosh!" James groaned. "I'm so sorry."

"You needn't be sorry son. You listen to Terrance. What he said is straight up truth. God won't thicken your skin but he will enlarge your heart. He'll make it possible for you to love your enemies. He did that for me. And that, my dear boy, is the source of real courage."

As Hollinswood stuffed his shirt back into his trousers, James stared blankly across the room. "It isn't cheap is it?"

"What's that?" Hollinswood curiously asked.

"The cost of faith." James looked over at Fr. Ted who was already looking at him, "Like you said, Father, what cost God much can't be cheap to us. Can it?"

"No son, it never is. The cross is where we go to meet him. Can't get to resurrection without confronting the cross."

"Baptism: That's what you told me baptism is about."

"That's right, son," Fr. Ted said through a soft smile.

"Gentlemen," Hollinswood broke in. "There isn't anything cheap in life. Mr. James Meyers, what was the cost of your former behavior?"

James cracked a sideward grin, "Prison."

"Indeed it was. Now then, let me ask you again, was it worth it?"

"No sir, it wasn't."

"So, what do you think is better? Letting God take charge and transform you or livin' in that old lifestyle?"

"No contest! I'll take the cross."

"Atta boy! I feel the same way son. And it's been a few decades since I made that decision. God has never let me down. He won't let you down either. Hold onto him son! Those thugs are not your enemy. Your enemy got beat here in that library a week ago. He got beat long before that when Jesus cried from the cross 'It is finished.' Yes indeed, God finished off the devil and eternal death in that declaration. As long as you hold onto God, that enemy can't hurt you. Even if those animals get you, God has your soul and that will live forever." Hollinswood nodded his head at the guys, "Gotta go gentlemen. More of that infernal paper work. God help me." All at once the tension fled the room as if Hollinswood swept it out with a dismissive sweep of his hand as he left.

"I needed to hear that," James said.

"So how do feel about things now," Fr. Ted asked.

"Like God's in charge and I don't need to worry about this crap."

"T, you looked like you got sucker punched," Scanlon said throwing an arm around Terrance.

"Did you guys see those scars?"

"How could we miss them," James snarled.

"I'd heard Bram had been through the racial mill. I had no idea…" Terrance didn't finish his words. He just sat shaking his head, his face drawn.

"Guys, we'll always be tested," Fr. Ted broke in to say. "That's another reason we need each other." Looking at James, "You see why we're *all* in this together – and I mean *together?*"

"I'm beginning to," James answered. "It's definitely not a solo act is it?"

"Not hardly kid," Scanlon snorted.

"So what's today's lesson?" James asked while twisting his head toward Fr. Ted.

"I believe my dear boy we just had it. Why don't you summarize it for us?"

James took a moment to reflect. Stroking his chin he ticked down the list of things that stood out most. "Our faith is very expensive. It is always tested. We're never far from the cross – or shouldn't be. And we aren't going to make it without each other."

"Perfect," Fr. Ted confirmed. "James you make sure those words get into your journal today. I want you to email that summary to each of us. Okay?"

"Yes sir. I'll do it right away."

"Well guys, a lot has happened. Let's pray."

The men bowed over the small coffee table in front of them. Fr. Ted made the sign of the cross. James did the same. "In the name of the Father, the Son and the Holy Spirit," Fr. Ted began. "Keep us safely in your embrace and may we never stray from it."

"Amen," the men said in unison. Each man then leaned back in his seat letting the moment and Fr. Ted's prayer work into their own spirits. What was tension was now peace, and nothing had changed. Well, actually there was change. James – and the others – had a fresh idea about who is in charge. It would get tested.

FIFTY-NINE

Terri took her seat as James and Fr. Ted entered the classroom. Others filtered in and took their seats, a few grabbing a cup of coffee from the stainless pot and a cookie or two. Terri passed when asked by one of the members. So did James. Fr. Ted took his seat at the center of the squared-off horseshoe table arrangement and waited for Kathy Swanson, the catechist, to arrive. Chatter spread across the room as the obviously familiar members took up their conversation pretty much from where it stopped last week. One of the men teased good naturedly with Fr. Ted. James accurately surmised him to be the godparent of one of the catechumen. About then a hand dropped onto James' shoulder and another onto Terri's. "Hi kids," a familiar voice greeted from behind them. The figure swung into the empty chair beside James. "Hi Mr. Raynor," Terri bubbled. "Great to see you."

"Well, did you two do your homework?" Raynor asked.

"Sure did," Terri chirped.

"Yes, sir," James joined.

The room's attention suddenly diverted to the door, as Kathy Swanson swept in like a force of nature and fell into the chair beside Fr. Ted. One of the ladies as if on cue handed her a cup of freshly poured coffee, which Kathy dutifully acknowledged with a kind smile.

"Sorry I'm late," she remarked while hastily pulling material from the backpack she had swung off her shoulder. "Traffic! Ugh!"

Her excuse didn't go unnoticed. "Yeah like it was worse for you than us, huh?"

Kathy glared mockingly at the smart aleck at the far end of the table, "Purgatory for you Mitchell," she snarled sarcastically. The room lit up with laughter.

James and Terri were both enjoying the friendly repartee, which broke whatever ice they might have felt as the newcomers. "Well, Fr. Ted, do you want to get us on course before Mitchell drags us further into the abyss?" Kathy asked poking at the round-faced Mitchell Davis who was very much enjoying himself.

"I hardly know if it would do any good with you two. How about you both meet me in the confessional?" Fr. Ted joked. Again laughter erupted and Mitchell slapped the table while laughing hysterically. "Okay folks, I think we've had our icebreaker tonight. Let's welcome James and Terri once again." Words of greeting came from all corners of the room accompanied with warm welcoming smiles and kindly nods. "Thank you," Terri said for both her and James.

"Let us begin in the name of the Father, the Son and the Holy Spirit," Fr. Ted said. As a group everyone made the sign of the cross, even the two self-avowed atheist agnostic types. "Lead us dear Lord to you. May our hearts fasten to your heart and our words please your ears. In the name of the Father, the Son and the Holy Spirit: Amen." With that brief prayer Fr. Ted formally opened the evening session. "We have only two more gatherings people before the final scrutiny. After that we gather for the main event – Easter Vigil. Kathy will be sending out instructions in your email. Be watching." Turning his head in Kathy's direction, "What's our lesson tonight professor?" Fr. Ted asked.

"This week we return to the Old Testament for a look at what our text titles 'The last seven commandments: Love of neighbor.'"

James came with his copy of the book as well as the Blue Book both of which sat on the table in front of him. Harold couldn't avoid noticing that the Bible belonged to the prison. After all it was plainly stenciled "Property of Marysville Correctional Institution." "Swiped the prison's copy, huh?" He joked jabbing it with his thick index finger.

"Borrowed, Mr. Raynor," James whispered in reply. Fr. Ted overheard the comment and saw the *borrowed* Bible. "Got to fix that," he mused quietly to himself, at the same time making a mental note.

"Before we dig into this week's material, let me ask if anyone has questions or comments from last week's discussion about 'Love of God'?" Kathy began. "It seems a few of you worried yourselves over veneration versus idolatry and others about whether doubt is ever legitimate. Who's still bugged about this stuff?"

"I am," one of the women said raising her hand.

"All right, Rachel, what's your concern?"

"I believe in God and I truly accept that Jesus lived, died and rose again. I don't have any real qualms about those things anymore. But I just can't get my head around why? I know I don't deserve such unmerited love. So does my doubt label me agnostic?"

"Go ahead, Father, you take that one," Kathy said jabbing Fr. Ted with her elbow. Chuckles swirled around the room.

"No Rachel that doesn't make you an agnostic. If it does, I'm agnostic with you. Here's why. Do you recall how last week's chapter began? It began with a quote from First John chapter four. Let's go back there together."

People began flipping through their books. "You'll find it on page two eighty-five," Kathy directed.

"Read it to us if you would, Rachel," Fr. Ted asked.

Rachel sat the book in front of her and read the passage aloud. Suddenly she paused, her eyes began to sparkle. "Oh my," she shrieked as if caught by surprise. "I'd read right past this part." Fr. Ted urged her to read it again. "Love consists in this: it is not we who loved God, but God loved us and sent his Son to expiate our sins. My dear friends, if God loved us so much, we too should love each other."

"What did you see this time that you didn't see before?" Fr. Ted asked her.

"I've been thinking it all backwards. I always thought that it started with us. It was up to us to love God before he would love us. I don't know why I missed seeing this. But what a revelation! It all truly starts from him, doesn't it?"

"So what do the rest of you think? How does Rachel's discovery strike you?" Kathy asked the group.

Others chimed in offering their impressions, adding to the question or simply processing their own uncertainty. "The plaguing question," Fr. Ted interjected, "seems to be why would God reach down to worthless people like us? Why would he take the initiative? It seems kind of backward doesn't it?"

"Fr. Ted if I may," the avowed and most vocal of the two atheist agnostics broke in.

"Certainly, Dave: What's your thought on the subject?" Fr. Ted asked recognizing Dave Remmick, a long-time philosophy instructor at the local college, a slender man of medium height, clad in a long sleeve denim shirt and Levis, with a halo of long white hair pulled taut into a ponytail, a trimmed goatee fastened to his chin. It was Dave's wife – a member of St. Ambrose parish – who urged him to attend the RCIA and find out for himself what the church really teaches. "If God is as loving as this passage suggests, why does he permit so many atrocities to seemingly go unaddressed? I'm not certain I see the love in that. It appeals to me more as indifference, like he wound up creation and left it all for us to figure out."

Dave's question provoked old nemeses to prowl James' mind. A question very much like Dave's had been his undoing. James waited for others to comment.

"Dave, I had that same concern for the longest time. But last Easter it came into focus for me," Mitchell stated. The jokester wasn't joking now. His expression was entirely concentrated, reliving his own trek up this difficult hill. "As you know, I'm a repeat. The first two times I sat in this classroom we'd come to this very chapter and I'd walk out. I couldn't reconcile the state of the world with a loving God."

"So you've said, Mitchell. What changed your mind?" Dave asked.

"More like changed my heart as well as my mind," Mitchell answered. Mitchell, like Dave, had been a confirmed atheist. His work as a lab scientist precluded in his mind the existence of any metaphysical being. Fr. Ted permitted him entrance into the Catechumenate after the season of Inquiry largely to allow him to continue his probing, so long as he did it honestly and with respect. The same courtesy had been extended to Dave. Neither man was considered a catechumen per se, but as people on a sincere and deliberate journey for truth – an extended inquiry for want of better

302

description, who were willing to allow the church to present its conclusions. That Mitchell had actually submitted to the Rite of Welcome was a major source of encouragement to those who knew him, Fr. Ted among them. That Dave was still asking questions, still searching with integrity for answers was clearly seen by those who knew him as evidence of doubt – but not as much doubt about God than doubt about his preconceptions. For the past few weeks he seemed to awaken to the plausibility of God. At times he even seemed to hope for it much like James himself did before he reached that inevitable crossroads.

"Did you attend the Vigil last year?" Mitchell asked Dave referring to the Holy Saturday Vigil that led into Easter.

"No, I didn't," Dave replied.

"Oh, I wish you had. I was still stuck in my cynicism but agreed to attend with my family. Here I sat, my arms smugly wrapped around myself, my head poked into the air totally indifferent to everything until." Mitchell paused.

"Okay, until when…or what?" Dave probed.

"The scriptures, Dave. Until the scriptures were read – sung really. I was surprised when they began in the Old Testament with creation. Odd, I thought, for Easter. As the lectors continued to read, the story began to take shape in my mind. It was no longer a stream of broken anecdotes about God; it began to seem like a cogent chain of events pointing directly at the Christ story. It occurred to me Jesus emerged very early in the telling – in the prophetic passages. To make a long story reasonably short, by the time the Epistles were read I was no longer comfortable with my long held antagonisms toward the biblical record. This wasn't a book of proofs, logical propositions or arguments for God; it was this remarkable narrative about his painful relationship with the cosmos – mostly with man the creature made in God's own image. I wasn't feeling very smug any longer. In truth, I was feeling overwhelmed with something I did not expect to encounter – a thread of truth that clearly held more explanatory cogency than any theoretical system of thinking I'd ever considered."

He paused a moment. "You see, Dave, my preconceptions were melting away right before me. God was no longer small but incomprehensibly immense. He was no longer an –ism, he simply *was*." Mitchell bit his lower lip and stared off into space, "He was simply there and magnificently frightening. Oh my Lord, Dave, when the organ swelled, the people rose, the lights brightened and the priest held the Gospel high above his head I knew beyond doubt I had been encountered by the living truth and I had to face it. What now?" Mitchell shook his head and let out a long sigh through a thin smile, "I found myself on my feet! I heard the Gospel story of Christ's passion like I'd never heard it before! My heart nearly burst inside me."

"Okay so what then?" Dave pressed.

"That night, after it was all over, I dashed out to find Fr. Ted. I had to tell him. Actually I had to confess. Dave, it was like Rachel's ah-ha just now, I thought I had to conjure God up in my mind and pretend I believed in him. How utterly ridiculous! He was waiting for me to wake up and see him standing right in front of my sickening contempt for him."

Mitchell tapped his chin, "I remembered Pascal. Fr. Ted had given me a book about him. He came to a similar epiphany. Until his death he kept a note pinned inside his coat. It was just a single word – Fire. I now knew what he meant. "

Dave had no words. The group had no words. Fr. Ted and Kathy had no words. Mitchell had just proclaimed the Gospel and there were no other words. Rachel had tears in her eyes. She wasn't alone. Terri was a blubbering mess. James held her hand and passed her the box of tissues. Fr. Ted smiled, "I treasure that moment, Mitchell. I'm glad you let us all know."

"I'm glad I finally let it out."

"Alright Mitchell, you've definitely left me with a lot to think about. I wish I were more capable of accepting mystery in the answer."

"Pascal helped me there too, Dave. He made a most meaningful statement that also stuck with me. He said 'If we submit everything to reason our religion will be left with nothing mysterious or supernatural. If we offend the principles of reason our religion will be absurd and ridiculous.'"

"That's quite an insight." Dave said nothing more. He fell back into his doubtful demeanor albeit with more to consider.

Dave respected Mitchell though he was a scientist for whom philosophy seldom gained credence. Tonight, though, Dave certainly found it interesting that Mitchell would broach philosophy while quoting a scientist. More so, Dave was beguiled by Mitchell's transparent reaction to the biblical account. He had to admit, there was more operating beneath the surface than he was presently willing to explore for himself.

"Rachel, how does Mitchell's story help answer your question?" Kathy asked gesturing to get Rachel's attention.

"I think it confirms that God reaches for us before we ever reach for him. I'm definitely going to pay more attention to the scriptures during Vigil. Thank you, Mitchell! Your story really spoke to me." Others expressed their agreement and appreciation also.

"So," Fr. Ted broke in, "Maybe we should hear from the new kids on the block. What say you?"

Terri looked at James. James looked at Terri. "You first," Terri said with a poke to James' ribs.

James swallowed hard before responding. "I'm a little nervous to say anything. This is all so fresh to me." He turned toward Dave, "Up to a couple weeks ago, I had the same questions as both of you guys," meaning Mitchell too. "I also doubted how a God of love could love a scum-bag like me. But like Mitchell said, I had no place to run any more. Every time I tried to run away from God it was like I ran right into him. He was everywhere. It was me who was messed up. It was like I was standing on my head thinking I was on my feet. Now I know. It's like for the first time in my life I'm right with him and right with the world. God has changed me. And I want him to keep changing me."

Even Dave let a thin smile signal his approval. Others in the group fairly radiated with appreciation. Rachel capsulated the moment, "I've really had to finally realize it's a matter of faith. God is everywhere, James; just like you said. We just don't want to see him."

James nudged Terri, "Your turn."

"Oh gosh, I don't know what to say. I'm such a baby believer myself. A group of nurses helped me find my way. I'd aborted my baby, but they loved me anyway. They showed me Jesus. And believe me, he's real. I love him so much!" Tears welled in her eyes again. James handed her another tissue with a broad smile like a proud friend.

"You know guys," Kathy broke in. "We were to talk about love of neighbor, but I think you all demonstrated it just now. Given the diversity within this group, the love you have shown each other is if nothing else evidence that something more than us has visited our space and made it possible to care about one another. Nobody flinched when Terri told us she aborted her baby. Nobody got in Dave's face about his doubts. Mitchell wasn't a jerk for a change." That drew a chuckle from the group. "Perhaps we should simply pray. What do you think?"

Heads nodded. "Fr. Ted, would you please lead us?"

Fr. Ted stood and gestured for the others to stand with him. Reaching out he took Kathy and Terri by the hand and called for everyone to join hands also. As he began others joined in, "Our Father who art in heaven hallowed be thy name. Thy kingdom come. Thy will be done, on earth as it is in heaven. Give us this day our daily bread. And forgive us our trespasses as we forgive those who have trespassed against us. And lead not into temptation but deliver us from evil. For thine is the kingdom and the power and the glory forever. Amen."

"Did you hear what you prayed?" Fr. Ted asked. "Did you hear yourselves plead for God's kingdom to come, his will to be done – be done here on earth as in heaven? Do you know what that all means?" Fr. Ted waited. No one responded. It was as if they knew he had more to say. "Folks, this prayer answers Dave's question about where is God when bad stuff happens. When we pray that his will be done on earth as it is in heaven; that means we've asked him to take charge. We've asked him to assert his will, and that it should prevail even if our will is crushed. Are we really ready to let him answer that prayer? If so, we'll find him showing up to meet the needs of the least and the lost. When he does it will be our hands, our feet and our hearts he will use to heal the sick, set the captive free and to proclaim the acceptable day of the Lord. So where is God when stuff happens? He's waiting for us to pray this prayer and let him use us in the answer."

Dave's attitude softened. "You've left me a lot to think about tonight – all of you have. Thank you."

*****

"So what did you two think of tonight's discussion?" Fr. Ted asked while hastily driving James back to Marysville ahead of curfew.

"Wow, I like those people," Terri answered from the back seat. "They seem so real!"

"I thought so too," James concurred. "They all seemed so comfortable with each other. Was it like that from the beginning?"

"Not hardly," Fr. Ted almost choked out the answer. "Dave could barely tolerate sitting in the same room with Mitchell. Rachel was the proverbial wallflower – wouldn't say a word for the longest time." Peering into the backseat through the rearview mirror, "Did you recognize the couple to the left of Raynor?" he asked Terri.

Terri's mouth suddenly fell open, "Oh my gosh!" she burst. "They were the ones who nearly lost their baby. The ones at my hospital! I barely glanced their direction. Oh my gosh!'

James spun around in his seat, "That was the couple?"

"I'm sure of it," Terri exclaimed, holding her face in her hands.

"You're right, my dear, that's exactly who they are," Fr. Ted confirmed.

"Did you know they'd be there? Did you know they were the ones? Why didn't you warn me?" Terri cried.

"Would you like me to introduce you to them next week?"

"Yeah, I guess but what would I say? I'm sure they didn't know I was watching them?"

"Tell them your story. Let them know how God used them. I can't begin to tell you what it would mean for them to know their little one's ordeal would lead someone – namely you – to God's son."

"Oh man, I don't know if I can do that," Terri cried, throwing herself back in the seat.

"Hey," James pressed. "You told me and look where it led?"

"One story often leads to another story, my dear," Fr. Ted coached. "It's like a chain and every link matters. Tell them."

"Look, I'll be there with you. We'll meet them together. Okay?" James offered through a gentle smile.

"Yeah, well okay," Terri haltingly agreed. "Oh wow, God sure doesn't make it easy does he?"

Fr. Ted nearly drove off the road he was laughing so hard. "No my dear he doesn't. But believe me, he's always ahead of us – never behind. He saw this coming too."

Terri stared out the window into the dimming gray of dusk as it slowly vanished into darkness. "This has to be a God thing," she muttered beneath her breath.

"Well kids," Fr. Ted said coming to a stop in the Marysville driveway. "You've both entered catechesis."

"Another cat-ate something word, huh?" James snarked.

"Learning rarely comes from a book. It most often comes in the form of encounters   encounters with God, with one another and with odd circumstances that affect us. All of those are catechetical moments – times of encounter that lead us to deeper understanding. Sounds to me like that's what you both experienced tonight. Right?"

"I suppose so," Terri said with a twist of angst in her voice.

"This whole thing since last week has definitely been a steep climb for me," James surmised. "It hasn't been comfortable but I wouldn't change any of it."

Fr. Ted gave his young protégé – catechumen as it were – a stiff pat on the knee. "Good," he said.

Terri stepped from the car and gave James a goodnight hug before taking her seat beside Fr. Ted. "So much has happened, Fr. Ted. He seems like a different guy altogether," she said while watching James disappear through the door.

"He is a different guy my dear girl. And you've changed too."

At that comment, Terri snapped her head around and stared at her grinning priest as he pulled away from the facility. She bit her tongue, though. Somehow she knew he was right. In time he would tell her.

SIXTY

"Never a solo act," James jotted in his journal late that night. "No one can make it on his own." A moment later he wrote, "Dave seemed like a train hit him after Mitchell's story. I know the feeling. I just hope he gives in and stops fighting." He reached for the book, *This is Our Faith*, and flipped it open to the creed marked by a scrap of yellow paper. He read it quietly aloud pausing on the words, "holy catholic Church, the communion of saints, the forgiveness of sins, the resurrection of the body, and life everlasting. Amen." Odd, he thought, that it would seem so easy to reconcile the notion of God in three persons but find these last confessions so difficult. They seemed markedly personal. In a couple of weeks Fr. Ted will expect him to recite these words – the entire Creed for that matter – after which he will undoubtedly ask, "Do you, James Meyers, believe what you have confessed?"

Easy to reconcile the triune God? It wasn't that long ago James denied the existence of God. Having made that step, however, the next one – the more personal one – seemed even more daunting. Could he cross the threshold of acceptance? He read the passage again asking himself at each stop if he truly believed it? "Holy catholic Church," he read softly aloud. "Yeah, I can believe that. It's been around a long time junk and all." He moved on, "the communion of saints." Again he halted before replying. "I have no idea what that means." He jotted it on a sheet of paper headed "Questions for Fr. Ted." Next was the hardest one to swallow, "the forgiveness of sins." James closed his eyes. "How can you forgive me, Lord? I don't get it but I know you have done it. I don't feel guilty anymore. Still, it might take me awhile to accept myself. Will you help me – please?" That's where he stopped. The remaining strains would have to wait. About then a guard practically frightened him with a loud rap on his door: "Lights off Meyers." James shot the guard a wave and immediately snapped off the light, rolled from his chair into bed still contemplating the Creed – and the evening's RCIA conversations. Forgiveness, he continued to ponder. It occurred to him as his mind slipped between sleep and awake that all of trust is wrapped up in this single notion that God could do what even he could not do for himself – forgive. Tears streamed down the sides of his face wetting his pillow. His only reasonable reply he whispered into the dark then drifted off – "Thank you."

*****

"I see you've dug into the reading assignment," Fr. Ted observed as he slid the chair from under the table, spying the book flagged with small torn pieces of paper. Terrance had already dropped into a chair across from

James in the mostly empty library. A couple guys sat off in the carrels on the far wall from them.

"You guys sneak in like the other day or come in the front door?" James asked mawkishly.

"We snuck in," Terrance answered. "The heat's still on if you get my drift."

"Dude, aren't you a little nervous showing up here?" James pried.

"Nope, not in the least," Terrance confidently assured as he swung his denim jacket around the back of a chair beside him. "Besides, who's going to thump a priest? As long as I hang with Fr. Ted, I'm good."

James rolled his eyes, "You're too much dude."

"Not to undermine your confidence Mr. Hall, but I don't think this brand of ruffians respect the collar as much as you might think," Fr. Ted warned. "We'd better be looking a little bit higher for our protection gentlemen."

"Yeah, well," Terrance sputtered, "I was just taking the bite out of James' worry before you jumped him with it."

Again James' eyes rolled while the other two exchanged friendly sarcasm.

"For what it's worth, I'm not worried. But I've got questions," James said dropping his hand on the pad in front of him.

"Okay, my son, what's on your mind?" Fr. Ted replied rocking back on the hind legs of the chair as was his custom.

"I was wondering why the catechumen don't get to stay for the rest of the service. Why not? Why'd we have to leave? Just some Catholic thing?"

Terrance punched Fr. Ted, "I'll let you handle that one. Bugged me too."

"Oh it's more, much more really than a Catholic thing, James. It ranges back in history to the earliest centuries of Christianity. Are you sure you want to go there? It's a rather long story."

"Yeah, I do. I just get the feeling it was for a reason – not just some ritual thing."

"It was. You see, during the first few centuries, up until Constantine, persecution – at times quite severe – plagued the church. Many people gave their lives. Others abandoned their faith for the sake of their lives. When Emperor Constantine declared Christianity legal within the Empire those who defected the faith wanted to return – this included clergy too. The question was how and on what terms. If these people had been properly taught, had made the surrender of their lives to Christ in baptism, why did they renounce him? Why did they go so far as to pervert the church's teachings in order to appeal to the government's desire to expunge the faith from the face of the earth? It was a hideous situation. Communities began to wrestle with the matter on their own – some imposing strict standards of reform, others more lax. Ultimately, for the sake of fidelity to the right and honorable teachings of Christ, a process known as the Apostolic Tradition was adopted and implemented in various ways across the Church." Fr. Ted stopped and twisted his face. "Okay, here's where it gets a little weird. It was the premise of the process that until the catechumen had been baptized that their 'kiss' – the symbol of peace and reconciliation – was unholy."

"Kiss?" James broke in. "Really?"

Fr. Ted nearly fell off his chair laughing. Terrance dropped his head on the table. "I warned you it was a little weird! The kiss, son, was the breath of God shared between members. Trust me, it's done differently today. In its place we offer one another the sign of peace. We look each other in the eye, shake hands and say 'The peace of the Lord be with you.'"

"I can buy that? But where did the church get that idea?"

"It came from Paul's admonition to greet one another with a holy kiss. What made their kiss holy was full surrender to Christ demonstrated in the waters of baptism. The kiss meant reconciliation and unity among the members."

"Alright, but why is it done during the service? Why not in private?"

"That's a good question. Paul warned the Church against participating in communion in an unworthy manner. He made this explicitly clear in his letter to the Corinthians. To enter the zenith of worship – the rite of communion – worthily meant to harbor only love for your neighbor so that you could in true conscience approach the Table together in peace. It called upon the Church to obey the one commandment Jesus left it – to love one another as he had loved us."

Fr. Ted pursed his lips – his words more deliberate. "Let me add, communion also meant you understood that by taking the bread and the wine you were surrendering yourself to Christ as you received him into your body, soul and spirit. That simple act is a prayer asking Christ to transform you to become in ever increasing degrees more and more like him. The way it plays out in life is through relationships – first with God and then with one another; hence to love one another as he loved us."

Fr. Ted flicked his hand in the air, "I've gotten a bit carried away but I don't want you to misunderstand something, James. The Church held and continues to hold that baptism is truly death to new life. It's not a metaphor or a vacant symbol. It is reality. And Holy Eucharist – the act and rite of communion – is to be undertaken in reverence and awe, because Christ is our salvation. It's for this reason the Church as early as the late second century lovingly, carefully, deliberately guided new believers into the faith, helping them understand its implications, its sacrifice, even its dangers, and above all to know in whom they put their trust – Jesus Christ son of God and son of man."

James hastily jotted a note. "It's like everything has a reason."

310

"Indeed it does, James. The entire point of mass is to re-enter God's redemptive narrative as full participants."

"Like living an endless story."

"Oh most certainly so, James! Some people live the dream; we re-live the grandest of all stories with an eye to Christ's return."

"I'm afraid that I've misunderstood some of this," Terrance confessed. "The seminary treats both baptism and communion as things we do in memory of Jesus."

"I know, Terrance. I was there once myself. But let's be fair. There was much in need of reformation in Luther's time, and he aptly put his finger on certain sensitive items, corruption of the sacraments among them. I assure you guys, the Church since the day of Pentecost understood memory and memorial quite differently. The point of the matter is to realize that both of these rites were initiated by Jesus himself – mandated really. During the Last Supper, Jesus implored the disciples to do this in remembrance of him. He called for the Church to make disciples of all nations by baptizing them in the Triune God and teaching them to obey all he had commanded them. Both of these mandates established the means for us to enter into his covenant fulfilled on the cross."

Fr. Ted grew increasingly animated as he went deeper into the depictions. He dropped the chair onto all four legs and stood behind it. As if lecturing students at Loyola he continued, "In the Gospel of John he told Nicodemus that unless we are reborn by water and Spirit we cannot enter into the Kingdom of God. And to avoid putting you guys through the misery of the real presence during communion, I'll dispense for now with any conversation about Jesus' difficult words in John chapter six or Paul's terse words to the Corinthians."

"But Father Ted, Jesus did say do this in *remembrance* of me! Doesn't that make communion a memorial? What else could he have meant?" Terrance challenged.

"Yes Terrance! But here's the rub. The Greek offered Jesus four words from which to choose. He chose a fascinating word, one appearing only three times in the entire New Testament – two of which come from him. It's a strange sounding word – *anamnesis*. In its essence it means do this as though Jesus were doing it with us here and now. It is re-enacted memory." Fr. Ted leaned over the table, "Think of it this way; what's the point of let's say Memorial Day?"

"To remember the veterans," Terrance said with a shrug.

"Yes! And how does our nation go about *remembering* them?"

"With parades, re-enactments, prayers at memorial sites and family picnics. So that's what this word anamnesis means?"

"Yes and more!" Fr. Ted affirmed. "It carries the strong implication that we are to import the past into the present as an eternal participation, one not restricted by time and space. It's like the veil separating the finite from the infinite; or better heaven from earth were lifted, and suddenly we find ourselves for that instant standing in eternity. Most importantly we are always to respect the truth that he is with us whenever we proclaim him." Fr. Ted squeezed his lips together as if searching for something. A thought came to mind. "Terrance, when you preach to your kids do you believe God is speaking through you?"

"Of course!"

"If he is as you say speaking through you while you preach, why then would you find him absent and ineffectual in the two sacraments that call us into communion with him – the ones he gave us to transform our lives into lives remade in his image?"

Terrance's countenance went blank. "Honestly I had never thought of these things – not in this way."

"So what about now? Going forward how do you think these new revelations will affect your understanding?"

"For sure I'll never think of baptism or communion the same again. I certainly won't take them for granted. And for sure I'm heading back into the Bible for more guidance."

"Very good Rev. Hall," Fr. Ted said with resonate satisfaction. "And I would encourage you to read the commentaries of the Church Fathers. They took their cues and instruction from the Apostles."

"Alright! I'll do that. I think maybe you've given me a thesis subject."

"You could certainly do worse my friend. But beware though: It could take you down a path you didn't anticipate. It did for me."

"But answer this for me," Terrance continued. "If the preparation for baptism was so rigorous what was baptism itself like? I mean back then – the ancient church?"

"I'd like to know that, too," James broke in.

"So you guys want to know how the Church did baptism in the early centuries, eh?"

"Exactly," James confirmed. Terrance nodded.

Fr. Ted paced the floor, a hand held to his chin. "Okay," he began, "Let me take you to the city of Milan in say the late fourth century, at the time St. Ambrose was bishop. The week before the vigil the faithful fasted and prayed. On the eve of Easter, the night of the Vigil they gathered in a public place – hundreds of them – for what was known as the *lucinarium* – a parade under candlelight through town to the church. Each person, a lit candle held cautiously against the night breeze, joined in singing praises to God as they marched steadily toward the church – a long mob of light snaking through the narrow streets of Milan." Fr. Ted paused and cocked his head. "It must have been quite a spectacle."

With a wave of his hand he continued, "Once they reached the church the faithful entered the sanctuary while the *electi*, those to receive baptism, stopped in front of the baptistery – a building attached to the church. Its door was shut. For as many as three years, these former catechumen walked by wondering when or if they would ever see inside, would they ever receive the sacrament."

Again Fr. Ted took pause, and like he was face to face with one of the *electi*; as if he himself were there in that moment explained, "Ambrose then went one by one to each of the elect tracing the sign of the cross on their ears, eyes, tongue, hands, heart and feet, calling upon God to open their eyes, to open their ears, to loosen their tongues, to enlarge their hearts, to move their hands and feet in fulfillment of his commission and commandment. He implored them to never abuse the gift of God's mercy, and to forever honor their baptism."

Both James and Terrance sat rapt as Fr. Ted lived out the moment in front of them. Once again he stroked his chin. "Then the door opened," he said while miming the gesture and with a note of heightened mystery to his voice. "The bishop and his deacons led the members into the chamber lighted by candles that flickered against walls etched with the images of the saints. They saw the font – an octagonal pool. They smelled the Myron – aromatic oil that would be poured over them."

Grabbing at the lapels of his jacket, "Each member had been clad in a coarse robe – ugly and uncomfortable, kind of like this worn out coat. It represented the sinful old man St. Paul spoke of – the one they were about to forsake; to throw off like an old rag." Pointing toward the ceiling he described, "An ambulatory – a walkway – something like a gallery above the font area, permitted godparents and catechists to observe. They were the witnesses."

Striding over to the doors leading into the library as if the library itself had been transformed into Milan's baptistery, Fr. Ted pointed to the floor mat. By now even the other two library denizens formerly seated in the carrels had walked to the edge of the stacks where they could observe the antics of this priest. "The electi," Fr. Ted stated shaking his finger at the mat, "were individually led to a bristly rug where they stripped off the ugly robe, knelt and were sealed in chrism – the fragrant oil – as a symbol of sealing them from the evil predators who sought desperately to avert their conversion. Like you once said, Terrance, there was still a cosmic war being waged."

He then swung around and pointing to the far wall said, "Once sealed the *electi* faced west – the place of visible darkness; the symbol of evil according to ancient tradition, where they were instructed to spit into the face of the devil. They were asked again if they renounced evil and the evil one." Abruptly, Fr. Ted turned on his heel toward the opposite wall. "Then they faced east the direction of Jesus' anticipated return and were asked if they embraced Christ. I envision it as a remarkable moment – a solemn moment."

Striding now to the center of the library where a ceramic tile bearing the state's seal was placed, he stared at it as if it were the baptismal waters: "Then they were led into the waters which had been blessed for the occasion – set aside as it were as the living waters of baptism. The bishop or his deacon met them in the waters. Each one then stepped down into the pool where they were immersed three times in the name of the Father and of the Son and of the Holy Spirit." As he said this, Fr. Ted swept his right hand in broad strokes making the sign of the cross. "When they rose, a deacon – likely a deacon anyway – led them from the water." Fr. Ted dropped to one knee, "Ambrose would then meet them, girded in a towel as Jesus might have been at the Last Supper, where he washed their feet. Why? Because even though they had been washed there remained the venom of the serpent in their heels. It had to be washed out! Oil, warm and fragrant oil, was now poured over the newly baptized from head to toe signifying the presence of the Holy Spirit who now sealed them as the surety of holiness and eternal life."

With a massive smile stretching his thick beard, Fr. Ted wagged a finger as he stood and returned to his seat, "Transformation, gentlemen! Death to new life! That's the shorthand version of how it went down in Milan. It was similar in other places. I've always been especially drawn to Ambrose's explanation of what had taken place. He told them, 'you have seen with your eyes all you can see, but not what is done.' What was done, gentlemen, took place in the subterranean depths of the human soul where inner transformation was forming an entirely new man."

James sat mesmerized listening to Fr. Ted: Terrance too. "Makes me want to be re-baptized," Terrance exclaimed.

"Oh no, Terrance! God calls us to enter his covenant one time and then remember it every day of our lives. *Anamnesis*, Terrance: Live in your baptism every day."

One by one Fr. Ted ticked off the items on James' list of questions with this single lecture.

"Well, James, you might have gotten more answer than you wanted. Did any of this make sense to you?"

James' mouth fell open but words didn't fall out of it. He shrugged his shoulders as much as to say, "Wow! That was unreal!" He glanced over the few hastily scribbled notes on his pad. "I think I have a lot to learn." James' eyes fell to the table and a strained look came across his face. "Am I even worthy of him?"

"No James you're not," Fr. Ted assured. "But neither is Terrance nor am I. None of us are worthy of the price Jesus paid – none of us."

"But he paid it anyway."

"That son is the illogical truth known as love – redeeming, sacrificial love. It is illogical because it does not reduce to rational explanation suitable for moderns who demand rationality. It is sacrificial because no one could possibly merit it. Jesus is the Father's unrequited gift to the cosmos, including each one of us. No sir, we don't deserve it. But do you know how to receive it?"

"Tell me."

"Humility and faith, James. Humility and faith. And a third thing," Fr. Ted said narrowing his eyes to a near squint.

"Ok, I'll bite."

"Cooperation! That's what Mary showed us how to do. In her humility she accepted on faith what seemed utterly unreasonable – to become the mother of the Messiah. In other words, she cooperated with God to bring to earth the Son of God. By following her example of obedient cooperation we come into relationship with God through the merits of her son."

"Hey dude," Terrance broke in. "It's taken me a long time to realize I can't earn it – God's approval I mean. I have to swallow my pride and accept my unworthiness. All I can ever do is present myself like I am – messy and needy." From Terrance these words meant a great deal. He understood where James was and what he was going through. "Kid it is never easy. Be patient with God and yourself. Just keep going. Don't stop."

"Cooperation," James muttered. "Okay, I can do that. With help from you guys, I can cooperate with him."

SIXTY-ONE

"What the...!!" James nearly leapt out of his skin! He spun around finding a chortling Warden Hollinswood standing behind him. James let out a relieved sigh, killed the mower motor and doffed the ear muffs clapped to his head. "You almost gave me a heart attack!" James exclaimed slapping a hand to his chest.

"Sorry about that my boy, but couldn't resist," Hollinswood replied still laughing. He'd dropped one of his massive hands on James' shoulder as James was blithely mowing the back grounds. "Got a couple of the fellas I want to meet you. James, meet Jason and Enrique. These guys got quite a charge out of Fr. Ted's library theatrics."

James jerked off the leather gloves to shake hands with the guys. "Nice to meet you both," James said. "Where ya from?"

"South Chicago," Enrique answered. "Tough neighborhood – what we calls the Wild Hundreds – gang turf mostly."

"You a gang member?" James asked naively enough.

"Hey dude, youz don't get sent to the Hilton if you 'aint."

"Hilton?" James asked cautiously.

"Prison! Youz a babe in the woods aren't ya?"

"I'm beginning to think that's all I'll be. So where you from?" James asked Jason.

"Fresno for me."

"You a gang member like Enrique?"

"Nah, I came from the other side of town so to speak."

"Jason here likes borrowing other people's cars," Enrique blurted, thumping Jason on the chest. "So we heard youz happy priest doin' his thing in the library."

"Cool! So you guys caught the act huh?" James snorted.

"Sure did. Is he like that all the time?" Jason asked with a sideward smirk.

"Pretty much," James answered. "He gets into it when he's on a roll. Great guy!"

"Seems like it," Enrique stated in an obvious Chicago-ized Spanglish accent.

"James these boys are part of our Bible study group here. Thought you should meet," Hollinswood said. "I'll leave you to get acquainted," he said with a backward wave as he strode up the steps and into the administration building.

"So you dudes are Christians?" James asked rather assumingly.

"I am," Enrique piped up. "Right here, in this house, I gave my life to the Man. Warden Hollinswood led me. Jason's still searchin'. The bro 'aint got a clue what he's missin'."

"So what's your hang up?" James asked.

"Long story," Jason snorted. "Not fit for public consumption."

"He means he doesn't want us to pry," Enrique said through a street tough smirk. "But he's closer than he thinks."

"So how long have you believed?" Jason asked throwing the ball into James' court.

"Not long – a couple of weeks."

"Dude, you're a bambino!" Enrique fairly yelled with excitement. "Hey bro, welcome to the familia! That's way cool!" He threw an arm across James shoulders like they'd been *famila* forever. "So what made ya crack man? When did you finally give up runnin'?"

"What makes you think I ran?"

"Hey don't smoke me dude, we all run. You know, like nobody falls without a fight."

From the looks of Enrique's scarred face, James' thickly built, well muscled new friend likely knew quite a bit about fighting. "Yeah, I ran alright – right into God. What I don't get and may never get is why? Why did I fight him? Fr. Ted said because we're all deceived. I think he's right."

"So youz joinin' the church? Youz goin' Catholic?"

"I am. And you?"

"Raised Catholic. My whole family's Catholic from way back. So answer me this, who's this padre dude? Is he gonna be hangin' around here more?"

"Yeah he is. You want to meet him?"

"Sure! Seems like a nice enough guy."

"He's a great guy! I owe my new life to him – and some other great guys."

"Hey look, James," Jason broke in leaning awkwardly to the side. "We know you're in a tough spot with the Lobos."

James' stomach suddenly wedged in his throat. He could feel the blood rush out of his face. "How'd you know that?"

"Enrique you tell him," Jason said.

"Mi hombres – you know my homeboys, they got the goods. But the news it 'aint all bad. These new Lobo hoods, they're all screwed up. Their alpha got nailed and sent up to Rikers. Nobody leaves Rikers if you get my drift. Not if you're made. Just soz you know. We got your back, bro. The dudes in the study – let's just say we've talked to the Man for ya – a lot."

"Okay, thanks. But you don't think I'm in trouble?" James asked in tremulous voice.

"Nah! Besides we'll know before they have time to find ya. And Warden Hollinswood – that's one cool dude. He's straight and strict, but he cares about us guys – kinda like youz Padre Ted. He's got us covered."

"Okay. Well, thanks for leveling with me…I think."

"Look, dude, we're in this together. In time you'll meet the rest of the boys. Tell youz Padre Ted weez liked the show," Enrique quipped in his South Chicago jive as he punched James' arm. "See around, dude." With that Jason and Enrique swaggered back to the far south building where they'd been repainting roof trim. James clapped the ear muffs on his head and fired up the lawn mower. It didn't ease his tension to know the word was out on the street and more than the Lobos knew about him. "Oh Lord, please don't let them find me," he prayed. "And thanks for these guys."

Just as he pushed the mower for another lap he spied Terrance strutting through the secured double gate, stuffing his wallet back in his pocket after the guard cleared him. Enrique and Jason caught sight of him too – ponytail and denim. They didn't turn around, just kept walking with an occasional glance Terrance's direction. "Whose those guys?" Terrance asked as he approached James, poking his thumb their direction.

"Guys from the Bible study here – Enrique and Jason. They caught the Fr. Ted show yesterday."

"Oh yeah, they're the dudes in the library?"

"Hey," James interjected, "They know about the Lobos."

Terrance's eyes narrowed. "What do you mean, they know about the Lobos?"

"They know about the head guy – the alpha – who got sent up to Rikers."

Terrance's expression went stone sober serious, his eyes taking that steel gray cast. "How'd they find out? Who ratted?"

"Enrique's connected with some gang in South Chicago – someplace called the Wild Hundreds. They found out and somehow got the word to him here."

"Wild Hundreds, huh?" Terrance groaned shooting a sideward glance at the two guys standing on the scaffold at the far end of the grounds.

"You know something about it?"

"A little. Some pretty mean gangs in that neighborhood. They don't typically show up around here unless they've tapped out. The Lobos picked up a few." Terrance pulled James behind a large oak tree. "So what did they tell you?"

"That the guys Enrique knows will inform him if anything's about to happen. He said the Lobos are really screwed up now – kind of like you heard from the gang cop."

"You mean Tony?"

"Yeah – him. Look Terrance, it scared the crap out of me again. Will this ever end?"

Terrance brushed a hand over his head, "Man I don't know. But God is our only real security here. You know that!"

"That's what Enrique said too. He said the guys in the Bible study have been praying for me. He said they all have each other's backs and Warden Hollinswood has our backs too."

"That's good. Your pal Enrique is right. The Lobos are pretty messed up right now. They're so disorganized they're starting to fight themselves. That bodes well for us. But be careful about what you share even with these guys. They may be brothers, but just keep your head on. Understand?"

"Yeah, I understand. What should I do with anything they tell me?"

"Tell Warden Hollinswood immediately. Don't wait! He'll take it from there. Look, like I said keep your head down and straight! Okay?"

"Sure. But man, I've gotta say you look like you saw a ghost. You alright?"

"Just a little punchy, James. That's all. I've seen too much if you get me."

"I suppose. Believe me; I hope I never see even half of the stuff you've seen."

"That's right, you don't! Well my man, it's in God's hands. We're in God's hands. Let's keep it there."

"For sure!"

"I'm gonna let Tom know about this stuff. He'll likely wanna contact Tony. Don't be surprised if you get a call."

"A call?"

"From Tony or even Tom: They'll know to call Hollinswood first."

Terrance broke into a reassuring smile, "You okay yourself?"

"I am now. Thanks for stopping by, T. You helped." James jerked his head like a thought flashed through his mind. "So why did you stop by?"

"I was just in the hood on my way to the State House to catch up with Fr. Ted and had a little time to kill."

"God thing?"

"No doubt a God thing!" Terrance gave James a slap on the shoulder, "Gotta go dude. Stay cool! God's got it all under control."

"You too," James said with a slap to Terrance's shoulder. Even though it might be a "God thing," James still couldn't shake off the edginess.

SIXTY-TWO

"Okay, James, how's the Creed memorization coming?" Fr. Ted asked as he pulled his now familiar chair up to the library table.

"Pretty good. But let me get something off my chest first."

"Alright; what's your concern?"

James looked around to see if anyone was listening. Speaking in a near whisper, and leaning half way across the table he said, "I read in the book, the *This is Our Faith* book about confession – you know, the rite of reconciliation. So I've got something to confess." His chest heaved, "Fr. Ted, I hate these Lobo creeps who want me dead. It's all I've thought about the last few days, especially since Enrique and Jason told me what they knew."

"I understand, James. Honestly, I don't much care for them either. But Jesus said to love our neighbors and pray for the creeps – in other words pray for our enemies. If by telling me this you are making confession, let me give you an assignment as part of atoning for the sin of hatred."

"Wait a minute! So hating these guys is sin? But they want me dead!" James glanced behind him again.

"Do you know what hatred is – really is, I mean?"

"Opposite of love I suppose."

"Actually it's more like the outgrowth of fear. So guess what perfect love casts out according to John's letter in the New Testament?"

"It must be fear then."

"That's right. Perfect love James casts out fear. So why do you think you hate these guys – the Lobos especially?"

"Because they scare the living you know what out of me!"

"Exactly! What we fear we hate because it torments us. The troublesome part of what you said wasn't just that you *hate* the Lobos but that they've distracted you to the point they occupy all your thoughts. In other words your fear of them has taken over what runs your life. That, son, is also idolatry. That they can torment you to the point they've taken your mind off God means they've taken his place – they've become more persuasive than him...and more powerful."

"Oh my gosh! I had no idea, but it makes sense. How do I beat it? How do I get those creeps like you said out of my head?"

"More importantly, James, the question is how do you keep God in your head – and heart – when the creeps come to mind?"

"Refocusing my mind, I suppose."

"Yes. Remember how Paul put it: 'I appeal to you therefore, brethren, by the mercies of God, to present your bodies as a living sacrifice, holy and acceptable to God, which is your spiritual worship.' But here's the punch line, 'Do not be conformed to this world but be transformed by the renewal of your *mind*, that you may prove what is the will of God, what is good and acceptable and perfect.'"

"Oh man, another tough lesson!"

"Yes, but don't get discouraged! Each day present yourself to God. Ask him to conform you to his way of thinking and behaving. Keep in mind he has everything under control."

"Okay, I'll give it my best."

"Let's look at the Creed for a moment. Can you recite the first part?"

"I think so." James tilted his head and scrunched his brow. Looking past Fr. Ted he began, "I believe in God, the Father almighty, Creator of heaven and earth."

"Stop right there! Did you hear what you just recited – and recited quite well I would add?"

"What do you mean?"

"Who is God according to the Creed? How is he described?"

James thought for a moment. "Father almighty and Creator."

"Let me ask you this, if God is understood in these terms, and scripture calls him a God of love, and if Jesus proved that point with his passion and resurrection, what about God would make him so impotent in your eyes that you'd spend more time worrying about the creeps as you call them, than centering your entire attention and energy on God?"

"When you put it like that it sounds kind of lame to even worry about those guys."

"Indeed it does. Look James, we're all confronted with stuff that seems larger than life to us, and more threatening than we can overcome. God gets that. That's why he calls on us to realize him – and only him – is God." Fr. Ted raised his finger to make a point. "When the disciples started fretting about things, Jesus reminded them that the Father feeds and houses the creatures of creation. He makes certain they are properly clothed, whether it's fur or feathers. So if he does this for the least of creation, what makes us think that we, who are made in his image, would be treated any differently, or that he might even treat us worse? It's utterly absurd to assume such a thought. So he tells them to 'seek first the Kingdom of God and his righteousness. And all these things will be added to you.'"

"Okay let me see if I get this. If I keep fixating on these thugs I'm really demoting God aren't I?"

"Well put! And that's also what makes worry idolatrous."

"Ouch! Man, I don't want to be guilty of that."

"So, do you still hate the Lobos?"

"Do I have be honest?"

Fr. Ted glared at James as if to say, "That qualifies as a stupid question!"

"Okay, I confess that I hate everything they're about them. But I think I can maybe not hate the creeps – the gang bangers themselves."

"That's a good first step – but not good enough. I want you come to the point you can pray for them. I mean pray that they might come to the same place you've come. Do you think that could be possible?"

"You keep saying all things are possible with God. Yeah, I think I can get there."

"That's my boy! Now, here's your assignment. Look up Matthew chapter six verse thirty-three. Read the verses before it and the one following it. But concentrate on verse thirty-three. Notice how it begins; 'Seek first!' The implication, James, is to seek the Kingdom of God and God's righteousness as if there were nothing else to seek; as if everything worthy in life is wrapped up in his kingdom and his righteousness. Remember the words of the Our Father? 'Your *kingdom* come. Your *will* be done, on earth as it is in heaven.' That kingdom, James, is our new home, and the only will done there is God's will. Praying this prayer acknowledges that reality. And what you're asking of God is what God wants most for us; that we should share in his kingdom even while we walk the earth, and live in his righteousness."

James slowly shook his head, "That's a big deal. I think that's going to be my personal verse – the one I'll live by."

"It's mine too, James. I recite it daily. It puts everything in its proper place especially when the creeps try to invade God's space."

Fr. Ted then prayed for James and James prayed a simple prayer after him: "Jesus I'm sorry I replaced you with these thugs. Please help me to love them like you've loved me. Amen."

About then the library doors swung open and the swaggering kid from Chicago and his more reserved friend pushed through them. "Youz must be Padre Ted. I'm Enrique. James here probably told ya we met," Enrique announced thrusting his hand at Fr. Ted. Fr. Ted shook his hand.

"I'd know where you came from even if James hadn't told me."

"Dat right Padre. What makes youz so sure? Wouldn't be my subtle accent would it?"

"Less than subtle jerk," Jason said stretching his hand to Fr. Ted. "Hi, I'm Jason."

"Ah yes, Jason from Fresno. You're the kid who likes cars," Fr. Ted said with a sly wink.

"Yeah, that'd be me," Jason answered shaking Fr. Ted's hand.

"Join us gentlemen," Fr. Ted invited pointing to the two empty chairs at the table. Enrique spun his chair around straddling it like it was his Harley, while Jason walked to the other side of the table and took a seat beside Fr. Ted.

"James here says youz mean a lot to him. Glad to hear that Padre. I'm kinda a youngsta believer just a little farther down the road than my man here. You gonna make a priest out of him?"

"Well, Enrique you don't waste time getting to the point do you?" Fr. Ted said with a chuckle peering at this stocky, cocky force of nature.

"Aint got time to waste, Padre. Life's too short."

Fr. Ted's interest moved to the quiet tall one seated beside him. "So Jason from Fresno, how'd you stumble onto this whirlwind?" he asked jabbing his thumb toward Enrique.

"He kind of stumbled onto me. Barely heard his name and the next thing I know he's got me roped into this Bible study here."

"So how's that gone?" Fr. Ted inquired.

"Not bad. Given me a lot to digest. I'm just not there yet."

"And where would that be?"

"Geez, you're as bad as Ricky!"

"Hey, don't call me that name. I've told youz never to call me that name. It's *Enrique*," Enrique said with emphasis. He noticed the quizzical expression on Fr. Ted's face. "My little cousin was named Ricky. He got whacked a year ago. May God bless em. Soz outa respect I don't mess with his name. I'm sure you feel me here don't ya Padre?"

"I suppose I do. But what do you mean he got whacked?" Fr. Ted knew the meaning but wanted to hear it from Enrique.

"It's South Chicago, Padre. People go missing. I'm sure youz get my meaning. My cuz screwed up. Got shot by some hoods." Enrique's face tightened. "I don't wanna talk about it, okay. Just let the boy rest. God love em."

"I'm sorry, Enrique. I didn't need to pry. You have my prayers," Fr. Ted replied.

"Thanks, Padre. No harm done. So we interuptin' a meet or somethin'?

"Just finishing up," James answered.

"Soz the good Padre here tryin' to make a priest out of ya? They do that sorta thing ya know?" Enrique asked poking fun at Fr. Ted.

"Maybe you should be a priest." Fr. Ted poked the fun back at Enrique.

"Hey Padre, youz might be on to somethin' there. My homeboys in Chi Town, they could use a priest from the hood. Whadda think? Do ya think I'd make an okay priest?"

Fr. Ted pushed his glasses higher on his nose, "Enrique I think you'd make a fabulous priest."

"Really? What makes youz so sure?"

"Son, you've the head, the heart and the guts. You don't back down, but you know how to care about people too. And it seems you truly know God."

Enrique stared back at the priest with wary suspicion. "Youz 'aint toyin' with me are ya? Youz mean doz things youz just said?" "He means them," James interjected. "Trust me. I know."

"Okay Padre. I'd like to talk. Would that work for youz?"

"Absolutely! You let me know when you're ready."

"I'll do dat. Count on it! But what about the kid here? He on your radar too?"

"That's up to James, Enrique. Just like you, he's got to discern where God's leading him."

"Cool! I dig that!"

Jason had been quietly taking in all this priest chatter. Fr. Ted could tell it was affecting him. "Jason, you're awfully quiet. I understand that, though. You're noisy friend here barely let's you get a word in edgewise. So what's on your mind?"

"Just listening. I'm still searching. Not sure what I believe yet."

"Fair enough, Jason. We've all been there. Let me know if I can ever be of help to you as well."

"I'll do that Father. I like your style. You seem cool with us cons. You don't seem to hold that over our heads."

"That's because I don't think of you guys as cons."

"He doesn't," James added. "He's treated me better than I've ever been treated. Showed me respect and helped me respect myself too."

"Nice," Jason replied with a soft smile on his face. "That's very cool."

"Hey weez gotta go. Thanks for lettin' us bust in on youz meet like this." Enrique announced. "Come see us some more Padre. I like youz!"

"I'll do that Enrique. I like you guys too. Blessings on you both."

"Alright. Seez youz guys later!" The doors whooshed open and the boys blew through them off to their day's work.

"So are you?" James asked Fr. Ted.

A confused look came across Fr. Ted's face. "Am I what?" "Trying to make a priest out of me?"

Fr. Ted broke into laughter. "Like I said, James, that's between you and God. I can help you figure it out, but let's walk first. Shall we?"

James understood exactly what Fr. Ted implied. "For sure. I'm still a babe."

"But a growing babe, son."

"Thanks! So will I be ready – for baptism?"

"Oh I think so, James. We'll begin talking about the preparations next Tuesday at RCIA."

"Great! I'm getting stoked about it."

"Not worried about making a public spectacle of yourself?"

"Nah, not anymore. I want people to see me take the plunge. It's kind of like making it real."

"Witnesses, James. They're the ones who remind us of our commitment to Christ. I'm proud of you young man. You've come a long way in a short time."

"Thanks! Youz been my Padre," James said smirking at an amused Padre Ted.

SIXTY-THREE

Terri tapped lightly on Fr. Ted's office door. James stood close beside. They could hear voices on the other side and then footsteps. A gleeful Fr. Ted opened the door and ushered them in. "Terri, I'd like you to meet the Ingrahams, Rick and Melanie."

Shyly Terri slipped through the door and stood in front of the couple. "I'm so honored to meet you," she said extending her hand to them.

"After what Fr. Ted told us, we've been excited to meet you," Rick said shaking Terri's hand. "We had no idea we were being watched."

"I didn't mean to pry into personal business, but the love you had for your sick baby just grabbed me. And the trust you put in God, who I didn't know – not at the time. But you really made a difference for me. I hardly know how to thank you." Terri was fairly gushing as tears glistened in her eyes.

Melanie reached for Terri's hand, "You have no idea what it means to us that you're here, that you've come to faith in Jesus. You've blessed us every bit as much as we've blessed you, Terri."

"I'm so glad. Thank you!" Terri exclaimed. "And how's your baby? I still pray for him and you."

"Oh, we can't begin to tell you what that means to hear. It's like God just knew we all needed each other. Our little guy is doing so well. He's our miracle son," Melanie said smiling lovingly at her husband. Rick gave Melanie's arm a gentle caress.

"I simply thought you should meet before tonight's RCIA session. I wanted you all to realize how marvelously God has connected the dots in each of your lives." Pointing at James, Fr. Ted added, "Even this young man has benefited from all of this."

"That right, James?" Rick asked.

"Very much, Rick. It was your story that helped Terri find her story that led to me finding mine. I guess you're right to think of your baby as the miracle God used to bring us to him and to each other."

"Well spoken," Rick responded. "God never lets us walk alone does he?"

"Obviously not," James smirked.

"Okay people, let's go meet the rest of the group," Fr. Ted coaxed holding the office door open.

Terri and Melanie walked together hand-in-hand with Rick and James a few steps in trail. Melanie shot a quick glance behind her before whispering in Terri's ear, "You and James make a cute couple. Any plans?"

Terri's face instantly blushed. "Oh we're just friends – that's all," she sputtered in a soft voice, fighting to regain composure. "But you really think we look good together?"

"Uh huh, I do. And I can tell James really likes you."

"Oh wow, Melanie, I don't know what to say," Terri stammered through her awkwardness.

"I didn't mean to embarrass you. I just thought you guys seem...well...meant for each other."

Terri didn't reply; just gave Melanie's hand a friendly squeeze, trying desperately to cool the rash of embarrassment in her face. As the ladies approached the room the convivial drone of voices filtered into the hallway. Though she didn't signal anything, and despite obvious awkwardness, Terri keenly appreciated Melanie's frank observation. It sent satisfying warmth through her – one that stirred both emotions of hope and emotions of fright.

*****

Fr. Ted had no intentions of simply letting a brief encounter in his office slip away as merely a private introduction. He had another motive in mind as well. "Good evening friends, please be seated. With permission I'd like to offer you a glimpse into God's intentions. Our text speaks of loving our neighbor as ourselves. There's a reason. In this room this evening that reason lives. Let me tell you how."

The room grew stone silent as Fr. Ted recounted the remarkable moments that brought the Ingrahams into Terri's life and in turn into James' life. There seemed an almost surreal sense to the recounting as if something – or someone – had plotted the intermixing of lives like a well presented drama unfolds its plot. How fluent, really, was the language of the Gospel proclaimed that, despite not a word spoken, Terri came to realize God stood above this anguished father and mother as they pleaded for their child's life. Around the room hearts melted and minds twisted in ways unforeseen. Even the seemingly indifferent, if not at times callously arrogant, Dave, couldn't avoid the simple irony of a truth reason could not contradict. All the empirical evidence necessary to judge for the event sat squarely beside him in four lives – four lives transformed by the ineffability of a grace most certainly beyond naked reason. There was mystery to it all.

Fr. Ted concluded, "And a little child shall lead them," referencing Isaiah's prophetic description of the coming kingdom, where God would put on human flesh as an infant – the child who would lead the world to a new awakening. Sober faces, several wet with tears, stared back at him.

Who could plausibly deny that the trauma of a baby's fragile beginning was meant for something far beyond the capacity of human imagination, and farther still from the fruitless conjuring of people intent upon denying the designs of a loving Designer? It was meant for redemption. God's story superseded all the doubts, the quaking fears, the intrepid helplessness of distraught new parents, to foreshadow a new day filled with more light, life and laughter than any one life had capacity to hold. It had truly spilled out and was even now, among those gathered in this plain classroom, still pouring its blessing upon those with hearts open to receive it.

"You see people," Fr. Ted directed, "the nexus, the sense of it all, was to unite four people desperately in need of a Redeemer; bring them to the cross where they came face-to-face with Christ, and to proclaim him to us all. This is the heart of the Gospel and beauty of life together in our common faith." The room fell silent once again. Fr. Ted's words hanging in their hearts.

"James, I'm curious," Dave broke the silence to ask. "Was it as apparently simple as Fr. Ted just described? I mean accepting the existence of God?"

James swept his hair back while gathering his thoughts. "No it wasn't. But the reason caught me totally by surprise. I was disbelieving in a god that doesn't exist – a mean, vengeful tyrant who decides who wins and who loses. That was who I thought God was. Everything I'd experienced pointed to that god. That is until I bumped into Fr. Ted, the posse, and Terri. They really messed me up." The room broke into laughter.

"I see," Dave remarked. "In other words they gave you a different god to think about."

"They sure did. They showed me the God I've come to know. And I really can't explain it well. When I finally broke it was like falling into arms that for the first time in my life actually held onto me. Mr. Rowland called it the wall against which I could lean, that wouldn't fall out from under me like everything else I'd tried did. He was right. I just feel stupid it took me so long to accept him."

"Thank you," Dave said through an unconvinced smile, but said no more.

Kathy Swanson took over. "This story has really touched me. I'd say it touched us all." She glanced around the room. Every head nodded agreement – even Dave's. "I think Easter may have arrived early for this group." Turning to Fr. Ted, "It's like you've said all along; Easter is about transformation."

"I'd even go so far, Kathy, as to call it the irony of all ironies, an epic paradox. For all the emphasis on Christianity being merely another ethical philosophy alongside those of so many other religions and philosophies, it is the only one where the deity dies for the lives of his subjects. It doesn't end there either. Because the deity doesn't remain dead – he rises from the grave with new life for all who believe in him." Nodding to the four young people seated together on his left, he said, "You are evidence in proof of this claim. Each of you is a miracle of death to an old life and resurrection into a new life – an entirely new way of living."

Scrunching his brow, Fr. Ted asked, "Kathy, do you remember a homily maybe four or five years ago I did on the subject of repentance?"

"That was four or five years ago, Father! I'm sure I don't, but probably will if you give us a hint about what you're thinking."

"Fair enough," Fr. Ted said with a chortle. "Repentance: It's more than a word. It means infinitely more than simply saying we're sorry for the sins we've committed against God and against one another. Oh for certain it carries the pain of remorse in its meaning. Coming to the realization that we've failed God's love and mercy will most certainly bring about remorse. And yet there's more. Like I've often and repeatedly quoted, Paul clearly and emphatically demands: 'Do not be conformed to this world but be transformed by the renewal of your minds that you may prove what is the will of God, what is good, acceptable and perfect.' I can't get past this passage. It cannot be overstated."

Fr. Ted brought a finger to his lips, as he contemplated what he'd just said. "Repentance is an odd word really. In essence it means to go beyond one's mind – literally to change one's mind so thoroughly as to have an entirely new mind in its place. It is utterly radical and accessible only by an act of faith – not an act of intelligent reasoning. But oddly, it is by means of this metamorphosis – this exchange of one mind for another – that allows for true clarity of thought. How do we prove the will of God? How do we come to account for what is good, acceptable and perfect? We come to it all by means of this remarkable about face, this taking on the mind of God. We only see clearly when we see through his eyes; when we accept him on his terms and stop every attempt to form him in our image."

Fr. Ted's face softened, "That, dear friends, is the upshot of tonight's story." Looking at James, "You haven't experienced the Rite of Election like the others who will be baptized and confirmed. But you are no less elected, son, and you will enter your name among those similarly elected. And along with these others, you will stand with your godparent for the final scrutiny this Sunday. In it you and the others will give evidence of this very transformation of mind and life. Are you ready?"

"I am, Father. I can't wait!"

The group applauded. "James," Mitchell broke in. "You might be a prisoner of the justice system. But in here you are one of us. I just want you to know that. I'm sure the others would agree." Again affirming applause rippled through the room.

"Thanks!" James said through cloudy eyes.

Fr. Ted rose from his chair, "The peace of Christ be with you all."

"And with your spirit," everyone replied.

"Stand with me," he directed his arms spread, his palms upraised. "Our Father…"

*****

James stood as his name was called. Harold Raynor joined him in front of the altar. Fr. Ted stepped from the platform and greeted them first addressing the congregation. "James Meyers has come confessing his sins, renouncing evil and accepting Jesus Christ into his life. It is the judgment of his godparent, the RCIA catechist and myself that he should be enrolled with the other elect for the Rite of Initiation where with his fellow elect he will receive Baptism, Confirmation and Holy Eucharist. Our bishop agrees expressing his consent in a letter addressed to me this past week. Please pray with James, Harold and all of us for his growth in faith, the transformation of his life that he, with us, will know and reflect Christ for the life of the world."

"James, while your participation might have come late, it has nonetheless been characterized by profound change in what you now embrace verses what you once embraced."

Fr. Ted diverted his attention to Harold Raynor. Reading from the text of the Rite of Election held before him by the acolyte, he asked, "As his godparent, Harold, I turn to you. Has James taken his formation in the Gospel and the Catholic way of life seriously?"

"He has, Father."

"Has he given evidence of his conversion by the example of his life?"

"He has."

"Do you judge him to be ready to be presented to this congregation and commended to the bishop for election?"

"I do."

Facing the congregation, Fr. Ted raised his arms, "Do you the faithful of this parish approve of James Meyers' election to the Rite of Initiation, which will bring him into the fellowship of Christ and His Church? If so say we do." A rousing "We do" filled the nave – filling James' heart at the same time.

"Let us pray." Again Fr. Ted raised his hands over the congregation. From the breviary he read, "Father of love and power, it is your will to establish everything in Christ and to draw us into his all-embracing love. Guide James along with his fellow elect in the days ahead: strengthen him and his fellow sojourners in their vocation, build them into the kingdom of your Son, and seal them with the Spirit of your promise. We ask this through Christ our Lord."

The congregation as one concluded with a loud "Amen."

"Now I would like the rest of the elect and their sponsors to join James and Harold at the front. While they gather will you my brothers and sisters quiet your hearts before God and pray in silence for these who will soon join with you in fellowship that they will possess a spirit of true repentance, a sense of their sin, and the true freedom of being children of God?"

James and Harold stepped to the side permitting the others to join around them as they all faced the altar. Fr. Ted took a position in front of them facing outward to the congregation. He then invited them to bow their heads and pray in silence asking again for God in Christ to forgive them their sins, to bring them to himself and to establish in their hearts the desire for Christ.

Moments elapsed – a palpable silence pervaded the atmosphere. Only a baby's fussing disturbed the spirit of reverence hanging over the congregation and those gathered with Fr. Ted. James felt Harold's hand on his shoulder. It had the steady feel of stalwart figure who had traveled this route ahead of him. Standing a few rows behind him was the posse, Terri and his parents among them. All the witnesses were present. This was the moment of final scrutiny, the rite that would lead the elect to Service of Light – the Easter Saturday Vigil.

"Let us pray," Fr. Ted began breaking the silence. "Let us pray for these elect whom God has chosen. May the grace of the sacraments conform them to Christ in his passion and resurrection and enable them to triumph over the bitter fate of death."

The lector standing at the ambo then called upon the faithful as she read from the text of the Third – and final – Scrutiny. "That faith may strengthen them against worldly deceits of all kind, let us pray to the Lord."

The congregation as one replied, "Lord, hear our prayer."

And thus the prayers continued ending with Fr. Ted standing on the upper step of the platform, his arms outstretched as he read from the prayer: "Father of life and God not of the dead but of the living, you sent your Son to proclaim life, to snatch us from the realm of death, and to lead us to the resurrection. Free these elect from the death-dealing power of the spirit of evil, so that they may bear witness to their new life in the risen Christ, for he lives and reigns for ever and ever."

The congregation heartily affirmed, "Amen!"

Fr. Ted once more stepped down in front of the elect, moving silently, slowly from person to person, placing his hands gently on their heads and calling upon the risen Christ to pour his Spirit into them and keep them safe from all harm. And then the final prayer, with his arms once more stretched out over the elect.

Before dismissing the elect Fr. Ted asked them to face the congregation, to see into the faces of those who stood in witness of their journey to Christ. Scanlon was the picture of uncomfortable poise – clad in a sport coat and jeans, his face fairly glowing with delight he sent James a quick salute. Terrance and Anne both winked, while Tom and Mary Rowland merely smiled their approval. Terri could hardly contain her excitement. Tears streamed down her face as she whispered, "so proud of you." Raynor gave James' shoulder a strong squeeze, whispering behind him, "praying for you son." For his folks' reaction he only needed to catch sight of his father's gleaming smile and affirming nod. All was right and the stage was set. Easter sat immediately ahead. New light and new life lie waiting in resurrection splendor.

SIXTY-FOUR

"We come bearing gifts," Fr. Ted joyously announced as he handed a wrapped package to James. The rectory was quite full tonight – the entire posse with wives and its newest member, Terri. James glanced her way with wary suspicion. "What's the deal? You know what this is about?" Terri just shrugged with a silly smug smile on her face.

"Open it!" Scanlon shouted.

"Yes sir!" James answered with a start.

Everyone sat with eager anticipation waiting for James to remove that last bit of paper. He turned the flat box over so its cover now faced him. "A Bible," he said in an unaffectedly calm voice – obviously stunned. "For me? My own?"

"And you'll notice it's not blue," Fr. Ted humorously added.

James pulled it from the box, "You're right. It's black." Carefully he inspected it, wiping a finger over his name brightly illuminated in gold leaf along the bottom edge. Opening it, he immediately caught sight of a small envelope. He opened it. Inside it read, "May this be the light that directs your path always toward God. With love and hope, your family in Christ." Everyone present had signed it – even his parents who weren't among them tonight.

Overwhelmed, he said the only thing that came to mind. "I don't know what to say other than thank you. This is the most valuable thing I have ever received. You guys are too much. I love you all."

Terri reached over and gave him a tender hug. Terrance and Scanlon slapped his shoulders like big brothers do. Tom Rowland stuck out his hand, "I'm very proud of you son. You've come a very long way."

James couldn't withhold himself; he leapt from his chair and threw his arms around Rowland's neck and began to sob. "You've been like a father to me and I'm so grateful. Thank you for believing in me. Thank you!" Rowland released Mary's hand and threw his arms around James. It might have been out of each man's character to fall into a manly embrace, but nothing could have been more appropriate. Scans and Terrance joined in the man-brace. Terri reached from her chair and laid a hand on James' back. Anne stood alongside Terrance, Mary beside Tom. Fr. Ted took a step back, clasped his hands in front of his chest, that broad, familiar smile stretching his salted beard. "Easter," he thought to himself. Inextinguishable Light bursting through darkness. "He is risen!" he whispered in a murmur no one but God heard.

"Well my son," Fr. Ted finally broke in to say. "I want you to get very cozy with that new Bible. We'll be discussing it quite a bit over the next few years. You'll find we've each inscribed a personal message on the few empty pages toward the front. Let us be your encouragement while you also encourage us."

"This is truly the happiest I've ever been. And I have each of you to thank."

"Listen little bro, you're not the only one to get something out of this whole thing," Scanlon asserted with a stiff tug on his ball cap. "I want you to know…" His words halted as a thick lump rose in his throat. "I'll just say, you've got guts kid. And it meant a lot to watch you fight all the way here." He dropped his head and wiped one of his thick mitts across his eyes. Terrance flopped an arm around his friend. James stuck out his hand. "I couldn't ask for a better big brother." He then glanced at Terrance, "For two big brothers like you guys." The men shook hands.

No one noticed that Fr. Ted had dropped into his comfortably worn easy chair, his legs crossed with that goofy grin spread across his face. "Family," he said. "Don't you just love it?" The room howled with laughter, each person finding his or her seat. James moved his chair a little closer to Terri. Anne seemed to appreciate the gesture. She just winked at him as if to say, "nice move."

"Easter Vigil begins at eight sharp on Saturday night. I trust you'll all be there," Fr. Ted stated as if anyone had a choice but to be there.

"Hoodlums too?" James asked looking at Terrance.

"You couldn't keep 'em away," Terrance confirmed with gangsta' bravado.

"And," Fr. Ted continued, "So will Warden Hollinswood who will escort your two newest acquaintances – Jason and Enrique."

"Way cool!" James exclaimed.

"Who's Jason and Enrique?" Scanlon demanded.

"Two guys I met the other day at Marysville. Jason's a kid from Fresno who's still figuring God out. Enrique is from South Chicago and thinks he wants to be a priest."

"A priest from South Chicago gang turf? That'll qualify as a miracle," Terrance busted in to say. "Think I've got to meet this dude."

"You will," James said with a smirk. "He knows where you came from too."

Terrance jerked the collar up on his denim jacket like a hood, "Tell him I'll be waiting."

Anne jabbed Terrance with her elbow. "Stop that. You're no wolf anymore."

"Not a wolf anymore huh," Scanlon crooned. "Just a whipped puppy."

Anne brought a hand to her face, "That's not what I meant, Mike. I meant…"

"Please dear," Terrance confided pulling his bride closer to him, "I think you've done enough damage." The room howled with laughter and the pun wasn't missed either.

"Alright you creeps! Knock it off!"

"Yeah, she's got your number," Scanlon said bobbing his head with a twisted grin on his face.

Terrance glared at his buddy but said nothing more. There was sufficient fuel on this fire. Discretion calmed the riot.

"Well, I'm glad we got that taken care of," Fr. Ted said restoring order to the room. "Tom, why don't you lead us in prayer? I think we need it."

Tom sat forward in his chair taking Mary's hand as he did. Around the room everyone joined hands. "Father in Heaven, thank you for the gift of life in your Son! Thank you for new life in this place! That the chair is empty no longer; that James has come to know you. Lead us to the cross and the empty tomb this Easter. Make us in your image. And help us to avoid making you in ours. In Jesus' eternal Name we pray, amen."

A soft "amen" from the expanded posse closed the evening.

James sat quietly to himself musing about all that transpired, including this night. How remarkable he thought. I am truly a new man.

SIXTY-FIVE

Standing on the grass a short ways from the fire where the Christ candle was blessed, James lit his candle from the person beside him then tipped it to light Terri's. Scanlon leaned over and whispered to Sally, "Feels like we're going inside a tomb." A short man standing in front of him turned around, "It is a tomb. But not for long."

It was a comfortably cool Saturday evening, but the atmosphere of the cavernous nave had a dank, somewhat eerie, nip to it. Since Thursday night after it had been stripped of all religious symbols, the tabernacle removed from its place and the crucifix draped in a red cloth, the church had been converted into the tomb of Christ. Even the furnace had been shut off, and the lights dimmed to their legal limit. A faint musty odor wafted about the old stone and wood interior giving off the fetid scent of decay. To James it reminded him of the frightening instant he entered the cold steel hell of prison. He felt his stomach tighten. Terri noticed his mood change and whispered softly, "It'll be okay." James looked at her. The tender smile on her face assured him it would be okay: First death then life.

The cantor intoned, "Christ our light," and the parishioners echoed behind him "Thanks be to God," as they followed the lit Christ Candle and the pungent fragrance of incense rising from the thurible into the darkened church reciting again in song voice the ancient verse. Reverently people slipped into the pews; James along with the other elect along with their families took their places in the front rows.

He was immediately struck by the reverence, the intentionality and sense of moment. Truly this was sacred time in a sacred place. Reverence, even an anxiety of expectation, pervaded the environment. There was no missing of the significance or point of it all.

James found his emotions piqued as the scriptures were proclaimed. He thought of Mitchell's story, finding his own reaction to them intriguingly similar. As the passages flowed from creation and the fall in the Garden of Eden, to the prophetic proclamations of the coming Messiah it was as if the road were opening in front of him. And then the crescendo! As Fr. Ted held the Gospel high above his head, suddenly the lights brightened, the organ swelled to life, the choir sang out the loud "Alleluia!" and people came from all corners of the church returning the symbols of Christ to their proper place. A man pulled the drape from the crucifix; another placed the tabernacle on its pedestal. From the tomb to Heaven the church transformed in an instant – death had been swallowed up and the Gospel account of Christ's passion and victory was read out with the congregation standing as one community united in Christ. Pangs of exhilaration raced along James' spine. He felt his heart swell as if it would burst. Soon it would be his moment to proclaim his faith and receive the ultimate initiation.

Fr. Ted ended his homily calling upon the faithful to pray for those now entering Baptism. The elect were dismissed to change into baptismal apparel – swimsuits mostly. Standing to himself, having changed out of his street clothes, James pulled the gray flannel robe around his shoulders and over the brilliant white gown. Grabbing a portion of it he muttered indignantly, "The old man; I'm going to toss you off like a bad debt."

"What's that?" Mitchell scowled overhearing James' comment.

"Oh I was just talking to myself."

"You sounded upset."

"Nah, not anymore." Tugging on the drab rag, "I'm done with this life."

"Ah, I see. Me too," Mitchell replied swiping at the gray robe hanging over his shoulders.

As the congregation continued singing the elect entered through the side door. A twinge of anticipation raced down James' spine. His moment had arrived. He walked to his place where Harold Raynor stood waiting for him – an unlit candle in his hand, a white robe draped over his arm and a proud smile spread across his face.

Fr. Ted took his place across the font, a large, black and white tiled octagonal pool set into the floor, a gold cross formed in tile at its center. Water streamed into the font from a dark stone fountain. Soon the entire congregation had gathered around the elect and their godparents reverently singing a haunting prayer – The Litany of the Saints. The cantor sang out, "Saint John pray for us," with congregation in reply, "Pray for us." When he sang the name of St. Ambrose, Fr. Ted's Patron Saint, James felt a warm sensation creep over him. It felt as though the past had merged with the present and that he might well be immersed by both the Bishop of Milan as well as the man he knew as Father and friend. He felt as if all of Heaven were present. It certainly seemed as if the space was filled with voices that somehow augmented the peoples' – unseen but no less present. He had worried he might feel anxious. Instead he found himself subsumed in unanticipated calm.

Fr. Ted stepped into the water, opening his arms to the heavens, gray clad *electi* standing around the edge of the font in front of him with the faithful packed in around them. Raising his voice he read in chanting song-voice from a thick book held by a young girl robed in white. "Father, you give us grace through sacramental signs, which tell us of the wonders of your unseen power." As he continued the lyrical chant of this ancient prayer, he dipped a porcelain cup into the water gently sprinkling it back into the pool around him. Receiving the lighted Christ candle from the outstretched hands of the acolyte, he lowered it until its unlit end broke the surface of the water. His voice strong and resonate sang, "We ask you, Father, with your Son to send the Holy Spirit upon the waters of this font." Stirring the waters with the candle as if bringing them to life, he concluded the prayer: "May all who are buried with Christ in the death of baptism rise also with him to newness of life."

"Buried" James thought. The word fastened in his mind. If the old James had not completely died, he reasoned he most certainly would moments from now. All the events of the previous weeks raced in Technicolor through his memory. The library table that had become an altar; the many conversations with Fr. Ted, Terrance and Terri that challenged his angry skepticism; Rowland's fatherly counsel; Scanlon's big brother encouragement; the sickening moment he entered prison – it all passed before him. Judge Abrams words "What happened son?" tore through his thoughts again. But here in this place at this moment he was startled by a realization that could not have been foreseen as he stood slump shouldered before the judge's bench so many months ago. Today he could look Judge Abrams squarely face-to-face and say, "I became a new man."

The swishing of water as Fr. Ted positioned himself to face the elect returned James to the moment. Pressing his glasses to his nose, Fr. Ted searched the faces of the elect, his arms reaching toward them. "Do you reject sin so as to live in the freedom of God's children?" he asked.

In unison the elect answered, "I do."

"Do you reject the glamour of evil, and refuse to be mastered by sin?"

Again, "I do."

"Do you reject Satan?"

"I do." With each scrutiny the responses grew steadily stronger. James' face contorted at the last one as if hissing into the face of Satan himself.

"And all his works?"

"I do!"

"And all his empty promises?"

"I do!"

"Then come and be baptized; be reborn into new life," Fr. Ted invited sweeping his arms over the water.

With trepidation as if unsure of what to expect, perhaps even anxious about the covenant they were about to enter – could they complete it? – One-by-one the elect shed the gray flannel robe and stepped down into the watery tomb where Fr. Ted greeted them. James closely observed those ahead of him. He read anxiety in some and apparent bliss in others. But when they came up out of the water they all seemed to glow. There was freshness about them and it seemed real.

It was his turn. With a shrug James threw off the gray robe and felt it brush his bare ankles as it fell to the floor. He reached for Fr. Ted's outstretched hand and stepped into the font. Unexpectedly the water was warm and he felt a soothing comfort about it. Fr. Ted placed one hand on James' back as he held onto his hand. Their eyes met. Tears welled. Father and son as it were – the sense of moment could not have been stronger, neither could the bond that had brought them together. His voice soft but strong, tender but admonishing, Fr. Ted asked, "James, do you believe in God, the Father almighty, creator of heaven and earth?"

"I do," James replied sweeping tears from his face.

"Do you believe in Jesus Christ, his only Son, our Lord, who was born of the Virgin Mary, was crucified, died and was buried, rose from the dead, and is now seated at the right hand of the Father?"

"I do."

"Do you believe in the Holy Spirit, the holy Catholic Church, the communion of saints, the forgiveness of sins, the resurrection of the body, and the life everlasting?"

"I do." James could barely choke out the last "I do" for all the emotion surging through him.

"Then kneel my son and be reborn to new life."

With tears welled in his eyes, James knelt down into the pool; the water pressing around him. Fr. Ted placed his hands on James' head and with a downward thrust shoved his head beneath the surface intoning the words, "I baptize you in the name of the Father." James barely heard Fr. Ted's voice as his head was thrust under the surface twice more in the name of the Son and of the Holy Spirit. Drenching wet he rose from the water and threw his arms around his mentor. "Thank you! Thank you! Thank you!" James exclaimed as he wept on Fr. Ted's shoulder. All those present applauded, many weeping with the men. James' mother threw her head into her husband's chest, sobbing with utter gratitude. Terri's shriek drew laughter from those around her and a massive brotherly hug from Scanlon. Anne clasped Terri's shoulders with her hands and whispered in her ear, "Your turn next year." Terri nodded agreement clasping Anne's hands. Terrance stepped to the pool and stuck out his hand. James grabbed it as Terrance fairly jerked him from the water into a manly embrace. Harold Raynor thrust out his hand, "Well done young man! Well done!"

Standing beside his freshly rinsed brothers and sisters, all dripping baptismal water, James took his place. Fr. Ted stepped forward, himself soaking wet, and with a large clear jar of warm fragrant oil began pouring it over the heads of the newly baptized – neophytes as they were called, new citizens of God's Kingdom. As he wiped the chrism as it is called through the hair and down the faces of each neophyte, he declared, "The God of power and Father of our Lord Jesus Christ has freed you from sin and brought you to new life through water and the Holy Spirit. He now anoints you with the chrism of salvation, so that, united with his people, you may remain forever a member of Christ who is Priest, Prophet, and King."

Oil streaked James' face and fell across his closed eyes, rimming around his lips. Pungent yet pleasant, he came quickly to recognize something Fr. Ted once said to him after reading a portion of one of Paul's letters. "James," he said, "Like the scriptures tell us, we reek of God's Spirit. For some it's the aroma of life. For others, it is the smell of death. But for us who know Him, it is the fragrance of His Spirit filling us, sealing us and endowing us with the gifts of God's Spirit." Through eyes blurred by the oleaginous chrism, he saw Harold Raynor unfold the brilliant white robe and proceed to sweep it over his outer garment. As it settled onto his shoulders, Fr. Ted stated, "Each of you has become a new creation and have clothed yourselves in Christ. Receive this baptismal garment and bring it unstained to the judgment seat of our Lord Jesus Christ, so that you may have everlasting life."

Raynor stepped forward again, this time handing James an unlit candle while Fr. Ted declared, "You have been enlightened by Christ. Walk always as children of the light and keep the flame of faith alive in your hearts. When the Lord comes, may you go out to meet him with all the saints in the heavenly kingdom." Closing the book, Fr. Ted looked into the sparkling, oily faces of the newly baptized. "Now my newly christened brothers and sisters, as St. Ambrose himself instructed the baptized in Milan, always live in your baptism." Pointing at the candles held by each one, he concluded, "And always let your light shine. May it never go dim or ever be extinguished."

Don and Kathleen, who only weeks earlier wondered if their lives would ever be whole again, clutched each other and wept. Their son, painfully lost was now wonderfully found. Life had begun again. They could barely contain themselves. Kathleen reached over to Terri, slipping an arm around her waist. Terri threw her arm around Kathleen. For all the look of it they were the picture of family. And why not? They had endured a great deal individually and now together. That they thought fondly of each other sweetened the moment. James brought them into each other's lives, and returned him to theirs.

After the confirmation rite, Fr. Ted dismissed the newly baptized to don their Easter clothes and return for their first Eucharist. Scanlon led the posse with many of Terrance's hoodlums close in tow to their seats in the nave. Terrance overheard Dirk whisper to Tag, "Man that was the coolest! Maybe we oughta go Catholic." To which Tag replied, "Not so fast dude. That's a God-thing. Besides, we've got a good thing going too ya know. We're all catholic; we're all his kids. Do ya dig?"

Dirk smirked, "Yeah, I dig. We're catholic enough."

Terrance whispered in Anne's ear, "Did you hear that?"

Anne smiled and grasped her husband's arm, "Not bad. I think your boys got it."

"Yeah, they got it alright."

SIXTY-SIX

James couldn't ever remember taking communion in his brief church life. So Fr. Ted's question caused pause for thought. "I don't know," James began. "The entire mass was like an out-of-body experience for me. The whole thing overwhelmed me. Eucharist was like nothing I can remember – but neither was baptism. For sure I knew God was there. It was like he was everywhere – like Heaven invaded earth or something."

The entire posse blew up in laughter. James enjoyed that they all convened in the Marysville Library, at the table where it all took form. Even Don and Kathleen sat with them, and one very curious Warden Hollinswood.

"So you made a Catholic of our boy?" Hollinswood remarked taking a verbal swipe at his good friend, a very tired but satisfied Fr. Ted.

"Nope, I didn't, Bram. God took care of those details. I just led the parade."

Hollinswood didn't let his friend off so easily: "So did ya make any converts of this group after that grand Easter spectacle?"

"Were you there?" James broke in to ask.

"Indeed I was James. Sat toward the back. All that incense gives me a headache."

"I had no idea. I'm stunned," James exclaimed.

"What! You don't think I'd miss a show like that would ya? C'mon my boy! Watchin' you take the plunge was truly a highlight. You made my year!"

"Really? Thank you!"

"Well what we've all got to realize, son, is that our God is bigger than any denomination, any movement and any heresy. We're just all one in His eyes."

"Amen!" Scalon burst in to affirm. Others added their voices to his.

"So y'all didn't answer my question. Who's next?"

Sheepishly Terri slowly raised her hand. "Me, sir," she said in a meek voice.

"Why am I not surprised? I would have guessed as much."

"Why's that?" Terri asked.

"Well some things my dear girl are obvious even to an old guy like me." With that Bram rose from his chair. "On that happy note my friends, I've got a date with that infernal paper work. Darn stuff never goes away." Slapping James on the back, "I'm so proud of you son. You've brought joy to these old bones. Glad for y'all really. God's ways might be mysterious but they're always worth waiting for."

As he turned to saunter his way out the door and back to his office, Terri leapt from her seat and threw her arms around Hollinswood's neck. "I just want to say thanks!"

"For what young lady?"

"For your kindness – and wisdom. I like you Mr. Hollinswood!" she blurted.

Bram's face twisted into a strange grin, "Well Miss Terri, I like you too. I think we've done good work together. Let's keep it up. Shall we?"

"I'd love that!" she exclaimed.

"So where do we go from here?" Rowland asked. "What's next for James and for this group?"

Fr. Ted rubbed his chin a moment and rocked back in his chair, "Let's ask God. I think there's another James around that our James needs to help find his way home."

"Before we pray," James interrupted to say. "I don't hardly know how to say what you all mean to me. Saturday night was unreal. I still have that smell on me from the oil Fr. Ted rubbed into my hair." James glided a hand through his thick hair. The others snickered. "I just hope that somehow I can repay you. I don't know how. But I promise; I'll try my best."

"James, you don't need to repay us," Rowland offered. "What you need to do, son, is walk with us like we've walked with you. You see, son, that wall we talked about some weeks ago; the one that I said would hold you up; it's right here in this room. It's all of us together, held together by God and each other. We lean on Him and he holds onto us – all of us. Do you understand what I just said?"

"Yes sir, I think I finally do. It's about trust isn't it?"

"It always is, James," Rowland affirmed. "It's always about trusting one another and being trustworthy. Trust, son, is a two-way street with traffic in both directions. If it's going to run smoothly, it cannot be clogged up with doubt and distrust."

"I see your point." Looking into the faces seated around the table with him, James witnessed in everyone the conviction they showed when he first met them. "You've all been faithful to me. I guess it's my turn to return the trust."

"Good," Fr. Ted interjected. "That's where it starts."

"Look kid," Terrance added. "Don't get too hard on yourself when you screw up. Believe me, you will. All of us have. That's when we need each other the most. Look, I want to spend more time with you. There's some guys here that need what you have – a new start. How about partnering?"

"I'd love it," James asserted.

"I'll be there with you guys, too! Count on it!" Scanlon boasted with a thump of his fist on the table.

Fr. Ted looked at his good friend, "Well Tom, it's been a great ride again hasn't it?"

"Yes it has. Are you suggesting there might be another one on the horizon?"

"Oh I'm certain of it. This time we'll have more company," Fr. Ted answered referring to the *new* posse.

"Well then. Bring it on!"

"Yes indeed! Bring it on!"

*****

Fr. Ted hung back in the library while the others went off to their day's tasks. Terri left too; time to get some sleep for the long night shift ahead.

"What's on your mind?" Fr. Ted asked James who seemed somewhat absorbed in thought.

"Something off the wall. You'll probably tell me I'm getting ahead of myself again."

"Well, out with it. Get it off your chest."

"What if I want to be a priest?"

Fr. Ted's eyebrows arched and his eyes blinked. "A priest, huh?"

"I told you it was off the wall."

"Why am I not surprised? You're always a mile down the road before anyone can catch up to you. But, listen; don't let my puzzled reaction make you think I'm not on board with you. Let me ask, when did you first start thinking about this idea?"

"Honestly, while sitting here just now, with everyone around me. And because I admire what you did for me."

"Just now, eh?"

"Well, it's crossed my mind mostly at night before drifting off."

"Have you mentioned this interest to anyone other than me?"

"No. Just you."

"James, I would be the last person to discourage you from the priesthood. It can be a lonely life, but a good life. I wouldn't want anything different. I love my calling. But that's the issue, James; the priesthood is a calling that takes time and deep introspective discernment to confirm. If you truly think God is leading you this way, I'd love to join you in that process." A serious look came over Fr. Ted's face. "But let me ask you something. What about Terri? Where does she fit in your life?"

James could tell Fr. Ted wasn't jerking his chain this time. He was dead serious. Cocking his head to the side, he shrugged, "Honestly, I hadn't thought about that."

"You mean in light of becoming a priest."

"In light of anything! Especially that!"

"Do you think that maybe Terri might influence your notion of becoming a priest? You know we don't marry. We're married to the Church." Fr. Ted lifted his eyebrows inquisitively, almost as if offering an insightful warning to his young protégé.

"Oh wow! How do I answer that?" James said squirming uncomfortably in his chair.

"James, even I can tell she means more to you than you let on. And for what it's worth, that young lady is quite taken with you."

"I know. Honestly, I'm quite taken with her."

"I'm glad to hear that, son. We'll get back to that. Now let me help you with your question. The priesthood is not the only way to serve in ministry to the Church."

"What do you mean?"

"There's the possibility of becoming a deacon. Deacons are ministers who serve the parish and assist the priest. And they are often married men."

"That's too cool! Do you think if I became one of those dudes I could maybe work under you?"

"Well, stranger things have happened," Fr. Ted said with a chuckle.

"That's…"

"Just a minute though. You've got a lot of school ahead of you. And a lot of spiritual maturity to reach. It's not easy, son. It's a life of sacrifice."

"But I could become a minister?"

"It's certainly possible."

"Even for a con?"

"James, the Church looks at each of us as sinners who are being saved by the mercies of Jesus Christ. We've all fallen short of his glory. How bad and how far is not the final arbiter of whether or not we can serve Christ's Church. The real matter has to do with surrender. Have we surrendered ourselves to Christ? Do we seek his will above our will? And what evidence do we offer that he has called us to serve as priests and deacons?"

"So what's the first step?"

"If you're truly serious, the first step is to place yourself before God and ask him? Ask him to show you what lies in your heart. I will help you."

"Okay. I get that."

"And…"

"And what?" James asked suspiciously.

"And I think you ought to chat with Terri."

"Huh?"

"Yes, I think the two of you need to have a DTR."

James felt the air fly out of his sails. "What the heck is a DTR?"

"A DTR my son is a Define the Relationship chat."

James felt his stomach tighten. "Man, I don't know if I'm ready for that!"

"Oh I think you are. And I know she is."

"Okay now I know you're meddling."

"Oh no, I'm not meddling James Meyers. You're the only naïve one in this conversation."

"What makes you so sure she's ready to have the D whatever you called it?"

Fr. Ted sat his chair on all four legs and clasped his hands on the table in front of him. "Because she has spoken to me, James."

"Huh?!"

"Let me finish," Fr. Ted said with a wave of his finger. "She wonders how she can help you; you know, where she fits in. James that young lady cares deeply about you, more than I think you know. I would encourage you to evaluate your own feelings for Terri, and be honest with her – certainly before you make any decisions or entertain any notions of what you will do with your post-prison life."

"Wow!" James said exhaling loudly while looking across the table. He could tell Fr. Ted was not playing with him. "Am I ready for that talk? Do you think I even deserve Terri?"

A broad grin spread across Fr. Ted's face, "Without doubt, son. You've got all the qualities; you just need to refine them."

"I wasn't exactly expecting this conversation."

"No problem. Neither was I." With his head tilted to the side, and with that silly smirk on his face, Fr. Ted put his young charge on the hot seat, "So what are you going to do about it?"

"Gosh, I thought getting baptized was going to be scary. This stuff scares the you-know-what out of me."

"James, be honest with yourself. And be honest with Terri. Above everything don't lead her on. Like I said, be honest with her and yourself."

"Yes sir. This won't be easy either will it?"

"Like I've said all along, the best things in life never are." Fr. Ted pursed his lips, "You want to know what I think?"

"That would be helpful."

"I think if you invite Terri to pray with you about God's plans for your future, she will jump at the chance. I think she'll even tell you what's on her mind."

"Are you telling me something I should know about what she thinks is in her future?"

"No, not really; I just know that she has a strong desire to serve God. That's all."

"Oh man, guess I'd better strap in for sure, huh?"

Father Ted just smiled.

"Well, that's life son. What I can do is shine a light on the potholes. The rest is up to you."

"Yeah, I get your point. No easy way out if you want the best is there?"

"No. But you're not alone, son. You've got plenty of company on that road with you. I think by now you should know that."

"Yes sir, I do – I finally do. And I'm grateful."

"Well then, I look forward to a good report."

"About?"

"The DTR, James. The DTR! In fact, I look forward to spending more time with both of you – that is if you'll let me tag along."

"I wouldn't have it any other way."

"Let me pray for you. And let's ask God if this idea of serving the Church is his or yours."

The men bowed at the table. So many important transactions had already taken place over its wooden surface. "Oh blessed Father, wrap your arms around these your children – James and Terri. Show them your direction for their lives. And help them always to look into your face to find the answers for their journey. Amen."

SIXTY-SEVEN

"Can we talk?" Terri asked her hands clasped tightly in her lap.
"Sure," James replied noticing his friend's tension. "You first."

"I think I need to know…" Terri stopped and fidgeted with a tissue in her hand.

"Know what, Terri?" James pressed.

"Oh this is really hard," she said, biting her lower lip.

James gently laid his hand on hers. "I'm listening and for what it's worth I'll respect whatever you want to say."

"Thanks. That helps." Terri turned her hand over to take his. "James, we've not been friends for all that long, but I think we've gotten pretty close. I never meant it, but I began to get these weird feelings." She rocked back and forth; obviously uncomfortable.

"Feelings? What kind of weird feelings?"

"James," she began staring into space. "I really, really like you." Her chin began to quiver, her eyes dropped to the hands clasped in her lap –his and her hands. "And I hope that you really like me."

James felt this strangely warm sensation come over him. "Terri, I do really like you. I owe you so much. You've been the one person I thought really understood me. You never judged me. It's like you accepted me when I couldn't accept myself."

"Really?" Terri said in a near whisper.

"Terri, I've been doing a lot of thinking. I've thought about you – and us."

Terri lifted her head. Her eyes blurred with tears. "Us?"

"Yeah, us. Fr. Ted told me we should have what he called a DTR."

"I know. He told me that too."

"You know what a DTR is?" James almost fell off his seat.

"Sure – define the relationship. Isn't that what you meant?"

"Yeah, I guess."

"Okay, I'd like to know," Terri said again staring into their hands unsure of what she might hear.

James' heart beat like it was about to bolt from his chest. He felt his face flush. His hands went clammy and his mouth dry as toast. He drew a deep breath, "Terri, I can't imagine taking a step without you. You mean more to me than any person I've ever known." He paused and stared anxiously into their hands with her. Like a smitten school boy caught in that painfully awkward moment; too far in to turn back he drew another deep breath. "I kinda hope we might become more than friends. I'm kinda hoping we might see if God has something more in mind for us – as us."

Terri's mouth flew open; her eyes widened and sparkled with tears pouring from them. She threw her arms around James' neck and shrieked, "Oh James, I've hoped for those words! Yes! Yes! Yes! I want to go there with you – to God about us."

James wrapped his arms around her. "So do you think your social media stuff might change?"

"You mean like to I'm in a relationship?"

"Yeah, to that."

"Do you want me to change it?"

"Yeah, I do."

Terri shrieked again. "Oh wow! I'll do it right now!" She pulled her phone from her purse, punched up her personal page and let the world know, "I'm in a relationship!"

The two kids sat staring into the other's face. "I never dreamed I'd meet someone like you," James said shaking his head. "I couldn't be happier!"

"It's a God thing," Terri chirped.

"It's a God thing!" James echoed.

*****

James picked up the pen beside the yellow pad on his desk and scratched out all the impressions that flooded his mind and emotions from the events of the past few days and hours – several hastily scribbled pages began to fill the pad. What he wrote only he and God know. But these few words concluded the entry: "The gavel fell once and I was sent to prison. It fell again I was set free. I am most definitely a new man – a God thing."

Made in the USA
Columbia, SC
14 July 2017